Incarnate

Book One of The Celestial Wars

A.N. Fox

* * *

This book is a work of fiction. Names, characters, places and incidents are the product of the author's imagination or are used fictitiously. Any resemblance to actual events, locales, persons, living or dead, is coincidental.

No part of this book may be reproduced in any form or by any electronic or mechanical means, including information storage and retrieval systems, without written permission from the author, except for the use of brief quotations in a book review.

To the chaos of childhood, parenting, and the whimsical
outlet that fantasy provides.

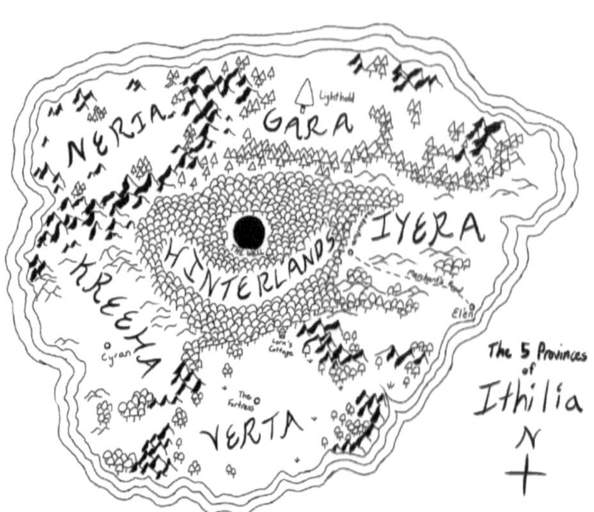

NERIA
GARA
Lighthold
IYERA
HINTERLANDS
THE WELL
KREEHA
Merchant's Road
Elen
Cyran
Lara's Cottage
The Fortress
VERTA
The 5 Provinces of
Ithilia
N

Find one whose soul is pierced,

Weeping, grieved, wrecked.

The darkness beckons them in.

Find those that seek their ruin,

Bent on vengeance,

Sorrow fills their every step.

Find one who has suffered,

Their heart torn from them,

Their world fallen apart.

For once the lost is found,

Then they can enter into the darkness.

Creatures and beasts ignored,

Those twisted and gnarled ends,

Rooted deep into the ground.

The madness relenting,

Only for the changing of the moon.

She can be a tricky sort,

To explore and seek the treasure,

Newly forged and powerful,

Emerges from the Well.

Quick! Quick!

Or it will be gone forever.

Excerpt from The Prophecy given by Ulmina of Iyera

* * *

One clap for the trees so high,

Two claps for the beasts inside,

Three claps for those crazy within.

Shh, Shh, Shh.

Glitter, Glitter

Gold, Gold

What magic will the Well unfold?

Silver, Silver

Shine, Shine

Hurry! Quick! Before your time,

Is up!

Common game played among the children of Ithilia

1

From the records of the scholar Oria of Iyera

Lorn of Verta fought the rising dread that accompanied his sleep. Every night his nightmares haunted him. The distant scream and screech of foul creatures echoed in his head. It was all imaginary. Well, not truly imaginary. The horrors he had experienced were real, but they were not here with him as he bedded down in this ramshackle barn. Traces of their abhorrent shapes formed in the shadows. Their monstrous forms never left him alone. Some nights they were all he could picture.

He readjusted his body on the scratchy hay pile. The small farming town was one of the poorer towns he had assisted recently. They had little to offer him, not even proper housing to stay the night. Lorn didn't care. He vowed long ago he would rid Ithilia of the twisted creatures that escaped the Hinterlands. He flopped onto his side, searching for faint outlines of the animals he shared this barn with. Their noises and gentle stirrings brought forth painful memories of a life he had long since buried away.

He was tired. His body ached. The fight earlier should not have drawn out as long as it did. But Lorn had grown arrogant, and the Feaster had ripped a chunk of skin from his shoulder as it attempted to haul him into the tree line. Lorn had evaded its grasp with a deft maneuver. Eventually the fight ended as Lorn pierced the Feaster through its heart. He didn't even bother cleaning up the unsettling body, its beady red eyes, and sharpened fangs glinted back at him. The black sludge of the creature's blood coated his sword and stuck to his clothes. Amongst claps and cheers from the townspeople, he retreated, barely acknowledging the praise, and dunked himself in the nearby river hoping to feel anything. When he emerged from the river dripping wet, he still felt nothing—only a hollow pit where there once was thriving life.

Lorn reluctantly fell asleep, his hand loosely clasped on the hilt of his sword.

Lorn rose early to the soft rays of light piercing through the gaps between the wooden slats of the barn. He rose to his feet and made to quickly depart. He did not require any fanfare or heartfelt goodbyes. A hesitant knock on the door caused him to pause.

"You may enter," Lorn said, his voice gruff from sleep.

A gangly teenager entered, his eyes darting between the haystack Lorn slept on and the sword he finished attaching to his hip.

"A letter for you." The teen stretched their freckled arm out to Lorn. His arm shook as Lorn pulled it from his grasp. Before Lorn could utter a 'thank you' the kid had scampered out of the barn, leaving the door clanging in his wake.

The letter was pristine, the white paper blindingly bright in the dark warmth of the barn. His fingers ran over the wax seal. It was a deep blue, an imprint of waves with a sun looming over it. He ran his fingers under the seal and tentatively opened the letter, unsure of what would be written. As he read, he couldn't help a feeling of finality, of facing an unknown destiny he needed to rise and acknowledge.

He was going to the province of Iyera to meet Lord Aldrich.

~

Lorn bit his tongue and held back a stream of curses. Of course, his arrival to the province of Iyera coincided with the MidSummer festival. When he entered the capital city of El'en, he shook his head in defeat when he noticed the exuberant decorations adorning the buildings. Strands of flowers dangled from archways, rooftops and over market stalls. Their vibrant, rich colors of pinks, oranges, reds, and yellows blurred his vision. It wasn't that he abhorred celebration, but it was a sharp pain to be amongst so many of his fellow MagicBlessed citizens watching their happiness, their lives unencumbered by so much pain and suffering that he shouldered.

Lorn left the inn feeling naked. He had argued with himself whether to bring his weapons but decided at the last minute to leave them hidden within his sparse room. The weapons would only draw unwanted attention to himself. Also, the guards at the castle would remove any potential weapon from his body when he reached Lord Aldrich. Lorn grabbed his cloak and wrapped it around him. The heat of the day was already unforgiving, but it was incredibly worse given the immense crowds. Yet, he needed anonymity. Everyone was out to celebrate the MidSummer Festival. The celebration occurred for one week every year to revel in their blessings from the Well–the very reason for their magic.

The crowds grew thicker around the market square, vendors were out hawking their wares and chefs were cooking for the gathered crowds. Lorn's stomach betrayed him as wafts of freshly barbecued meat and fish tempted him to stand in line. Yet his stomach soured as soon as he remembered his purpose here. The meeting with Lord Aldrich. His fingers twitched over his left pant's pocket, a habit to reassure himself that he was meant to be here. He wanted to reread the lines again and again.

It was the start of a mystery he wanted to unravel. Yet as he pulled the string to unspool it and reveal its true meaning, he felt like he would be diving deeper, tangling himself in the threads. Why would Lord Aldrich have need of a hunter? Have need of him? He knew little of the Lord of Iyera, only the evidence around him. His people were well-cared for, happy, and prosperous. Just as much as any other province of Ithilia. The Well was not the only reason they were gifted with magic, it was a means of security. The soils were always rich, the fish plentiful, and the crops, minerals, gems in abundance–everything prospered.

It was a mystery to Lorn why he received summons from a lord he had never met before. Yet he couldn't stop the empty feeling of his stomach or the electric energy that gathered around his body. The feeling of something being set in motion.

He urged himself forward, his broad shoulders allowed him to easily navigate the growing crowd. As Lorn left the marketplace behind him, the pulsing sound of a drumbeat began, soon followed by the sound of fiddles. Cheers broke out as people flooded past Lorn, aiming to dance and revel together. He looked over his shoulder and quickly eyed the growing crowd, trying to quell his bitterness and instead replacing this emotion with appreciation. He *did* appreciate seeing the smattering of MagicBlessed of Iyera gathered to celebrate— children, adults, everyone clustered enjoying the small pleasures of this life. Yet it was a blatant reminder of everything lost to him.

His lips tipped at the sides as he watched a family magic ice out of the air and form it into a deer for their daughter. Her child-like wonder lit up her face at the precious gift. Lorn's heart cracked at the precious scene. People flamboyantly displayed their magic, creating designs in the air with their preferred magic type. Everyone would be drained, their magic depleted by tomorrow. Their current generation's magic strength was a fraction of what their ancestors were. The original MagicBlessed to come from the Well–their source of origin–were rumored to have immeasurable amounts of magical power. Every generation since then had been watered-down, their essence of Magic used in small finite amounts, the user quickly exhausted.

Lorn failed to realize he was standing still amongst the sea of people going in the opposite direction. He turned his head forward and a figure slammed into him. He nearly fell and reached out a hand to steady himself. Lorn was broad and sturdy, the person merely upset his balance. Instinct reared, he reached for his weapons and grasped on nothing. Lorn steadied his breath and flexed his fingers, happy to not be equipped with his weapons for once. If he had, the person who slammed into him might have had a knife held to their throat. With Lorn, his trained body acted first, and his mind raced to catch up after.

"Apologies," Lorn muttered, dusting himself off. The person continued walking away unperturbed, cloak pulled over themselves, their features shadowed from the harsh light of the day.

"Well Happy MidSummer to you too," Lorn grumbled, ignoring the lack of courtesy, as he continued his walk towards the castle. His jet-black hair flopped into his face, and he hastily brushed it back with a hand.

* * *

~

The capital of El'en was a seaside city bordered by the Wyra Ocean. Navigating its roads required constant use of steep inclines. The hilly landscape mixed with the unrelenting summer sun caused him to have a thick sheen of sweat. Away from the busy crowds he removed his cloak. The reprieve was instant. The occasional breeze from the Wyra Ocean helped to cool Lorn off. He was not used to such temperatures. Lorn came from the province of Verta, their soil rich for farming, the land mostly flat broken apart with soft hillsides and the occasional grove of trees providing shade. The sun seemed to burn fiercer here, his golden skin threatening to darken to a deeper hue.

Iyera was famed for its beautiful ocean, plentiful fish, and its isolated castle atop the hill. The market square was directly west from the castle— the jewel of El'en—lay upon the top of the hill. If anyone wished to reach the castle, they needed to climb up the hill, weaving back and forth through the switchback roads. Small houses and gardens dotted the side of the road, each fully decorated with flowers for the MidSummer celebration. The throng of people lessened as Lorn trekked up the hill. Everyone was gathered around the market square or outside their houses. No one was planning to head to the castle today, except him. Lorn reached the crest of the hill and beheld the breathtaking jewel of El'en.

The castle was a thing of beauty. He grew up away from massive civilization, in the quiet farmlands and lush forests of Verta, and the grandeur of the city never became old. The marble white castle was built upon a cliff of rock, with a bridge leading from it to the main part of the city. Over time the rock face beneath the bridge eroded away leaving the castle to sit on its own with only the bridge connecting it to the city, as if held up by external magical forces.

Wave after wave rose to meet the base of the castle and crashed against the sharp rocks that jutted out. The bridge and castle matched, each made from white marble, pristine and blindingly clean. The harsh summer sun reflected off the castle, almost forcing Lorn to shield his eyes. Compared to the small towns he had visited; this castle was a beacon of decadence.

Lorn made his way across the bridge, his footsteps slowing as he approached the castle. The bridge was wide enough to allow at least ten horses and their riders to march though. Touching a hand to the edge of the bridge, Lorn paused, reflecting on the amount of craftsmanship involved. Entranced by the waves crashing below, he leaned forward. Growing up, he listened in disbelief to tales of the vast water that encircled the land. The cottage he grew up in was deep inland, the ocean was a beauty he rarely experienced. The waves undulated far below the height of the bridge were hypnotic, rising and falling, rising and falling. One fall from here would surely kill a man, the jagged rocks below a death sentence. He edged forward, his body halfway over the side of the bridge. Lorn stared hypnotized by the waves. They called to him. His fingers loosened, and their grip began to slip. He needed to get closer to the ocean below. A breeze caressed Lorn's face as a soft voice whispered, "Lorn."

Lorn quickly shook his head and scrambled away from the edge. He glanced around looking for who the voice belonged to. No one was near him on the bridge. He reached for his head. He felt light and dizzy, as if he were in a trance. *The summer heat must be affecting me*, Lorn rationalized. He retouched the summons in his pocket, a brief reassurance to himself and a reminder of why he was here. Lorn strode forward, sparing one disconcerted glance over his shoulder as he crossed the bridge, leaving the crashing waves behind.

~

The castle grounds were equally as immaculate as the exterior. Bluebells and crocuses grew unchecked along the edge of the castle while jasmine climbed up the sides. The wind carried the scent of the flowers and Lorn breathed in, steadying himself. Cypress and olive trees lined the pathway interspersed with water fountains. The bubbling of water paired with the crashing of the ocean waves should have been a peaceful reprieve for Lorn, yet his stomach was twisted in knots.

Lorn's hand helplessly itched to grab at the summons in his pocket and reread it, feeling the need to double check he was supposed to be here. Searching, he found the main entrance hall where he assumed the lord to be. Two guards outfitted with metal armor bearing the crest of Iyera—a sun over waves—stood entry at the open door. Their bored faces barely glanced at Lorn's summons and pointed him in a vague direction behind them. Lorn took a breath and moved ahead, unsure of where Fate was leading him.

~

As Lorn stepped into the throne room he couldn't help but gaze at the wondrous room before him. Intricate tapestries depicting the history of Ithilia hung upon the walls. Large glass windows adorned the walls and the sunlight poured through. The refracted sunbeams highlighted the gnarled beechwood throne sitting at the far end of the room. Magic seemed to imbue the room, emitting a heightened glow. The bluebells and crocuses he spotted outside were arranged in ornate vases depicted with the Iyerian crest. Although it was an austere throne room, it was not cold, but rather celebrated the warmth of the city. The city of El'en's beauty was carried inside.

A handful of guards lined the throne room, standing to attention. Their faces unable to mask their emotions, many appeared crestfallen to be excluded from the raucous celebration outside. Lorn's gaze swept the room, his attempt at appearing unimpressed failing as each time he looked, he spotted something even more intriguing.

A man occupying the far end of the room caught his attention. The man was watching Lorn, scrutinizing his every move. This was the Lord of Iyera, Lord Aldrich. As he looked upon the lord, he knew why this man was in charge of Iyerian province. He was above average height, light brown skin with wavy almond colored hair that came down to his shoulders framing his handsome face. He wore a white tunic, comfortable-looking dark green pants, and a richly designed coat which tapered to his frame. He had a presence about him. Everything about him exuded a regal charisma. Lord Aldrich leisurely strolled towards Lorn, a hungry curiosity fixed on his face. Startled, Lorn's foot slipped back a step. Lord Aldrich's eyes were unsettling. As Lorn met the Lord of Iyera's dark brown eyes, he felt as if was falling into a fathomless depth.

"Ah you must be Lorn," Lord Aldrich stated. "Rumors of your skills have spread throughout all five provinces. I must admit, I am not easily impressed." He flashed a quick smile, an attempt to set Lorn at ease.

Lorn locked eyes with the lord unsure of his motives. They were the eyes of a predator locking in on an interesting new prey. An inner alarm rang throughout his body, and his magic withdrew in terror. Lorn admonished himself, reminding himself of the lord's benevolence and that all was well. Despite his attempts to relax, an unease crept throughout his body like the hold of a creature's sharp talons.

"According to my advisers you grew up near the Hinterlands. Is that correct?" Lord Aldrich asked.

Lorn cleared his throat, "Yes my lord, that is correct."

He went on, "Is it true you slew the creatures that have revealed themselves from the Hinterlands?"

"Yes my lord, I grew up near the Hinterlands and some of the foul beasts would venture out. I had to learn quickly, otherwise I would not be here." Doubts ran through Lorn's head. Why would he call me here? Does he want me to kill a beast plaguing their lands?

Lord Aldrich thoughtfully advanced towards Lorn, paused and asked one more question. "Did you truly kill a Howler?"

Lorn's heartbeat sped up and his palms began to slick with sweat. The room was darkening slowly, his mind reverting back to that time, back to that memory.

"No! Run Lorn!" A scream pierced the air as the monster's claws tore apart her stomach. Blood seeped into the ground, her scream echoing throughout the dense forest. He was the only witness to this atrocity. Lakesh's pleas were a blight amongst the sanctuary of trees. The never-ending sound of her cry reverberated back to him.

"Lorn?" he questioned. Lord Aldrich's voice ripped Lorn painfully back to the present. The throne room began to feel more solid underneath his feet. Lorn gave a hollow stare back at Lord Aldrich. A long, slow breath eased from his body.

"Yes I killed a Howler." Lorn's statement held nothing. No anger. No fear. Only words.

The Lord of Iyera held Lorn's stare taking note of something within. Lord Aldrich blatantly scanned him taking into account the weather worn leather boots, pants faded with smears of old blood from hunting, and loose shirt with a thick cloak. Whatever he noted, he approved.

"Come with me, hunter of the Hinterlands. I have a proposition for you." The lord turned and walked out of the throne room. As Lorn made no move to follow, Lord Aldrich steps slowed as he turned around. "If you desire a chance at an adventure, a chance to discover something no one in the last millennium has ever witnessed, come with me." Lord Aldrich paused, letting his words sink in. Lorn attempted to keep his face neutral, but the things Lord Aldrich discussed were unheard of. A temptation to discover the unknown.

Lord Aldrich continued, like a hunter setting a snare. "I have heard rumors of your skill and prowess. I know there is nothing left for you in your life. You could have a chance at greatness if you choose to follow me."

2

"The Ladies and Lords are in their seats of power based on many factors; lineage, magical prowess, or some arbitrary unknown variables the rest have not been privy to."

How the land of Ithilia came to be by Ursu of Kreeha

Lord Aldrich walked briskly through a chamber door on the right side of the throne room. Lorn considered his options. He could leave now, go back to his small rundown cottage in Verta, continue to hunt, and live with the phantoms of memories that plagued him daily. He could leave this castle, leave this city and be done with this nonsense. Or he could choose to follow Lord Aldrich. The urge to follow him pulled like the undertow of the ocean below the castle. Despite any futile efforts it was natural for him to be pulled into the depths. His feet began to walk of their own accord, his body listening to some inner demand his mind could not yet understand. He picked up his pace, his steps trailing Lord Aldrich. He left the throne room behind and followed Lord Aldrich up a spiral staircase.

Countless hallways and passages passed by with neither one of them speaking. Only the celebrational cheers from the city and the echo of their footsteps resounded in the empty castle corridors. Lord Aldrich turned to his left and opened a large wooden door. The hinges creaked as the door swung open and inside was an impressive study. Bookshelves lined the walls, filled to the brim with books of all sizes and styles. Ornately gilded books, leather bound books, along with loose sheaves of paper, notes scribbled and hastily put in between the pages.

Various maps depicting Ithilia hung on the wall. The maps were aged, withered, and curled but each province of Ithilia was drawn with clear precision. Lorn's eyes roved over the maps, and he drank in the beauty of the five provinces intricately painted before him. He spotted the province of Gara with the thick forests and perpetual rain, Verta's vibrant green farmlands, the majestic deserts of Kreeha, the icy fortress of Neria, and finally the large coastal province of Iyera.

A large circular wooden table stood in the middle of the study surrounded by two men and a woman. The man standing on the left had weathered skin, hard blue eyes, and a muscular lean body. The other man next to him looked to be one of the oldest men Lorn had ever met. This is a spectacular feat considering the MagicBlessed have longer lifespans compared to most. The man's spine was bent, altering his height, but his eyes held an intelligence and sharpness, bordered with deep wrinkles and age spots. The woman stood next to the two men, her hair pulled back into a loose braid. She assessed Lorn with cold, gray eyes. The woman barely stood at five feet tall, yet a deadly energy exuded from her. Out of the three people at the table, Lorn's instincts, which always guided him when hunting, flashed in warning at her presence. Lord Aldrich's hand extended, gesturing for Lorn to enter the study.

"These are some of my closest advisers," Lord Aldrich explained. "Meet Gravers, my personal guard, Oron, my closest adviser, and Lilit, captain of my guard. What we are about to share with you, we have studied for years. We have toiled for this information and deem you worthy enough to share it with you."

Lord Aldrich paused to look at each of his advisers. None of them interjected, so he continued, "If you are to accept this quest, you will not be able to share this information with anyone." Lord Aldrich's eyes met Lorn, his gaze unwavering and absolute. Lorn cocked his head to the side, trying to ascertain what the quest might entail.

"How can I accept anything if I do not have any information about it?" Lorn asked. "I can hardly be expected to accept this quest if I don't even know what I am doing, or what is expected of me." His voice rose involuntarily, and he forced himself to remain level-headed. "It would be madness to agree to something this significant without first understanding the terms." Lorn finished, his gaze slowly sweeping the room, trying to glean any bit of information from Lord Aldrich's study.

Lord Aldrich circled the table and stood next to the advisers.

"I cannot tell you any specifics yet, except that it will be extremely dangerous. You will be pushed to your physical, and mental limit." Lord Aldrich paused and examined the window behind Lorn. The province of Iyera lay bathed in the afternoon sun, glory rays highlighting all the buildings and the distant market square. His gaze shifted back to Lorn like a decision had been made, and softly said, "You might not even come back alive."

Lorn exhaled a breath quickly and his weight shifted from one foot to another. He glared at each of the people in the room. "Why is my potential death worth going on this quest?" Lorn questioned. "You know nothing about me Lord Aldrich. Why involve me in the first place? I come from Verta." Lorn paused, thinking about his home province. A province of simplicity. A province focused on farming and providing food for the other provinces to survive off of. The people were hardy, but most lived a simple life. Yes, he had a great skill in hunting, but why would Lord Aldrich want him?

The Lord of Iyera locked his unsettling eyes on Lorn. He could not help the shudder that crawled up his spine. "I cannot give you the answer to all of these questions you wish to know, unless you first swear an oath to me." Lord Aldrich was unflinching, his stance rooted to the floor. He would not sacrifice any more of his information. "However, I can tell you one thing. This quest will take you into the Hinterlands." He let the statement sink in. Lord Aldrich's advisers glanced at one another, unsure of how Lorn would respond.

Lorn let out a dry laugh. "Surely you are lying. You are simply testing me to see what I will and won't do." Silence followed. Lorn looked closely at each person in the room. "Don't tell me you are serious! This is pure suicide. Of course, I won't return alive! I will step one foot into that abominable forest and be killed." Lorn paced the room running a hand through his jet-black hair.

"Do you have any idea what creatures lurk inside that forest?" he demanded.

~

Lorn reflected to when he was at the Hinterlands border. He wanted to disappear.

He wanted to be gone from the world. The overwhelming tide of grief ebbed and flowed. Lorn felt as if he was drowning. Lorn willed his body to move closer to the Hinterlands, to end it all. His wife was gone. Her beauty never to grace the world again. He would never return home to her laughter sounding through the air. He would never see her flash of desire directed at him, her dark golden skin beckoning to him in the twilight hours, her insightful gaze as if she were viewing his very soul. Day after day Lorn trekked farther, reminding himself that he wished to be reunited with his wife. Eventually he made it to the border of the Hinterlands.

The air he breathed was thick and stale. His magic felt dull in his veins, tampered by the toxic surroundings. His body resisted going in, his stomach roiling as nausea set in. The utter sense of wrongness, the twisted feeling of the Hinterlands coursed through him. Lorn forced his feet to move forward, yet his body refused. He had hunted down creatures that strayed too far from the Hinterlands— those that plagued the surrounding towns. Yet he had never stepped foot inside. Lorn fell to his knees staring into the immense forest looming before him, burying his head into his hands as tears streamed down his face. The dirt and blood from the last few days' journey clung to his skin like a shroud. Hours or even days passed. Lorn had no concept of time as he knelt there, his sorrow washing over him. A single plea from his mouth escaped, "Please, my love." Memories of Lakesh flashed through his mind. His rough calloused hands running through her strands of hair, the color of fresh tilled earth. The tender share of a kiss as he felt her sigh in his arms. The two of them sparring together, practicing with wooden batons he made from the forest bordering their cottage.

His steadfast, lovely, courageous, partner, wife.

In that moment, a part of Lorn's soul cracked and was buried at the edge of the Hinterlands. He wanted to continue, go into the wild Hinterlands, and never return. Those who entered either died or came out mad. Lorn begged the wilderness around him for release. He yearned to enter and never return. He attempted to stand, stumbling, his limbs aching and tender from being still too long. Lorn's ravaged mind was already set to enter the Hinterlands, yet as he attempted to take his first step, he felt a pull.

The mangled, grief ridden soul that remained, told Lorn not yet. He couldn't take a step forward. He damned his body, despite how much he wanted everything to end, he couldn't force himself to do it. Something else, Fate, or the Goddesses above whispered to him, not yet. Lorn screamed into the vast emptiness in front of him. No bird songs, or the chittering of animals joined him.

He was alone, with only his rage and frustration that roared throughout the never-ending forest ahead. Defeated, exhausted, and confused, Lorn chose to listen *to Fate this time and turned around. Each footstep a betrayal to the soul he buried at the edge of the Hinterlands.*

~

Lord Aldrich and his advisers stood silent as Lorn worked through his memories. He stalked over to the open window and looked out at the MidSummer festival. The noise of cheers and bouts of rowdiness carried on the wind like letters from faraway provinces. The citizens below, oblivious to the turmoil happening above. Light footsteps sounded from behind.

Lord Aldrich cleared his throat, a weak attempt to bring Lorn out of his thoughts. "I know of your skills as a hunter. I know what happened to your wife." Lorn head jerked up. A fire deep within burned in Lorn's eyes. A small feeling of magic gathered and crackled throughout the room, yet Lord Aldrich continued his honeyed persuasion. "I know you are broken. I know not long ago you craved to end your suffering." The Lord of Iyera walked closer to Lorn daring to put a hand on his shoulder. "If you swear an oath to me, to not speak of this quest to anyone, and to follow me, then I can tell you everything." The unwanted touch of Lord Aldrich jarred Lorn to the present, his eye's traveling between Lord Aldrich's and then to each of his advisers. Gravers, Oron, and Lilit all were holding their breath, their gaze unwavering. Lorn locked eyes with Lord Aldrich and gave a barely perceptible nod.

No words were needed to comment on his own suicide, for it would be a death sentence for him to willingly enter the Hinterlands.

3

"An oath binding is something sacred and precious. It is rarely seen outside of a traditional wedding ceremony."

The Book of Magical Oaths and Promises by Trevi of Gara

"Good, good" muttered Oron. "We must now do an oath binding ceremony." Despite Oron's curved back he moved quickly from behind the circular table. Oron's deep red robes swished as he walked, his slippered footsteps padding over the marble floor. "Let us do the oath binding now, that way Lorn will be fully aware of the quest and everything it entails. We have a lot of explaining to do and there is no time to waste." Oron stood across from Lorn and studied him. "Have you done an oath binding ceremony before?" Oron asked.

Lorn's jaw clenched, his teeth grinding. "Yes, my marriage ceremony."

Oron paused, his eyes downcast. The room held its breath unsure how Lorn would react, like he was a rabid animal they needed to treat carefully or else be bitten. "My apologies, it slipped my mind." Despite Oron's careless remark, his apology was sincere and Lorn unclenched his teeth, providing a sharp nod in return.

Satisfied, Oron turned and his fingers delicately moved across the book spines. He pulled a massive tome out from the shelf, shuffled back to the center table, and gently opened the weathered pages. As he searched, Oron explained, "Our magic originates from the Well. It is our entire source of magic and provides prosperity throughout our lands. It is why we are so long lived." Oron gave a dry chuckle, pausing briefly from his search to raise an eyebrow at Lorn. "The magic enhances who we are and each of our magic manifests differently. The original MagicBlessed born from the Well were the most powerful beings in this world. Since we are generations removed from them, we only have a kernel of the magic they displayed." Oron paused, his eyes rapidly scanning the book page in front of him. "One way to utilize the magic is in the form of an oath binding ceremony." Oron fingers scanned the worn page in front of him. "Your magic, your very essence will be in an agreement with Lord Aldrich's own magic." Oron's eyes drifted from Lorn to Lord Aldrich and nodded once. "What you promise in the oath, you must keep or there will be terrible repercussions. Do you fully understand the oath binding ceremony?" Oron awaited his confirmation.

An even breath eased out of Lorn as he surveyed the people gathered here. Oron appeared hopeful, while Gravers and Lilit looked ready to carve daggers into him. He finally glanced at Lord Aldrich whose face remained neutral. The motley combination of emotions was enough to set Lorn on edge, unsure of whether to tip forward and free-fall into the unknown abyss below or crawl back to the sanctuary of his preferred darkness.

"I will accept an oath only to secrecy, and nothing else," Lorn said. "I do not know exactly what this quest entails, however I will not have my magic, *my soul*, be at the mercy of someone else. I do not know what I am doing, however I promise to try and accomplish the task you set out for me." Lorn faced Lord Aldrich and met his gaze. "Clearly you aim for secrecy, since you will not give me any more details about the quest."

A beat passed where both stared at the other, Lord Aldrich listening to some internal discussion Lorn wasn't privy to and when Lorn was about to leave, Lord Aldrich nodded, conceding. "Very well, once you take the oath, you will be sworn to secrecy but there will be nothing else required of you. After the oath, you may choose whether you wish to pursue the quest or not."

Lorn hesitated and ran a hand through his errant strands of hair. He understood the severity of taking an oath binding. If he did not uphold his end of the bargain, the magic entwining him with Lord Aldrich would force him to endure a devastating reaction. Failed oath bindings revealed themselves in a variety of deadly ways. That is why oath bindings for a marriage were serious endeavors. Most couples did not go through with a traditional oath binding due to the severe repercussions.

Since Lakesh's death, his life had been a blur. He hunted the hellish creatures that strayed from the Hinterlands. Different towns required his aid, and he dedicated his time traveling to each one dispatching the twisted beasts. Often Lorn didn't accept any payment besides food and a place to sleep. His life had become a penance to make up for the beast he did not kill in time to save his wife.

He had felt it. When she was ripped apart by the Howler, he felt the oath binding snap. The comforting presence of her magic, their promises to each other, dissolved. His vows to her gone, just like her spirit.

Every day he woke up envisioning her lying next to him. Her body fit snugly next to his. His arm comfortably rested over her stomach. Lorn would lightly trace his fingers over her side, teasing, tickling. Lakesh would slowly stir and turn to face him, a smile beginning to play at the edge of her lips. "Good morning my love," Lakesh would sigh at him. Lorn would blink, and her phantom spirit would slowly fade away with the rising of the sun.

Why not embark on this quest from the Lord of Iyera? Every day has been miserable, every hour, every day spent fantasizing about Lakesh. Hollow. Empty.

"I will do the oath binding ceremony. Let us begin," Lorn announced, springing into motion. Any longer spent standing idle would result in him second-guessing his choices, retreating to the cold and empty embrace of a ghost who haunted his daily life.

Oron witnessed the uneasiness in Lorn and sought to help him. "Lorn and Lord Aldrich must face one another and clasp hands." The old man demonstrated holding his arm up at an angle with his hand curved as if to hold a cup. They copied Oron's demonstration clasping hands as if they were brothers returning from a successful hunt. Oron approved of how their hands were positioned and began reciting from the tome, his voice low and clear. Although it was the middle of the afternoon, the light seemed to dim slightly in reverence to the ceremony. "You must repeat after me. I, Lorn, promise to keep the full extent of this quest a secret." Lorn recited the line and immediately he felt a deep pull from within his spirit. A tendril of magical light flowed confidently along his forearm, snaking up to circle around their clasped hands. The magical light, pure and white, pulsed waiting for the other person's magic to arrive.

Lilit and Gravers took a sharp inhale, oath binding ceremonies outside of marriages were incredibly rare. To witness someone's magic manifest into a physical form was beautiful and enticing to watch. Seeing his magic given form gave Lorn comfort, despite the tension in the room. Everything melted in the background as he focused on this gift, this small thing of beauty that still resided within him.

In the background, Lorn faintly heard Oron drone on, "I, Lord Aldrich, accept your promise to keep the full extent of this quest a secret." Lord Aldrich repeated his line and his own magic burst forth. His magic, the color a deep mossy earth color, circled around his arm coming to wind around the clasped hands. Both of their tendrils of magic encircled around one another, pulsing, moving. Everyone in the room watched as the threads of magic partook in a silent dance. Once the thread of pure white and mossy green were fully entwined Oron spoke, "So the oath has been said, and if it is broken, unspeakable horrors will occur to the oath breaker."

Lorn gasped feeling as if his magic was tethered with an invisible branding. The entwined lines of magic slowly unraveled, rewound and traveled back up the bodies of each person. Gradually the tendrils of magic returned to their hosts, and Lorn took a steadying breath. The room remained the same, even though he felt different.

Something had changed fundamentally, his magic, the essence that lay deep within him altered.

"Let us explain how our world will be changed forever."

Lord Aldrich walked over to the open window, peering down at the city below. The sun was beginning to lower in the sky, the cries of celebrations still resonating in distant waves below. He closed the window and motioned for everyone to sit. "I'm sure you have many questions right now, and I will try my best to answer them now that you have taken the oath." Lord Aldrich looked at each person around the table, locked eyes with Oron and nodded. Oron pulled out an old, stained map of Ithilia and placed it on the table.

"Everyone here is familiar with the topography of Ithilia." Oron placed his finger in the center of the map. "This is the Well, the source of all of our magic." His finger traced the outside of the Well. "Here are the Hinterlands. This impenetrable forest prevents anyone from going in and reaching the Well." Oron shifted back into his chair assessing Lorn. "There is a prophecy," Oron leaned forward his eyes glinting, "a prophecy that something will appear from the Well."

Lorn's fingertips pressed into the surface of the table. "That is unheard of," he whispered. "Nothing has come from the Well in over a…"

"A millennium," Lord Aldrich finished. "We know this sounds like some fanciful dream, but we can assure you this is true. There is no trickery."

"Do you know what is coming from the Well? Or why you chose me?" Lorn's questions bubbled over like a pot left too long on a stove. He wanted to ask more but forced restraint on himself.

Oron and Lord Aldrich exchanged a brief look and Oron stated, "No, we don't know precisely what will appear, but we do know it will be one of the strongest items of magic we have ever encountered within the last thousand years." Oron attempted to straighten in his seat, his face a grimace. "I understand this is an undesirable quest for anyone. We are asking you to brave the Hinterlands, reach the Well and return to us with the item." Oron appeared as if he was about to say more.

Lord Aldrich intervened, "You will be heavily compensated and live the rest of your life as comfortably as you would like. Your name will be famous amongst all the MagicBlessed."

Lorn stood up abruptly from his chair, the wood screeching against the marble floor. "You never answered my second question." Lorn paused looking at each of the people seated at the table. "Why must it be me? I fail to understand why you can't send one of your own advisers, or soldiers to go instead?" Lorn scoffed, wanting to turn away from the audience at the table that scrutinized his every move.

A sharp female voice spoke up. "Oh please," Lilit sneered. "Gravers and I would easily go into the Hinterlands and spare bringing your sorry ass here in the first place." Lord Aldrich turned to his adviser, his eyes narrowing at her, willing her to behave. "We cannot go, because the prophecy was alluding to someone like you." Lilit disdainfully eyed Lorn, taking in his old, bloodied clothes. "How the prophecy was referring to you, I will never understand. *You* clearly are broken, and how *you* even manage to hunt those creatures is beyond my understanding" Lilit's cold gray eyes hardened with each declaration, but Lorn couldn't let her mockery continue. His fingers instinctively grabbed for the hilt of his sword, but it wasn't there. Gravers gave a quick smirk, clearly enjoying the verbal battering Lilit was doing.

Magic stirred in the room, as if someone were accumulating too much static electricity. Lorn gathered energy to himself, his anger fueling the rise of magic.

This was not going to end well. Lord Aldrich glared at Lilit. "That is enough Lilit! Thank you for that enlightening response." Lord Aldrich rolled his eyes as he turned to look back at Lorn. Lilit bared her teeth at Lord Aldrich but relinquished and lay back in her seat. The magic that gathered in the room slowly dissipated, but the tension in the room remained.

Attempting to diffuse the situation further Lord Aldrich stated, "What Lilit was trying to say is that the prophecy states there can only be a few who may enter the Hinterlands unharmed during a short period of time."

Gravers snorted and interjected, "You mean less harmed. Those creatures will still be harmful, but he may still escape without losing his sanity or his life."

Lord Aldrich spared a quick glance at Gravers and continued to speak as if he was never interrupted, "We believe you fit the prophecy. It seems, it was referring to someone with your hunting skills, and your background." Lord Aldrich's face remained impassive, but Lorn noticed a quick look shared between Lord Aldrich and Oron. There was more they were not telling him, but he placed that thought in the back of his mind to revisit later.

Lorn considered his options. He swore an oath to Lord Aldrich, but that only pertained to him remaining silent about the quest and the prophecy. He did not have to pursue it. He could let the item stay there untouched. But Fate above, a quest to reach the Well? No one has ever touched or looked upon the Well in a millennium. He would be the first and only. This was pure insanity, but he had nothing to live for anymore. Why not bring this item of magic back to the Lord of Iyera? Even better to come back alive, successful and shove it in the face of Lilit.

Everyone in the study looked expectantly at Lorn and awaited his decision. "I will need time to decide," Lorn announced. He walked back to the table hovering at the edge, he looked down scanning the map of Ithilia. In the middle of the map the words The Well, were written with a careful hand, as if the artist was aware of the reverence they needed when drawing the map. It lay there enticing him, but then his eyes caught the jagged abruptness of the Hinterlands jarring him from fantasies of grandeur. The Hinterlands encircled the Well, dark and foreboding. The temptation of the Well and the glory associated with being the first successful MagicBlessed was strong. However, one look at the surrounding Hinterlands soured any idea of venturing further.

Lorn's hand flattened on the table, as he gave a sigh. "Give me one night to think about it and I will return with my answer in the morning."

Oron eased himself out of his chair, stood and walked over to Lorn, and reached his aged hand forward and gently patted Lorn on the shoulder. "It is only fair we give you time to consider, but we cannot give you any longer than that." His head shook slightly, disappointed. You must make haste, because you only have one turn of the moon to reach the Well and escape from the Hinterlands, Fate willing."

Oron's bleak declaration was a silent dismissal for everyone. Gravers and Lilit left immediately, not even sparing a glance at Lorn. Oron stepped out of the room giving Lord Aldrich and Lorn some privacy to speak. "You can stay in the castle if you wish," Lord Aldrich offered. "We can easily make up one of the spare rooms for you."

While the offer was tempting, Lorn declined, preferring to roam the city to clear his head. Lord Aldrich escorted Lorn outside.

"We will await your answer tomorrow at noon. Come straight in. The guards will be alerted to let you in. I hope all the information you heard here today has persuaded you to consider the offer." Lorn nodded his head and turned away from Lord Aldrich. "Oh, one more thing Lorn." Lorn paused, glancing back. Lord Aldrich's dark brown eyes narrowed a fraction. "Do not forget about your oath binding." A shadow passed over Lord Aldrich's features bathing him in momentary darkness. He appeared unbalanced; his face hungry. Lorn blinked and the shadow passed, Lord Aldrich's features returned to the charismatic lord. Lorn locked eyes with him and gave one decisive nod back. As Lorn turned to walk back across the marble bridge, he couldn't help but feel the dark, hungry eyes of the Lord of Iyera following him all the way across.

4

"Prophecies can be tricky to interpret correctly, they are often told in images, scattered words, it is our duty to understand and record it."

From the journal of Ulmina located in the Hall of Prophecies in Kreeha.

The sun dwindled in the sky. As it sank below the horizon, it bathed the city in hues of pinks, oranges, yellows, all the buildings highlighted by the fading sun. Lorn trudged back to the main market square, unable to take in the beauty of the city, his mind too overwhelmed with replaying the strange afternoon. His options laid before him like forks in a road, unsure of which path to take.

Lorn paused in his musings, realizing his footsteps led him to a cliff overlooking the ocean. The cliff face was jagged with bits of rock jutting out into the air. Small tufts of grass and flowers lined the edge. He walked over and sat down near a small patch of grass, his legs dangling over the jagged precipice. With solid ground beneath him, Lorn was able to let go of a breath he was holding, the tension in his shoulders softening. The soft summer breeze caressed his face. Lorn closed his eyes, and enjoyed the feeling of shutting out the world, only the soothing ocean waves below sounding in his ears.

As he opened them, he spotted his wife beside him.

Lakesh looked at him, adoration and sympathy pouring out of her.

"Hello, my love," Lorn barely choked out, tears beginning to form in his eyes. Lakesh smiled, her unabashed, brazen smile that he loved so dearly. "I don't know what to do." Lorn took in a ragged breath, not daring to look away from his wife. If he looked away, this illusion, *she*, would disappear. He wanted to savor this fleeting moment with his phantom wife as long as possible.

"What do you want, Lorn?" Lakesh asked kindly, tilting her head at him, her rich brown hair flowing freely, framing her beautiful golden brown face. His name on her tongue, like a caress of his soul.

"You." Lorn started to reach out his hand and retracted it, knowing better than to touch her.

"You have many decisions before you."

"I know, and I don't know which is the right one to make. Lord Aldrich and his advisers are hiding something. This feels reckless, but what else is there for me? You are gone. Every day I wake up and dream of you. Even now you are here!" His voice grew ragged at the blatant honesty. The truth laid bare to his phantom wife. He couldn't bear how pathetic he felt right now, speaking his concerns to his dead wife. This wasn't even truly her, yet he couldn't let go. "I am empty and hollow. I have nothing left to give this world." His voice wavered, beginning to crack. Not wanting to break eye contact, he stared at her, willing her stay this time. For this moment to be forever, for her not to disappear into the fading twilight.

"I believe you have a bigger part to play in this world. I think you should go on this quest." He shook his head slowly in disagreement. Lakesh countered, "You know I am right. Even your own heart and soul betray you. You know deep within. Something is calling you to the Hinterlands. It has been ever since that day." A small, knowing smile crossed her face as her hand reached out to touch Lorn's cheek. His eyes threatened to close, as he savored the fleeting invisible touch. As he imagined her soft touch on his cheek, his own tears finally broke free and gently streamed down his face. Lorn focused on Lakesh's dark brown eyes. Her eyes were one of comfort, a face he found solace in.

He finally gave himself permission to close his eyes, clinging to every little detail about her. Memorizing each touch, each look. The sun finally sunk below the horizon, the last rays of summer peeking out. Lorn remained with his eyes closed, the delicate summer breeze rifling through his hair slowly drying the rivulets of tears that ran down his cheeks. When he opened his eyes, he found himself alone on the seaside cliff top. The sounds of celebration in the city below and the constant crash of the ocean waves were his only companions.

~

The Midsummer celebration was beginning to hit its peak. Countless bodies packed the streets. Lorn tried to navigate the busy market streets, attempting to make his way back to the inn. Delicate paper lanterns adorned the buildings, strung from one side of the street to the other.

Bursts of light flashed sporadically as people gifted with fire magic demonstrated their skills with shapes and designs filled the air to impress the gathering children. Lorn caught quick smiles shared between lovers and friends. He almost stumbled as a pack of children ran underfoot. The children disappeared as he caught his bearings, laughter echoing down the alley. Their child-like playfulness lifted his veil of sorrow.

Thinking about Lakesh often sent him in a downward spiral of emotion he had to climb out of tooth and nail. Ever since her death, Lorn struggled to truly fit in with MagicBlessed society. Lingering on the outskirts, he was only called in to deal with the feral beasts that escaped the Hinterlands. Taking part in the pleasantries and celebrations of their community took too much effort, his pain a secret knife to his heart.

The scent of food carried on the heat baked wind leading Lorn to the food vendors. The vendors were busy preparing their food for the long lines of hungry people. Sweet pastries, barbecued meats, roasted vegetables, grilled fish, bowls of noodles and more were being prepared. Lorn's stomach rumbled as he passed all the food stalls. Realizing he hadn't eaten anything since that morning, he pulled out one of the few coins he had left and paid for a grilled fish resting on a bed of rice. He found a secluded bench and wolfed down the fish, which was flaky, delicate, and heavily spiced. Satiated, Lorn looked around at the crowd gathered in the market square.

Tonight was the first night of the Midsummer celebration. For the first and last night of the week, everyone would be up until the late morning hours celebrating. Tomorrow, everyone would be lazily dozing in their beds recovering from their overindulgences. Once the sun reached its zenith, the endless cycle of celebration would begin again with the streets packed shoulder to shoulder. During the whole week of the Midsummer celebration, people were carefree, work halted—apart from the food vendors who tried to make the most coin possible.

Wishing to retire and rest in his rented room, Lorn shouldered through the crowd to the local inn, situated two small streets off the main market square. The densely built structures muted the sounds of celebration coming from the main market square. A few people milled about outside of the inn, enjoying the cool summer night. Lorn entered and nodded to the woman behind the desk. Groups of people were scattered around the tables, preferring to eat their dinner inside. Lively chatter filled the room, the familiar buzz of people sharing stories and experiences. Tired from the day and ignoring it all, Lorn walked up the stairs to find his room, seeking the comfort of his own counsel. The inn was small and only held three rooms for people to rent out. Lorn entered the third room, closing the door behind him. A habit born out of precaution; he locked the door.

The room Lorn rented was small, but he had stayed in far worse. As long as he had a place to sleep, he didn't mind. Whatever meager offerings townspeople could give him, Lorn accepted it graciously, happy to be ridding the world of the vicious Hinterland beasts. Oftentimes he spent his nights sleeping in barns next to the farm animals or sleeping outside under the comfort of the night sky.

A small bed occupied the right side of the room, a wooden dresser directly across from it. Next to his bed were his small bag of belongings. Lorn never required much to travel with, a few changes of clothes, travel rations, and his weapons. Atop the dresser was a pitcher of water, a small basin, a crude bar of soap and a fresh cloth to wash with, courtesy of the innkeeper. In the back of the room was a window, overlooking a small alley behind the inn. The window was cracked open allowing the cool, welcome breeze from outside to air out the increasingly stuffy room.

Dirt and sweat from the long day clung to him. Thankful for the thoughtful innkeeper, Lorn strode over to the dresser. He poured the pitcher of water into the small metal basin, wet the cloth, lathered the soap, and started methodically removing all the dirt from the day. By the end Lorn was sluggish and tired. Before going to bed, Lorn removed his weapons from behind the dresser. Knowing he was going to meet the Lord of Iyera today, he didn't bother bringing them along. They would have been confiscated upon entry. With the Midsummer celebration, he didn't want to garner any negative attention, looking as if he was armed for battle.

Lorn pulled out his bow and arrows. The bow familiar in his grip, his fingers ran over the curves and notches from the hours he toiled on it. He carved the bow himself from an oak tree on his property, his father helping him to pick out the best tree possible. He remembered the tilt of his father's mouth as Lorn sought his approval over the wood he picked for his bow.

Returning to the task at hand, Lorn counted the arrows and double-checked that none were missing. Laying his bow aside, he pulled out the few hunting daggers he had, and lastly his longsword. The longsword was something he couldn't craft himself, but he recalled when his mother escorted him to town. His mother and father always stressed the importance of having a proper weapon and learning how to defend oneself. It had cost a large sum of money and Lorn had treasured it from the day he received it from the blacksmith. The steel shined back at him, a mockery of what blood would stain it in the future.

Lorn was exhausted but followed his nightly ritual. He patted the dagger strapped to his right leg and ensured a second was underneath his pillow. His head hit the soft down of the pillow and he fell into a rare, dreamless sleep.

~

Lorn's eyes flashed open. He was not alone in his room. The room was bathed in darkness, except by the open window where the moonlight beamed through. Lorn lay motionless on his side, his hand slowly curling around the hunting dagger under his pillow. Whoever was in the room, was standing behind him, nearly silent footsteps moving slowly toward him. Lorn feigned the steady rise and fall of his chest and waited, hearing the footsteps draw closer. A slight hitch in the intruder's breath warned Lorn to act now. He rolled off the bed away from the intruder and stood upright clutching the dagger in his hand. The intruder was dressed all in black with a cowl over their head obscuring their features. None of the features were discernible in the darkness. The intruder backed up, wary now that Lorn was awake.

"This will be easier now that you are awake," a male voice whispered. A voice that hinted at secrets being hidden and prized. "Tell me why you met with the Lord of Iyera. Tell me everything that went on, all of the information you discovered, and I will let you go." He circled the bed, closing the gap between him and Lorn.

The glint of the intruder's blade warned Lorn that he wouldn't be free, no matter what was promised. Even if he wanted to share the information, his oath-binding prevented him from uttering a word of the quest. If he did, cosmic retribution would rain down on him. Lorn looked around the room and assessed the situation. The window was still open. The intruder must have scaled the building and come in through there. Lorn cursed himself for being so careless, not used to dealing with the conniving traits of people rather than the predictability of wild beasts. He had locked the door, but completely forgot about the open window.

The intruder crept towards Lorn, intending to trap him in the corner of the room. Lorn realizing the intruder's intent, quickly slashed at him, creating more space for himself. The intruder jerked back barely avoiding Lorn's dagger. Although Lorn was more accustomed to fighting creatures and beasts from the Hinterlands, he still knew how to hold his own against another person. Growing up, his parents had relentlessly trained him in everything he knew today. Their strict tutelage was what allowed him to slay the rampant beasts from the Hinterlands. Even after he married Lakesh, he continued his training and trained her too.

Steadying his breathing, Lorn studied his opponent. The intruder tried to get Lorn off balance by moving into his space and swung his dagger upwards. Lorn deflected with his own dagger and maneuvered himself so he was steadier on his feet. Lorn had a bigger build and less to lose compared to this intruder. Whereas this intruder needed information, Lorn only needed to survive. Luckily, he has been surviving his whole life even when darkness threatened to swallow him up.

Powering through the intruder's defenses, he knocked his arm aside and plunged the dagger into the intruder's shoulders. Lorn was not aiming to kill the man, he only wanted to injure him enough to find out more details on why he was here.

The intruder released a sharp breath as the dagger plunged in, blood drenching his cloak. His cowl shifted back enough for Lorn to vaguely glimpse his face. It was oddly plain, no discerning features, his skin white, pale, and his eyes an unremarkable brown. The intruder was born to be a spy for his features were so plain, enabling him to blend in easily.

"Why are you following me?" Lorn had the intruder pinned to the wall with his weight and his hand forcefully still on the dagger ready to twist if the intruder showed any signs of struggling.

"You had a meeting with Lord Aldrich. Who wouldn't be curious about that?" the man grunted out.

"Who are you and who do you report to?"

The intruder gave a mocking smile. "There are many who read the ancient scriptures and prophecies. Many who know something is about to happen, something that will alter Ithilia. Lord Aldrich is cunning enough to have figured it out." The intruder paused, grimacing in pain as his wound continued to bleed. "I am no one, and I have no answers to give you."

Displeased with his answer Lorn slightly twisted the knife in his shoulder. The intruder's body tensed from the pain. "You will tell me what you know."

The intruder looked unblinkingly at Lorn. "That will never happen." So quickly that Lorn couldn't react, he was pushed backwards, his body flying towards the bed. The intruder went to the window and leaped down onto the road below. Lorn raced to the window, scanning the street below. The intruder was already gone, like a wisp of smoke disappearing into the air.

Lorn cursed himself for letting the intruder slip away. A magical manifestation of physical strength was rare. The provinces coveted and prized it amongst their spies, captains and guards. That was the only way he could have slipped out of Lorn's grasp. Lorn paced the room, his mind racing with what happened. It was still the middle of the night. He realized he wouldn't be allowed in the castle at this time. He would have to wait in case anyone else decided to come back from the other provinces. Lorn grabbed his weapons, sat on the edge of his bed, and began to methodically clean his dagger, waiting.

~

Although Lord Aldrich instructed him to return at noon, Lorn departed the small inn during the early hours. He stayed up the rest of the night, thinking through all his options. Lord Aldrich and his advisers failed to mention anything about being hunted by people. Lorn didn't know he would be facing a different sort of beast, and the Hinterlands wasn't the only danger he would encounter. His anger fueled his steps as he raced through the town up to the castle traveling the same switchbacks from the other day. A single day that felt like a lifetime ago. How much had altered since his last trip up to this castle?

The sun was barely peeking over the Wyra ocean as he made it to the castle, the sky slashed open and blood red painted the dense clouds. Guards stationed around the entrance stopped him immediately.

"Get Lord Aldrich out here, and if he doesn't come, then tell him his hunter quits!" Lorn seethed. With his longsword strapped to his back alongside his bow, daggers glinting off his thighs—he was a sight to behold. Fully equipped, Lorn was every bit the beast-hunter the rumors claimed him to be.

The guards looked questioningly at one another, but eventually conceded. One scurried off to inform Lord Aldrich. Surrounded by the same garden from yesterday, flowers blooming and the nearby fountains bubbling, the sounds and smells did nothing to quell his anger. He continued to pace in front, focused on calming his breath as he tried to take in the beauty around him. His blood pounded in his veins. Lord Aldrich knew of this danger and yet let him leave without any warning. He could barely hear over the roaring in his ears.

One of the guards tentatively stepped forward and interrupted Lorn's pacing, telling him to come into the castle. He was escorted back into the same study from yesterday afternoon. Dismissing the guard, Lord Aldrich now stood alone in the room.

All the anger bottled up inside of Lorn erupted. "I was nearly killed this morning. Did you know someone would be following me?" He stood his ground, staring at Lord Aldrich. Lorn already had an underlying suspicion that Lord Aldrich knew about the danger.

Despite the early morning of Lorn's interruption, Lord Aldrich was perfectly presentable. "We suspected people from other provinces might be interested in the information. If you agreed to go, we would have warned you about spies potentially following you and wanting information." He waved an errant hand in Lorn's direction, a slight flickering of his fingers betraying any sign of irritation or surprise. "I certainly did not think you would be attacked already."

"I only hunt beasts and foul creatures. I do not enjoy hurting or killing people," Lorn said stiffly. "If that is what you want from me, I refuse to follow your quest."

Lord Aldrich slowly shook his head. "I do not want you to kill any people. This was... unexpected." He paused, deciding his next words carefully. "I would have told you about the potential attacks, but I did not realize they would act so quickly. I'm sorry about this whole situation, but I hope you will consider the offer and pursue our goal." Although Lord Aldrich was calm, almost feigning indifference, Lorn caught a fleeting glimpse of fear in his eyes. This quest was important to him, to his advisers, and to this province. This newly forged magic item could create a new era of prosperity in the land of Ithilia.

There were no noisy distractions or other people to drag Lorn's attention to, only this mysterious lord. His anger fizzled out as quickly as it had arisen. Something within him was pulling him towards the Hinterlands and he could not ignore it any longer. He knew he should listen to the call. Lorn ran a hand through his hair, loosening a breath. "Yes I will go into the Hinterlands and bring back the magic item that appears, but you must tell me everything about the dangers I could be facing."

Lord Aldrich gave a feline smile, one that did not complement his face but distorted his features. "Alright, how about some breakfast first?"

5

"The magic of the MagicBlessed can manifest in many ways. Usually all have access to the basic elements of nature such as wind, fire, water, earth. These can present themselves uniquely per the individual. Magic may manifest a bit strangely. It is assumed the magic forms from their personal interests or personality traits. For example, a person with the skill of manipulating the earth may be a great chef. They can bring each item created to the peak of freshness."

Excerpt from *The Secrets of our Magic* by Yorune of Gara

Lord Aldrich led Lorn through the castle to a private dining room. The room was covered with floor to ceiling glass windows allowing the bright morning sun to filter in. The castle grounds and city below were quiet, too many people out late last night reveling in their Midsummer celebration. They would all be sleeping in and gently stirring later in the day. Only the faint chittering of birdsong pierced the quiet. In the middle of the room lay a quaint wood table, with four chairs scattered around.

"Please relax and get comfortable. I will alert the cooks to bring food up directly to you." Without waiting for a response, Lord Aldrich left the room.

Lorn sat in one of the chairs and his muscles slowly unwound all the built-up tension from his eventful morning. He looked at the expansive windows drawn to the faint line of the Iyerian countryside and a pang of longing for his home shot through him. A home that could never truly return to him.

He longed to be outside again, far away from city life with the cold air tingling his skin, the fresh scent of the dew-coated grass. Visiting the city of El'en was impressive and gave him a rush of excitement, but he found himself quickly drained, stifled, and yearning to be out, alone with only the wilderness to comfort him. Lorn realized he would be leaving soon enough, but the wilderness he would be in was one of death. Huffing a breath, he reminded himself he was the one who chose to pursue this quest. It was his choice to potentially forfeit his life in the unforgiving Hinterlands. Was it his choice though? Choosing to acknowledge it or not, deep down he felt this inexplicable pull towards the Hinterlands.

A polite knock on the door interrupted his reverie as an older man popped his head in. "We have your breakfast, sir. May we come in?" Lorn nodded his head as plate after plate was carried into the room. He stared in disbelief at the amount of food brought in. The older man spotted the look on Lorn's face and explained, "Lord Aldrich said you would be hungry and to serve you the very best." Lorn thanked the older man and examined the plates in front of him, determining which one to devour first.

The table he sat at could barely hold all the food they placed on it. Decadent breakfast pastries, fluffy buttery eggs, fresh rolls, piles of ripe fruit and heaps of crispy bacon splayed across the table. Lorn's stomach growled loudly, encouraging him to take a bite. He tried to think back to a time when he last had a meal like this. He couldn't think of a time, many of his meals after Lakesh's death had been purely for sustenance. There was no enjoyment, only an innate need to stay alive.

Before her death, they lived on the outskirts of a nearby town. While they had a farm with access to food, they usually ate sparingly. The winters could be harsh, and food was needed to be stored throughout the winter. Their meals were still lovely, but in much more modest portions. Taking a large bite, his mouth exploded with flavor. Without a care for decorum he shoveled the food in, trying to pace himself. The food rivaled nothing he had ever had before. Pondering over it, Lorn came to the realization the chef's magic must relate to food. While many MagicBlessed could conjure basic elements such as water or fire, some magic manifested in more particular ways, such as fighting, or cooking. The chef could imbue the food with better taste, essentially bringing the food to its ripest and freshest state.

Lorn leaned back in his chair, satiated and impressed. The current generation of MagicBlessed held a small amount of power and their magic depleted quickly. Lord Aldrich must have alerted the chef to use any magic reserves on Lorn's breakfast. His righteous anger quelled with a full belly.

A few hours had passed since he showed up this morning and Lorn felt content and full. He was just about to roam the castle when Lord Aldrich strolled in. He wore black pants, a loose black tunic and an elaborate coat. On the coat was a small stitching of a sun. The rest of the coat was a swirl of different colors, blues, turquoise, cerulean, and small strips of white and black woven throughout. Lorn studied the coat for a second and realized all the blues represented the ocean. The coat captured the roiling essence of the ocean below Iyera's castle, a subtle but powerful hint to the province's origins.

"Are you ready?" Lord Aldrich asked. Lorn briskly nodded and made to follow. They returned to the study from the prior day. Gravers, Lilit, and Oron already sat around the table waiting expectantly.

"We heard you had some problems already," Lilit's cold gray eyes narrowed, taking in Lorn's disheveled appearance, and the small bits of dried blood on shirt. Lorn's jaw clenched, ready to give an acerbic retort, when Gravers gave a small chuckle.

"Well at least he's still alive, and hopefully the other person is worse off," Gravers clapped a firm hand onto Lilit's back, a subtle warning. Lilit gave a faint snarl and threw his hand off her lithe form.

Lord Aldrich rushed in, before things could escalate too quickly. "We don't know who tried to attack you in the night. Did you see anything notable about them, or what the person looked like?"

Lorn paused to reflect on the chaotic moment of the prior night, but like a steel trap he never let the image of the attacker fade from his mind. "He was oddly plain. Unremarkable even. His skin was white, pale and he had brown eyes. He wore a cowl which covered his features, until I stabbed him in the shoulder. I believe he escaped, because he was able to use his magic to aid his physical strength."

Lord Aldrich and his advisers looked at one another, each shaking their heads, their expressions grim. "That description doesn't sound familiar to any of us. Whoever sent him is trying to keep themselves hidden. Now I know you want answers. We believe we are the only ones who have the information given to you about the Well. However, the rest of the provinces could have an inkling of the knowledge we have, and they want to know more."

Lorn thought back to the encounter with the intruder. The man only knew that Lorn had met with Lord Aldrich, but what he really wanted was information about their meeting. What Lord Aldrich was saying rang true. "Will more be pursuing me? I was recruited by you to enter the Hinterlands. To hunt beasts, not men."

Oron gently shook his head. "While there may be people pursuing you into and out of the Hinterlands, we do not think anyone else besides you can enter. The people who try to follow will either be killed by the beasts or driven mad."

Lorn glanced down at the dried blood on his shirt. "I will not kill another person, if that is a problem then you need to find yourselves another hunter." Lilit rolled her eyes but Lorn ignored her. "I do not mind harming them to slow them down, but I will not end a life." Lorn stared at Lord Aldrich. "That is a line I will not cross."

Lord Aldrich's fathomless eyes held Lorn's gaze. "I'm hoping it will never come to that."

With his boundaries set and clear, Lorn sat down at the table and the official meeting began. Oron and Gravers detailed the quickest way to reach the Hinterlands. Everyone decided even though Lorn was being pursued, he should still venture alone. He would be less conspicuous going on his own, compared to being accompanied by Lilit and Gravers. Lord Aldrich would provide Lorn with a horse and supplies. Since no one had entered the Hinterlands and survived, they assumed Lorn would need to pack plenty of food and water. Food sources could be difficult to come by.

Although Lorn can summon small amounts of water with his magic, he did not want to rely upon that ability. Worried about the toll on his body from using magic, and the unreliable nature of magic inside the Hinterlands, they agreed he should be prepared. Lord Aldrich offered Lorn new weapons, but Lorn declined, preferring his worn weapons, their touch as familiar to him as his own body. With their limited timeframe, Lorn was to leave tonight under the cover of darkness and travel as far as he could go until he reached an inn. He would stay there, have a quick meal and buy a new horse. With the new steed, he would continue traveling until the next farthest inn. They assumed a combination of speed and stealth would keep Lorn safe until he reached the Hinterlands. Once at the second inn, he could truly rest and travel on a more traditional schedule. When he reached the edge of the Hinterlands, he would release his horse, and he would enter alone.

This route took him straight through Iyera. The group discussed the advantages and disadvantages of staying or avoiding the main road—Merchant's Road—and eventually decided for him to stick to it. Taking too long, looping through small side roads and off path could be disastrous for the horse and Lorn. With the limited window of time, there was only one turn of the moon for Lorn to enter the Hinterlands and get out. During their discussion, there was a constant unasked statement including a when and if Lorn ever escaped alive. It lingered in every statement like a foul mold hidden in your food, tainting the mere taste of it. If he returned, Lilit and Gravers would try to meet with him at the inn closest to the Hinterland border of Iyera, near the city of Shadow Acre.

Once the details were finalized and they were all in agreement, Lord Aldrich led Lorn to a sleeping chamber. Just like everything else in the castle, the room was decadent and filled with items that flaunted the wealth of his province. The room was roughly the size of Lorn's old cottage. A giant bed filled the room with a window on the far side, thick drapes blocking the sunlight. A washroom was attached to the room, with shelves overflowing with soaps, and oils held in ornate glass bottles.

"Wash and sleep for the remainder of the day. Tonight and the next few weeks will be spent without any luxury. Let me know if you need anything." Lord Aldrich left the room, allowing Lorn privacy.

Realizing he was coated in the intruder's blood, he walked over to the washroom and turned on the tap for the bath. Hot water on demand was a luxury Lorn rarely experienced. His rural cottage on the border of Verta and the Hinterlands was far removed from any big cities with proper indoor plumbing. All of his prior baths were painstakingly prepared by hand with buckets of water heated over his giant hearth. He experimented with the various bottles of oils, sniffed each one and decided upon an earthy, rosemary scent. As the bath filled, Lorn discarded his clothing, which reeked of the past week's travel. Lord Aldrich had promised him new clothing anyway.

Lorn turned the tap off and gingerly stepped into the massive bathtub. Tendrils of steam rose from the water as he lowered himself in. Once submerged, Lorn rested his head on the back of the tub, closed his eyes and savored this final luxury. He had never experienced such richness in his life, not out of refusal but out of practicality. Life in the country didn't lend itself to such self-indulgences. Considering his life may be over once he entered the Hinterlands, he decided to enjoy this moment.

When the bathwater cooled, Lorn reluctantly got out. A stack of towels lay stacked next to the bathtub. He grabbed one, quickly dried off, and walked over to the bed. The heavy drapes hid the bright sun of the day from view. If he was going to ride a horse all night, he needed to recover now. Lorn laid in the bed and his body sank down in the softness of it like he was resigning himself to a cloud. He had barely pulled a blanket over himself as he succumbed to sleep.

~

The forest moved past him in a blur of brown and green. A darkness crawled alongside him, shadowing his footsteps. He was heading back home. Their quaint cottage lay on the outskirts of town nestled on the edge of the woods. Lorn had been out hunting, his bow casually slung across his back. His mind too distracted, he failed to catch the deer he was tracking so he decided to come back home. It was barely noon and the sun was scorching overhead. Lakesh would be tending to the animals, probably mindlessly humming some tunes as she worked. He smiled, imagining her voice carried on the wind. She wasn't a beautiful singer, but the heart she put behind it made the songs endearing to listen to.

Everything was unusually quiet. His stomach lurched and his body quivered. Something wasn't right. Sprinting he came closer and closer to his cottage.

Every thought emptied from his mind as he found Lakesh pinned underneath a foul beast. Howlers were a myth, something joked about in taverns as patrons were well into their cups, not something real with his beloved pressed to the ground underneath one.

The creature stood nearly seven feet tall, its body contorted into harsh lines and shapes. Its elongated snout ended with deadly sharp teeth. Saliva dripped down the creature's blood-flecked mouth as Lakesh struggled under its grasp.

The beast bore burn marks around its face indicating Lakesh's magic had been used. The creature's lanky fur matted to its twisted face, it stood on its back two legs, its body lean and muscular, but its lack of food twisted its shape into a grotesque mockery. Ribs were outlined in its mangy fur. Fur of a lifeless color, like a body drained of blood, gray and ashen. A lone dagger protruded from the creature's leg, blood seeping down onto the ground, the Howler unphased.

Lorn's pride for his wife flared. She had held her own against this formidable beast. Lakesh pulled out another small knife, a knife she used for a menial farmhouse task kept along the inside of her apron. She pulled her arm up sharply, slashing the beast across its concave chest. The beast's luminous yellow eyes went wild with pain and it lashed out with its claws, catching Lakesh's face. The claw marks gouged her face, the blood gleaming red, smearing across her beautiful golden brown skin. Lakesh screamed at the beast, a scream of pure feral energy. Fighting, her body wriggled underneath attempting to find an escape.

Lorn looked on in horror, his feet stuck to the ground. Lorn fought harder and harder, but his feet remained, unable to move, unable to intervene. The darkness and shadows held onto his feet, entwining itself around his body. The shadows held Lorn back, his body heaving, struggling to break the bindings, as he watched his wife. Lakesh's eyes flashed over to Lorn. "No! Run, Lorn!" Her final words extinguished as the beast ripped her open and ended her life.

The darkness and shadows encircled his body and whispered in his ear, "You did this." Lorn flinched, unable to look away from the destruction of his wife. "Her suffering. Her life. Gone, because of you." Lorn's mouth opened in a silent scream. The darkness entered him and did not leave.

6

"The light dims on this treasured day,
I would have hoped you stayed.
But our ways must part for now,
I'll search for you somehow.
You are seared in my soul.
Never again to be whole."
Random singer at the Midsummer festival

Lorn jolted upright, his chest heaving. He brandished the dagger in front of him and quickly scanned the room for any danger. Loosening a breath, he collapsed back in bed, and ran a hand through his hair, his grip relaxing on the dagger. A quick knock at the door had him instinctively raising the dagger protectively in front of him again. The door creaked open, and Oron's bone white hair popped into view. "It is time to go," Oron said pointedly ignoring Lorn's defensive position. He left the room and closed the door behind him.

Lorn tried not to spend any time thinking about his nightmare. He still felt the coils of darkness around him. Squeezing him, encircling him. He studied his arms looking for any marks or bruises of the haunting nightmare. Nothing.

Trying to shake off the feeling of unease creeping over him, he dressed quickly and chose a light pair of brown pants, a long sleeve cotton shirt, and leather boots. Although the weather in Iyera was light and temperate most of the year, the weather of the Hinterlands was an unknown they couldn't predict. Unsure of what to expect, he packed a heavy cloak, and another set of warmer, wool clothing. After equipping his weapons, he headed out to the stables where they had agreed to meet. The sun barely dipped below the horizon as Lorn made it outside. The light coated the sky in one final glow. Lorn tried to hide his awe. How did Lord Aldrich become so accustomed to such beauty in his province every day? The sounds of the Midsummer festival carried all the way up to him. While not as loud as last night, the celebration was still going strong.

The stables were as immaculate as the rest of the castle. The ground was inlaid with paving stones, laid down in a precise circular design. The stables were constructed of wood and metal, with the beechwood smoothed and marbled with rich browns. The stables housed roughly ten horses with the rest of Lord Aldrich's horses housed in a stable on the outskirts of El'en near their military barracks. Each horse was well cared for, their fur coats glistening, their bodies healthy and muscular as they lazily chomped hay in their own stalls. Lord Aldrich, Gravers, Oron and Lilit stood outside of one of the stalls waiting for Lorn.

"This is your horse for the first night. Once you reach the inn, remember to switch her out for a new horse," Lord Aldrich explained, rubbing the horse's neck. While he was speaking, the horse popped its head out and began gently nibbling on Lorn's shoulder. The mare had a smooth chestnut coat with her mane an even deeper brown. Lorn looked at her and stroked along her neck. A bucket of carrots lay at his feet. He reached down and grabbed one, handing it out to the horse. She eagerly accepted the treat, munching away happily.

"Remember you only have one turn of the moon to get into the Hinterlands, reach the Well and get back out," Oron added. Lorn nodded, he had repeated the plans in his head multiple times. He was familiar with everything.

Lord Aldrich tipped his head towards Lilit and Gravers. "They will be waiting for you at the closest inn to the Hinterlands when you are finished. Do not look for them, they will find you. They will attempt to be inconspicuous, just in case others are trying to intercept you coming out."

"Good luck, Lorn. You will need it." Gravers shook Lorn's hand, his icy blue eyes fixed upon him.

"Try not to die while you are in there," Lilit snarled, disdain dripping off every word like blood from a wound. Lorn's magic flared and urged him to fight her, to force her to back up her words with actions. Lorn scolded himself. He needed to reign in his anger and not let an entitled captain rile him up.

Lilit must have noticed a change in his eyes for a deadly smile stretched across her face, one implying mutual destruction. Her hands lingered around the hilt of her sword ready to engage. The mare began to whinny, sensing Lorn's frenetic shift in energy.

Lord Aldrich glared at Lilit. She shrugged and relaxed the hand on her sword. The intensity in the air, the crackle of potential magic dissipated as if the incoming breeze had swept it out of the room.

"We will have our fun soon enough hunter." Lilit strode past Lorn and knocked her shoulder into him. Although Lilit stood a good head shorter than Lorn, he stumbled as if someone twice her size had run into him. He reached out a hand to steady himself on the walls of the stable. Lilit glanced back over her shoulder, smirking as she left the stables.

Lord Aldrich cleared his throat. "I apologize for her behavior. She is jealous of not being able enter the Hinterlands herself. She shouldn't have used her magic against you." Lorn brushed himself off, nodded and accepted the weak apology. He was ready to depart. Before his walk to the stables, he had wanted to enjoy all the luxuries the castle offered, yet now his body was jittery, ready to leave and face whatever challenges awaited. Once the horse was saddled and packed with supplies, Lorn threw on his heavy cloak and mounted the horse. "If we do not hear or see you for one month, we will assume you are dead. If something goes wrong, try to send a message," Lord Aldrich reminded him keeping pace alongside the horse.

Lorn led the horse away from the castle towards the bridge. The night blanketed the entire city of El'en. Lights flickered in the distance, as torches and lamps lit up the streets. Without any goodbyes or well-wishes, Lorn rode his horse away and crossed the pristine marble bridge, the ocean tearing underneath.

~

With the Midsummer festival still occurring all week, Lorn decided to avoid going directly through the market square. It would be packed with people, difficult to navigate, and easy for someone to track him without him noticing. He kept his hood up, his features indiscernible in the darkness. Descending the winding roads from the castle Lorn led his horse around the edge of the market square, his pace slow and measured. By avoiding heavily trafficked areas and traversing side alleys he finally reached the outer limits of El'en without incident. Buildings were spaced further apart, and the roads widened. People who lived on the edge of the city chose to either congregate in the market square or stayed home preferring to celebrate quietly. The city gates loomed in front of him, the metal portcullis raised. He relaxed his shoulders away from his ears, using his years of hunter-trained senses to be alert for anything amiss. The men and women on guard duty tonight eyed him speculatively but let him pass. He urged his horse into a trot, increased his speed, and left the beautiful city of El'en behind.

Lord Aldrich, his advisers, and Lorn all agreed for him to travel at night. They wanted fewer people tracking his movements and believed a lone rider would be less noticeable as the Midsummer festival went on. The Merchant's Road leading from El'en to the next inn was incredibly well-maintained. It was smooth, with no holes or bumps for his horse to twist their hooves. As he got further away from the city, the sounds of the festival faded away. Only the steady beat of his horse's hooves and his even breathing filled the air.

Houses dotted the streets as he rode. The inside of each house illuminated from within, like a brief storybook picture of the countless lives gathered there. A small amount of bitterness coated his tongue as he imagined all the happy families, safe within their homes, blissfully unaware of the dangerous tasks he performed for them and the joy they were able to have because of him.

He pictured himself as one of them. Inside. Safe. Candles lit within, and a smile on Lakesh's face. She would reverently cradle their child, the babe wrapped in blankets blissfully sleeping. A peaceful quietness would encase them, a small moment of stillness. With their hands entwined, Lorn would gently raise her hand to kiss the back of it.

A quick jolt from his horse caused the fantasy to crumble away and the stark reality settle in as Lorn gained awareness of where he was. He shook the bitterness from his body like a dog ridding himself of unwanted water on his coat. This was his purpose. This was why he hunts beasts from the Hinterlands—to protect these families so they can remain safe in their houses, unaware of the quiet evils lurking outside.

Lorn set a blistering pace as he rode throughout the night, taking in the scenery of Iyera. The province was beautiful. Bordering the Wyra ocean provided the province with a temperate climate, allowing countless flowers and plants to grow everywhere. He rode over small rolling hills, each hillside lined with rows and rows of grapevines. The moonlight gilded the edge of the trellises supporting the grapes, highlighting their delicacy. The grapes in El'en were highly treasured and coveted, providing some of the most delicious wine in all five provinces.

Lorn vowed to remember everything, remember every bit of scenery, every bit of land. When he went into the Hinterlands, he might never come out again.

The night lightened as day returned, and Lorn finally arrived at the first inn. He led his mare into the small stables behind the inn and found a young stable hand to help his horse. After he instructed him about the proper care of his mare, Lorn slipped a few coins into his hand and headed inside.

His whole body ached from riding all night. He wished he could rest now, but Lorn knew he needed to continue. All he wanted was a quick, hot meal and to purchase a new horse. The innkeeper was a friendly, older man who informed Lorn that breakfast was being prepared. The inn was quiet, small groups of travelers were clustered around the tables. Bleary eyes, and yawns were common among the groups. No one paid attention to Lorn as he found a secluded table in the back and sat down. Lorn let out a quick breath as he rearranged his legs, the muscles stiff and sore from riding all night. He glanced around surreptitiously, checking to see if any of the inhabitants from the inn were watching him. Nothing unusual, nothing stood out. Lorn was not accustomed to this concept of cloak and daggers stealth. Sitting in a corner, hiding, attempting to be discreet was beginning to mentally wear on him, always seeing enemies in place of strangers. Even though his body was exhausted, he couldn't help but feel on edge as if a hidden pair of eyes were watching him and waiting for the moment to strike.

A door banged open, jolting Lorn as his eyes darted to the door, his hand hovering around the hilt of his dagger. A middle-aged man bustled out carrying hot trays of food, the steam curling up in ribbons. Lorn's hand dropped from around his dagger, his breath coming out in a slow exhale. A plate of food dropped unceremoniously in front of him. Eggs, sausage and bread. Lorn's stomach growled in response, and he dug in, washing the whole meal down with a warm cup of tea.

Lorn fought the aches twinging his body as he stood up and walked back to the stables to find his fresh horse for the next leg of his journey. He saddled the new horse with his supplies and was ready to depart. Lorn was always hesitant to be dependent on his magic, but his body ached looking at the horse he needed to ride. Spending another full day on a horse was not appealing. He did a mental scan of his body and slowly sent out his magic to refresh his tired muscles. Cautious, as to not overdo it, he used just enough of his magic to feel his muscles recover from stiffness. The use of his magic was akin to soaking his muscles in a hot spring. The memory of the soreness still echoed in the body, but it was tolerable. Lorn led his new mare out of the stables, mounted and went down the path heading west, towards the Hinterlands.

Traveling during the day provided Lorn with a much better view of Iyera, however the hot summer sun beat down on him as he went. He rested a few times, allowing his mare to drink from any streams they came across. He encountered more people on the road during the daytime, and continually reminded himself to be cautious, to trust no-one. Never in his life had he treated others with such outright suspicion, but he did not need another encounter like the one in El'en.

The days and nights blurred together. As dusk began to settle, Lorn reached a new inn, fell into a dreamless sleep, and rose as the sun did to prepare his horse to leave. He ate quickly, trying not to linger too long at any one place, trying to appear as if he was calm and just a normal traveler trying to get home. Every time he entered an inn, uncertainty claimed him, his eyes darting, looking for people out of the ordinary, people trying to hunt him before he reached his destination. At night, he took extra precautions, locking the doors and arming himself with weapons before he went to sleep. Nothing. Besides the constant paranoia, his days were spent enjoying the last remnants of the Iyerian countryside.

On his fifth day of travel, he finally reached the town of

ShadowAcre. The land of Ithilia was prosperous due to the magic of the Well that pulsed throughout the kingdom like its lifeblood. However, there were towns like ShadowAcre, run down, and disused. Why it still existed Lorn had no idea. As he rode by on his horse, he passed by buildings, warped and worn from time and close proximity to the Hinterlands. Maybe the foul magic of the Hinterlands had plagued this town, the residents as aged and lifeless as the buildings they inhabited. Lorn pulled his cloak tighter, trying to dispel any unwanted attention from the residents. As he passed they eyed his horse and clothes. Even though Lorn dressed plainly, the quality of his clothes stood out in this drab town. Tonight, he would need to be alert, not for anyone from other provinces following him, but from these desperate townspeople robbing him.

The light of the day slipped away like the snuff of a candle and thick clouds began to roll in overhead commandeering the sky. Lorn could feel the air thick around him as if it had trapped all the heat from the day. His face and body were covered in a thin sheen of sweat. His light cloak added to the sweat, but Lorn refused to remove it, wanting to remain inconspicuous as he passed through this sad town.

Lorn spotted the inn—an old, weathered building made of rough stone with many blocks chipped and broken. He led his mare to the stables and went inside, the door hinges creaking as he opened it. The innkeeper was as weathered as his building. The sharp angles of his face did nothing to help his small beady eyes as they narrowed at Lorn. The innkeeper eyed Lorn up and down, distrust dripping from his expression. Lorn's body was honed from years of physical labor and fighting beasts. He often forgot the physicality of his presence, and he attempted to cover himself with his cloak, hiding his weapons, and curling his shoulders inward. He allowed the exhaustion from the last week to appear on his face, as if he was only a weary traveler looking for a room.

"Do you have an available room?"

The innkeeper ran a hand through his thinning hair. He eyed Lorn a bit longer, and slowly nodded his head.

"You don't plan on causing any trouble do you?" the man asked Lorn, his voice gravelly as if he rarely used it.

Lorn shook his head and forced all of the weariness into his voice as he replied, "No, I just need a warm meal and a good bed. Then I will be on my way."

The innkeeper must have deemed his answer was good enough as he led him to his room, keys jingling as he walked and muttered under his breath.

"Excuse me, is everything alright?"

The innkeeper glanced back at Lorn as if forgetting he was there. "Yeah," he mumbled. "Just a lot of strangers have stopped by lately. Seems..." he paused fumbling for his keys as he showed Lorn his room. "...odd. Something's about to happen." He glared at Lorn. "Which is why I don't want any trouble from you."

Lorn held up his hands, trying to appear meek. "I only need a place to rest, and some food would be appreciated." The innkeeper narrowed his gaze as if measuring the veracity of Lorn's statement. "I won't cause any trouble," Lorn added quickly. "I will be gone in the morning." The innkeeper gave a gruff mumble and walked away leaving Lorn to his room.

The room resembled the rest of the town, old, outdated, and lacking any sort of life. But seeing as it was Lorn's last time sleeping inside for a while, he was going to appreciate it despite its lack of comfort. The bed lay in the corner of the room, Lorn eyed it, knowing he wouldn't fit well on the tiny bed provided. A small window was over the bed, the moon and stars hidden behind the deep purple and gray storm clouds looming overhead. The room held the heat of the day inside, stifling, Lorn conceded and removed a few of his layers until only dressed in a black tunic and loose-fitting pants. He spotted an overused towel next to a small basin to wash himself with, and a questionable bar of soap. Lorn sponged the lukewarm water on his face, neck and arms.

While he washed, he thought about what the innkeeper mentioned. He would need to be careful if there were extra people around. It could be a coincidence that other people were traveling at this time, but Lorn had a feeling it wasn't.

A loud crack split the sky a signal for the rain to be unleashed. The roof pounded with the drumming of the falling rain.

A similar beat sounded in Lorn's chest. He knew the quest he was following. He knew what he had agreed to. Yet, standing here in the town of ShadowAcre on the edge of the Hinterlands, the finality of what he was about to do began to settle. Numb and detached. That is what he was until a week ago. Until he was given the summons to go to Lord Aldrich.

After Lakesh was killed, he roamed from village to village assisting those who could not defend themselves. Any creatures that escaped the Hinterlands, he would slaughter. The only feeling he had in the last few years was one of rage as he let himself succumb to the overwhelming desire of his bloodlust as he killed creature after creature. Once the creature was killed, his bloodlust, his anger, would trickle out of him as if he was a fire being banked to embers, then crumbling into ash. Left to be blown away, empty without a purpose until another village needed him.

This summons, this quest had sparked in him something he had not felt in years, something other than anger. This feeling right now was one of excitement, and dread. This internal tug had always been leading him to the Hinterlands. By tomorrow he will have stepped foot inside. Lightning flashed through the small window and another crack followed. The building creaked and a heavy thud sounded outside as another stone slipped from the foundation of the building. *Hopefully this building makes it through the night*, Lorn thought ruefully.

Hunger led him out of his room, keeping one dagger hidden in his boot and the other tucked in his pants. The inn was too hot to keep his cloak on from the day and he assumed there would be very few people inside, hoping the storm would force everyone to retreat to their respective homes. Lorn entered the small dining room. Crammed inside were three small tables that had seen better days. Two of the tables were small and circular, placed in the corners, and one rectangular table took up the center of the room with benches on either side. A man sat at one of the circular tables, his shoulders hunched. Empty beer glasses littered the table. Lorn decided to occupy the other small table. The innkeeper walked out with a bowl of soup and a mug of beer. He hastily placed it on the table and returned to his front desk, out of view.

The soup was murky and had what looked like vegetables floating around in it. There was potentially a bit of chicken in it. Lorn picked up his spoon and ate his first bite. The soup sludged down the back of his throat and the vegetables disintegrated in his mouth. Living on the road, Lorn had eaten much worse and this was the only fresh food he would have for a while. He grimaced and continued eating, trying to wash down the soup with his tepid beer.

The small windows in the dining room flashed from the outside storm. The lightning seemed to strike to the very core of who he was. A beacon. A warning of what was about to come. He lost himself in a daze as he reflected on the strikes. The warning clear to him. Each flash a voice telling him to leave, leave, leave.

On the next flash of lightning the door banged open as a group of people came clamoring in.

"I told you we would be caught in the storm," a lilting female voice scolded.

"Forgive me, if I thought we would be able to outrun it," a voice dripping with sarcasm retorted.

"Let's at least get some food while we are here and waiting out the storm," another voice commented.

"Agreed," a deep voice added.

Water dripped everywhere and the group was oblivious to the innkeeper's displeasure. They were outfitted in plain traveling clothing and cloaks.

The innkeeper looked at the group of people gathered in front of him, practically seething.

One of the people stepped forward and removed her hood. She was of average height, slim figure, her long raven black hair falling down her back with some stray hairs plastered to her face. Her light brown skin glistened from the rainfall outside. She sauntered forward and eyed the innkeeper.

"Excuse me sir, I apologize for the mess we have made in your fine establishment. Would it be possible for us to pay for four meals and four drinks while we wait out the storm?" The innkeeper rolled his shoulders back and stood up a little straighter. The woman complimenting his inn must have softened him towards her.

Lorn chuckled to himself, clearly this group wasn't completely oblivious to their behavior and the innkeeper's reaction. The woman's eyes, the color of warm honey, looked beseechingly at the innkeeper.

"Oh alright," the innkeeper muttered. "But I have no more rooms. You may stay inside until the storm lets up." The woman gave an innocent smile, looked over her shoulder at her companions and smirked.

After exchanging money, the group walked to the dining room each removing their hoods.

"Very smooth, Xira," the other woman whispered as they sat at the rectangular table in the center. This woman towered over Xira and was of an equal height to her male companions and just as broad. The woman had long red hair braided down her back, her pale skin shone in the light and her dark green eyes leveled back at Xira.

"You should be thanking me. Otherwise, we would still be out in the storm," Xira said, lifting her chin toward the window where the lightning flashed outside and the rain pelted down.

The red haired woman lifted her hands showing her palms to Xira. "Hey, I said a storm was coming and *they* thought we could avoid it." She pointed at her companions.

One of the men laughed, a short huff of air coming out through his nose. "Alright Anwin of the mountains, I beseech your apology, for being so shortsighted." The man stood and mockingly bowed. This man had to be taller than Lorn by at least a head, his body thin, lithe and graceful, as if he were a willow tree, able to endure the elements by easily bending and adapting. Still bowing, his thick locs surrounded his face and ran down the length of his back. His brown skin shone gold in the flickering torch light. He lifted his gaze, his russet eyes a challenge to Anwin to see who would cave first with a waiting, expectant smile.

Xira rolled her eyes, but a faint smile was fighting to appear on her face. Anwin returned the man's stare. A grin broke like a ray of light through a storm of clouds. "Oh c'mon Reed. You can come sit down now. I accept your *humble* apology." Anwin laughed, playfully punching Reed in the arm.

The last person in their group stayed seated. His eyes lit up as he enjoyed his friend's banter. Even sitting down, this man held an air about him. Something was different, as if Lorn's magic could sense the otherness of him, the strength in him. Despite the cloak, the man's muscular body was still highlighted in the shape of his clothes. His dark brown skin was gilded in the torchlight, as he looked at each of his companions. "At least we are inside now and can eat." His voice resonated throughout the room. A voice of power, one that would inspire courage and cause weaker men to tremble.

"We might die from this food," Reed whispered jokingly as he peered over his shoulder to look at the empty beer glasses and Lorn's questionable soup.

The innkeeper walked out from the kitchen depositing the group's food on their table. Once the innkeeper was out of earshot, Anwin looked at Lorn. "Hey, do you feel sick from this yet?" Lorn, surprised to be addressed by the group, glanced back at her questioningly. "Well, you have clearly finished most of your bowl of soup," Lorn looked down to check, "and we wanted to know how high our chances of survival are?" Anwin and the rest of the group looked at him expectantly, waiting for an answer.

Lorn knew he shouldn't interact with anyone, and he hadn't so far besides small pleasantries, but they seemed like a friendly group that only wanted to pass the time in this bleak town.

"I haven't died yet, so I would take that as a positive," Lorn answered.

The group nodded, satisfied with his response, looked back at their own food and began to eat. Lorn thought that no matter how he responded, they would have eaten their food. They dug in ravenously as if they hadn't had a meal in a long time.

As time went by, Lorn was reluctant to leave his table. This strange group intrigued him, and they had an ease about them that was nice to be around in this stagnant town. Eventually the man at the corner table retired to his own room, staggering on his way out. It was only the group and Lorn in the dining room. The rain poured down steadily. Despite the thunder and rain crashing overhead, a single bone-chilling howl pierced the night. A lone reminder of what awaited Lorn tomorrow, the Hinterlands lingering so close as if waiting to swallow him up. Lorn and the group glanced at the window, attempting to discern any images outside. But everything was muddled and dark and the storm raged on.

The idle chatter in the dining room fell silent and Xira cleared her throat. "So stranger, what brings you to the town of Shadow Acre?" Her honey brown eyes looked at Lorn. A seemingly innocent question. Lorn knew he needed to give everyone he met false information and with a practiced breath he recited the same information he gave everyone else who asked at prior inns.

"I'm heading back to my home in Verta. I had some things to take care of in Iyera." Lorn finished giving his same repeated response, something most people would be satisfied with. The group appeared to be relaxed as if just talking to a stranger in an inn, but Lorn noticed how they strained to hear his response.

Xira nodded. "It must be rough, coming to visit a town like Shadow Acre, one so close to the Hinterlands."

Lorn kept his face neutral as he gave a noncommittal noise in response. Reed added, "Plus one might never know when it will rain." He gave a quick glance at Anwin and smirked. Anwin rolled her eyes and raised one eyebrow at Lorn.

Lorn was torn to leave the group, but he felt that if he stayed, the group would continue to ask questions, and he couldn't answer anymore without giving himself away. As he stood up, the man of power, the one he never heard a name for, looked at him and said, "I hope you have a safe journey to your home." Lorn nodded and left the room, feeling as if the man knew exactly where Lorn was headed tomorrow.

"I don't know, he might have been wrong, I might have been poisoned from this food," Anwin whispered as Lorn disappeared down the hallway. The group's resounding laughter followed him to his room.

7

"Sleep...what a welcome thought."
Excerpt Unknown

Even though weariness seeped through his bones, Lorn struggled to fall asleep. The combination of the staccato rainfall, the small bed, and stifling heat of the inn had Lorn tossing and turning. He wanted to savor this last night of small comfort. Once he entered the Hinterlands, he would not be enjoying beds, fresh food (despite how questionable it is), and the casual comfort of having people around.

Although Lorn has always preferred solitude, there was a sense of reassurance, of contentment in the presence of other people. The feeling of not being alone in this world. The solace of having people around him, laughing, enjoying themselves, and enjoying this life filled him with ease. It was one of the reasons he spent his life hunting down creatures terrorizing villages—for him to be included, for him to be a part of a family that never would be, and have his life be ingrained in these daily routines. The Hinterlands would be a loneliness he had never anticipated.

~

The morning sun beamed through the window and woke Lorn. One eye eased open followed by the other, his limbs stiff as he gently stretched. The tiny bed was unforgiving and hard beneath him. His lack of sleep last night would not benefit him today. The bright sun had been what awoke him. The storm from last night had disappeared, leaving behind voluminous clouds bathed in pinks and oranges of the rising sun. A stark contrast to what he would be facing today. He squinted and looked beyond the horizon to see the faint edge of the Hinterlands. Its presence beckoned him. His stomach tightened in response.

Today was the day he would enter that forsaken place. Fate save him. Lorn sent a quick flare of magic throughout his body to ease his aches and reminded himself to conserve his magic for the Hinterlands. He hastily dressed, grabbed his weapons, and headed out of the room to grab his last warm bit of food before he plunged forward into the unknown darkness ahead.

The dining room was empty, any trace of the group last night gone, as fleeting as the storm, a blur of energy then gone. Lorn continued checking, looking around the room and out the window into the small town as if he could sense the group and know if they were still here. Disappointment spread. Lorn tried to dismiss the feeling. He barely interacted with them. Why should it matter if they were gone?

The innkeeper walked in carrying a tray of Lorn's food. Another questionable dish it seemed. "They aren't here," he said. The innkeeper must have noticed Lorn glancing around.

"Do you know who they are, or why they were here?"

The innkeeper halted and shrugged. "I don't ask too many questions around here. Being so close to...that." He nudged his head in the direction of the Hinterlands. "We often get strange people passing through." The innkeeper ran a hand through his thinning hair and hesitated. He cocked his head at Lorn as if weighing the information he was about to share. "I have seen people lose themselves to the Hinterlands. Those foolish enough to think they can master the forest, those arrogant enough to think they can survive it and reach the Well. Glory seekers." He snorted and narrowed his eyes at Lorn. "That group is probably just another one." The innkeeper straightened and left, leaving Lorn to contemplate over his cold and questionable breakfast.

The breakfast was a dull plate of eggs and sausage. The eggs cold and dry, the sausage equally cold and dry. *So much for this being my last warm meal,* Lorn thought as he scarfed down another bite of food determined to eat it despite the awful flavor.

The group he encountered the previous night could have been a fluke, yet he felt something deeper, something pulling him towards them. The same feeling that pulled him towards the Hinterlands. Lorn was unsure of how it all connected. The group appeared to have no ill intent towards him. They could have easily accosted him, given their group of four. A sense of power, strength, and camaraderie exuded from them. Lorn released a sigh. His mental efforts would be better focused on his upcoming task of entering the Hinterlands.

Whether from the thought of the Hinterlands or the food he ingested, his stomach began to sour. Lorn stood up and left, giving a brief and friendly wave to the innkeeper. The innkeeper grunted his response and failed to reciprocate a wave back. Lorn saddled his horse, led her out into the main road of Shadow Acre, and spared one pitying glance for the dilapidated town as he rode off, the gloom of the Hinterlands before him on the horizon.

~

The main road out of Shadow Acre went on only for a few miles before it became overgrown with scrub brush. He led his horse tentatively through the thick thorns, dismounting multiple times to lead her further on. Once within walking distance to the Hinterlands, he unsaddled the horse, shouldered his supply pack, and let her go free. He didn't want to lead a horse to slaughter, for that's what it would surely be if she followed him into the Hinterlands. This way, she would be able to roam anywhere she chose. He brushed his hand along her mane bringing his forehead to hers.

"You are free to go now. Thank you for carrying me this far." The soft brown eyes of the horse looked back at him as if acknowledging everything he said. "But don't linger around here. Make sure to enjoy lush green fields away from this place." Lorn gently patted her and turned away. Whether by instinct or fear, his horse shied away from the Hinterlands and retreated to the path they traveled on.

Lorn surveyed the woods looming before him. About an hour before he would reach the border. Lorn hesitated briefly, hefted his supplies onto his shoulders, and continued his long trudge towards the ever-present darkness.

As he walked, Lorn heard the rogue cries of the beasts within. Each felt like a talon scraping down his spine, a premonition of what was to come. Soon he would be entering this nightmare. The morning dragged on as the diseased trees grew closer together into the suffocating woods.

He had arrived at the edge of the Hinterlands. A clear demarcation line, one side full of plagued trees and the stifling of magic, the other full of abundant life.

The ancient, gnarled tree limbs twisted together. The air was thick and heavy, the fresh winds and open air blocked from entering. Moss was overgrown on the tree branches, devouring the trees alive. No other creature stirred. The area was eerily quiet as Lorn's footsteps echoed in the emptiness. He was an intruder within this empty decay.

His steps faltered. No one had entered the Hinterlands and come out alive. They were either physically torn apart or became insane from the monstrosities they witnessed. He stood there rooted to the ground, numbness enveloping his body. This decision, this path he was on, he agreed to—it was pure madness.

Doubt crept in like tiny vines, hooking around his limbs slowly encasing him until he was covered. Heaviness weighed him down. His feet were immovable stones. He couldn't move, could barely breath as his chest remained still, air barely escaping. The vines tightened. The darkness from his dream slithered along Lorn's body and whispered in his ear, *You will fail. You have already failed your wife. You will die there. No one to mourn you. No one to care that you are gone. You are nothing.* Despair flooded through Lorn. He couldn't move, couldn't filter through all the memories that flashed through his mind. The images were a kaleidoscope of horrific memories blurring together, crashing into prisms that created new dimensions with which to haunt him.

The days immediately following Lakesh's death when he couldn't bother to move, couldn't bother to eat. The months after when he ruthlessly hunted monsters, allowing bloodlust to fuel him and sustain him. Images continued whirling in his head. Like a dam holding back water, it broke under the strain releasing all of the sadness, all of the desperation.

It filled him.

Plagued him.

The darkness laughed, its ancient voice cold and oily, like the deepest, most horrific facets of a person pulled out and given form. The images and memories barraged him. Lorn kept spiraling unable to pull himself out from the pit that the darkness had carved in his mind. Down and down, he fell, while standing on the edge of the Hinterlands, still trapped within the torrent inside his head.

Do not give in to it. A small voice urged him. *Fight it. Resist it.* Lorn tried. He tried to pull anything from the depths of his soul to combat the darkness and despair flooding through him. Nothing came to mind as the memories and images bombarded him, every moment he had ever felt weak, powerless, numb. Every moment where he allowed the darkness to override him. It kept coming.

Are you not the one who was called here? FIGHT IT! The voice bellowed out at him, breaking him out of his stupor.

The veil of darkness lifted for only a moment to reveal a faint glint of light. It was an ember of hope in this cavern of darkness and Lorn reached for it, reverently encasing the light with his hands. A small memory appeared before him, a treasured moment from before, from before all this misery started.

It was of him and Lakesh. Their cottage had a small pond nearby. It was a blistering summer evening and they had decided to go for a walk and cool off near the water. Summer was always a rigorous time of year. Many crops needed to be tended to, the animals cared for, and the long summer sun allowed them to work tirelessly throughout the day. So many tasks accumulated, and they hadn't spent much time together without an extra chore interfering.

Lakesh had offered a walk, a mischievous gleam in her eye. They strolled towards the pond and enjoyed the familiar quiet of the countryside with never a need to converse—only enjoying the contentment that encased them. The buzzing of summertime bugs filled the quiet, along with the rustling of nearby grasses as rabbits darted to and fro. Too soon the pond came into view, a small river led into it, the water bubbling over the rocks as it came to a halt. Cattails pierced through the water's surface, swaying in the breeze as if welcoming them into this private sanctuary. Tree branches gently intertwined overhead, allowing them a brief respite from the hot summer sun bearing down. Underneath the clear water, small blurs of orange and gold darted back and forth.

Lakesh looked at him, a slow smile crested over her face. She quickly shucked off her boots, pulled off her socks, and plunged her feet into the water. A soft moan escaped from her lips. His body twinged in response, but he stayed still, enraptured to her every movement. In the fading summer light, her skin glowed like molten gold, a beacon of radiance. Lorn copied her. He removed his boots and his socks and joined her in the water. Lorn stood behind her, and began unbraiding her sweat-soaked hair, running his fingers through the dark brown tresses, allowing them to spill from between his fingers. His hands massaged her scalp, releasing all the pent-up tension from the constant chores and strain.

Another moan broke from her lips, her head bowing so he could continue his ministrations on her body. His hands ran along her supple curves, and Lakesh leaned back into him. Lorn would always be there to support her. He lowered his head to press a kiss to her neck, breathing in her earthy smell. Lakesh glanced over her shoulder, a question in her eyes. Pulling herself away from Lorn, Lakesh held his gaze as she peeled off her shirt, and the band around her chest.

Lorn's breath hitched, as he beheld his glorious wife. He would never tire of this. Never tire of her. She gave a small knowing smirk, and unbuttoned her lightweight skirt, tossing it to the side of the pond.

Without any warning she dove into the pond, laughing as she emerged. Fish scattered frantically beneath the water, seeking shelter. "Come join me Lorn." Lakesh's voice light and carefree, beckoned him. Lorn pulled his tunic over his head revealing his muscular body honed from years of farm work, and hunting. His skin had darkened from the summer sun, now the color of burnished copper. Lorn stepped out of the pond, maintaining eye contact as he stripped off his dust worn pants. Completely bare to her, Lorn strode forward into the pond to join his wife.

Lakesh treaded water, her feet skimming the bottom. Lorn held her sultry gaze and met her in the middle of the pond. He leaned down and softly kissed her, a small promise of things to come. The kiss had been an unleashing as they kissed longer and deeper. Each taking their time to explore one another. Minutes or hours seemed to pass as they each held on to each other, floating in the pond basking in the last rays of sun from the day.

As they joined, their breaths mingling together, their bodies becoming one, they glowed with the love they shared for one another, the love that would always be there. The hot summer sun faded below the horizon, bringing with it a cooling relief. It painted the sky in rough brushstrokes of pink and orange. Lorn and Lakesh let the hours pass lazily making love as evening progressed to night. Both flushed, they lay next to each other on the edge of the pond. Their shoulders touched, both of them inseparable like their bodies knew they were never meant to be apart. One by one the sporadic glow of fireflies joined in the night sky, illuminating the beauty of Lakesh. Lorn wanted this moment to last, wanted to savor every second with his beautiful, and fierce wife.

The memory rippled in front of him, a buoy to help pull him out of the sea of darkness threatening to envelop him. All the despair he felt earlier lingered, yet Lorn was viewing it from a distance through a lens. The warmth, and love from the memory pulsed through him, its energy bright and golden as the morning sun. It fought against the darkness consuming him, like a light casting out the darkness, banishing it. Lorn held onto that precious memory, reliving it and feeling everything. Reliving the feel of his wife's delicate hands in his, her laughter, her soft lips, every image, every feeling. He submitted himself to it.

Reliving every moment of her.

The love pouring out from him strengthened him and tamped down the darkness. Until the despair, misery, and darkness were smothered, the golden light within emerging triumphant.

Lorn gasped, gulping in a huge breath of air.

A breath of life.

Unsure of what just happened and what he just went through, the twisted woods of the Hinterlands stood before him still. The sun had barely moved in the sky. No time seemed to have passed, even though Lorn felt as if he just witnessed years of his life. The heaviness in his body had vanished along with the darkness, and he was able to move freely. In fact, he felt lighter than he had in a long time. Lorn didn't want to consider what any of it meant, what the darkness was, or the voice that spoke to him. He stored the information away for later, stared ahead, and began his quest as Lorn stepped foot inside the Hinterlands.

8

"The creatures of the Hinterlands are assumed to be a mutated form of existing animals. It is curious, many speculate as to where the creature came from..."

Excerpt from *The Speculations of the Hinterlands* by Brinall of Verta

Lorn stepped over the threshold of the forest and nausea gripped him. His magic was smothered, as if the heaviness plaguing the air had settled inside him. Despite the protests of his body, Lorn plunged forward ignoring the warning signs of his body. Each step was shaky. Each breath too loud, too intrusive. The further on he went, the more the tree branches melded together and doused the sun overhead. No light pierced the thick canopy above, as if the pureness of it couldn't be seen by those that dwell in the depths of this dark forest. Rogue cries from creatures shattered the silence.

Checking the sound of his footsteps, he crept from tree to tree. Wary of his surroundings his eyes darted everywhere unsure of what to expect. The Hinterlands was an unknown entity. Lorn had faced the occasional creatures that escaped from its confines, but to experience it fully, was completely different. His senses were off; his awareness, his body, especially his magic. Everything felt distorted and manipulated. Lorn took a deep breath to regain his composure. He needed his focus. This was only the beginning. He was determined to reach the center of the Well, find the magical item and return to Lord Aldrich. Under a strict timeframe, Lorn had no time to waste on extra precautions. The moon was already halfway through her transformation. He calculated he had about seven days to get to the center of the Well and grab the item and about seven days to get back out again—very little room for error.

Determining the passage of time was tricky due to the lack of light coming through the trees overhead. Shocked he had not encountered the beasts or mind tricks that have been rumored to exist in the Hinterlands, he kept his guard up unwilling to be lulled into a false sense of security. Finding a thick grove of trees growing together, he rested and ate some of his provisions. The base of the trees was a perfect spot to hide. Sitting down he gulped a quick swig of water and had a small bite of his dried jerky. He doubted he would be able to hunt inside the Hinterlands. The twisted and emaciated creatures wouldn't provide any healthy meat for him to consume. He counted his provisions, ensuring he would have enough for the journey back.

A small voice carried on a distant wind. "Lorn," it whispered as it passed through the gnarled trees. Pulling out the hunting dagger sheathed at his side, Lorn hastily put away his supplies. He crouched behind the trees and glanced around assessing the area.

The Hinterlands was a place where people die from the creatures or go insane.

"Lorn," a distinctly female voice whispered again, the wind whipping around Lorn, urging him to follow.

Lorn braced his body against the cluster of trees, refusing to be misled. His grip on the dagger tightened, as he scanned the area for the source of the voice. That unmistakable voice, a voice he would always hear in his dreams.

It was a voice he heard every morning when he awoke without her beside him, his soul aching and hollow. Lorn stayed rooted to the spot, unwilling to be led into a trap. Lakesh's voice sounded real. The temptation to run to her and see her was overwhelming. Against Lorn's instincts, he remained hidden within the copse of trees and closed his eyes. Following the pace of his breath he repeated to himself, *This is not real. She is not alive. This is not real. She is not alive.* It became his maxim, causing his eyes to crest with unshed tears. Each reminder was a phantom Howler talon gouging into Lakesh's stomach. Her death replayed in his mind. Following the course of his breath, he repeated himself. Each time the voice became more distant, until suddenly Lorn was left with only silence around him.

Choking down a ragged breath, he opened his eyes and glanced around. Nothing stirred, and he couldn't detect anything connected to the disembodied voice. Still crouched behind the gnarled trees as cover, he rose and peeked into the forest beyond, nervous to see what showed itself. Lorn released a breath held tight within him and began to creep out from the trees. Step by step he emerged. He inched forward but his next step didn't connect with the ground as he was thrown into the air.

Lorn was lifted and launched across the tree line, his body sent sailing. He crumpled against the hard earth, the breath knocked out of him. His mouth gasped for air, like a fish hoping for water. He managed to get to his knees, and he looked around frantically for his dagger, cursing himself for dropping it as he was lifted into the sky. The creature dragged itself towards him. Lorn looked at the creature with disdain, knowing full well what he was facing.

He had encountered these creatures before a handful of times. They would hide in the local town's tree lines and farmyard barns, preying on the animals inside. They could devastate a town's only supply of meat and dairy. The townspeople took to calling them Feasters, because of their constant drain on their supply of animals.

The one looming before him was bigger than any he had seen before. They resembled enormous bats, except everything was eerily stretched out and exaggerated. The scrunched face held tiny crimson eyes and a bared mouth with tiny rows of needle-like teeth. Protruding from each side of its back were two wings, crafted from its thick leathery skin. At the end of each wing were two black claws gripping the ground. The Feaster's hunched body ended with two legs also displaying massive claws. The beast took off, flapped its wings, and launched itself towards Lorn. The Feaster's mouth opened hoping to get a bite of Lorn's tender flesh.

Disoriented, Lorn patted the ground searching for his dagger. He hastily scrambled to his feet, an attack plan formulating quickly before the Feaster drew too close. He needed to wait until just the precise moment. Once the Feaster couldn't alter its flight, Lorn quickly dove to the ground and rolled underneath the talons of the beast. A single sharpened talon shredded his back. The Feaster released a shrill scream—frustrated at losing its prey. Lorn fought the urge to scream as his flesh peeled from his back and scrambled away from the

Feaster's deadly talons.

While the Feaster was dangerous, it could not make agile movements. Lorn hoped it would be enough for him to get to his weapons. Lorn sprinted for the cluster of trees where he had been hiding. His dagger. A weapon. He needed something to defeat this creature. The Feaster landed on the ground facing away from Lorn. It moved quicker on the ground and began turning around, using the elongated talons to find purchase on the forest floor.

Eyes roving, he searched and finally spotted his pack of supplies, and the familiar glint of his sword. He grasped the sword and turned around to face the Feaster. Lorn took in the creature, its tiny needle teeth grimacing as drool and spittle flecked down the edges of its jaw. Quickly glancing around at the forest, Lorn noted the thick tangle of trees that constrained the Feaster's movements. The Feaster released a scream and charged Lorn. It stayed rooted to the ground for its attack, using its talons on its wings and back legs to propel itself forward.

Lorn held his ground, his sword raised, patiently waiting. He needed the beast to come to him, needed it to be clumsy around the thick Hinterland trees. As the Feaster neared, its talons eagerly reaching for Lorn, he dodged to the right sprinting for the next clump of trees. The Feaster's talons closed on air as it hastily landed on the ground. Its piercing red eyes enraged as it had lost its prey once again.

With barely any time to recover, Lorn maintained his breathing and assessed how much maneuverability the Feaster had within this dense forest. There were only a few patches of the forest clear enough for the Feaster to fly. Once the Feaster was on the ground, precious time ticked by, with its back exposed to Lorn. The Feaster turned and faced Lorn, rage and hunger twisted its face. Again, Lorn departed from the safety of the trees, brandishing his sword at the Feaster. The Feaster charged. Lorn stood his ground and prayed to the Goddess above that his timing would prove correct. He waited as the winged creature drew closer. Lorn needed precision. He needed the Feaster to believe its prey was an easy thing to kill, yet he would not be an easy victim.

Another breath, another moment.

The Feaster reached its long black talons towards Lorn, eager to rip him apart. *One more breath* Lorn reminded himself. The moment when the Feaster would have ripped into Lorn's skin, Lorn sprinted left to the trees providing sanctuary. Circling the tree and using it as a shield, he spied the Feaster's exposed and vulnerable back.

As Lorn had predicted, the Feaster landed on the ground and was clumsy to turn around. Lorn seized this moment and struck hard and true into the creature's curled back. The Feaster shrieked with a feral cry and frantically turning its head to snap at Lorn with its gnashing teeth.

Lorn pulled the sword out from the creature's back. Sickly black blood thickly dripped from the blade as he lifted it up and slashed it down on one of the Feaster's wings. The creature screamed, stumbled, and tried desperately to bite Lorn. The Feaster fell to the ground. It curled in on itself and black blood coated the forest floor. Standing over the Feaster Lorn paused, his sword poised over the creature's heart. The Feaster's face relaxed, as death hovered waiting to claim another. Confusion flickered briefly across Lorn's face as he brought the sword straight down into the Feaster's heart. The body stilled. The Feaster was dead.

Unsafe to linger, Lorn grabbed a cloth from his bag and cleaned the thick black blood from his sword. While he cleaned his sword, Lorn couldn't help but stare at the body of the Feaster. It was a feeling of almost gratitude which passed across the creature's face. Puzzled, Lorn grabbed his supplies, eyes darting around checking his surroundings, as he left the gnarled body of the Feaster.

Worried about other beasts being attracted to the cries of the Feaster, Lorn hurried away from it maintaining a delicate balance of stealth and speed. The cries of the creatures within the Hinterlands haunted him, echoing throughout the dense forest. Unable to discern the time of day, he was unsure of how long he had been traveling.

Such little time spent within the Hinterlands, yet his body was sore and bruised as if it were his first day spent sparring as a novice. His body ached and smarted every time he stepped forward. The twisted tangle of roots along the forest floor left him stumbling as exhaustion settled in. He bit back a hiss of pain as he placed his feet back underneath him. Blood trickled down the expanse of his back, his clothing stuck to his skin at the base of the wound. His shoulders twinged with pain from his fall and the Feaster's dangerous talons. He needed to rest, but how to get rest in this environment of constant danger? This journey to the center of the Hinterlands to retrieve this item was pure madness. Shaking his head at himself, he searched for shelter.

Lorn came across a thicket of trees on top of a small hill. At the base of the trees on one side was a hollow, providing a small bit of protection from the prowling beasts. The thick roots of the trees twisted around one another creating a lattice on the ceiling of the makeshift shelter. Lorn squeezed in and pressed himself as far back as possible. Dropping his supplies, he grabbed out his extra cloak and wrapped it tight around himself. An undefinable chill permeated the Hinterlands. It crept along his body coating it like a second skin he was unable to remove. Despite the chill Lorn did not risk starting a fire. There were too many unknowns, too many beasts. It would be an unwanted beacon shining to every creature within the Hinterlands. Lorn pushed his back against the hollow, grimaced against the pain, and sat upright. He tiredly scanned for danger. Eventually he drifted off to a fitful sleep.

Lorn awoke the next morning to deep aches throughout his body. The attack with the Feaster left him stiff. Bruises of purples and blues covered his body. His restless night of sleep did not aid him in his recovery. Tossing and turning the whole night, he would startle awake finding himself in the bleakness of the Hinterlands or awoke to his heart racing, and him wielding his dagger against some imagined danger.

Stretching to release the constant ache, Lorn noticed the whole Hinterlands was covered in a thick mist. It obscured the forest and he had the eerie sense of standing in a void. Releasing a defeated sigh, he grabbed his belongings. Traveling through the mist provided an extra layer of difficulty. Unaware of the specific dangers residing in the Hinterlands, Lorn needed his vision, needed all his senses to help him get through this alive.

Lorn closed his eyes, sending his mind to assess the state of his body. His torso and shoulders took the brunt of the damage from yesterday's fight. He tentatively sent a flare of his magic to those areas, removing some of the lingering pain, hopeful the bleeding had ended. Afraid to use up too much of his magic, he only sent out a tiny amount, wanting to reserve as much as possible for what lay ahead.

Calling upon his magic in the Hinterlands felt strange. Using magic in the five provinces was natural like an extension of your body. It took time and practice to fine tune it, but the magic was there eager to be molded and used. Here in the Hinterlands, his magic felt distant like a phantom limb he was trying to regain control over. It was disconcerting, but Lorn strained using the extra effort to send out his magic for healing. Tentatively prodding fingers at the damaged areas, he was content with the meager results and moved on from the cluster of trees where he spent the night.

The mist lay thick and heavy over the forest. Lorn's neck ached from constantly swiveling his head to check his surroundings. Hidden tree roots snaked their way around Lorn's feet, the beast's muted cries came from all directions. Lorn attempted to move quickly, but the mist diminished any chances of that. As he walked through the Hinterlands, he kept his mind alert, yet he was walking around with a feeling akin to being lost. His usual keen sense of direction he had throughout this life was now muffled. He wouldn't know if he had been turned around or walked in circles. Frustrated, Lorn was about to sit down when he heard a familiar voice.

It was the sound of home, the sound of his heart. Must he be constantly haunted by the voice of his wife? Seeking cover behind a tree, Lorn looked around, searching for the source of the voice. Nothing showed itself. He risked closing his eyes, if only for a moment to calm his beating heart, to calm the blood roaring in his ears.

"Lorn." Her voice permeated the air around him, sinking deep into his bones. It pulled him, awakened him. Opening his eyes, he saw orbs of light within the thick mist. They highlighted a path for him to follow. The orbs wound into the mist, beckoning for him to follow. Despite Lorn's own reservations, he couldn't resist the sound of her voice any longer. Weary and hurting, a string, a pull deep within him led him away from the safety of the tree, following the path of lights.

Lorn was a ghost floating along, following them. Mesmerized and determined to continue, he disregarded any concern for the beasts within the Hinterlands, disregarded everything. He could only follow the song of her voice.

It wrapped around his heart and pulled him forward. It whispered to him, urging him along. As he followed the enchanting lights the rest of the Hinterlands melted away, there was only one true path for him to follow.

They trailed throughout the forest, leading Lorn deeper and deeper.

He stumbled after them, searching for an end, searching for the source of her voice. Lorn reached the last orb of lights floating serenely in front of him. Lifting a hand, he reached out towards the light, eager to see his wife. His fingers graced the edge of the orb and it immediately burst into small fractions. A firework of light exploded around Lorn, blinding him. He shielded his eyes and upon opening them the path of lights vanished and reappeared as an ethereal ring encircling a small pond. The water before him was pure and clear. Its surface lay undisturbed, not a single ripple to be seen. His feet moved forward of their own accord entranced by the pond's beauty. The lights flickered as if by some unseen wind. He knelt at the edge of the pond and stared deep within. Nothing showed in the water, not even his own reflection.

"Lorn." Her voice beckoned to him. It was coming from within the pond. He needed to reach her, see her again. Her voice was a lure he could not resist, and he plunged both hands into the water.

Upon touching the water, he was transported.

9

He stood within a small cottage. Items of comfort were strewn about the room. A fire merrily crackled away with a pot of stew hanging on it. Knitting was laid across chairs, small, whittled objects decorated the space. It was home. His home.

Lorn glanced down. He was wearing his tunic and pants for doing farm work, not what he was wearing in the Hinterlands. Worn boots lay by the door. He hastily slipped them on and ran outside. His farm was exactly how it had been before Lakesh's death, life bursting in abundance. Familiar animal sounds dotted the air. Crops were growing in their garden and the orchard trees were heavy with fruit waiting to be picked.

He ran.

Lorn frantically scanned the area outside, searching for a sign of her. No sign of her in the garden and nothing in the orchard. Empty.

Lorn passed by the barn and the call of animals greeted him. Then he heard it. A familiar laugh coming from inside. He rounded the corner and saw her.

She patted one of their goats and a lingering smile rested on her face. His wife. Shock paralyzed him. Unable to move, he could only look upon her beauty. He looked upon her like she was his compass, his only direction and path in life.

Lakesh glanced up at Lorn, the smile on her face widening. That smile directed at him, broke any of Lorn's reservations. He forced himself to take a step, then another—closing the distance between them. Lakesh cocked her head at him but continued to smile, slight confusion and concern appearing on her face.

Neither said a word as he approached, his steps were slow and measured. Once Lorn stood next to her, he reached out his hands. They shook slightly as he extended them towards her. The previous times when he touched her she would disappear, a light extinguished, a phantom that only existed within his mind. He did not want to break this illusion. His arm remained extended towards her, unable to touch her, unable to decide. If he could keep this illusion, he would rather spend all his days looking at her, interacting with her, if it meant he'd never be able to touch her again for fear of the illusion being shattered.

Lakesh's brows furrowed, worry seeping in. Her eyes probed Lorn's silently asking a question he was unsure he could answer. With his arm extended, Lakesh stepped forward and put her face within the curve of his palm. She closed her eyes, savoring the feel of Lorn's rough hands holding her steady. When she opened her eyes, Lorn's eyes were filled with tears.

Her touch was a release as Lorn realized Lakesh was there in front of him. Solid. Real. His hand moved across her face, as his other trailed to the back of her head. Their eyes never left each other's.

Standing there, staring.

Lorn would never tire of looking at her. He would never take another moment for granted. Overcome with emotion, he pulled her towards him for a rough embrace. Time seemed to stand still as Lorn refused to part from her.

In the solitude of their barn, with goats circling them aimlessly, Lorn clutched Lakesh tightly and she let him. As if reading his mind, she let him hold her without question. His hands wandered over her body, memorizing each touch, each movement. Lorn reluctantly pulled away from her and looked upon her face once more. "Lorn...what's gotten into you?" Her hands ran along the sharp planes of his face. "I didn't think letting you get some extra rest would have you acting so strangely." She held both sides of his face, eyes peering into his. "Are you well?"

Unable to respond, Lorn merely nodded his head. His throat thick with emotion, he didn't want to concern her. He hurriedly pulled her to him for another hug, his arms squeezing tight, refusing to let go. "Yes, I am now."

He breathed in her rich scent of the earth—soil, plants, the faint smell of animals. Lorn wanted to remember and cherish every bit of her. He wanted to be lost in this daydream forever.

She was here.

She was real.

"Well next time I won't let you sleep in if it causes you such distress." Lakesh laughed lightly. The longing for her reached a breaking point, as Lorn leaned down and kissed her. Gently their lips came together, a soft invitation, an exploration. Lorn couldn't help himself as the kiss turned deeper, their tongues seeking the other's. Lakesh parted from Lorn, her hands resting on his chest, a slight pant mirrored in her own.

"We have quite a few chores to do first." A coy smile flitted across her face. "We finish those, then maybe we can continue this." Her hand playfully went down the front of Lorn's chest towards his pants.

"Of course," Lorn agreed, catching his breath.

Lakesh turned away to grab a milk pail. She glanced over her shoulder at Lorn, her hair spilling down her back. "Would you like to do all the chores together today?"

Lorn's breath caught in his throat. He didn't care what type of place this was, as long as Lakesh was here within. The gratitude of being together in this space overwhelmed him. "Yes, I would love that, Lakesh." Her name rolled off his tongue as familiar to him as the land around him.

It was a homecoming.

Lakesh's eyes lit up and she motioned for him to join her.

They worked together throughout the rest of the day discussing everything and nothing of importance. The day carried on and Lorn was still in the presence of Lakesh. He did not question it, enjoying every detail of her, every nuance. Everything was comfortable and familiar, the routine with which all the countless farm chores were completed, their conversation. No effort at all, as if no time had lapsed, as if nothing had taken Lakesh from him. After they finished their chores, they retreated inside and readied themselves for dinner. Lorn lit candles and picked wildflowers which overgrew near the side of their cottage. The flowers crept out from the sides of the house, bursting to be seen. He presented them to Lakesh, who reacted like she had been given the finest jewels and gems from Gara. They talked long into the night, as if nothing was amiss. The only important thing was each other and they held onto that.

Their plates of food empty, and their bellies full of food, they laid down on a plush blanket, made from wool from their own sheep, in front of their roaring fire. Night descended, the stars shone through their window and the cottage lightly glowed from within by the warm fire and the soft light of the candles. Lorn sat upright with Lakesh's back to his chest. The firelight gilded her dark copper skin and added an ethereal beauty to her, like she was crafted and sculpted from the earth around their cottage. Lorn traced his hands along her arms, strong from all the farm work. He followed all the way along to her hands. His fingers delicately touched the tough work-earned calluses, sliding back and forth over the delicate skin of her forearm. Despite the heat of the fire, goosebumps coated Lakesh's body. Lorn bent his head to softly press his lips to Lakesh's neck.

He moved slowly, determined to take his time. Lakesh tilted her head slightly exposing her neck further to his ministrations. Lorn's hand came around the front of her body, giving light pressure to her throat. A slight reminder of belonging to each other. Lakesh's breath sped up, as Lorn's hand drifted to her chest, softly kneading and teasing her peaked nipples. Lorn uttered a low growl, pleased at her response. Both still wore their clothes from the day. Lorn unbuttoned the back of her dress, the top falling away exposing her breasts. He brought both hands up to Lakesh's nipples and began teasing and playing with them. She arched into his touch, silently urging him to continue. His hand descended down her chest plunging underneath the top hem of her skirt, finding her soft curls of hair. His fingers gently skimmed over her core. Her breath hitched, her hips pushing up towards his hand, eager for more.

Lorn's muffled a chuckle against her skin. "Just like that?" His fingers lightly rubbed over Lakesh again and she emitted a frustrated moan. He hovered over the entrance to her core, one finger parting her flesh and entered slowly.

"Yes," Lakesh hissed between clenched teeth.

"More?" Lorn whispered in her ear.

Lakesh submitted, nodding her head. Lorn added another finger into her and began pumping back and forth. Lakesh allowed her head to roll back supported by Lorn's shoulders. As he moved, her hips followed, a rhythmic dance they both were synchronized to. His thumb swept back and forth over her top bundle of nerves, eliciting deep moans and bigger hip thrusts from Lakesh, while his other hand flicked her dusky nipple in time with the pumping of his hand. More and more franticly their movements were rushed and hurried as Lorn wanted to elicit every pleasurable sound possible from Lakesh. He steadied her as she was lost in her pleasure, her body melting allowing Lorn to support her. Lorn knew she was near her peak, he kept his pace, his lips lightly gliding over the side of her neck.

"Lorn, yes, please..." Lakesh's plea went unfinished as her body tightened around Lorn's fingers, and she released a soft cry. Lorn kept his pace throughout her climax, wringing out every last bit he could. Lakesh's body went limp against him, catching her breath.

Still supporting Lakesh, he laid her down on the blanket beneath them, peppering her with kisses. Their mouths met in a quick joining. He trailed kisses down her body and lingered in places. He ached to memorize each part of her, unwilling to forget any aspect of his wife.

Never again.

Each kiss left Lakesh gasping, craving more. When Lorn reached the apex of her thighs he looked back at Lakesh splayed out before him, her long dark hair fanned around her face, her eyes searing into him, he had never seen anything more beautiful. As their eyes locked Lorn pressed a kiss to her mound and began to worship his wife. He licked her slowly, patiently allowing her body to adjust to another round. She gasped and moaned. Her hips pushed into Lorn's face encouraging his sensual rhythm. Once she was near her peak again, Lorn sat back on his heels and unbuttoned his own pants. He quickly shucked them off, his hardened cock springing free. This union was focused on her pleasure, and her being here and alive in front of him. He nearly forgot about his own arousal until this point.

Free of his constraints Lorn came up to meet Lakesh, bracing himself on his forearms over her. He cradled her face with his hands, his eyes tenderly taking in Lakesh. The fire danced casting shadows and light around the two of them, a silent observer encouraging and embracing them. Lorn kissed Lakesh deeply as he entered her, their mouths meeting as one. His movements were slow and languid. There was nothing else for him, only this moment, only her. They both moved together, familiar with each other's bodies after years of marriage. Time stood still as they joined and moved and when they both reached their peaks, they came together clutching each other tightly. Their bodies glistening faintly with a sheen of sweat. Lorn looked down upon Lakesh, her face coming down from the throes of ecstasy. His black hair fell in front of his face and he kissed her one more time—cherishing this chance, this gift from the gods and goddesses above. Lorn rolled off her and laid beside Lakesh, pulled her back to his chest and cradled her as the sounds of the crackling fire lulled them both to sleep. His arm stayed across her, a warning to all who might dare to take her from him.

~

Days passed and Lorn remained with his wife. He treasured everything they did together, even the mundane tasks, as long as he could be with her. The farm, their cottage, nothing was altered, like a shrine preserved in time. Lorn refused to question it. Sometimes when he worked alongside Lakesh, a small voice would sound in the back of his head telling him this wasn't real, and it could be taken away. Ignoring reason, he damned the voice. He only wanted to be here with his wife. What did it matter if this was real or a fantasy? He was where he belonged.

Lorn lived this fantasy for five days.

Then it ended.

Lorn lay in bed next to Lakesh, uninterested in starting the morning chores. He wanted to stay here curled up next to the warmth of his wife. She rolled over sensing he was awake.

"Good morning, my love," she whispered, eyes softly drifting to lock with Lorn.

"Good morning," he said, pressing a kiss to her forehead. As he pulled her closer and squeezed tightly, he felt a strange sensation in his stomach. Puzzled, he released Lakesh and searched his body for anything off. He cried out in pain as the sensation tightened, like his body was caught in a vise. He patted his body furiously and desperately searched for something to fix, some source of injury.

Lakesh instantly jumped out of bed. "What's wrong Lorn?" She came over to his side of the bed, concern riddled on her face.

"No, no, no, no," Lorn muttered. He knew. He knew his time was up. This fantasy could not last forever. The pain intensified— his whole body was being crushed. Forcing himself to stand up, he scanned Lakesh's face, memorizing everything one last time—her dark rich brown eyes, the soft feel of her hair, her full lips. He brought his hand to her face, his thumb gently stroking her cheek.

"I love you Lakesh." He bent forward to kiss her and felt a tight grip and pull at his navel. His world melted away. Lakesh, the cottage, everything gone. Darkness blanketed him. Thick trees encircled him.

He was back in the Hinterlands.

Lorn fell to his knees, his face in his hands. Frustrated sobs escaped his mouth. His fingers tightened, gripping his hair seeking to pull it from its roots. Vaguely remembering where he was, Lorn put an arm over his mouth to muffle the deep sorrowful scream he released. Everything hurt, his body, his heart.

"I am sorry for your pain." A voice next to Lorn spoke.

Disoriented, Lorn scrambled to his feet searching for his supplies, a sword, a dagger, anything. Fingers clutched the worn hilt of his sword, and he jumped back brandishing the weapon. The figure before him stood covered in a thick black cloak, shadows writhing around their form. Their face was completely covered, indiscernible. Lorn stood there shaking, unable to decide how to act. How was there someone else within the Hinterlands?

"I pulled you out." The figure nodded towards the pond in front of them. "Any longer and you would have died." They stood there, content in the silence that surrounded them. Lorn took a breath to still his shaking hands. He cast rapid glances between the pond and this figure in front of him.

"What is that?" Lorn gestured to the pond.

"It is... a fantasy." The figure paused and turned their body toward the pond, their back to Lorn. Their voice reverberated throughout the forest, deep and powerful. "It is this life, but with your greatest happiness, your greatest joy granted to you." The voice was tinged with sorrow. "If you stayed within, you would have withered away body and soul. It is not real—only a fantasy. Do your best to remember that." The voice turned sharp, reprimanding Lorn. They stalked towards Lorn, the shadows following and curving around them, like a wild animal staying close to its master.

Lorn eased back a step, sensing an other-worldly power from this figure. He searched the face, sought anything familiar, anything of note, but he was unable to find anything due to the darkness shrouding them. All he could feel was power emanating from them in waves, their magic somehow different and altered.

"Why are you here?" they asked slowly, the sound echoing throughout the entire forest. Lorn hurriedly searched for creatures coming out to get them both. The person's voice was so powerful, something was bound to come out of the forest after them. "Nothing will come for us," they assured Lorn.

Mystified, Lorn distanced himself from this person, this figure. He eased in a circle, keeping his sword in front of him.

"I repeat, why are you here?" Each word was enunciated clearly and drawn out. Shadows swirled around the figure, cloaking, hiding, altering them.

"I was sent to retrieve something." Lorn said, monitoring his surroundings, avoiding the large groups of trees where he would surely be trapped if he needed to escape.

"Hmm." The figure paused, appearing to consider Lorn's response. Silently, they turned and strode away, melting into the darkness of the Hinterlands. Lorn bit back a cry. What had just happened? Who was that?

Locating his supply pack on the ground, Lorn hastily shouldered it and ran from the magical pond which now lacked the illumination that had beckoned Lorn in. Far enough away from the temptation of the pond, Lorn crumpled to the forest floor. His head bowed in towards his knees, dry sobs wracked his body and all his anger and frustration bubbled to the surface. Anger at having lost Lakesh twice —at having an illusion bring him so much happiness, at being unwillingly brought back to this cruel world he had no love for anymore. He pounded his fist against the ground in defiance and rage. He vowed he would make it to the center of the Well, if only to spite this world.

Once his overwhelming emotions subsided Lorn did a mental check of his body. He had no gauge of how long he had been within the alternate reality. He was struck by hunger and thirst, but it was manageable. Lorn estimated he was in the illusion for less than a day. He only had roughly four or five days remaining to reach the center of the Well. Pulling his rations out of his bag, Lorn slaked his thirst and hunger.

When finished, Lorn rotated in each direction to gain his bearings. He always had a knack of finding his direction no matter how lost he became. An inner voice he always listened to pointed him in a direction, so he set off towards the center of the Hinterlands, to reach the Well.

10

"There are two reactions from those who enter the Hinterlands. Either they never come back out again, assumed to have been eaten by the creatures within. Or those who escape go completely mad. We have tried to interact with them, but they are incoherent and cannot see what is right in front of their face."

Excerpt from *The Speculations of the Hinterlands* by Brinall of Verta

As he walked through the Hinterlands, Lorn reflected on the mysterious figure. Who were they and how were they in the Hinterlands? Were they even real? They vanished into the air. No MagicBlessed person had that kind of power. Lorn mulled over his thoughts again and again, hoping to reach an answer.

Nothing.

Nothing made sense anymore. His reality had shifted dramatically over the last few weeks. He was standing on the precipice of a cliff undecided whether to cling to it or free fall into the unknown. Instead, he was caught in between, stuck between these two crumbling realities.

An exposed tree root clipped Lorn's foot and caused him to stumble and fall to his knees. Lorn cursed himself for losing his focus in such a deadly environment. He quickly rose when he heard a bone-chilling howl echo throughout the dense forest. The howl seemed to bounce off the trees and pierced Lorn's ears. His body froze, he knew that sound anywhere. It was the same creature that killed his wife.

It was the sound of a Howler.

The Howler must have caught his scent. Lorn calculated how much time he had. The howl seemed far enough away for Lorn to set a trap. He did not want to be surprised this time.

This time he would be ready.

Howlers were difficult to kill, their immense size and strength paired with their intellect made them deadly. They had a bloodlust which fueled their insatiable hunger, not a true hunger—only one satiated by malevolence and spurred by pure cunning. Lorn removed his supply pack and his cloak, laying them against the base of a tree. He rubbed dirt and dried blood on his discarded cloak embedding his scent further. Being careful not to reopen the wound on his back, he rubbed the remaining blood into his cloak. He needed the Howler to target this, instead of him. Lorn checked to make sure his sword was in its scabbard and his daggers attached to his belt. He hurriedly grabbed his bow, looping it over his shoulder.

Another howl pierced the air. Lorn needed to hurry, his heartbeat in his ears pounding a drumbeat of his impending demise. He spotted a tree close by. He climbed, gritting his teeth, dug in his feet, and searched for any footholds. The bark on the tree was firm and unyielding. Lorn's nails began to bleed slightly as he climbed, coating parts of the bark in his blood. Higher! He needed to be above the Howler. Any advantage could save him. He studied Howlers relentlessly after Lakesh's death but was unable to find one in order to get the vengeance he craved. The lie he told Lord Aldrich rang through his head along with the guilt over his ineptitude to kill the Howler. Many believed he had killed the Howler. It tore him up inside—the inability to admit his failure of a truth.

Confident in the height of the tree, Lorn crouched and carefully moved out onto a sturdy tree branch overlooking his supply pack. A sniffing noise filled the air. Branches snapped and the tree shook as the Howler appeared.

Revulsion filled Lorn. Lakesh did not deserve to be killed by the likes of this filth. This twisted creature deserved only death. The Howler paused nose in the air, searching for Lorn's scent. It stood on its hind-legs. Lorn held his breath, hoping to withhold any scent to from reaching the Howler. He prayed to the long-forgotten gods and goddesses for success.

Its head swiveled and checked the surrounding area. Its body was sucked in and emaciated. The elongated snout pointed in the air. The Howler paced towards Lorn's pack. Lorn dared to creep closer on the tree branch, waiting for his moment to strike. The Howler lowered to the ground back onto all four limbs to inspect the pack. Now was Lorn's chance while the dense leaves shrouded him, while the Howler was turned away from him distracted, the decoy working. Lorn discreetly raised his sword overhead, ready to leap from the tree branch and strike the Howler down. His muscles twinged with anticipation. The Howler needed to move a little further for Lorn to get a perfect strike.

The Howler abruptly turned its head, nose sniffing rapidly. Lorn paused, waiting for it to turn back to the cloak and pack. Instead the Howler followed Lorn's path up the tree, until its revolting yellow eyes locked in on Lorn, witnessing him poised and ready to attack. Its eyes widened as it let out a shrill cry. The cry was deafening and Lorn had to stop himself from shielding his ears.

The Howler bounded towards the tree, easily using its long claws to climb up towards Lorn. Since the element of surprise was gone, Lorn reassessed the situation. His sword wouldn't do well within the dense tree branches, while the Howler made easy work of climbing up the tree. It would have the advantage in the trees. It was built for climbing, built for destroying. Its luminous-yellow eyes homed in on Lorn seeking to kill him. Lorn eased back a step, one hand holding his sword, the other pulling out his dagger. He cocked his arm back, prepared to throw it and embed it into the beast.

The Howler reached the tree branch Lorn was on, and it tested its weight, its eyes and mouth hungry for Lorn, ready to devour. What it sought after was finally within reach.

Lorn released a sharp exhale and threw the dagger, aiming for the Howler's chest. The Howler did not see it sail through the air. The dagger struck true into the Howler's chest, with only the handle sticking out. Black blood leaked out of the Howler's chest.

A cry of primal rage rose from the Howler as it leaped onto Lorn, knocking them out of the treetop. Its razor-sharp nails tore through Lorn's clothing and ripped into his flesh. He had no time to register the pain. Lorn's blood coated the Howler's nails as they both grappled in the air falling to the forest floor below. Lorn gripped the Howler tight.

They crashed to the ground, the Howler pinned under Lorn. Lorn's ears rang and his vision blurred from the impact.

Despite the fall, Lorn found he still gripped his sword. Dazed, he slashed wildly at the Howler. It easily shook Lorn off, thick black blood dripping out of it. Instinct and years of training taught him to roll out of the way of the Howler's attack. Lorn stabilized his feet and stared down at the glowing yellow eyes of the Howler. It remained on all four legs, crouched, and reared back ready to attack again. Instead of going straight for Lorn, the Howler darted around the surrounding trees, aiming to disorient Lorn. Keeping his feet beneath him, staying light on them, Lorn kept the feral creature in his vision. The Howler weaved and darted through the trees swift as an arrow, trying to find a weakness in Lorn's defense, testing him like a cat playing with a clever mouse.

Lorn spun, keeping the beast in his eyesight, his sword raised, waiting for the moment to strike. The Howler's massive body jumped off two tree trunks and pounced at Lorn. Lorn dodged and sidestepped, his sword sliced upwards, catching the Howler in the chest. Its chest was riddled with black blood and his dagger still protruded from it. The Howler released another shrill cry causing Lorn to falter slightly, his foot slipping on an exposed tree root. Lorn fell to the ground and the Howler seized its chance.

The creature moved even faster, urgent to end the fight. Lorn scrambled to get on his feet, but saw the Howler closing in. Its jagged teeth glinted in anticipation. The Howler leaped, a victorious leap, ready to tear into Lorn. A steadying breath rippled through Lorn. He tightened the grip on his sword as his other hand reached in front of him, fingers splayed.

His magic was tampered from the oppressive heaviness of the Hinterlands, yet Lorn searched deep within himself, calling it to him. It was faint and reached for Lorn and he pulled on the thread of his magic unspooling it, freeing it from its binds. A bright searing light from Lorn's hand pierced the forest and blinded the Howler. Lorn rolled out of the way as the Howler faltered mid strike. It crumpled to the floor, unable to see. Lorn stood lightning fast, raised his sword, and brought it down beheading the Howler. The gruesome head still fixed in a snarl rolled beside his feet as the world faded to black—Lorn passed out alongside his foe.

~

"Lorn."

"Lorn."

"Come on. Keep up little one." Lorn's eyes opened, and he saw familiar rolling green fields around him and ran after his mother. She was tall and lean, her body honed after years spent farming and practicing swordplay alongside her son and husband. Her light brown hair was braided, streaks of gray poking through the strands. She placed her hands on her hips and assessed the field in front of her, her lightweight trousers swishing back and forth in the breeze.

"We are practicing our magic over here today." She gestured to the hay bales behind her. Bright red targets dotted each of them. "Every child in Ithilia needs to master their magic. And..." She bent down in front of Lorn and met his gaze, "... we must see how yours manifests." She rose, marked a spot in the grass, and began counting her steps to the hay bales. "While I'm setting up, why don't you explain to me how our magic came to be?"

Lorn spoke, his voice young, the pitch still high, "Our magic comes from the Well. It is a gift."

"Good, Lorn. Now what does everyone's magic look like?" Lorn's mother continued her routine, marking the ground and counting steps.

"Everyone's magic manifests differently. Typically, it forms as an element, but it can take other forms. It depends on who they are, their personalities, and their interests. Almost all MagicBlessed have healing powers, but some can also conjure strength and speed," Lorn recited, having practiced multiple times.

"Very good, Lorn. Now, would I be able to conjure a giant fireball?"

"No, because your magic manifests as water."

"True, but what about a spark? Could I conjure a small flicker of fire?" She paused waiting for Lorn to answer.

"Yes, you could summon a small spark."

"Tell me why that is."

"Because almost all MagicBlessed can conjure a small amount of the basic elements."

"Which are?"

"Water, fire, earth and wind."

"Precisely right Lorn." She smiled at Lorn, her joy radiating like a beam straight to him. She walked directly behind Lorn, gripped him by the shoulders,

and turned him to face the hay bales. "We will try to see if your magic manifests today. If it doesn't we can try again another day." She lingered a moment, and one hand squeezed his shoulder reassuringly. "I have a feeling today will be the day."

Lorn heard her footsteps receding. He squared his shoulders to the hay bales. He cleared his mind, allowing himself to focus on the targets.

"Allow your mind to clear, take a breath, and give it a go." His mom encouraged him, and he imagined the warmth she radiated, the joy she directed at him, her everlasting endurance, pride, and hope.

Lorn's small arm extended forward, and he pointed at the targets. His mom stood expectantly behind him. He remained focused on her love, and he felt a surge of power rise to greet him, and magic coursed through him. It needed an outlet, a release. The magic burst from his hand and a beam of light encased the target. His mouth dropped open in shock, the magic continuing to flow out of him, He aimed the light at each of the targets, stopping when he reached the end. He turned back to face his mom, disbelief riddled his body, and she stood there with a huge smile plastered across her face.

"Light." She walked over to him, picking him up, hugging him, and twirled him around. "Your magic is light," she gleefully screamed, spinning him around.

~

Lorn's head pounded. He groaned and forced his eyes to open. Everything hurt. He lay there, recollecting his thoughts. He had just beheaded the Howler.

The Howler.

His body refused to listen as he tried to move. He had overextended himself. Lorn was about to twist his head to look, when he heard a rustling of leaves. He looked left in the direction of the sound and he saw something he couldn't comprehend. The Howler's body and head had been gathered and moved. A figure towered over it—the person from earlier. Their shadows twisted and twined around their body.

Then a peculiar thing happened, the person began to sing. Their voice echoed throughout the forest, a song filled with sorrow and lament. He didn't understand the language, it was as ancient, primal, and mysterious as the figure before him. Lorn remained still, allowing the sadness of the song to wash over him. He was a pincushion, the singer, the hand and the song, needles of sorrow that burrowed into his skin.

The figure's sonorous voice filled the Hinterlands, weaving in and out of the trees. Everything stayed still to listen. Even the figure's shadows halted their movements, embodying solemnity. The song ended and merged into another, and another. Lorn silently rode out the waves of emotions, listening patiently to the songs.

When the singer was finished, they knelt beside the Howler, and delicately placed a hand along its chest and pulled out Lorn's dagger. Despite his need for survival, Lorn was overcome by a moment of guilt. He had killed this creature and caused this person to suffer.

They stood and raised their hand towards the Howler. It became encased in a mass of black shadows. Then the shadows retreated and the Howler was gone. They stood there for a moment, a quietness lingering. The figure abruptly turned around and stomped to Lorn, their angered footsteps causing him to shudder. He still couldn't discern any of their features, the cloak and shadows covered them completely.

They marched over to Lorn still wielding his dagger. He tried to scramble back, but the intense pain crippled him. They threw the dagger with a skilled hand, embedding the blade into the forest floor. The dagger lay inches from Lorn's body, not a mistake, but a clear warning, one of anger.

"Wait," Lorn gasped, reaching out his hand towards them. Pain roiled through his body as he tried to come up to a seated position.

The figure did not halt but strode past while ignoring Lorn's plea. The shadows writhed around them and they vanished.

Questions assaulted him, but it hurt to think over these things when his head pounded with each breath.

After many failed attempts, he finally rose to his feet. He needed rest immediately. Each step weak, his body protested his every movement. He achingly maneuvered to grab his dagger, and the dirt and blood encrusted supply pack he used as a diversion. Unable to move any further, Lorn decided to find rest against the trunk of a tree. He didn't care that he was exposed for his urge to rest outweighed any need for survival. The significant use of his magic and his brutal fight with the Howler had drained him. Even though the MagicBlessed were gifted with magic, each generation became more diluted. Many factors cause the MagicBlessed to reach their own personal level of burnout. Battle-worn and exhausted, Lorn had reached his.

Huddled against the trunk of a tree, he gingerly reached in his pack to pull out water and a small hunk of jerky. He desperately needed to refuel his body, to give it more energy instead of the magic eating away at him.

His headache flared with each bite of jerky. The pounding continued in rhythm with each chew. He persevered, knowing the nourishment from the food would ease his suffering.

Yes, food, water, and rest. Then he will recover. Bite after bite, he consumed more, his energy waning. His eyelids grew heavy, his body slackened. He took one last sip of water from his pack and fell asleep.

Lorn startled awake. His headache lessened, but his body felt like it was rusted all over. Exhausted and tired, Lorn thought back to how many days he had left. Only a few more if his count was correct, for him to reach the center of the Well and retrieve the item. His magic now replete, he sent a small wave coursing through his body, to revitalize him, and speed the healing of any deep wounds he suffered.

Lorn inspected his shoulder, testing the torn and bloodied skin with his fingers. Fresh blood coated his fingers from the mangled shreds of skin flapping loosely. He took a sharp inhale as his fingers probed the wound. Definitely tender, he would have to wrap it. Worried about the Howler's claws and chance of infection, Lorn sent an additional wave of smothered magic to his shoulder, hopefully burning away any infection. Lorn checked the rest of his body. Patting his hands down, his ribs were tender. He lifted his shirt to reveal a battering of bruises, evidence of his fall from the tree. Nothing but time would cure that, yet he poked his fingers to see if any ribs were out of place. Everything seemed in order. He would just have to patiently wait to heal. The rest of his body appeared to be fine, only aches and pains he would need to endure.

Lorn searched his bag for some clean cloth and water. He was coated in a thick layer of dirt from the Hinterlands and splatters of the Howler's vile blood. Eager to be clean he removed his cloak and tunic. Nothing could be done about cleaning his clothing, but at least he could clean himself.

Pulling his reserve of water out from his pack, he poured it onto the cloth and pushed it onto his shoulder. He squeezed his eyes shut, muffling a pained groan. The wound stung. The dirt and blood was stuck to Lorn and stubborn to removed. Lorn added more water, letting the cloth soak on his skin, loosening up the impurities. The wound stung each time he cleaned it, the dirt and blood slowly washing away. Once clean Lorn tore some extra cloth from his bag into long strips and wrapped it around his shoulder. He knotted the ends and inspected his work. It was the best he could do right now. Satisfied he put his torn shirt back on, careful not to rub the dirt and blood back onto his wound.

Rifling through his bag, he pulled out some dried fruit. The dried fruit was a delicacy in the Hinterlands and he took his time savoring each bite. While eating, he allowed himself to briefly think of everything that transpired. Who was this cloaked person and why were they here? How were they able to vanish right in front of him? How were they in the Hinterlands? No records or stories ever mentioned such a thing.

Lorn knew very little about the history of Ithilia due to his rural upbringing. He couldn't answer any of these questions. As far as he knew, he never heard of anyone else being able to enter the Hinterlands, or vanish in a mass of shadows. Perhaps Lord Aldrich knew the answers to these questions. Lorn had suspicions Lord Aldrich and his advisers were withholding key information from him. They might have known about this entity.

Frustrated with his lack of answers, Lorn hastily threw his fruit back in his bag and began methodically cleaning his weapons. The Howler's blood lay thick and congealed on his blades. Each swipe the blade's metal glinted through the muck. Lorn used this moment to recenter his mind and to not get caught up in the torrential downpour of his thoughts.

He was only sent here for his ability to hunt and survive. He was not a scholar, or renowned for his mind. He needed to ignore all of the questions bogging him down and focus on reaching the Well alive. Lorn resharpened his blades, placed the glinting steel back into his scabbard, and his daggers along his belt.

Shakily he stood, his body stiff from sleeping against the firm tree trunk. Twisting back and forth, lightly stretching his stiff muscles. Lorn rotated his shoulder, taking care to move slowly, testing out the bandages he had wrapped around. Shouldering his pack, Lorn stepped forward, determined to reach the Well. He ignored the protests of his body, taking step after step in the stillness of the

Hinterlands. Lorn stopped a moment, silenced his footsteps, and cocked his head to listen to his surroundings. He heard nothing.

Not a cry of beasts, not the rustling of twigs and leaves.

Nothing.

He thought back to when he last heard the common sounds of the Hinterlands. Nothing had come about since the figure sang the lament. The Hinterlands was always unsettling, but now it felt eerie, like a vacant graveyard—like he had imagined all the creatures and inhabitants within. Lorn walked slowly and cautiously, keeping his eyes on the surroundings.

Did the mysterious person's songs cause the beasts to subside? Whatever the reason, Lorn remained wary, but trudged forward, the air festering and stagnant. He wished to be free of this place, but he needed to make it to the Well first. He faltered for a moment unsure of which direction to go. Steadying himself, an inner voice steered him to the Well and he obliged.

11

"As the dim light fades from view, I can only look forward. The Meadows of the Undying lie there in front of me, welcoming me home. I am hesitant to leave the world behind, but excited for what lay ahead."

Last journal entry from the Scholar Oria of Iyera

Hours trickled by as Lorn trekked up and down the undulating hills of the Hinterlands. He passed by trees devoured in the overgrown moss, their slow growth suffocating the trees, causing them to buckle and curve.

The Hinterlands remained silent since the figure's mysterious lamentations. It unnerved him. He expected the random shrieks of the beasts and rustling movements in the forest. Sounds were warped and magnified within, including the silence.

Paranoia set in.

All sense of time had shifted. Lorn felt like he was trapped in a hourglass. The time kept moving around him—he was aware of it yet saw no changes in the daylight. The forest blocked all light, and Lorn was stuck moving in this forever gray forest, missing the warmth of the sunlight on his skin.

He hadn't encountered any other creature, any sort of sound. This was its own form of torture. Lost and wandering left alone with his own thoughts in this forest wasteland. Each step muffled on the overgrown forest floor as he pushed onward. Illusionary sounds played in his head. He imagined shadows and creatures. They passed his line of vision, yet he could not hear anything to confirm his suspicions. Flashes of worry spread through his body like a slow acting poison. The constant paranoia drained his energy. His mind attempted to reconcile the fact there were no creatures present. Yet leaving him in a perpetual state of distress, his instincts reared up anytime he perceived a threat.

Lorn found a spot to rest for the night, or what he considered to be night. If he escaped the Hinterlands, he was determined to make a roaring fire and never leave it. The Hinterlands was not a snowy, freezing landscape, however an undefinable chill permeated his body.

The Hinterlands was uninhabitable—it discouraged life, warmth, and happiness. The gray veil lingering in the Hinterlands leached away his essence every second he was stuck in this forsaken place. As he lay there, he wished for many things to be different. Dismayed, he readjusted his position and dismissed those thoughts. They brought nothing but sorrow.

When he awoke, he blearily trekked on, ignoring the thoughts plaguing his mind. He tucked them into a tiny corner, despite the flurry threatening to pull him under. The dark thoughts loomed in the back of his head, waiting for a weakness to rear up. Lorn made progress across the Hinterlands. His inner compass told him he was getting closer to the center. Hope began to flicker like a small candle lit in the darkness. His chest felt lighter than it had been in weeks. He held on to this feeling, allowing it to kindle him from within.

At the peak of a small hill, he spotted the thick tangle of trees lessen. Small bits of sky poked through in quiet rebellion, a reminder of the joy and purity the outside world contained. This wonderful sight spurred an extra surge of energy.

Lorn had a vague sense of proximity to the Well. He was close, and yet he wasn't dead. A thin smile fought to appear. He could reach the Well, retrieve the item, and then make the journey back. As quickly as his happiness appeared, it withered away. He would still need to make the dreaded journey back. Lorn hoped he might find sanctuary in the center of the Hinterlands. Perhaps the Well could offer him refuge.

With nothing besides paranoia to occupy his mind, he turned to thoughts of Lord Aldrich and his advisers. During the last couple weeks of travel, he tried not to contemplate Lord Aldrich. They were going through all this trouble to retrieve an item from the Well. Historians, ancient tomes, and withered scrolls all documented how nothing has revealed itself from the Well since the Hinterlands came to be, about one thousand years ago. Curious as to what would reveal itself, Lorn thought back to any knowledge he had of magically imbued items.

Fabled stories and legends of lore whispered around crackling fires told of a variety of weapons ranging to even the mundane. Simple items pulled from people's homes could be imbued with magic from the Well. Lorn was unsure of the exact process involved. There must be some other factors, because magical weapons weren't commonplace. They were extremely rare.

The rarest of magical items appeared from the Well itself. No MagicBlessed rituals were involved. Only a gift presented directly from purest source of magic. What could be so precious that Lord Aldrich and his advisers sought it out? Sought him out? Puzzled, Lorn walked on and followed the brief glimpses of light, a balm to his weary soul.

Reaching a break in the tree canopy, from glimpses he could spot night had descended. Stars twinkled from the small peeks. Lorn spotted an alcove hidden by the surrounding trees and decided to rest for the night. It would be unfortunate to die being so close to his journey's end.

A bolt of excitement coursed through him. He could feel it. Sense it. He was close. His hunter's instinct and internal compass told him he would reach the Well by tomorrow. He was almost there. Lorn's eyes closed, wondering what the mysterious Well would look like. He fell asleep, a kaleidoscope of colors splattering his dreams.

Lorn woke abruptly the next morning, a burst of nervousness and anticipation skittering throughout him. He readied himself quickly and set off. Each step brought him closer to the Well. He saw larger gaps in the foliage as he neared, like the center of the Well fought back against the intruding darkness. Each sight sped him along and gave him a burst of hope. Optimism flowed through him. He could do this. He would do this.

Lorn plunged ahead, his hope fueling his determined steps. Not a whisper or a sound permeated the dense forest.

Lorn's optimism stopped abruptly as he heard the movement of paws on the forest floor, and a deep, distant growl. Lorn prowled closer, edging from tree to tree. What he saw up ahead, chilled him down to his bones.

It reminded him of a bear, yet appeared much bigger and deadlier, its features distorted. The bear-like creature's face was twisted in anger. It paced back and forth guarding what lay behind it. Lorn didn't need to see it to know the Well lay just behind that creature. He needed a plan to get past it. He was so close to succeeding. Lorn backtracked, finding a secluded area to set his items down and plan.

Could he sneak past it? He doubted the creature would let him pass. What kind of opponent would this creature pose? Its sheer size and muscles proved it would be difficult. He was nearing his breaking point, both physically and mentally. He couldn't simply muscle his way through it. Lorn debated going around and seeking another way through to reach the Well. He considered the option, but the dwindling light poking through the canopy of trees overhead, warned Lorn he did not have much time left, possibly less than a day. If he couldn't go around, then he would have to go straight through. Lorn didn't think he had the strength to face the bear creature head on. Even from a distance, the bear was massive. He would likely be killed. If he couldn't face it head on, maybe he could face it from a distance? He still had his bow and arrows. Yet what if the arrows weren't enough to pierce the animal's hide?

Many unanswered questions swamped Lorn's mind. Nothing would ever feel right. He needed to pick an idea and follow through with it. Crouched down, Lorn formulated his plan, ate one last meal, and prepared himself. By the end of today he will have either reached the Well or be dead. He sent a quick prayer out to the gods and goddesses, and a heartfelt thought out to his wife.

"I love you Lakesh. At least I am doing something with the remainder of the life granted to me. If I die, I will happily greet you at the Meadows of the Undying."

Lorn strode forward, prepared to greet death.

Lorn hopped from tree to tree, using the wide moss-covered trunks to shield his body from the twisted bear. He tried to reach the correct distance for his aim and held his bow in a relaxed grip, gauging where and when he needed to shoot. He needed to stay as far as possible from the bear, but still close enough to hit his target. His goal was to fire repeatedly, and pray the arrows struck true. If he was too close, there wouldn't be enough arrows to fell the bear, and if he was too far away his arrows would alert the bear and possibly miss the target.

Satisfied with the distance he found, he pressed his back up against the tree trunk and hid himself. The bear continued its relentless pacing. The matted fur was a dark brown almost black. Its paws were the size of the wheels used for his horse carts. The bear's body easily towered over Lorn.

Soft rays of light filtered through the leaves. He needed to act now. The light would be gone and he would be fighting blindly, the darkness another enemy he didn't need.

He pulled an arrow from his quiver, nocked and allowed himself two slow breaths in and out.

Nothing more.

At the exhale of the second breath, he revealed himself from behind the tree, centered his arrow on the bear and released. The arrow flew straight and true, embedding itself deep into the bear's formidable body. The bear released an earth-shaking roar, the ground vibrating underneath Lorn's feet. Searching its surroundings, the bear frantically looked for the intruder. Its nose lifted to the sky. It caught Lorn's scent and faced him. While the bear howled its displeasure, Lorn wasted no time, pulling another arrow from his quiver and strung it.

He let it fly.

The arrow whistled through the air, piercing the bear a bit lower than Lorn hoped, in one of its legs. The bear reared back and charged towards Lorn. Its powerful legs propelled it forward, rage contorting its face. Lorn refused to cower and readied another arrow. The arrow barely grazed the bear's back. Lorn kept his footing, and released two more arrows, hitting the mark each time. The bear-like creature plunged relentlessly forward, arrows sticking out of its flesh.

Lorn had to move and soon. The bear would be upon him, and he was no match for the sheer size of it. One more arrow, and then he would have to reassess. The bear closed in on him, Lorn released his arrow, and it stuck straight in its chest. The bear bellowed its displeasure but kept on. It was mere steps away. Lorn darted around trees across from him, hoping the cover would help slow down the bear's attack. The bear charged on the space where Lorn was, its giant paws swiping the air. Lorn quickly nocked another arrow, peered out from the tree, and shot again. The arrow lodged in its back, along with the others. The bear growled in pain, swiveled to find Lorn, and raced towards him again. The bear gained on him quickly and Lorn barely rolled away in time.

No, his plan would not work. The arrows were not slowing the bear down, only angering it.

Enraged at the tree for shielding Lorn, the bear swiped at it, and the ancient tree burst into splinters. Fragments of it rained down, the tree fell, shaking the ground with its withered remains. Lorn scrambled to his feet. This creature was unstoppable. It did not slow. It did not tire.

Anger, rage, and hatred emanated from the beast. Lorn wasted no time hiding behind another tree, storing his bow along his back. The bear charged and Lorn sprinted to the next. He wanted the bear to keep shifting its focus. Lorn sprinted diagonally from tree to tree. The bear chased him, knocking, and demolishing each tree Lorn hid behind. Lorn needed a plan, he couldn't run and hide forever. He needed to defeat this creature, yet it was so formidable. If countless arrows embedded in its body did nothing to it, what would?

Lorn kept sprinting, creeping closer and closer to the opening where the Well was. The more Lorn outran the beast, the more enraged it became. He was almost there, yet how to rid himself of this bear? Lorn barely dodged the next swipe of the bear, rolled and sprinted to the next tree.

The bear roared.

A roar to awaken.

A roar to signal the end of Lorn's life.

Lorn froze and stared at the trees around him. The ground shook from the weight of a thousand claws, talons, paws tearing at the ground. The shrill cry of beasts filled the forest. The bear waited, knowing victory was close at hand.

Lorn's stomach dropped. He had never anticipated this. The bear on its own was enough. A challenge he might never have won but, to have all the beasts of the Hinterlands surround him, he would not come out alive. Lorn ran to the center of a small clearing among the trees as the beasts corralled him. All manner of creatures appeared in the Hinterlands. Those he had fought in villages, and others he had never encountered before.

They all stood there, their fangs dripping with saliva, waiting for the command to come forward. All of them were twisted mockeries of creatures that existed outside of the Hinterlands, such as wolves, snakes, mountain lions, bats. Yet they were mangled, their hunger and something else distorted them. Lorn knew this was the end. He would never survive.

"I will see you soon Lakesh," he whispered and pulled out his longsword. There were too many beasts to face, so he faced the bear-like creature. Despite knowing his death was imminent, he still would fight until the very end.

The bear watched like a general assessing a battlefield. It was so unlike the rage-filled monster that chased Lorn moments ago. As if attuned to the bear's thoughts, the beasts broke off one by one to attack Lorn. The years of pent-up rage and frustration over his wife's death unleashed Lorn's fury like a gathered bolt of lightning. He was light. He was death. The beasts unaware of the threat in front of them advanced. Lorn's bloodlust overcame him, thought evaporated, and only a primal predator remained.

Lorn's sword lashed out and he painted the forest floor with black blood. His sword was an extension of his arm and this fight was a dance he had long-since memorized the moves to. Each slash, swipe he was alive. His body thrummed with the expert use of magic and blade fully harmonized. It was a fitting way to go, fighting against the creatures that took away the joy of his life.

Lorn gracefully moved and beasts felled in his way. He succumbed to his inner rhythm, his steps sure, confident. He was a force to reckon with. Scratches and bites found their way to him, but he waded through, ignoring the pain, ignoring the blood dripping down his arm, drenching his body. More and more creatures attacked, and he danced to the bloodlust singing in his body.

One of the beasts raked its long yellow claws down Lorn's back. He cried out, turning and slashing. Another bit deep into his back, tearing into muscle. He dropped to his knees. Dirt, and blood mingled. This was it. The end for him.

A small smile crested his face, a single tear rolled down his cheek. "Lakesh, my love, I will see you again." He closed his eyes, and waited for the beasts to rip him apart, to end him. There was a stillness that rippled in the air. He looked around, his vision blurry, the light in the forest dimming. Night descended and he too would disappear like the light of the day. He welcomed it.

The beasts stayed in place, unmoving, as if listening to something else present. Slowly the creatures parted, like a stone being dropped in a pond. Ripple after ripple the creatures moved aside as a figure walked through. It was the same person he had encountered. The cloaked figure.

Their shadows writhed and swirled at their feet, eager to be used. Step after step they approached, until they towered over Lorn. Lorn's bloodlust and adrenaline drained out of him like a puncture wound. Left feeling the ache and rupture of every wound inflicted on his body, his back felt slick and wet, the blood steadily coursing down. His eyes struggled to remain open. The figure surveyed the creatures torn apart at Lorn's feet and crouched down to meet Lorn's gaze. Lorn's sight was unsteady, he swayed on his knees, struggling to hold up his body.

The figure placed their fingers underneath Lorn's chin, forcing his gaze to steady on them. Surprised at the firm feel of their fingers, he expected a phantom instead, their grip to slip through him. The shadows slipped away from their face, revealing herself to him.

The cloaked figure was a woman. Lorn didn't know what to expect entering the Hinterlands, but he was shocked at this. His eyes widened, as she stared at him. She placed both of her hands on the hood of her cloak and reverently brought it down. He was met with a sharp and angular face, geometric tattoos on each cheek. Rich brown eyes searched his face. They were tinged with deep sorrow. Lorn knew because when he looked at himself, he saw the same thing. Her onyx hair was braided around the top of her head and framed her light brown face, turned sallow from the lack of light in the Hinterlands. Unspeaking, she stared at Lorn, evaluating him. He dared not speak. The shadows flickered around the bottom of her cloak, restless despite her own stillness.

She elegantly rose and walked back to her place among the beasts, her steps full of purpose. She halted in front of the bear. They stared at one another, the bear's face once full of rage and anguish, exhibited calm. They brought their foreheads together, bear and woman and closed their eyes. The woman clasped both sides of the bear's face, her fingers gripping the fur in a tight embrace. The Hinterlands was shrouded in silence, everything enraptured, watching the curious exchange. Even the wind and night sky were silent observers to the meeting.

The woman's shadows climbed up her body, slithering over the bear's figure, and continued to grow. Bigger and bigger the shadows formed touching each beast encircled around Lorn. Soon every creature had a black shadow swirling around them. Even the slain beasts' bodies on the ground were covered with her shadows.

The woman screamed an ancient word to the night sky and the shadows enveloping each beast caused them to vanish. All except the bear.

The woman and bear bowed their heads to one another again and parted. The bear looked past her and towards Lorn. It growled a single warning, turned, and stalked away. Nothing remained except for the destruction of the forest trees.

Lorn could scarcely breathe. What had just happened? The woman and Lorn looked at one another, transfixed. She gave a curt nod, a small sign of encouragement for Lorn to stand up. Lorn had no chance to breathe a thank you, before the shadows swallowed her up.

She was gone.

The forest felt dimmer with her spirit gone. Whatever she was, Lorn thanked the gods and goddesses above. She had saved and spared his life. Lorn couldn't even begin to fathom what had just happened, and how she was connected to it all.

Shakily he stood and headed towards the Well. Each step sent a flare of pain through his body. His mind was foggy. He felt himself losing consciousness. He forced himself to keep his eyes open. He stumbled forward. Tree roots hidden in the night tripped him, catching himself a few times until he finally crashed to the ground. Pain blinded him. He lay there curled on the ground, blood leaking out of him. He needed to make it. Gritting his teeth he rose again, step after step. The thickness of the Hinterlands began to thin. He was so close. He could do this. His whole body was slick with his blood and sweat and pain was his companion as he forced another step. He passed the final tree line, stumbling upon a beautiful meadow.

He made it.

The Well lay in front of him.

12

"Records from long ago indicate the Well has not always been surrounded by the Hinterlands. I wonder what it would be like to gaze upon its beauty. The records say the written word cannot do it justice. Pity I will never be able to look upon it myself."

Excerpt from *The Well and its Origins* by Ghipp of Iyera

Lorn dropped to his knees.

The Well, he had finally reached it.

Once out of the Hinterlands and the gloom of its disease-ridden forest, he entered what looked to be a small meadow. Soft grasses, and small flowers dotted the landscape. There in the middle lay the Well. It was a tremendous pit in the ground and inside was glorious. The magic was both viscous, fluid, and solid, a spectrum of all colors and none, swirling and stationary. Its existence is a contradiction of all components, yet wholly itself.

This was the same magic that flowed throughout his veins.

This was the magic that sustained the land of Ithilia. In the center of the Hinterlands was this gem, this sanctuary.

The night seemed to be holding its breath in anticipation. The stars overhead seemed to shine brighter. Lorn, abandoning all concern for his wounds, quickly got to his feet and looked around, searching for the magic item that was destined to appear. He had lost all sense of time within the Hinterlands but felt confident that he had shown up exactly when he needed to. He only had one turn of the moon to arrive here. He reassured himself he had done it. Where was the magic item?

As if on command, the matter within the Well moved and swirled. The colors morphed, changing—something began to form. Entranced, he looked on, unsure of what was going to appear. The colors altered and a bright white light pierced through the center of the Well, a purer light than even his magic could summon. The entire Well lit up, the light engulfing the darkness of the night. It pierced straight upwards into the sky a giant beam of power. It called seductively to Lorn's magic. He fought the urge to be drawn into the deep well of magic and shielded his eyes against the intense light. Lorn blinked his eyes rapidly to clear the white flashes that still danced in his vision. He was desperate to see what all his work had amounted to, what he had fought for. When he could finally see clearly, he was speechless.

Standing on the shapeless matter of the Well was a woman.

Lorn collapsed to his knees. The woman stood there, casually surveying the land. She spotted Lorn and walked towards him. She stepped across the rippling Well, her shoulders back, and her head held high. Her feet pressed lightly to the surface of the Well and the magic beneath her, embraced her, unwilling to let her depart. Eventually her slow, measured steps brought her to Lorn. His head bowed, he refused to gaze upon her, worried if he did, he wouldn't leave this place alive.

"Who are you?" A soft melodic voice rang out.

Lorn hesitated, unsure how to respond to this person, if she even was a person. Unsure of proper protocol, unsure of what to do, he slowly raised his head to gaze upon her.

She was forged as if the night had declared her queen and the stars had bequeathed her a crown. Her skin was the color of midnight itself, her eyes a liquid silver as they pierced Lorn's gaze.

He swallowed, averting his eyes. His thoughts were flustered, so he decided upon honesty. "I am Lorn, a hunter. I was sent to retrieve an item from the Well." His eyes trailed over to the Well behind her. She followed his line of sight. As she looked at the Well, Lorn stole a quick glance at her again. Her hair had soft, springy coils with a hue that matched her eyes—a vibrant silver. She turned back to face him, her eyes unsettling him. After a few moments her gaze softened as they continued to stare at each other. The hunter and the goddess.

"Excuse me, my lady, but what are you?" Lorn asked, surprised at his own boldness. An otherly power emanated from her and he knew, if she chose, he would be dead upon her command.

She loosened a sigh, glanced at the meadow, then surprised Lorn by looking at the sky.

"The moon is beautiful tonight." She paused, taking in each detail of nature. "The stars are bright. They shine so brightly right now. I can almost feel them." Her arms, sculpted from the night sky, reached towards those faraway stars. In awe, she drew back her arm and began studying it, turning it this way and that to look at the fine details. "I do not know what I am." She tilted her head, assessing Lorn, those silver eyes piercing through to his core. "I feel as if I have been in a great sleep and only now, I have been awakened. I now have a body." She paused as if searching for the correct words, "But my mind… my mind has been here for a long time."

Lorn was completely shocked by this woman, this being, appearing from the Well, he had failed to notice she was completely naked. Averting his gaze, he reached into his bag and grabbed out his spare cloak. Wordlessly he held it up for her to take. She raised an eyebrow in question.

"Is something wrong, Lorn?" She continued looking at him, unmoving.

"Um, this is for you, my lady," Lorn's face turned warm, as he stammered, searching for the correct words. "You have no clothing, nothing to keep you warm or safe from the environment. Would you please put this cloak on?"

Slowly she reached for the proffered cloak and began putting it on.

"Why do you kneel?"

"Because I do not know what you are, and your power…" Lorn shifted his eyes barely catching glimpses of the woman above him, "Your power… it overwhelms me. I can feel it in the air. I can feel it all around you, as if I am in the eye of a storm and if I move, I will be lost to it." Lorn forced himself to still his shaking body. His fingers clenched around the ground. Searching for something to hold onto, something to weigh him down, to prevent him from being swept away by her immense power.

"Will you please stand? I am not a goddess or a god. I would rather you look at me and talk to me normally." Her voice betrayed a hint of irritation. She shifted her weight from one foot to the other and knelt beside Lorn. Her fingers went underneath Lorn's chin as she tilted his eyes up to meet hers. "Please." She invited him, her arm extended towards him to help him rise.

He nodded, untangled his limbs, and reached towards her hand clasping it as she helped to raise him up. His body jolted in response. The power of her magic invaded him. Lorn felt like he was in a vast ocean, lost in the ever-flowing current of her magic. She was pulling him in, and he was not strong enough to survive. He quickly released her hand and discreetly stepped away from her.

Her brow wrinkled with confusion. "Your power of magic is too strong. I can't even touch your hand without feeling it threatening to overwhelm me."

She nodded slowly, thoughtfully and regarded her body.

"My name is Aza," she said softly, as if speaking to the wind and night sky around them. "Let me make a campfire for you, and we can talk." She strode away and found a spot in the meadow devoid of flowers. She circled her hands, raised one, and a warm crackling fire appeared. Aza gracefully sat down cross-legged and beckoned for Lorn to follow. He lingered, his footsteps slow and painful. All the injuries he had experienced in the Hinterlands made themselves known, his excitement and adrenaline now faded. The faint itch of dried blood seemed to cover his entire body.

Aza stared, frankly assessing Lorn. "I did not realize you were injured. Would you like me to heal it?"

Lorn winced and gently touched the gash across his forehead. Blood coated his fingertips as he pulled them away. Lorn nodded. He sat down next to her in the soft meadow grass, his body protesting his every move, feeling the torn flesh, his muscle and sinew exposed. Sitting down, his breathing labored, he looked upon Aza. Her beauty was startling, and a smattering of silver freckles graced the bridge of her nose and her cheeks.

She lightly placed her arm upon his and her whole body glowed with a soft white light. A sharpness pierced Lorn, as he felt his wounds begin to heal. The skin knitted back together, all the aches in his bones were erased. She released her grip on him, dropped her hand back in her lap and gazed at him expectantly. "Better?" Aza quirked an eyebrow at him, waiting for a response.

"Yes, thank you. The beasts in the Hinterlands are formidable."

"The... beasts?" she asked.

"Yes, this area is surrounded by a thick set of woods known as the Hinterlands. Beasts and creatures roam the Hinterlands and protect the Well. As I came through, I was set upon by many different types of creatures, which is why I came to you injured."

She gave a noncommittal sound in response. Aza seemed distracted, half listening to the conversation, with another part of her tuned to her inner self. She leaned back resting on her hands and gazed up at the sky above softly humming to herself. Lorn looked at her waiting for some type of reaction, yet Aza was content to remain that way, so Lorn attended the fire. It crackled wildly in front of them, the warmth comforting Lorn. He had been so afraid to light a fire inside the Hinterlands, often he would be left feeling cold and stiff from nights sleeping on the hard ground. Being here in the meadow left him with a sense of peace and calmness despite the groundbreaking realization that he would be returning Aza to Iyera and back to Lord Aldrich.

His heart raced. He would have to return Aza to Lord Aldrich. What would he think of Aza? Lorn's body swayed, his vision darkened. Too much. He had done too much. Lost too much blood. Aza turned her head, glancing at Lorn struggling. Her voice was a soft command. "Sleep, Lorn."

He shook his head, adamant to keep conscious. Her hand reached out to touch his forehead. "Sleep, Lorn," she repeated, and a darkness swept over him. Lorn crashed onto the soft meadow grass, his body limp.

~

Flashes of different images played through his mind. Twisted creatures. Blood. A piercing light. A cloaked figure. The images repeated themselves. Lorn stood on the outside of the flashing images, a silent observer. He turned, viewing each one. More and more images pushed together. Lorn spun in circles catching glimpses of each one. They blended and merged, the colors bleeding together, the images overlapping. "What does it all mean?" Lorn whispered.

"Lorn." A voice wove into his mind.

Lorn's eyes opened. A bright clear sky welcomed him back, not one of darkness and decay. Confusion warred within. He blinked slowly, trying to recollect his memories. He had made it to the Well. He was alive. Lorn sat up and abruptly ran his hands along his body. His wounds were gone. He felt...refreshed. His head swiveled back and forth, and he remembered the Well was surrounded by a peaceful meadow. The fire in front of him had died out, small embers glowing a deep red. Lorn closed his eyes and remembered Aza. His eyes flashed open, and Lorn rushed to his feet searching for her.

He turned around and spotted her closer to the Well, but instead of rushing towards her, he chose to stay in place and observe. She had healed him, but he had no idea what to think of her. How would Lord Aldrich react to Lorn bringing Aza back? More importantly, what was she?

Aza seemed to be wandering aimlessly around the Well. Her grace and beauty were staggering. As Lorn stared at her, he felt like he was missing something. There was something bigger at play and he was just another piece on a cosmic game board.

Aza still wore Lorn's cloak. It loosely covered her body. She walked barefoot through the meadow grass, stopping occasionally to stare at the Well. Or the sky. Or even her own body. It was like she was hearing and seeing everything in a completely different way than Lorn.

Propelled by curiosity, Lorn made his way towards Aza and the Well. As he neared, he felt the tremors of magic pulsing in his body. The Well called to him. Mesmerized, Lorn advanced towards it. He felt alive. The magic in his body yearned to get closer. Lorn stood speechlessly at the edge.

The magic roiled and writhed—countless colors moved as one. Unbridled power washed over him. It was a calling to who he was as a MagicBlessed person. It was like the magic wholly agreed with who he was and it penetrated to his core.

The magic inside the Well was neither solid, liquid, or gas but appeared to be a strange combination of all three. He stared, allowing himself to bask in the beauty, bask in his triumph of reaching the Well.

Lorn tilted his head back, allowing the sun's piercing rays to cleanse him. His journey through the Hinterlands was a stain on him. Sorrow and despair reigned heavily. Being here, near the Well and Aza in this quiet peaceful meadow was Lorn's tonic.

Lorn raised his head back, and found Aza next to him, slight concern showing on her face. She reached a hand towards Lorn about to touch his shoulder, reconsidered and let her hand fall limply by her side.

"Are you well?" Her silver eyes flashed to him, examining him. They began to fill with pity, as if she could sense the trauma that riddled his life. He nodded. It wasn't a lie. For the first time in a while, he felt well. The overwhelming numbness after Lakesh's death had faded, replaced by a sharp, acute pain like a leg fracture healing incorrectly. He only needed to experience the pain of the break again for him to heal properly in the presence of pure magic. He was well. Confused and filled with many questions, but he was well. Aza's face relaxed upon hearing Lorn's answer.

"And you? Are you well?"

Her eyebrows furrowed and she looked lost in her thoughts. "I do not know how to answer that."

Lorn gestured to the spot in the meadow with their supplies and burnt-out fire. "Would you like to sit down and talk? I think we both need to understand each other. There are many pieces of this story we don't understand."

Aza agreed and they sat down facing one another. Lorn pulled out rations from his bag, grabbed the dried jerky and handed a piece to Aza. She took it, graciously nodding her head in thanks. They munched on their food, wondering where to begin. "How about you explain everything," Aza suggested. She curiously scanned Lorn, trying to discern any information from him, as if weighing who he was and who she would discover him to be.

Lorn began his story. He explained the summons he received from Lord Aldrich, and how he was told of a rare magical item appearing from the Well. Aza nodded and followed along, some parts confusing her. Lorn went slowly, repeating himself whenever confusion appeared on her ethereal face, or when she turned quiet and contemplative. He often needed to bounce back and forth in his retelling.

Aza's memory and understanding of Ithilia was riddled with holes. Lorn tried to tread carefully, not wanting to displease her. He wasn't scared of her power, oddly enough. He was scared when she became lost in thought, as if she wasn't truly a part of this world—lost in the questions of her own existence. She cycled back and forth between different realities, and he didn't want to cause her any pain. Each time she shifted between listening to him and listening to something within herself. She appeared lost like she was unsure of her place in the world and wasn't meant to truly be here. The sun moved across the sky, close to setting by the time Lorn was finished. Aza magicked another fire. It crackled and sparked, the light a beacon throughout the darkened meadow. They sat there absorbing all the information Lorn shared.

"What do you make of Lord Aldrich?" Aza's voice broke the reverie of the still evening. Lorn considered her question, glancing around at the Well, the meadow, and the Hinterlands. "I'm not exactly sure. His province is well cared for—if that is any sign of his true nature. He claimed that he and his advisers have been studying the prophecy for years, expecting a magical item to appear." Lorn shifted his body to turn and look at the Well. "If he only knew what would appear instead...you." Shaking his head, he looked back at Aza. "I can't give you a clear answer because I truly don't know him that well. He summoned me and gave me a quest. I followed it because my life was filled with emptiness." Lorn sighed, he did not want to be dishonest with Aza. "To be honest, I have felt a pull towards the Hinterlands for a while. I can't help but think this is all Fate designed." He pointed his hand at Aza. "You cannot be a coincidence." Lorn loosed a frustrated growl and stood to his feet. "There is something more, something at play I cannot see. It is like smoke. The more I grab at it the more it slips out of my grasp." He paced back and forth. The fire cast erratic shadows behind him.

"And you, Aza, how are you here?" Lorn realized his voice was rising in frustration, paused his relentless pacing and looked at Aza. "What is your story?" Lorn quietly asked.

Aza watched Lorn unraveling. "I don't really know how to answer that question." She casually examined her body, tracing her fingers along the contours. An exasperated sigh escaped her lips. "I don't know Lorn. While you slept, I have been asking myself these same questions. My memory is frustrating. It is like water in a sieve. It holds for a moment, then everything slips through." She unfolded her legs and stood across from Lorn. "I feel power thrumming through my veins." Aza turned her arms over, displaying her forearms to Lorn. "I feel it there, never ceasing. It calls to me." She walked decisively over to the Well, her toes cresting the edge. She stared intently at it, like all the answers to her questions resided there. Aza clutched a hand to her head and whispered, "Everything is muddled. I wish I knew why I was here. Yet, despite everything, you feel familiar." Aza turned back to face Lorn, silver eyes entreating his hazel eyes. Her face scrunched, she waited for a response from Lorn. Lorn didn't know what to tell her. He had a similar feeling, like he was meant to be here at this moment. He was meant to find Aza. A thread connected them. A thread crafted from the gods and goddesses long ago. Aza continued, "I expected you to be here. I knew you would meet me here when I appeared. I was not surprised."

"There are many mysteries we have yet to figure out. Let us plan our return to Iyera, if you are willing?" Lorn's question hung in the air between them.

Aza stole a glance at the Well and turned back to Lorn. "That is the odd thing. I trust you. My mind races through emotions, people, and places—I do not often put my trust in others. Yet...I trust you." Aza squared her shoulders and walked towards their campfire. "If you think we should head back to Iyera, I defer to you. You and I are linked somehow."

Lorn joined her and they discussed a plan for returning to Iyera. They talked long into the night, the moon and stars providing them company. Lorn shed some of his clothing and shared it with Aza. Despite Lorn standing a little over six feet tall, Aza fit in his clothing. She was statuesque. The clothes weren't exactly right, weathered and encrusted with dirt from the Hinterlands, but they were enough for now. Lorn tried to give Aza the cleanest bits of clothing he could find. One pair of his pants and a black tunic fit her well enough.

They decided that when they escaped the Hinterlands, she must cover herself. Her silver hair and eyes stood out and would startle people. He didn't want her to become a spectacle. She would keep his cloak and interact with as few people as possible. Lorn remembered that Gravers and Lilit were supposed to meet him at the inn in Shadow Acre. They were both gruff and unsettling and he didn't want any danger to come to Aza. Yet her power was so immense, Lorn had a feeling if Aza was left to fend for herself, she would come out the victor. They would still need to prepare themselves to fight their way out of the Hinterlands too. Scenarios played through Lorn's head. So many factors to consider, but he knew they would face any obstacles together.

Worn out and exhausted, they agreed to settle for bed. As Lorn laid down to sleep he had a brief thought about Aza that rang true. She had the familiar feeling of a friend.

Across the campfire, Lorn spotted Aza preparing for sleep, her face towards him.

Lorn thought he saw the same look on her face, one of disbelief at finding a long-forgotten friend.

13

*"A good nap under the warmth of the summer sun can cure me
of all wounds both internal and external."*
    Journal entry from the traveler Qaron of Gara

The following morning, they both woke slowly and stretched under the light, morning sun. Lorn grabbed more rations from his bag. Worry beginning to creep over him like an unsuspecting predator. He was running low on food. He had not expected to share with another person. They would have to leave soon and maintain a good pace. Familiar with suffering from hunger in the past, he could go without eating some of his meals, but Lorn wanted to be able to defend himself and Aza, if needed. The less energy they had, the more vulnerable to attacks they would be.

Lorn had no idea how people would react to Aza's appearance. True they wouldn't know she was created from the Well itself, but while standing in proximity to her for even a few minutes a person would understand she was different. Others would sense and feel her power. Lorn thought back to when she first offered him a hand to stand. Touching her was overwhelming. The power threatened to consume him. Countless worries wove in and out through Lorn's head. He had gone so long without ever worrying about anything, including himself. She was this prized rarity, her magic a gift that he felt he needed to protect. So many questions, he wondered if their the answers would ever come to light.

Today they would be returning to the five provinces, which will require them to cross the Hinterlands again. Lorn hoped Aza's appearance was not a beacon for the beasts. Lost in his thoughts and pacing aimlessly, he found himself at the edge of the Well. Every person in Ithilia had dreamed of standing where he was now. To witness and be in the presence of pure magic. He memorized it, seared it into his memory, never wanting to forget any part of this. He had made it. He was still alive.

Aza's footsteps moved behind him, startling him out of his reverie. "Are you ready?" She stood shoulder to shoulder with him, staring at the Well, like it called to her in a language only she understood.

His eyes lowered and he realized her feet were bare. "I'm sorry, I have been careless. We need to find you some sort of shoes to cover your feet." Aza examined her feet, looked back at Lorn, and shrugged. It seemed such a normal reaction to exhibit, Lorn couldn't help but smile.

Aza reminded him of a powerful goddess, one he grew up hearing whispered stories about over a roaring fire in their hearth, goddesses crafted from the world itself. Yet her mannerisms were normal. "You have seen the strength of my magic. I can heal the wounds I sustain." Lorn hesitated, preparing to interrupt, but Aza held up a hand. "I promise, it will not bother me. And if it does, I will let you know, and we can try to remedy it. Besides you have scavenged every leftover scrap of fabric to clothe me." Aza jerked her head back at their campfire. "Ready?"

Aza had no belongings except for the clothes Lorn had lent her. Lorn extended a hand holding out one of his daggers to her. "Will you take this?"

Aza hesitated, confusion evident on her face. Lorn clarified, "To protect yourself." She smirked, extended both of her hands and delicate flames whipped out of her fingertips. The flames beckoned to him, drawing him closer despite the danger of being burned. The fire intensified and it grew until it crested into an inferno. Lorn warily backed up, the heat scalding him. Sweat dripped down his face. A trickle of fear crept over Lorn's spine. Aza was lost to the power at her fingertips.

"Aza," Lorn breathed her name. She didn't hear him, focused on her power. "Aza!" Lorn shouted, hoping to bring her back from the brink.

Aza blinked, startled, and looked back at Lorn. Recognition dawned on her face as she realized where she was. "I'm sorry, I didn't mean to frighten you. The magic calls to me. It is easy to become lost in it."

"What does it feel like? Many MagicBlessed only have a small reserve of magic to pull from, and it drains us quickly." Lorn pulled his hand up to demonstrate. An orb of light appeared in the center of his palm, and it quickly diminished. "Even that small amount of magic is tiring for many of us."

Aza paused, searching for the words to explain to him. "It feels like...a river rushing through me. The water can flow softly, the current slow. Yet other times, the river can become a torrent, going faster and faster and it needs release, it needs to break off to slow it down. When I use my magic, it slows it down. Yet if I succumb to it, I feel like I am in the river merging with it. I can't tell where the magic ends and I begin." Aza noticed Lorn's wariness and a flash of hurt passed across her face. Aza's voice was soft. "Please do not be afraid." It was a plea, as if her greatest fear was being ostracized.

Lorn had faced a variety of beasts and creatures, the trials of the Hinterlands, and a mysterious cloaked figure with unknown power. He could face Aza without fear. He could face his new friend without fear. "I was afraid for a moment, afraid of what was happening to you." Lorn ran a hand through his hair and chuckled, "Clearly you don't need a dagger, but if you want one, all you need to do is ask."

Aza smiled tentatively and followed Lorn's lead. They left the peaceful meadow, the flowers swayed in the breeze, as if saying farewell. Lorn spared one more look at the Well, wishing he had more time to stay and bask in its beauty.

They reached the tree line where the Hinterlands began. A distinct line between life and decay, the thriving meadow filled with soft grasses and delicate flowers and a twisted forest with moss threatening to suffocate the life out of the trees.

Heaving an impatient breath, they crossed the threshold. The gloom of the Hinterlands descended. All the ease and relaxation leached out of their bodies. Aza and Lorn shared a look and began their journey back to Iyera.

They were quiet while traversing the Hinterlands. The day before Lorn had explained to Aza about all of the beasts and challenges they might face once inside. She had followed along, somewhat understanding Lorn's explanations amid her occasional blank stares and far off glances.

They traveled for the whole day and encountered nothing. Lorn was puzzled, the Hinterlands still had the same dark, smothering presence. His magic felt tampered, and his senses felt dull. Yet he had grown accustomed to the sporadic shrieks, and growls of the beasts that haunted the forest. Lorn thought back to when he entered the meadow. He had not heard a beast cry after he had reached the Well. After his interaction with the cloaked woman. Tired and exhausted after a full day of walking, they both stumbled into a small cove of trees. The chill of the Hinterlands, and their lack of food had worn them out.

"I will take the first watch," Lorn told Aza.

She blearily nodded and clutched her knees to her chest. Lorn grimaced, upset at being able to do nothing for her. The bottoms of her feet were ripped and shredded, from branches and thorns after a day of travel. Aza sent a flare of healing magic. Like a moth to the flame Lorn watched as Aza used her seemingly endless magic.

Frustrated at Aza's distress, Lorn asked, "Are you sure there is nothing I can do for your feet?"

Aza shook her head. "This is fine for the time being."

"You are not fine. Your feet are torn apart."

"Yes, it does sting, but it is a nice release for my magic. Holding it back all day is somehow worse and can be its own form of torture." Lorn shook his head but didn't want to pursue the matter further. She could make her own choices. He didn't need to pester her. Aza immediately laid down, her body resting on the hard earth. She placed her hands underneath her head like a pillow and fell asleep.

Lorn's own weariness blanketed him. His eyes fought to close. Instead, he stretched and tried to bring some movement to his body to combat his tiredness. The night was going to be long. As he looked over at Aza, her chest rising and falling with each breath—she was worth protecting.

Late into the night, Lorn shook Aza's shoulder to awaken her and switch shifts. He regretted doing it, but his own tiredness was overwhelming. She sat up cross-legged, her body alert and watchful. Lorn laid on the ground and fell asleep. He dreamed of nothing.

The next day progressed much like the first. They barely spoke for fear of encountering something in the Hinterlands, and each night they fell asleep instantly, one taking watch and the other resting. Two more days, and still there were no encounters. Lorn was grateful. They were slowing down, physically and mentally from their depleted food rations, and were lucky to have one meager meal each day. Combined with the strenuous hiking, their bodies needed more.

Even though Lorn was grateful to not encounter any beasts, it was still unsettling. He knew the Hinterlands. He had tracked beasts and helped local towns with the infestations. This was not natural. They were close to reaching the outskirts of Iyera, he estimated they had roughly one day remaining. Lorn told Aza and they decided to make camp for the night in a small hollow. It was the same as every night prior. Lorn took the first watch while Aza laid down to sleep. The forest was dark, the shadows playing tricks on Lorn. He dismissed the thought. He was tired and ready to be back in the five provinces.

Another movement in the shadows, and a twig snapped. Lorn shook his head and moved to alert Aza. She awoke immediately, her eyes concerned as she saw Lorn. "There is something out there," he whispered as quietly as he could. He motioned for her to move towards him. "On the count of three, wield your fire and I will fight with my sword."

Aza nodded her head in agreement. "One, two, three!" Aza's fingertips lit up with fire. The light briefly blinded them both. Lorn gripped his sword, trying to discern what lay waiting in the shadows. Lorn turned in a circle. Surely, this wasn't real. This couldn't be. How did they all get here without alerting him?

Surrounding Aza and Lorn were all the beasts of the Hinterlands. Their gazes fixed on them, eager to devour. Lorn spared a glance at Aza. She seemed unafraid, the fire coiling around her fingertips. One beast broke through the formation and sprinted for Lorn. It was a Howler. He would not let it get close to Aza. Lorn rooted his feet and gripped his sword, focusing in on his opponent. The Howler was on all fours, gaining speed faster and faster. It leaped. Aza screamed her fury. A magicked wall of wind blocked the Howler from Lorn. The Howler smashed against the formidable barrier and crumpled to the ground—stopped in its tracks.

Lorn raised his sword, ready to slash down on the beast when Aza cried, "Don't."

Lorn hesitated. He wanted to listen to Aza, but this might be his only opportunity to kill the beast. Frustrated, he glanced back at Aza as she stormed towards them. Her magicked wall of wind separated them from the beast.

"Don't," Aza repeated and put a hand on Lorn's shoulder. He felt the rumbles of her power course through him briefly. She lifted her hand and approached the Howler. In a silent command, she raised her hand and the wall of wind vanished. Lorn was uncomfortable with her in such proximity to the Howler. The other beasts looked on, remaining in their formation. The Howler lay twisted on the ground, breathing heavily. The collision with the wall had stunned it. Aza took small steps towards it and crouched down at its eye level. She reached a hand forward like a child aiming to pet a stray dog. The Howler snapped its jaw at her, the teeth sharp and dripping saliva. Aza pulled her hand back just in time. Lorn couldn't stand there a moment longer. He stepped forward his sword ready to cleave this beast in two.

"No, Lorn. Trust me." Her voice firm—a solid command.

Lorn struggled but forced himself to obey. His fingers restlessly curled and uncurled along the hilt of his sword. Face to face with the foul creature, Aza stared at the Howler. Suddenly she reached out both hands and clasped the Howler on both sides of its face. Startled, Lorn stepped forward, but saw the Howler relax in Aza's grip, like a beast tamed by a lullaby. They stayed in that position, locked into each other's eyes. Eventually, Aza let go. The Howler stood on its four legs and trotted back towards the outside of the circle.

A swishing sounded behind Lorn. He paused mid-swing and forced his sword to change directions. He swung around wielding his sword to find the mysterious cloaked woman behind him. He lowered his sword, stunned to see her again. She ignored Lorn; her eyes homed in on Aza. The woman cocked her head to the side, assessing her. With measured steps she walked to Aza.

Aza was entranced and let the woman come to her. The other creatures and beasts waited patiently, held back by some unspoken command. Lorn didn't know whether to intervene. He stood and watched the strange scene play out. The cloaked woman extended a hand to Aza. The woman waited, with her hand hovering there. Aza tentatively reached out and their hands clasped. Aza screamed, her cry filling the forest. Lorn rushed to her side, pulling her away from the cloaked woman.

"What have you done?" Lorn demanded.

Aza's eyes were closed, her body limp. Lorn struggled to hold her upright. The cloaked woman said nothing, but looked on, her features forlorn. Her mouth downturned, the woman turned her back on them both. Lorn thought he caught a slight tear in her eyes.

The shadows swallowed her up and in the blink of an eye all the beasts disappeared. Aza still lay in Lorn's arms unmoving. He checked her neck for a pulse. Her heartbeat was still going steady. Lorn released a sigh of relief. He picked her up and laid her down in the hollow of trees, watching over her for the rest of the night.

Tired, he was so tired, but he needed her to wake up.

Wake up Aza, he prayed. Aza's eyes fluttered open. They were unfocused, lost. "Aza, look at me." Her eyes flashed to Lorn. "You are safe now," he reassured her.

Aza sat up slowly, a hand going to her head. She closed her eyes in concentration. "What happened, Lorn?" Her eyes remained closed determined to shut out everything around her.

"What do you remember?"

"I remember a woman. She seemed so familiar. She walked up to me. She wanted me to clasp her hand. I did. Then nothing." Lorn listened intently, trying to discern any new bit of information. "After you locked hands, you screamed. It terrified me. It was a scream of anguish, of pain and suffering." Lorn gave a knowing look. "Then you passed out. The woman vanished along with all the beasts." Aza shuddered, the pain evident on her face. "Are you well?"

Aza took a deep breath in and released it before answering Lorn. "Yes, but the way you described my scream, that was everything I felt. When we touched hands, I felt the pain, the anguish, the suffering, everything. It was darkness. Not a comforting darkness, but one of despair. One of emptiness." Aza shook her head trying to dispel what haunted her.

"We can stay another day here, if you need the rest."

"No," Aza said forcefully. "I do not wish to be here any longer. I only need a minute to recover and then we can head out"

Lorn agreed and helped Aza to stand. He looped one hand around her shoulders, and the other clasped the hand near him. Immediately upon contact, the power of her magic threatened to consume him. Lorn gritted his teeth and kept his hold upon Aza. Once she found her footing, Lorn released her, trying to mask the effect her power had upon him. Small beads of sweat gathered along his forehead. He discreetly turned around to wipe them off and catch his breath. Lorn turned back to face Aza and saw a pitiful look.

"My power...is it truly too much for you to touch me?" There was no point trying to hide the fact, Lorn nodded his head.

Aza released a sigh and stretched her limbs. "Well then, I will have to be more careful and not pass out so often." She smiled, her face transformed into one of complete joy. "Plus, what would you do without me to protect you?" She laughed at her own joke, her melodic voice carrying away any darkness the Hinterlands brought. Lorn knew Aza was trying to make him feel better. How deeply affected he was by her magic. He enjoyed her lighthearted and teasing nature, and he smiled back at her. He ignored the gnawing feeling of how isolated she must feel, with her vast power and the magic in her veins.

"Ahh, yes. How would I ever survive?" He gave a small laugh and they set off, to finally leave the Hinterlands behind them.

14

     Musings of a wandering poet

They moved quickly, the dense forest no longer weighing on both of
their minds. Hope spurred them forward. Lorn was ready to leave the
Hinterlands behind. Like a bad taste lingering in his mouth, he forgot
how much the Hinterlands affected every part of him. He was eager to
be past this and see what lay ahead.

The heaviness of the Hinterlands lifted with each step they took
towards Iyera with Lorn's infallible sense of direction leading him on.
Lorn and Aza walked in companionable silence, both determined to
leave this behind. Nearing the end of the day they came upon the
sharp edge of the Hinterlands. A clear barrier between forbidding and
safety. Aza and Lorn shared a look. Excitement filled both of their
faces. Dredging up any remaining energy, they began to run.

They raced and weaved in between the gnarled trees, both of them
gracefully leaping over exposed roots, their steps light. They were
phantom spirits, drifting towards their salvation. Lorn glanced at
Aza, her arms pumping back and forth, her strong legs propelling her
forward. Aza must have felt Lorn's prying eyes, because she looked at
him in response. Aza raised an eyebrow, a slight curl to her lips. An
invitation to an unspoken competition. They dredged any reserves
from the depths of their spirits, and they sprinted.

The edge of the Hinterlands lay within their reach. A lack of food left

Lorn's head pounding, yet he flew forward. They dare not laugh, but a bubbling of mirth began in Lorn's body, his chest aching to draw breath. Running by Aza's side with wild abandon out of the Hinterlands he felt free.

Each met the other's stride. The Hinterlands melted past them, everything a blur. The open evening sky beckoned them forward. Their salvation. Lorn and Aza raced past the oppressive Hinterlands forest, leaving it behind them.

They were free.

Lorn felt the heaviness leave his body, like splinters being eased out from his skin. He stumbled, gasping for air, not only from exertion but from the oppressive force that hung over him.

He was light.

Free.

He had made it out alive.

Aza was bent over, her hands clasping her knees taking deep breaths. Between ragged breaths, Lorn smiled, a full genuine smile. Aza responded with one of her own. They were both alive.

Unbidden joy rippled through his body and Lorn let out a giant whoop. The sound was full of defiance. A shout of what it meant to be alive. One of defiance and joy despite the tumultuous trials the gods and goddesses had forced upon him. Aza joined him, their voices calling and answering to each other. A protest, a proclamation of their brilliant lives, shining. Two lonesome stars shining in the all-consuming darkness around them. They did not balk. They did not cower. They both reveled in their victory, allowing themselves to be free, shouting their voices into the darkening sky above.

Their jubilant cries faded, descending into soft chuckles. Without a word, they aimlessly walked away, their backs to the Hinterlands. Each of them lighter, their sorrows still present, yet each carrying the other forward.

~

Once the Hinterlands was only a speck on the horizon did Lorn and Aza stop. Night had fallen and both were exhausted. Lorn had not slept the night before, and his feet dragged heavily. They were close to the town of ShadowAcre but needed to rest for the night. Aza magicked a campfire, and Lorn crumpled to the ground. Neither bothered to keep a watch. Without the threat of the Hinterlands everything seemed safe in comparison. Their eyes closed instantly, both too tired to speak.

Bright rays of sun pierced Lorn's closed eyes. How long has it been since he saw the uninterrupted sky? He had become used to the gloom and darkness of the Hinterlands and welcomed the warm sun. They needed to reach town and replenish their supplies. His stomach grumbled, agreeing with his thoughts. Lorn leisurely stretched, taking his time to enjoy their safety. Rolling over and up into a seated position, he saw Aza still sleeping.

The weight of her power lifted in sleep, she looked peaceful. While never showing it, Lorn had noticed Aza carried a slight strain on her face. It must be the burden of her magic. He shook his head. If she is only ever able to relax while she is sleeping, how much control must she have on a daily basis?

Lorn allowed himself to recline and rest as the bright summer sun rose in the sky. Based on his weeks of travel he calculated it must be nearing the end of summer. He basked in the heat, purifying his body against the endless chill from the Hinterlands. Lorn mulled over what came next. What will happen to him? To Aza? Will they part ways? Will she stay with Lord Aldrich? Each thought bubbled to the surface, bringing with it a new one. He tried to shake them away. There was no need to rush as the answers would come in time. Aza agreed to meet Lord Aldrich and to be taken to the capital El'en. Lorn would agree to her wishes. Perhaps when Aza and Lord Aldrich meet, more answers will click into place.

This morning was not a time for these worrisome thoughts. This morning was one to relish in their escape from the Hinterlands. To cherish seeing the brilliant expanse of sky above him. Those thoughts pestering him could wait until the middle of the night, when he lay in doubt over his decisions in life. But not now. Not with this glorious day ahead of him. The feeling in him was unfamiliar, one of actual anticipation of the days laid out before him.

Aza stirred, her eyes blearily opening. "Good morning," she yawned, placing a hand over her mouth. In one fluid motion Aza sat up and rubbed her hands over her eyes and back through her silver coils. Aza grimaced. Lorn looked down at his own clothing. Both looked rough, encrusted with days of dirt and travel worn, they needed a proper inn. He also needed to find Aza suitable clothing. His eyes trailed down to her scratched feet. Clothing and boots too.

"We should reach ShadowAcre today. We can find you proper fitting clothing, boots, food and an inn to stay the night at." Lorn surveyed Aza deciding to revisit their briefly touched upon topic from earlier. "I don't want you to feel uncomfortable, and it is your choice to decide, but I feel you should hide your identity." Aza opened her mouth to speak, paused and reconsidered.

She pursed her lips together thinking, then raised an eyebrow at Lorn.

"Give me one reason why."

"For Fate's sake, you look like a goddess incarnate." Lorn opened his hand towards Aza. "Any MagicBlessed can feel that you are different." Lorn paused, his hand bracing his chin while he thought. "Other provinces were willing to kill for Lord Aldrich's knowledge of a magic item from the Well. Imagine if now, that item wasn't an item, but a person of seemingly infinite power"

Aza gritted her teeth, annoyed and interrupted, "I am not some tool to be used!"

"Exactly!" Lorn vehemently agreed. "You are not a tool, and I fear people will view you as such."

Aza released a quick exhale through her nose, frustrated at the conversation. She avoided Lorn's eyes, choosing to look at the sparse and dry chaparral landscape around them instead. Lorn remained looking at her, willing her to make eye contact. Aza eventually conceded.

"Fine," she muttered, throwing her hands in the air. "I will try, but..." Aza gestured at their surroundings, "...I want to see and experience all of Ithilia."

Lorn softened at her admission and the undisguised yearning in her voice. "I promise, we will try, but I also want to keep you safe."

Aza scoffed, "Protect me? I can protect myself. Or do you need to be reminded of my power?" Her silver eyes flashed in a challenge.

Lorn shook his head," I know you can protect yourself. Your power could bring all of Ithilia to its knees." Lorn faltered, debating on the correct phrasing he wanted. "Would you want to be pursued your whole life, just for what you are?"

"For now."

"What?"

Aza sighed. "For now, I will try to remain covered and hidden. I understand your point, although I don't like it."

"Thank you."

Lorn knew she was frustrated with the discussion. She already had firm control of her magic and now she had to control how people might perceive her? He knew it was unfair—for them to be free of the Hinterlands and she could not embrace herself completely.

A heavy silence preceded while they dismantled what few items they had set up for camp. Lorn estimated they only had a few hours to walk before reaching town. They set off, ambling their way through the roughly hewn path. Rogue bushes and brambles scattered through their path. The town loomed closer, and Lorn looked to Aza ensuring her cloak shielded her face. He turned his face to the sky. The sun was heavy overhead, it's heat stifling. Wordlessly, Aza kept on, even though Lorn knew she must be near overheating in her cloak.

They had done it. Lorn had returned to ShadowAcre. The dilapidated town greeted them. The streets were empty, save for a few stray cats meandering the streets, searching for scraps of food. The cats howled their displeasure, scattering as Aza and Lorn neared. Lorn spotted the inn he stayed at prior and motioned for Aza to follow.

Only one week ago Lorn had left this building to enter the Hinterlands. One week yet it felt like a lifetime. The experiences, the pain, the awe, the mysteries, everything. Lorn pushed open the creaky inn door and found the innkeeper, his appearance as craggy as before. He leaned over his desk, deeply considering papers strewn before him. An uninterested glance was sent Lorn's way, until Aza stepped over the threshold. The innkeeper's head snapped up, determined to assess the person behind him. Lorn thanked Aza's sense as she gripped the hood of her cloak and cast her head down to prevent him from glimpsing her features. Discreetly, Lorn stepped in front of Aza, blocking the innkeeper's view. The innkeeper narrowed his eyes, suspicion evident in his face. Lorn cleared his throat, bringing the focus back to him.

"We would like a room for tonight. One bedroom with two beds please."

"You are back." The innkeeper's rough voice stated.

Surprised at being remembered after such a short time, Lorn spoke, "Yes, me and my friend are weary from traveling. Do you have a room available?"

The innkeeper grumbled, his speech indiscernible, and led them to a room. They followed the gruff old man as he showed them to their room and abruptly left, a slight limp peppering his steps. The room was a mimic of the one Lorn stayed in prior apart from two beds instead of one. Two weathered beds filled the room. A small chest with a crude clay pitcher of water and a bar of soap rested on it. A tiny window on the wall showed the late summer sun.

Aza and Lorn gazed at the pitcher of water with longing. They reeked, days of travel and dirt coated their skin.

"You can wash up. I will go search for some food."

Aza flashed Lorn a grateful smile as he left the room. Lorn went in search of the innkeeper. After some discussion, he persuaded the innkeeper to scrounge up some extra food from the night before. Lorn pressed a few coins into the innkeeper's hand and waited in the dining room, wanting to give Aza a chance to wash herself and not be rushed.

The innkeeper emerged from the back room with a small tray filled with food. Bread, cheeses, and a small array of fruit dotted the tray. Lorn thanked him and quietly thanked the Fates for edible food. He inquired if there were any stores that sold clothing. The innkeeper reluctantly pointed out a small shop around the edge of town. Lorn returned to their room, the tray of food testing his resolve. His stomach grumbled. They had barely eaten over the last few days. He needed to rest and recover. They both did. Lorn knocked on the door, awaiting confirmation to enter. Aza opened the door, her skin glistened from washing. Relief crossed her face as she took in the tray of food Lorn held.

"Yes, food!" She rubbed her hands together excited to begin. Lorn set the tray down on the tiny dresser, shifting the clay pitcher to make room.

They dug in, grabbing bread and cheese. Lorn had to restrain himself from eating too quickly. Although the bread was hard as a rock and the cheese stale, it was delicious. Aza and Lorn ate their hard-won meal and discussed what to do next. Lorn mentioned the clothing store nearby. Aza's eagerness was apparent, she clearly wanted her own clothing, something that fit her.

Aza eyed Lorn up and down. "Perhaps you need some time to wash up?" Her eyebrow raised as she fought a smile. "Where's the dining room? I can give you some privacy. Then we can head to the clothing shop together." Lorn agreed, pointing Aza in the direction of the dining room.

"Please be safe. I won't be long."

Aza waved him off, dismissing his worry. "I will be fine. You can relax."

Lorn watched her turn down the hallway and sighed reluctantly, closing the door. Dirt coated his entire body. He desperately needed a quick wash. Lorn grabbed the pitcher of water expecting to find it empty. Strangely, it was still full of water despite Aza washing. Lorn cursed himself. Of course, she used her power to wash. She summoned any water she needed to wash the dirt off. Curiously, she could have washed herself off at any point during their journey. Yet she waited to wash herself when Lorn could too.

Shaking his head, he removed his shirt, picked up an old washcloth nearby and began scrubbing his arms and face. Layer by layer the dirt came off. It wasn't perfect and he craved a bath, but it would suffice. Grabbing his journey-worn shirt, he regretfully put it back on and went out the door to look for Aza. He found her sitting in the dining room, her back to him facing the window. He slowed his steps and watched her. She was captivated, her back rigid unmoving.

Worried about how she would react if startled. By some internal instinct Lorn whispered, "Aza?"

Her shoulders raised as she turned abruptly to look at Lorn. Her face had a seriousness to it that Lorn couldn't understand.

"Would you like to go to the clothing shop?" Lorn's voice trailed off. He peeked behind her trying to see if anything in the window had disturbed her.

"Clothing shop..." Aza looked down at herself, confusion riddled in her tone. She shook her head, a small reassuring smile replacing the seriousness on her face. "Yes, the clothing shop. Let's go." Aza rose from her seat and passed next to Lorn. Heat poured off from her like a living furnace. If their skin touched he feared he would be burned on the spot. Lorn staggered back. His hand reached out to touch her but veered back the sweltering heat too much to bear.

"Aza are you well?" Concern for his friend, overrode any sense of his own well-being. Aza sent him a bleary, dazed look.

"What are you talking about Lorn?" Aza batted his hand away, the heat scorching. She was a furnace. Dry heat emanated from her body.

Frustrated, Lorn ran a hand through his hair, the strands beginning to stick to his forehead from the heat she was producing. "You are burning up Aza. You are somehow producing heat. Do you not feel it?"

Comprehension dawned on her face like an ember catching fire, she realized what was happening. As quickly as it came, the heat dissipated, a fire being smothered.

Aza loosened a deep breath. "Better?"

Lorn didn't understand what happened. No MagicBlessed he knew of could summon an internal heat and suffer no harm from it.

"Aza, are you well?" he repeated. His hands ached to reach for her and reassure himself that she wasn't burned from the inside.

"Yes, I'm fine." Despite her tone, a distant look appeared in her eyes, like she was experiencing something years away.

"Would you like to talk about it?" Although they were hastily slammed together, Lorn felt an odd sense of duty to protect this lady with his life. Lorn hoped she would let him shoulder some of her burden.

Aza thought for a moment, the silence a chasm between them as Lorn waited for her answer. "No," she said quietly. "Not yet..." she paused searching for the words eluding her, "I'm not really sure I understand what to say about it." Aza patted her body reassuring herself, a hand absentmindedly drifted to her forehead. Lorn might have missed it if he wasn't solely focused on her, but he caught her slight wince. Something happened, and he wanted to help. Going against his instincts, he heeded her statement, ignoring the pressing matter of her discomfort.

"Let's head out to the clothes shop." Lorn led the way out through the inn, Aza trailing behind. He was shaken, conflicted. He didn't want to alarm her, but something was going on, and he was going to find out and fix it.

15

"Clothes are essential. They provide an identity. Who you are can dictate what or how you wear it. Each court has a different sense of fashion for those held in high regard. They can disguise you, or elevate you, if done correctly."
Journal entry from Melina of Kreeha

The clothing shop was a small distance away, constructed from discarded pieces of lumber, a forgotten extension of the town. The worn dirt path wound them around the edge of town and the heat from the late summer day pressed in around them. Despite being uncomfortable Aza still donned the cloak to hide her features.

They entered the cramped shop. Bits of fabric and clothing haphazardly strewn about the room. They peered around the piles of clothes and debris searching for the owner. A small, wizened woman appeared from the back room. Her arms held copious amounts of material, blocking her vision.

Lorn tentatively called out, "Hello?"

Startled at the sound, the woman shrieked, dropping the fabric on the floor. Her cheeks flushed, she raised a hand to her chest.

"Give a woman a fright, why don't you?" She cast a stern face in their direction, fighting to catch her breath. Aza and Lorn stood there, unsure of how to proceed.

"Well?" The woman stared at the two of them awaiting a response. She made a dismissive sound in the back of her throat and continued the conversation. "I'm assuming you would like something to wear."

Her eyes meticulously examined them. Whatever she saw, she disapproved. She shook her head. "You aren't from around here. I take it you need travel clothes?"

Lorn found his voice and answered, "Not for me, but for my friend." He inclined his head towards Aza who lingered beside him, not daring to speak or bring any attention to herself.

The woman bustled around the shop counter, nearing Aza and Lorn. Lorn protectively stepped in front of Aza unwilling to let the woman get any closer.

"How am I supposed to dress your friend if I don't know their size?" She put both of her hands on her hips contesting Lorn. He rolled his eyes and stepped to the side. He measured this obstinate woman and decided she was no threat.

"C'mon now." The woman impatiently gestured for Aza to remove her cloak. Hesitating, Aza reached for the hood of her cloak and removed it revealing her face.

The woman gasped, her eyes widening. She composed herself rather quickly, straightening her small stature. "Well, best to remove all of this clothing, none of it fits you properly." She expertly ran her hands over Aza's clothing, plucking at certain areas and making *tsking* noises in her throat. Her eyes made it all the way down to her feet. "And no shoes!" The woman glared at Lorn, and her warm brown eyes turned razor sharp, silently cursing him for his negligence.

She looked back at Aza, her eyes softening. "I am Melina, my dear, I will get you fixed up right quick." Melina reached an arm around Aza, her hand contacting Aza's skin. She immediately recoiled. Her head tilted back to look at Aza anew.

Horrified, Aza winced and apologized. "I'm sorry, I'm afraid you can't touch me."

Melina only nodded her head and muttered a soft *hmm* under her breath, her lips thin and pressed together.

Aza's voice was quiet like a feather on the wind. "I'm Aza." A hopeful pause, waiting for Melina to respond.

"What sort of clothes are we looking for?" Melina asked.

A small sigh of relief escaped Aza as she answered. Her shoulders sagged with the weight of meeting someone new. Lorn scrounged the small shop searching for a chair to sit in while Aza was freshly outfitted. He found one piled under countless fabrics. He gingerly lifted them and placed them on the nearby counter.

Despite Melina's age, she moved like a desert storm. Small and subtle at first, then a giant downpour. Aza gracefully embraced everything Melina tried to dress her in, with Melina skirting around trying to make small changes and additions. Melina wanted to dress Aza in the most decadent outfits, but Aza's protests sent her towards practicality. Aza stressed to her many times how they were traveling and needed practical clothes. Melina tried to cover her disappointment, commenting on Aza's exceptional beauty and how it was a travesty not to wear one of her creations.

Lorn looked around the shop, curious at how a small, dilapidated town held such a formidable seamstress. Lorn inquired as to why she was here. Melina's eyes crested with silver as she blinked away unshed tears. She shook her head freeing herself from the weight of heavy memories, and explained she used to design for the court of Kreeha but the loss of her children led her to this town. She still designs for the different provinces and accepts requests, but she chooses to stay here surrounded by the pressing gloom of the Hinterlands and this small inconsequential town.

After pressing different fabrics up to Aza, and whittling down their options, Melina had decided. "Your clothes and shoes will be ready tomorrow morning. Now out, out, I have a lot of work today." Melina shooed them out the door, a last lingering glance of curiosity set on Aza.

The door closed, pushing them out into the harsh daylight compared to the calm darkness of her shop. Lorn squinted his eyes again at the brilliant light and turned to Aza. "That was...interesting."

Aza redrew her hood, concealing herself as they wandered back to the inn. Upon arrival Lorn convinced the innkeeper to grab more food for the two of them. They ate in their room, laughing and sharing light-hearted stories of their past and what few memories they could contribute.

Free of the heaviness of the Hinterlands with food in their bellies, and the feeling of safety, they talked. Aza inquired about Lorn's childhood, the five provinces, the sights he had experienced, everything. She was filled with an insatiable curiosity, eager to learn about this foreign and not-so-foreign land.

The room shifted from the bright hues of the day to softer pinks and finally the comforting dark of night, as they lay in their separate beds. Lorn tried to ignore what Aza had experienced earlier, the heat she gave off, her background and instead asked about her.

Anything she could remember she shared—which wasn't much. Although Aza couldn't contribute to any meaningful stories, her memories vague and faded like worn-out fabric, Lorn over-shared so Aza wouldn't feel the need to give more than she could.

They stumbled into sleep, their talking and late-night ramblings slowly easing like a spigot being turned off, the flow turning from a rush to the small drip of whatever was left.

The following morning, they woke up slowly, easing themselves into the day. There was no sense of urgency. They had somewhat comfortable beds, cramped lodging, and mediocre food— glorious conditions compared to the Hinterlands. Once ready, they headed back over to Melina to grab the new clothes.

They entered the shop, clothes still strewn about. Melina's small frame burst from the back room, an easy smile forming on her face, her gray hair pulled back in a loose bun, flyaway strands escaping to frame her face.

"I'm glad you are back. I was busy working into the night over these items. I wanted them to be ready in time." Melina cleared an overflowing space on her desk and dropped the items in her hands down. Her tan hands lingered on the pile as she looked hopefully at Aza.

"Alright my dear, I have two practical outfits for you, a pair of boots, and a new cloak." Melina eyed Aza's cloak. "I'm sure that thing is way too hot for this weather, and I understand you are aiming for discretion." Melina cocked her head towards the back of the shop. "Get dressed back there, make sure it fits."

Aza grabbed the stack of clothes and shouldered her way through piles of clothes to the back of the shop. Melina waited until Aza walked to the back of the shop and came to stand beside Lorn. The old woman peered up at Lorn, her eyes searching for something within him.

"Now I don't know everything that is going on. Clearly, she is special. Different." Lorn raised his eyebrows not expecting this conversation. "You take care of her. I do not want to see someone as special as her so... bedraggled."

Lorn opened his mouth to interrupt.

"Don't interrupt me boy. That girl came in here with no shoes on and both of your clothes filthy." She shook her head, gazing back at where Aza was changing. "You take care of her," she repeated. The conversation finished, Melina turned back to face the doorway of the changing-room. The rustling of clothes filled the silence as Aza changed. Lorn held his tongue, swallowing his pride. Melina couldn't know all the intricacies of what they had gone through. He would endure her scorn and listen to her advice.

Footsteps sounded as Aza strode through the cramped clothing shop. No longer dressed in ill-fitting clothes lent by Lorn, Aza was impressive. Melina was worthy of her craft, the clothes fit Aza's shape perfectly. They were molded for her. She wore simple brown pants and a white tunic. Aza was statuesque, her shoulders rolled back, her head held high, she looked as unique as her origins suggested. Not forced to hide and cower beneath a cloak, she radiated.

Lorn held a hand up to his mouth, thoughtlessly biting the tip of his thumb. *This* was Aza. She could not be hidden like a shiny trinket. She deserved to be free and not rely on secrecy.

"Thank you, Melina." Gratitude filled Aza's face. "It is beautiful. You have such a gift." Aza's hand flitted over the fabric, her gaze following where she touched.

Melina batted her hand in the air, as if knocking aside Aza's sincere compliment. "'Tis nothing." Melina's eyes scanned Aza. "You would be radiant in anything, my dear."

A quick smile flashed across Aza's face, her hand tucking a loose silver coil behind her ear. "Nevertheless, it is appreciated." Aza turned, admiring the fitted clothes. "What is the material? It is light, comfortable..." Aza trailed off, unable to explain further.

"The cotton is from the highland sheep in Gara."

An unexpected gasp released out of Lorn's mouth. "You must be joking?" Lorn sputtered out. "I'm sorry for your effort, but I'm unable to pay for that material."

Melina waved him away. "You can pay me the same amount you would normally for the clothing." Lorn clamped his mouth shut, shocked by this woman's generosity. Aza shook her head, her eyebrows drawn together. "I don't understand, how much is this material?"

Lorn began to explain but Melina cut him off. "It is of no consequence." She walked briskly across the room grabbing a small package wrapped in white linen. "I can do with my materials what I wish." Her defiant gaze met Lorn. "A special material for a special lady. Her eyes cast over to Aza and softened. "I do not know what you are, but you are special, my lady." Melina marched to Aza and pushed the wrapped package into Aza's hands. Tentatively, Aza reached out, a question lingering in her face.

"I know you are traveling and have no reason for pretty clothing, but when you do, please wear this. I think it would suit you beautifully."

Aza nodded, accepting the package with a trembling smile on her face.

Aza could do this. People's reactions would be visceral. Worry crept into his thoughts, like a leak in a roof. She would be worshiped, adored, and revered. He thought back to when he first saw her appearing from the Well. His first reaction was to kneel so what about others? Would this be her life? Or would people react in opposition? Hating her, jealous of her raw power, or her beauty? Would she be a mine of rare ore? One that is harvested over time and used constantly?

Lorn's reservations drifted away as he looked upon her face. Pure joy and gratitude shown at the woman's selfless gift-giving. Lorn snapped himself out of his loud thoughts as Aza's melodic voice filled the room thanking Melina. Gathering the extra garments in her arms, Aza headed out of the shop with Lorn. The pair of them spared one last look at Melina and her lonely, weathered and worn shop situated in this forlorn town.

Out of earshot from Melina, Aza fidgeted with the hem of her shirt. Her eyes squinted against the radiant sun, she cocked her head at Lorn and asked, "Can you tell me about the highland sheep of Gara?"

"I'm surprised she even had such fabric at her disposal. I have never seen it in person." He eyed Aza's clothing, appraising them from his casual distance. "The highland sheep are fiercely guarded and only a small stock is left. It is rumored only the highest of nobility wears it because the cost is exorbitant."

"It is quite a gift then—to be so freely given."

A contemplative quietness developed as they walked back to the inn. Lorn ran a hand through his hair and a frustrated sigh passed his lips. "Aza wherever you go people will react in two ways. Either they will respond with complete adoration and amazement, or..."

"Or?" Aza stopped forcing Lorn to halt his steps and meet her eyes.

"Or they will despise you. Hate you for the blatant power you possess."

They stood in silence and Lorn shifted his weight from one leg to the other under Aza's scrutiny.

"I see." That was Aza's only response as she began her walk back to the inn.

~

After another night spent at the inn, Aza and Lorn discussed and formulated a plan for their next steps. They left the following morning after quickly shoveling down another questionable meal. They followed the winding dirt path out of town headed east, towards the capital of Iyera, El'en.

Lorn kept a constant watch for Lilit and Gravers. They were supposed to be waiting for him. At the next inn, he pondered if he could try to send a message to Lord Aldrich. Lorn and Aza hiked on foot, the sun climbing in the sky. Throughout their walk Aza questioned Lorn about the surroundings of Iyera. Flora, fauna, buildings, anything and everything Aza soaked all of the information, a flower eager to bask in the first summer rays. Lorn delighted in sharing Ithilia's beauty with her.

His past experiences crossing back and forth over similar terrain, he had been blind to the beauty. Unfeeling, he traveled to small towns and cities, numb and unaware of what was around him. Aza reminded him of the beauty that surrounded him, of the beauty Lakesh cherished in nature. Something he should never have grown numb to. Like the ache of an old wound he discussed the environment and memories of Lakesh surfaced. The day passed quickly as they found a small inn placed upon the road.

Pity and remorse lay heavy in Lorn's stomach as he looked at Aza. She released a small huff of air and put on the cloak Melina had made for her. The black fabric shadowed Aza's features as they walked up to the inn. Light spilled out from the windows as they neared the door. Voices carried out on the warm summer air.

Lorn cast a worried glance towards Aza. There was a fully occupied inn ahead of them. Keeping Aza disguised would be difficult. Aza gestured for Lorn to continue, reassuring him, giving him a pointed look to continue. Lorn's hand hovered over the door. *Here goes nothing*, Lorn thought and pushed ahead. The air was filled with the warmth of bodies pressed into a small space. The tang of alcohol tinged the air. A large group occupied the tables, plates empty, and glass mugs filled with ale. Their raucous laughter clanged in the room an unwelcome volume for such a peaceful night outside. A clinking of glasses followed their celebration.

No one noticed Lorn and Aza slink into the inn. Lorn scanned the room, searching for the owner. He was eager to get away from the main room.

"Hey, bring us another refill." The group cheered their agreement. A man rushed haphazardly out of the back room, carrying pitchers of fresh ale for the table.

"As if you haven't had enough Igor," the man grumbled.

"Ach, no such thing," Igor belched, giving a rough slap on the back of another man.

A petite blonde woman next to Igor added to the clamor, "Plus you have the finest ale around."

"Well, there is no other ale around," Igor spewed out, his laughter crass and obnoxious. A sound too loud for this small inn to accommodate.

A nervous energy settled in Lorn's stomach. These people were well into their cups and rowdy, not a combination he would have preferred to encounter tonight.

Lorn leaned back to whisper discreetly to Aza, "Try to stay back, I don't like the feel of these people. We will just book our room and try not to interact."

"Why not just leave and we can camp outside? Aza questioned.

Lorn noticed a few curious eyes had strayed and spotted the two of them. "I don't think we can anymore." Lorn straightened up as the harried man rushed over to them. He looked to be about late-middle age, his hair ruffled, falling in his face. His cheeks were blotchy with bits of pink and red on his pale skin.

"What would you like?" The man seemed out of breath, his question barked out.

"A room please, with two beds," Lorn responded quickly, hoping to attract little attention.

"Lucky you, one last room left." The man's head flicked back to the group in the dining room, their voices getting louder. "This group booked most of the rooms." Lorn exchanged coins with the man, and he gestured to the hall behind him straight through the group of people. "Rooms back there, last door on the left."

Lorn nodded his thanks, itching to leave the prying eyes of the group clustered in the dining hall. More eyes lingered on them. Like flies they swarmed, one by one, interested in the newcomers who had arrived. The man hurried away, presumably to gather another round of drinks.

Igor stood up, his steps unsteady as he recovered his balance. The drinks were clearly taking their toll. His hair was cut short to the scalp, and he had a trimmed brown beard. His light blue eyes were glazed with his heavy alcohol consumption. He staggered towards Lorn, and clumsily clapped a hand on his shoulder. Lorn gritted his teeth and cocked his head granting this man a moment to talk before he reacted.

"New friends, come and sit with us." The invitation swirled in the air like his stale breath, invading their space. Igor peered behind Lorn, trying to discern Aza's face in her hooded cloak. His eyes meandered back to Lorn.

Lorn gave a curt nod toward Igor. "Thank you for the invitation, but we are ready to rest. We have had a long journey." Lorn sidestepped out of the man's grasp moving past him. Lorn expected the ale-addled man to drop the conversation. What he did not expect was the man's sun-scorched hand to lash out quick as a viper and grip Aza's upper arm.

Aza froze and jerked her head in his direction. Her hood fell back from her face, unveiling her and unveiling her power. Igor cringed, releasing his hold on Aza. Aza's eyes were not the soft silver Lorn was used to, they had changed. Anger and disbelief roiled beneath the surface. Her silver eyes changed to one of attack, like the silver of a blade ready to strike.

The whole room was silent, a captive audience waiting to see what would happen next. "Next time, you will think before touching someone without permission." Aza locked eyes with the man, palpable disdain pouring from her.

Embarrassed, Igor recoiled, but his willful ignorance led him forward. His eyebrows furrowed as he took in Aza's appearance. Lorn's hands fidgeted around the handle of his sword, ready to strike if the need arose. Dazed, Igor reached a hand forward as if encountering a mirage. "What are you?" his rough voice asked, disbelief coating each word.

Aza's eyes bored into his, the silver seas inside crashing. "I am not of your concern." Her voice permeated the air, a heavy command laid down for all to hear. If there were any in the room who doubted Aza's power, it would be banished instantly. Her power flooded the room, as if she had released a gate. It coiled around each person, tempting them to press her further.

She scanned the room, looking at each person individually before reigning her power back in, a leash she had firm control over.

"Let's go." Her voice brooked no argument. With her shoulders back and proud, she strode to their room, every bit an elegant ethereal goddess.

Lorn followed behind her, uneasy at turning his back on this group of scorned and drunken individuals. Those shamed and angry tended to lash out. Lorn risked a small glance over his shoulder and did not like what he saw. Blooms of heat filled their faces, embarrassment, anger and confusion. They will need to lock their doors and listen with bated breath for this group to leave. He would not be resting easy tonight.

Aza and Lorn filed into their room, shutting the door behind them. Aza glared at Lorn. He staggered back under the weight of her gaze. She drew in a deep shuddering breath, her eyes closed, like shutters over a window. A soft exhale passed through her lips. Opening her eyes, a soft silver looked back at Lorn.

"Are you well?" The question lingered between them, hovering unanswered.

Aza turned, taking in the amenities of their room. Time dragged on, Lorn was about to ask his question again, when Aza spoke, "Yes I am. They are inconsequential, mere animals to put in their place."

With many words left unspoken, Aza and Lorn prepared for bed.

Before drifting off, Aza's voice pierced through the dark, a soft whisper, a question to the night. "Are you afraid?"

Lorn knew what she was implying. Was he afraid of her and her power? No. Was he afraid for her? Now that was a different question entirely.

Lorn confidently answered back, "No." His firm whispered response filled the room. There was a quiet shuffling of bed covers as Aza adjusted herself, her face glancing over to look at him. Her silver eyes and hair glistened like a beacon in the dark. "Good."

Lorn pressed his lips together, slightly tilting up at the sides. He watched her eyes shutter closed, her breathing heavy and deep.

He had viewed himself as a monster for years. There was nothing for him to fear.

~

A voice buried deep within Aza spoke, waking her. Instinctively, she always listened. Her magic, her survival depended upon her listening to her inner voice. It protected her and she yielded to it.

Her eyes flashed open.

The room was coated in the darkness of the early morning, a small lantern lit up the corner casting grim shadows. The group from earlier stood in the light each wielding a dagger. Lorn was pinned against Igor, a sharp dagger held against his throat. The sickening gleam glinted at her, mocking her. The handle caught Aza's eye. Finely crafted gold glinted back with small gems inlaid along the handle. Aza rose from the bed slowly, maintaining her composure. These pests will be dealt with soon enough.

Beside Igor stood the petite blonde, the innkeeper, and a few others, presumably their other travel companions. Aza leveled a cool gaze at each of them. Lorn's face was filled with fury, his body twisting to find release from Igor's grip. Aza raised a hand to Lorn, a message for him to relax.

Igor sneered, "About time you woke up." Aza let nothing show, her demeanor icy and unruffled. "Now I don't know what you are, girl, but you are going to come with us."

Aza said nothing but narrowed her eyes allowing the chaos to shine from within, the power that often lapped at her heels.

Igor swallowed and continued, "Now none of that! If you show even one ounce of magic, I'll slit your friend's throat." Igor tightened his hold on Lorn, the blade digging into his soft golden skin. A single bead of red dripped down his throat. "There are a few provinces I can think of selling you to."

Aza kept silent, his words silently fanning the flames of her anger. Let this idiot dig his own grave. Let him speak and condemn him and his friends. Her magic ached for release, an incessant itching feeling under her skin. It was practically begging her to be freed. These people deserved it. Threatening her, threatening her friend. Wanting to sell her? Yes, her magic would find a release and it would be them.

"Now come over here nice and slow." Igor motioned for the petite blonde next to him to move forward. She gripped a length of rope. Aza scoffed. The entire group froze, their grips tightening on their weapons. Igor tugged Lorn closer, the blade nicking his skin.

Aza splayed her hands out at her side, palms faced out. "How am I supposed to walk towards you if you are all skittish from a single sound?" Aza smiled grimly. "Do you feel it?" She eased her power out, a small trickle coursing through her veins, curling around their bodies.

Igor's face paled, his hand loosely shaking. "If you do not stop, his throat will be slit!" Igor's hand stilled waiting to see if Aza would heed his warning. Aza locked eyes with Lorn, a subtle nod and message. In a flash, Lorn pulled his hands up providing leverage to move Igor's blade away from his throat. Aza curled her fingertips and the whole group clutched their throats. Their eyes bulged. They glanced desperately at Aza and Lorn. Lorn stepped away, standing firmly next to her.

Aza felt it—felt everything. The wind and air swirling within their beings. She stripped them of it. They didn't need it anymore. One by one they dropped to their knees, clutching their throats. They dared to threaten her. They dared to threaten her friend. Never. They did not deserve this life. Aza's magic caressed her, welcomed its release. It beckoned her forward. Called to her.

"Aza!" Lorn shouted. The roaring in her ears grew, drowning out Lorn's pleas. He stepped in front of her, going face-to-face. His face unwavering, he held his ground. She saw his mouth forming her name. Why couldn't she hear it? He kept forming her name, his expression calm, but his eyes focused on her. "Aza," Lorn called. His voice sounded far away, a distant bell being tolled. She had no time to focus on him, she needed to feel her magic, her power punishing those who threatened them.

"Aza! Stop!"

She heard it this time. The pleading in his voice. She faltered, her magic coming to a halt like a stopper being put into a bottle.

"Why should I?" Aza asked. Her unwavering voice filled the room, a question demanding an answer.

"There are other options besides death," Lorn calmly explained. She understood, but she hated it. How reasonable he sounded. He held her stare, the turmoil he must see within her silver eyes.

She lifted her chin high, unbothered. "They snuck upon us in the night. They threatened you. They threatened me. They wished to sell me to the highest bidder." Aza clenched her fingers together, restraining her anger. She turned a steely gaze to the limp coughing figures on the ground. Gasping for air now that she had released her grip on them, they avoided looking at her, all except Igor. Rage and humiliation, those are the two emotions she gleaned from him. She cast her eyes back to Lorn. "And yet...you would like me to spare them?"

"Yes, let's think of something else. This is not who you are."

Igor lunged, a dagger in his hand, plunging toward Lorn's unsuspecting back.

Aza clenched her fingers, the magic called to her, and she let herself go. Without any strain, she pushed Lorn aside with a cast of air. He crashed to the floor, his hands catching himself before falling on his face.

Frost coated her fingers as her magic swelled, an invisible inhalation in the room as the magic bent and moved with her. Her exhalation sent the magic to warp around Igor and his group. They each were encased in ice.

Frozen.

Lorn planted his hands and scrambled to his feet. Aza watched as he situated his feet, shock on his face. His mouth hung open, eyebrows raised. His jet-black hair fell in front of his face as he hastily pushed it back to better see what Aza had done.

Shakily he walked over to the frozen statues. Igor and his dagger were captured midair. Lorn tapped a hesitant finger against it, then turned to face Aza. She stared at him, allowing him to see the storm brewing in her eyes.

"You are wrong Lorn. *This* is who I am." She flexed her hand open and abruptly clenched them shut. The ice figures shattered behind her.

The light from the lantern cast the room in harsh shadows and light. Each ruptured ice fragment the only tombstone these interlopers would receive.

16

"There is no greater task than protecting those you love. Protect them and hold them close, for there will always be outside forces ready to wreak havoc down upon you and those you cherish."

Excerpt from a torn and discarded scroll

The weak light of dawn crested the horizon. The early morning chill left a trail of goosebumps on Aza's skin. She couldn't shake the feeling that coated her whole body. Lorn's back was a silent judgment and Aza couldn't dismiss the eerie disquiet that had rooted itself within her. Aza slowed her steps. She couldn't stand to see Lorn's furtive looks. His judgment, his disbelief. After she had shattered the bodies of their attackers, the room coated in shards of ice and blood—Lorn was silent.

His eyes said everything.

He disapproved and a hint of fear was visible in his hazel eyes. After everything he had done for her, he now feared her. Aza sighed, kicking a small pebble on the ground in front of her. It rolled forward, coming to an abrupt halt on one of its edges, like her, caught in whatever stasis this was.

She would not apologize. She was protecting him, protecting herself. She had warned Lorn she could defend herself. Those people thought to sell her! To use her! She gritted her teeth and began to bite down on her tongue. Already she could feel her magic coiling ready to strike at any potential aggressors. It fed off her anger and the injustice.

There was nothing to be done about the bodies, fragments of them lay around the room. Lorn and Aza had packed up quietly, a tension between them. The groups' horses lay stabled outside. Lorn released them out of the pen so they could graze freely. Aza didn't even have the courage to ask if they should use them. He went through the motions silently, keeping Aza in a perpetual freefall of her own thoughts.

She would not lower her head in humility. Her back remained straight, her shoulders back and head forward. No, she was not proud of what she had done. It was necessary.

Images flitted through her mind. She pressed a hand to her forehead, a dull ache growing. Ever since she had materialized from the Well, she experienced these flashes. Distorted images, raw emotions, blurred faces bombarded her.

Her magic pulsed beneath, an answer to her distress. Throughout the morning, she caught herself ready to speak and share the information with Lorn, but he was closed off his back to her.

Sometimes the images that assaulted her were blurry, nothing clear or concrete, more of a vague feeling attached to them. Yet, in the inn with the group encircling them she saw a clear image overlaid. Soldiers and a forest. When Aza stared at the bits of people burst into ice, she saw a forest floor instead. The jagged image overlaid, like a sheer gauze placed over skin. She knew what was underneath, yet the image on top was difficult to discern, clear in some respects, but elusive overall. All she felt was hollowness and emptiness. The soldiers lay lifeless, unmoving, the forest floor bathed in their blood. A deep red coated the brown forest floor. A marred spot in this otherwise peaceful area. When she blinked, the image had disappeared, only left with chunks of blood and ice. She ached to discuss what she saw with Lorn, hoping he would bring some level-headed clarity. Instead, hardened with pride, she walked in silence, each left to their own thoughts.

Lorn veered off the main road, finding a broken tree trunk to sit on. Trying to hide her surprise, Aza followed him. He dumped his pack on the ground, rifled through it and pulled out a small pack of food and water. He held out his hand, a silent offering. Aza took the food, trying to discern Lorn's intent. She would not be ashamed of her power, ashamed of who she is.

Frustrated, Aza turned her back on Lorn, searching the surroundings. Searching for what? She was unsure, but she hated this silence. This lack of certainty of where she stood with her friend.

Her friend.

Was he her friend anymore? Was he disgusted to be with her? She couldn't bear it. Despite them just meeting, their friendship had locked into place. It was natural and comforting, like slipping into Melina's clothing. It just felt right, like Fate had destined for this to happen.

Footsteps scuffed behind her, his boots methodically scraping the ground as he walked. Lorn stepped into her line of sight. His angular face blocked her view of the gentle hills. Instead, she only saw his hazel eyes with a flicker of concern. No, it couldn't be. His jet-black hair fell back in front of his eyes as he carelessly ran a hand through it, slicking the hair back. A few scars lined his golden face, the white lines carved into his skin.

He stretched his hand forward, uncertainty on his face. He moved slowly, intentionally, making sure Aza watched him the whole time. Then his hand contacted her arm. Lorn's face tightened, she knew her magic overwhelmed people and contact worsened it.

"Are you well?" His eyebrows furrowed with concern, his eyes softening.

Aza rocked back, shocked at his question. He wasn't even going to discuss what happened at the inn? An imperceptible nod of her head. Yes, she was well. Confused? Frustrated? Yes, but she was not going to regret killing people who wished her harm.

"Can we sit and talk for a bit?" Lorn's voice remained steady. Aza wanted to maintain her cold indifference, but Lorn was not approaching her like a skittish animal. He was confident, calm. She searched his face. He did not seem afraid, only patient. Lorn waited, allowing her time to process. She noticed his body was loose, not even gripping his sword or his hidden daggers. He was genuinely not worried about his well-being, he still trusted her.

Aza agreed, retreating to the fallen tree log and utilizing it as a makeshift bench. Lorn sat beside her. His back bowed, forearms resting on his thighs, he steepled his hands in front of him. Aza held back her questions, waiting for Lorn to lead. He wanted to talk. She would allow him to start.

Lorn released a pent-up sigh, and his voice broke the silence, a stone tossed into a pond creating ripples. "Why did you do it?"

Defensive hackles rose along Aza's back, one by one. Her shoulders tensed. Her magic seethed.

She could not stand looking at Lorn's face, there was no anger, no resentment. His question was simply that—a question to understand her motive. She flicked her head to take in the distant hills. They rolled, undulating in the distance, their shades of green basking in the late summer sun. How she wished to escape there, to escape his sincere question.

"Do I even need to explain?" Her voice was cold as steel. Unwavering.

Aza kept her view on the hills, she could not look at his calm demeanor. For Lorn to even consider other options for those foul people was unthinkable.

"I was protecting you!" Aza shouted, her magic writhing beneath her. She was unable to restrain her magic and flowers bloomed beneath their feet. A colorful bed of flowers for the log bench they both sat on. Pretty things, yet if one looked closely, they were coated in thorns.

Unphased, Lorn kept his sight on her and did not even acknowledge the beautiful flowers underfoot.

Feeling a brief reprieve, she continued explaining her voice fighting to remain level, "I was protecting us. I stopped when you talked to me." Aza wrung her hands together, frustration building while she thought back to that night. "I debated letting them live. I really did." She vehemently locked eyes with Lorn, willing him to believe her. "Because of you. You were genuinely concerned about their well-being, despite everything they had done. Then, Igor tried to kill you, and I knew then. They were unfit to live." Cold fury burned in her eyes.

Restless and upset Aza pushed herself off the log bench and strode away towards those beckoning green hills. "They did not deserve a second chance. They heard you speak for them. Attempt to give them mercy. And still..." Aza scoffed, shaking her head in disbelief. "I do not regret it." Aza turned, gazing down at Lorn. "Nor will I. I will not feel remorse over defending myself or those I care about." A promise lingered in the air, a promise of punishment for those who wished to cross her. A sharp tug in the back of her mind, but she buried those demanding unanswered thoughts away.

Lorn stared at her with a critical eye. "I do not expect remorse from you."

Aza's eyebrows furrowed. She thought Lorn refused to speak with her during their quiet trek due to him being upset.

Lorn spoke with conviction, "Nor do I want remorse from you." Lorn rose from his seat, taking measured steps towards her. He hesitated, looking at the flowers blooming underfoot evidence of her immense magic. "I have never killed anyone and I do not wish to, ever in my life." Lorn's eyes glazed over with unshed tears.

Aza knew very little of Lorn's heartbreaking past and it pained her to watch her friend unravel.

"I do not know these people, or what lives they led. What families they left behind, relationships, mothers, fathers, sons, daughters, lovers..." Lorn's jaw tightened as his gaze swept up to meet Aza. "I understand your reasoning, but I think there may be other options to pursue other than bloodshed."

Aza opened her mouth to speak but Lorn held up a hand and continued, "They were foul people..." Lorn paused, caught on his next thoughts. "But I do not want to stoop to their level."

"Yet you feel comfortable with *me* stooping to their level?" Aza's question came out of her mouth with a biting edge to it.

Lorn raked a hand through his disheveled hair again, pushing it out of his eyes, a sharp exhale coming out of his nose. "Yes." Lorn paced back and forth, his feet copying the same pattern. Entranced, Aza watched him. "I know it doesn't make sense. This whole Fate forsaken thing doesn't make sense." He paused in his steps and looked at her. "I am still not afraid of you, even though I feel your magic now. You could kill me now without a second thought. But somehow, we were meant to meet. Fate or, the gods and goddesses have connected us somehow."

Lorn threw his hands into the air motioning to the world around them searching for the elusive beings he mentioned. "Aza, your magic is a gift, but something is happening within you. It is like you stand at the edge of a cliff and I am here to pull you back from it. To anchor you." Sincerity rang through his voice as he pleaded with her. "I do not want you to fall," he whispered softly, a silent plea.

Like the wind whipping through a small candle flame, her anger and frustration dissipated. The lingering smoke of confusion filled the air.

"May the light guide them. The call of the mountains bring them home. The everlasting sky above cradle them. To the soft snows that drift from above, to the roaring fires that burn beneath. Magic bless you."

The eulogy rose unbidden to Aza. Lorn furrowed his eyebrows, a mix of confusion and surprise warring on his face.

"I may have killed them without mercy, and I do not know if they have any families, but I hope this gives their spirits peace in the Meadows of the Undying."

Lorn cocked his head and asked, "Where did you learn that?"

Aza shrugged her shoulders. "Does it matter?"

Lorn stared at her and concentrated, trying to push pieces together to see if they fit correctly. He shook his head dispelling any lingering doubts or thoughts. "No it doesn't. Not now. Are we ready to continue?" A tentative smile broke across his face. It was a smile of trust and friendship.

Aza nodded, falling in step beside Lorn as they walked away. Lorn's question lingered in her head, why did she offer that eulogy? And where did it come from?

They trudged along in silence, although a different one than when they set off that morning. There was no awkwardness, no tension. They plunged forward nearing the capital of Iyera, the city of El'en, only a week of travel remained. Fighting the spring in her step, she was excited to witness the wonder of the city of El'en.

Images flashed through her mind of a shining city atop a cliff, the castle a lone building out among the wild surf below. She tried not to focus on the images for too long. They came unbidden to her mind and often left her with a myriad of emotions. Excitement, confusion, a kaleidoscope of feelings and emotions warred within her, magic pulsing along the outside of it all.

When Lorn had asked her what she was after emerging from the Well, she genuinely didn't know. She didn't know how to explain it. She didn't have memories or concrete thoughts on anything prior to her existence from the Well. Yet...

She couldn't place it. Something was missing, something she needed to know and to find. Perhaps that is why she followed Lorn to meet Lord Aldrich. She could forge her own path in Ithilia without dragging Lorn into her aimless mission. Curiosity propelled her along with an insatiable need to figure out who she truly was and why she was here.

~

Traveling with Lorn was a joy. The scenery was beautiful and breathtaking. The colors were heightened. Everything buzzed with the faint thrum of magic. However, it seemed tainted, like witnessing everything through a fog. Her mind struggled to latch on to any source of familiarity. Noticing her struggle, Lorn would point out a landmark, explain it and the idea then clarified in her mind. She chafed at the lack of knowledge, the vague abstract memories she struggled to place.

Soon. She would receive answers soon. Every step towards Iyera may lead to unlocking more about her past, about who she is.

Lorn and Aza found a secluded spot off the road to camp. The last interaction in an inn left a sour taste in both of their mouths. Lorn unbundled his pack, handing Aza a blanket. Aza accepted it graciously and laid down staring at the twinkling stars overhead. They glistened and sparkled, beckoning to her. Mesmerized, Aza focused on a particular cluster. The outline called to her.

"Aza!" Lorn's voice abruptly halted her musings.

Jarred out of her stupor she turned to look at Lorn. Irritation crept into the edge of her voice. "What?"

"I have been trying to talk to you for the last few minutes." Lorn rolled onto his side checking her. "You haven't been responding, so I admit you had me a little worried." A sheepish grin spread across his face.

"I was lost in the constellations overhead. Can you tell me what this one is?" She raised her arm and pointed to a specific group of stars.

Lorn chuckled. "It is kind of difficult to determine which one you are talking about, what does it look like?"

Aza shifted her hands in the air, attempting to discern a general outline of the stars. "It looks like a... man," Aza finished lamely.

Lorn adjusted his position to get a better view. "Yes, I know which one you are talking about." He smirked at her. "Lucky for you, my parents taught me all about the constellations." He laced his fingers behind his head. "Growing up on a farm, there wasn't too much excitement, but on a clear night," he paused, a smile in his voice, "we would lay outside, and my parents would swap stories about the stars and even the gods and goddesses of long ago."

Aza perked up, she knew very little of the gods and goddesses and wished to know more. She liked listening to Lorn's even baritone voice. As he spoke, his words painted the night sky, Aza laid back and listened as he answered her questions both asked and unasked.

"The constellation you are talking about is the hunter. He is associated with...well the hunt. Pursuing those he covets. He will stop at nothing to get what he wants. He craves the chase and the power of being in charge. If you look over to the right, he is being guided by the compass constellation. Goddess of navigation, she is his guidance, his voice of reason. The two of them are always entwined, they each need the other. For what is the compass without the hunter or the hunter without the compass to guide?" Lorn spoke with the practiced voice of someone who is reciting the words they themselves heard repeatedly. Aza imagined Lorn as a child nestled between his mother and father staring up at the sky, a look of wonderment plastered across his face.

"Now, some people say the constellations are actually fashioned after the gods and goddesses of long ago. I have heard some people claim the hunter to be named Cruvo and the compass to be his partner Issi. They were actual people who walked around and interacted with the MagicBlessed." His voice took on a note of awe.

Aza allowed herself to be washed over with his stories, the scene playing out before her eyes, but for the first time, she decided to interject with a question. "If the goddesses and gods were real, where did they go?"

A long pause filled the night before Lorn finally answered, "I don't know. It was a question I always asked my parents too."

They both fell into a contemplative silence and slowly drifted off to sleep. That night, Aza dreamed of stars and vague faces staring back at her, urging her forward.

17

"Have we always been the MagicBlessed? Or has there been a time before? Are the gods and goddesses only figments of our imaginations? Or were they here? Have they stood where we stand, looking out over the creation of their land?"
Journal entry from the astronomer Lilia of Gara

The next morning, they packed up camp and departed. Lorn continued to search for signs of Lilit and Gravers. The main road, Merchant's Road, had few travelers on it. He would try to glean any information about the people who passed by, but they were just like them—fellow travelers on their way to other destinations. He had no way to send a raven to alert them of his success at surviving the Hinterlands or of the surprising appearance of Aza.

A heavy feeling settled in the pit of Lorn's stomach. Would bringing Aza to this court be beneficial for her or bring about her ruin? Lorn thought back to the inn and the altercation. His shock at her actions. She was someone or something not to be trifled with. He admired her convictions. These people tried to wrong her, and she showed them otherwise. It wasn't the path he would have chosen for himself, but who was he to judge? He himself had become a shell of a man, a husk of his former self, succumbing to the bloodlust because it was the only way for him to feel anything.

How would Lilit and Gravers react? Lorn had few interactions with them, all unpleasant. He tucked his anxious thoughts into the back of his head, willing himself to focus on the path in front of them.

Lorn caught Aza's figure out of the side of his eye. Since the inn, she had been more withdrawn. Something was haunting her. He would catch her clutching her hand to her forehead, a slight wince crossing her face. Lorn tightened his jaw, clenching his teeth together. Soon. Hopefully they would receive answers at the city of El'en.

The following days blurred together. Lorn and Aza hiked along the main road passing through small towns. They avoided staying at inns altogether, wishing to avoid any confrontation, anything that would arouse suspicion. They followed the same routine, if anyone crossed paths with them Aza would discreetly shield herself using her cloak to cover her features and mask the use of her magic. If they encountered a small town, Aza would stay near the edge, waiting for Lorn to go in to barter food and goods. They had a smooth system and were pleased with how it turned out. Lorn would catch Aza staring at the towns and the people, a look of yearning plastered on her face. Caught in his gaze, she replaced her longing with one of boredom. Even still, Lorn saw it and his heart ached for her, unsure of how to give her what she needed.

Lorn and Aza kept on towards El'en. One afternoon while walking the dirt road, Lorn spotted riders ahead. They drifted to the edge of the road and Aza casually raised her cloak to cover her features and mask herself. Lorn shifted his shoulders, appearing to be in deep conversation with her. It was all an act, one to discourage travelers from being too friendly and asking nosy questions.

The steady sound of hooves clopped towards them. The riders were almost level with them. Lorn couldn't see the riders, because his body was turned toward Aza, but he felt a nervousness in his stomach; something was amiss. "Aza," Lorn whispered, "are they moving on?"

Aza discreetly tilted her head to peer around Lorn and shook her head. "They are both staring intently at you. It is a man and a woman."

Lorn decided to take a risk and turned to look at the mysterious travelers. Instinctively he moved his body to block Aza from sight, his body thrumming with energy. His hand lay within reach of his sword. His relief faded then immediately returned.

Lorn attempted to mask his features. "Lilit, Gravers, I have been looking for you."

Both were pristine sitting atop their horses, like they recently departed from their pampered castle, while Aza and he were filthy from days of hard travel. They wore light chainmail, the insignia of Iyera stamped along the center, a sun with waves cresting beneath it. Gravers and Lilit shared a conspiratorial look, and each dismounted from their horse.

"We have been searching for you as well," Gravers said. His weathered skin had deepened in color from riding in the late summer sun. This caused his light-blue eyes to appear strange in his face— unsettling. A grim smile crept along his face. "We feared the worst. We all thought the Hinterlands had swallowed you up just like anyone else."

Lorn kept his face a mask, all the thoughts and feelings blurring through his head. Lorn had to consciously stop himself from rolling his eyes, Lilit and Gravers would not have cared if he died. "Well, everyone but Lord Aldrich," Gravers added.

"Excuse me?" Lorn questioned.

"Everyone thought it was a fruitless task. Everyone but Lord Aldrich. He believed you would be successful." Gravers cleared his throat.

Lilit narrowed her eyes at Lorn, disdain dripping from her. "Do you have it?"

"Have what?"

Exasperated, Lilit sighed, "The magic item, you idiot!"

Lorn's thoughts raced. This was the tricky part. He didn't know exactly how to explain the situation they were in, and he wasn't inclined to introduce Aza to these two.

Lilit interrupted his thoughts. "And who are you traveling with?" Lilit leaned in close to Lorn and whispered, "If you have been blabbing about this quest, I will personally gut you." Her eyes sparkled with a promise of violence. "Need I remind you about your oath binding?"

Aza stepped out from behind Lorn and glared at Gravers and Lilit. She removed the hood and with it, all pretense of her hidden magic. Lorn felt her burgeoning magic spilling out around them, enveloping them. Although Lorn didn't want to admit it, he was impressed by Lilit and Gravers. They barely shifted their stance, despite the overwhelming presence of Aza's magic which made Lorn want to offer submission to her.

Lorn barely noticed a look pass from Lilit to Gravers with the hint of a smile playing about her lips. As quickly as he saw it, it vanished, replaced with her cold veneer.

"I'm Aza, and I would prefer if you did not threaten my friend." Her eyes blazed with the promise of destruction, her magic a beautiful snake coiling around them, tightening ever so slowly.

Lilit's whole being lit up. She was not daunted by Aza's display of power. Instead, there was an eagerness in her face. "I can threaten whoever I want, especially when he was promised to secrecy." Lilit sneered at Lorn.

Aza's magic pulsed around them, rising to the bait Lilit was placing. Graver's voice cut through. "Enough Lilit!" Graver's voice was like a bell. It resonated with command. Aza's magic dissipated.

"There is more to the story if you will let me explain." Lorn said.

Lorn sent a pleading look at Aza, hoping she will let it go for now. He gestured roughly to a spot off the road, to allow their horses to graze and their voices to not be overheard.

Lorn summarized his journey through the Hinterlands, leaving out any extra details. They only needed to know the bare minimum. He explained how treacherous the forest was, his encounters with the wildlife, and how he reached the center. Instead of finding an item, he had found Aza. Lilit and Gravers remained silent during the exchange. During certain parts, Lorn detected furtive glances and subtle gestures pass between of them. He wasn't sure what to make of it. Lorn ended the story with him and Aza traveling to reach El'en.

When Lorn finished, Gravers rocked back on his heels and let loose a long whistle. "Well, that is quite a story. Let us rest here a moment, then we can all head back to El'en." He walked to the horses, unpacked some of their supplies, while sneaking glimpses of Aza from the side of his eye. They quickly ate, everyone ignoring each other, the conversation stilted. All of Aza's and Lorn's easy-going conversations dried up in their present company.

Lorn was grateful to see a horse and be able to travel on one again. His legs ached from the countless hours he had walked. Lorn packed his supplies onto the horse and mounted it. They would each ride two to a horse for now, going at a light pace so the horses wouldn't be strained, but still achieve a quicker pace than if they walked on foot. Lorn offered his hand to Aza as she climbed and sat in front of Lorn. Gravers and Lilit mirrored them with Lilit sitting in front of Gravers. She glowered, clearly unhappy with the seating arrangements.

Aza cocked her head at Lilit coldly assessing her. "If you would prefer to ride with me, you can sit in front, and I can sit behind." She smirked and raised her eyebrows waiting for a response.

Lilit's jaw clenched, a nerve twinged along her forehead. "I'd prefer my own horse," she muttered.

Aza haughtily turned her head to face the road and urged the horse forward. Lorn kept his face unreadable and leaned forward to whisper in her ear. "If you keep baiting her, this will be a long journey." Lorn tried to keep the smile out of his voice, instead adopting one that was mock stern.

Aza leaned back, aware of her contact with Lorn, avoiding any skin-to-skin contact where her magic would be too much for him. "She is a terror. Also, I don't trust them." Lorn nodded his agreement. Aza furiously whispered, "If these are the people who work closest with Lord Aldrich, I will have to keep my guard up." She paused. "I just have a feeling of unease." Lorn pondered over what she said and found he agreed. He couldn't shake the same feeling.

Lilit and Gravers suggested staying at a local inn they passed by. To Lorn's vehemence, they agreed to camp further out from the town. They found a small river trickling into a pond. Animals flitted around the edges, searching for a respite just like them. A grove of trees heavy with lemons grew beyond the pond. The light dimmed overhead as the sun sank below the horizon, the chittering of birds and animals the only sound of comfort.

Aza and Lorn were uncomfortable around Lilit and Gravers. They were unable to talk freely. Instead, they shared furtive looks, gleaning hidden information only by the occasional glance. Aza lit a fire while Lorn caught fish from the pond. They all savored a fresh meal, the flakiness of the crisp fish satisfying his hunger. He even grabbed some of the lemons nearby and used it to add flavor to the meal. Coming across fresh food while traveling was difficult, and if they had a chance to savor a meal such as this, he would. Lorn encouraged Aza to try a bite with the lemon added and she exclaimed in delight. Lorn smiled to himself, satisfied they could have some semblance of normal with Lilit and Gravers around. With their bellies full of fish, they laid down near the crackling fire, the stars and moon shining down overhead.

~

*　*　*

Aza tossed and turned, unable to sleep. The newcomers disturbed her, and she couldn't exactly pinpoint why. Obviously, Lilit was not friendly, but there was something deeper hidden right beneath the surface. The horses whinnied and Aza bolted up. Whether it was from her immense powers, or something else, she sensed the horse's distress. Everyone else lay around the fire, still asleep. She checked the sky. It was past midnight but still far from dawn.

There! Something rustled among the lemon trees. If it was an animal, she could scare it off before it became a problem for themselves or the horses. If it was a person...well, she could scare those off too. She pulled her cloak over her hair, to hide the bright silver of her hair and crept towards the lemon trees. Shadows danced, distorted along the ground. Aza crouched flitting from tree to tree. She remained behind the trunk of one and peered out. A shadow moved, hopping from tree to tree just like her. The shadow was the outline of a person.

Suspicious Aza followed the moving shadow. She heard nothing else. Whoever was moving was skilled at moving silently. Deeper into the lemon grove she went, curiosity leading her in. When she came to the edge of the grove, she saw no one. Aza scanned the horizon only to see the soft rolling hills and small farmhouses dotted in the distance, gilded by the soft light of the moon.

Perplexed, Aza turned back ready to admit defeat. Upon turning two women faced her, their stances proud and unafraid. Aza's magic instinctively released. A circle of fire wrapped around each womans' legs, arms, and throat.

"Who are you?" Aza asked, each word punctuated clearly for them to understand. There was no mistaking her tone. Answer or die.

The fire encircling the women lit up their faces. One had a broad face, pale skin and red hair braided around the top of her head. The other was shorter, deep black hair braided in a similar fashion to her companion, delicate features rested upon her light brown skin.

The shorter woman with the black hair spoke, "My lady, my name is Xira."

"And why Xira, were you and your companion luring me out in the middle of the night?"

"We are sorry for the deception, but we came to warn you."

Aza raised an eyebrow at her, her voice skeptical. "Warn me about what?"

The woman next to Xira responded, "We saw you traveling with Lilit and Gravers. They work for Lord Aldrich. Please, you cannot go with them."

Xira nodded in agreement, as carefully as she could with a flame around her throat. "We know what you are. Lord Aldrich will exploit it. He will use you."

Aza filtered through all they said. What was their motivation? Why were they here? Who was to be trusted anymore?

"Why would you come to warn me?"

Xira and her companion stared back at Aza, unflinching despite the danger around their throats and limbs. She saw they were unafraid of her. Aza's respect for them grew. She did not appreciate people who looked on with fear in their eyes.

Xira answered, "Because it is the right thing to do. We cannot see someone as special as you get used, by someone like him."

"How do you know this? How do you know about me? Because if you know what I am, you know I could never be used." Aza's flames grew. They each looked down at the growing flame, sweat beginning to form on their faces and bead down their throats.

"My lady, we do not have all the answers to your questions but trust us when we say we do this for you." The red haired woman spoke with conviction.

The scuffling of footsteps broke Aza's concentration. People were approaching and she did not want them to be seen. Aza did not enjoy the secrecy and lack of information, but a shred of truth lingered in what they shared with her. Their statements embedded in her like a splinter she couldn't pull out. She could see in their faces, they openly believed Lord Aldrich was not to be trusted. Also, Aza appreciated they did not shrink from her powers. They kept their composure, trusting her.

"People are coming," Aza hissed at them. "I will think about what you have told me, but you need to go." She released the chains of flame from around their throats and limbs, ushering them away. Unsure of why she should protect them, she allowed them to flee.

Xira paused, assessing Aza. "If you ever need us, look to the mountains. They will call you home." Xira and her red-haired companion sprinted quietly off into the night, their forms disappearing.

The trees rustled as Lilit popped up beside Aza. Her cold gray eyes narrowed, taking in Aza and the surrounding area. "What are you doing out here?"

"I couldn't sleep, so I came out here for a walk." Aza had to tilt her head down to look at Lilit. "I don't need to explain my actions to you." Aza turned her head away dismissively, which she knew would infuriate Lilit. Gravers' heavy footsteps tramped next to Lilit. He waited for someone to respond.

Lilit prodded Aza with another question. "I heard voices and saw fire, what were you doing?"

Aza sighed, frustration edging into her voice. "Not that I need to answer you, but I was talking to myself and practicing my magic." Aza lazily brought her hands up and a flame flickered around Lilit's throat, hands, and feet. Lilit's eyes widened and she clenched her fists. Her anger was barely restrained, and Aza relished it. Just as easily, Aza released the fire from Lilit and walked away.

She glimpsed Lilit clenching the sword at her side, Gravers touched her shoulder whispering, "You need to let it go." He whispered something else too quietly for Aza to hear, but she walked on, unaffected by their presence.

Gravers raced back to Aza's side. "I understand Lilit can be...difficult, but we are trying to protect you."

Aza laughed, a dry laugh with little joy in it. "Based on what you have seen, do you think I need protecting?"

Gravers faltered, stumbling over his words. His icy blue eyes showed little feeling, he could care less about Aza. There was something else there hiding underneath the surface and Aza needed to uncover it. "No, but I would hate for Lord Aldrich to discover something had happened to you on the journey home."

Aza nodded only to satisfy their questions and queries for now, not aiming to pick a fight. She would do what she pleased, she needed no protection. Clearly their protection was a front for something else.

So many questions floated through her head but for every question she pondered, two more formed. When they got in sight of the campfire, Lorn was standing guard. His eyes immediately softened upon seeing Aza unharmed. His face hardened when he spotted

Gravers and Lilit escorting her back.

Lorn's eyes held Aza's, a silent plea to acknowledge her safety. She gave a firm nod and laid down on her makeshift bed. Lorn turned to Lilit and Gravers. "Why were you both following Aza?"

Gravers quickly responded, "We noticed she was gone from her bed and thought something had happened." As an afterthought he added, "We are here for your protection."

Lorn said nothing, but Aza pulled the blankets up around her and smirked. Their protection, what a joke. Something was going on, so many questions needed answers. She needed to discuss with Lorn about what happened and these two strange women. When would they be alone without prying ears to overhear? Aza let the crackling of the fire drown out the questions plaguing her mind. Yet all she saw when she tried to fall asleep was the delicate face of Xira, her dark black hair, and honey-colored eyes reciting the words, "The mountains will call you home."

18

*"Each province has its own distinct feel and culture. This has
been established since the dawn of the Well."*

Excerpt from *How the Land of Ithilia Came to Be* by
Ursu of Kreeha

The rest of the journey back went quicker with the use of the horses. They alternated between riding and walking to give the horses a reprieve after bearing the weight of two riders. Aza had no time alone with Lorn. Lilit and Gravers were always within hearing distance. It was like they knew Aza was hiding something and didn't want her to be alone.

Even at night, Aza couldn't speak to him. Lilit and Gravers remained close to her with heightened vigilance after the first night of her supposed wandering. She knew Lorn didn't understand the full significance of that night. He assumed the story Aza told was correct that she had decided to go on a walk during the night.

She was restless, the questions consumed her, threatening to drag her under in the depths of their unknown answers. While they traveled, she wasn't taking in the vastness and beauty of Iyera anymore. Instead, all of the questions and riddles danced in front of her. Her mind tried connecting them, answering them, but each night she was left increasingly frustrated. Once they had privacy, she hoped Lorn would have insight and be able to help her decode this mystery.

One of the main questions haunted her, a wisp of doubt implanted by the two women in the dead of night. Was Lord Aldrich trustworthy? Should she continue journeying towards him or leave?

Both the women seemed sincere in their warning to her. Should she heed it?

Her mind was wearing her out with the constant running in circles. For now, she would go to El'en, and gather her own conclusions. If he was truly awful, she could leave with Lorn and go find other areas of Ithilia to explore. Aza allowed herself to hope. Hope to find answers about herself, answers about her memory, who she was, and why she was here.

~

The city gates were impressive. Giant blocks of white marble stacked upon one another. It glistened in the morning sun. No wonder the city of El'en was given the moniker the jewel of Iyera. The portcullis gates were already raised due to the early hour.

Upon the guards seeing Lilit and Gravers, their captain and their lord's private guard, they straightened their stances, nervously casting glances to each other, whispering. They gave a curt nod and rode on. The city had the soft rumblings of the morning duties taking place, people waking and going about their day. Uncaring about secrecy they cut through the main road of El'en heading straight for the castle. Aza tried to reign in her magic. It was a feeling akin to wiggling your ears. Once she had mastered the correct muscles to use she was able to have better control over it affecting others. She had it on a tight leash, afraid of scaring the innocent townspeople. She held onto the edges of her hood, aiming to keep her identity hidden. For now.

A handful of townspeople stared and gawked, whether it be from Lilit and Gravers or they had sensed Aza's unusual aura under the safety of her hooded cloak. The townspeople nudged each other, their heads nodding in the group's direction. Aza saw some of the people do double takes, disbelief on their faces. Maybe they caught glimpses of her stray silver hair or felt her magic, like ink dropped into water. It was something she couldn't hide, and the spread was apparent. Luckily there were few people out and they made quick time through the city.

The main market square behind them, they climbed up a winding street, houses clumped together on one side, and a cliff side on the other.

Aza gasped. The expanse of the ocean lay on the other side of the jagged sandstone cliff. It was beautiful. It stretched deep into the horizon, no end in sight, the sky a perfect match overhead. Occasional clouds punctuated the sky. Aza closed her eyes and took a deep breath. The tang of ocean brininess filled her.

This. This is what she wanted to experience. The beauty of this world. Enraptured by the ocean, the questions which bogged her down ebbed away as if the ocean carried her worries out beyond and toward the distant shores. She let it ease her burdens, if only for this short time.

Lorn leaned in behind her. "I feel the same."

Aza turned her head over her shoulder to look at him, maintaining her balance on the horse. A soft smile played over her lips. "It is indeed beautiful," she spoke softly, the words trickling out of her mouth like the soft pull of the wind around them. She righted herself on the horse and proceeded to view the ocean, allowing herself this small reprieve —if only for a moment.

The castle was only accessible by a lone bridge. Aza stared in wonder at them, as the bridge and castle mimicked the city gates. Bright white marble sparkled in the morning light. Its radiance was brilliant as the light caught each facet of the marble highlighting its elegance. Nearly blinding her, the city gates were only a small interlude before the grand finale of this magnificent castle.

Understanding dawned as she realized this was the jewel of El'en. This is what everyone spoke of. As they crossed the bridge, Aza peered over the side of her horse marveled at the distance of the ocean below. A faint whisper seemed to call from the depths.

When they arrived, a few guards nodded at Lilit and Gravers gesturing them forward. They both dismounted from their shared horse and looked expectantly at Aza and Lorn to do the same. Aza felt the space behind her vacant as Lorn dismounted. He reached out, an offer to assist her if she needed it. Her eyes locked with his. Throughout this whole journey she never felt nervous over what was to come, but now in this moment she was unsure. Unsure of everything and if being here at this moment was necessary. Was she risking herself and her friend by coming here? Should she have tried to discuss what happened a few nights prior? Aza tried to keep a lock on all these emotions roiling inside, but Lorn must have seen something on her face. He kept his gaze on her and gave her a small reassuring smile and a faint tilt of his head, indicating all was well. An answering smile rose on her face as she graciously accepted his proffered hand.

Together. They would do this together. Ever since she had spotted him kneeling before her in the Well, he had never balked in his unrelenting loyalty and friendship. He had never left. He would be here now as her support in this bewildering situation. She needed answers and the jewel of Iyera, the city of El'en, would be the place to start.

Lilit and Gravers escorted them through multiple side doors. They veered through narrow passageways, unlocked doors, and climbed upwards. Nooks and crannies of staircases were hidden within the castle walls. They climbed up and up. Sometimes a window would be placed within these hidden walkways and Aza could spot the ocean crashing beneath them. A small wooden door, warped with age and disuse lay before them.

Lilit turned to Aza and Lorn. "Wait here. We need to talk with Lord Aldrich first, then we can let you in." Without waiting for an answer, they entered and shut the door.

Like children listening in on their parents hushed conversations Aza and Lorn leaned closer trying to eavesdrop on the conversation. She only heard murmured words back and forth. Aza leaned back just in time as the door abruptly swung open. Gravers faced Aza and stepped aside gesturing her into the room.

The room was as disused as the door leading to it. No furnishings decorated the tiny walls. Only a lone desk with a few books placed atop it sat in the center. Two minuscule windows crept along the top of the wall filtering in the weak morning light. Aza squinted through the graying light of the room and found a man leaning against the back wall.

He wore a richly embroidered tunic, a deep burgundy color with threads of gold weaving in delicate filigree around the edges of the fabric. His casual stance belied a confidence thrumming through him. "Lilit, Gravers, give us privacy." He flicked his eyes to them. They left shutting the door. The room was settled with stillness as everyone surveyed each other. Aza assessed Lord Aldrich, her eyes taking in every detail. He straightened himself off the wall, his stance casual, shoulders back and eyes leveled at her. Aza searched for something, hoping her memories would be triggered by something she saw. She felt like there was something missing, something she couldn't place. Her eyes moved up to take in his face. He was youthful for a lord in power. His skin was a soft light brown like it was lightly dusted in the rich spices from Kreeha. He had a strong chiseled jaw, and his hair fell down his face in soft waves to his shoulders. Then she looked into his eyes.

Aza jolted and Lorn reached behind her to grasp her elbow keeping her grounded.

"What's wrong?" Lorn searched her face for the answer, but Aza shook her head, unable to speak.

She straightened and stared back into Lord Aldrich's unsettling eyes. Whatever she had seen, whatever spell she had undergone was gone like a wisp of smoke.

She now felt pain, terrible, blinding pain.

Lord Aldrich feigned no emotion, his face stoic, a polite mask of concern at Aza's discomfort. Echoing Lorn's sentiment he asked, "Are you alright?"

Something was amiss, but Aza played his game. "Yes, I must have had a muscle pain or something." She waved off her own debilitating pain and reached a hand forward. "I'm Aza, I have been eager to meet you, Lord Aldrich."

Lord Aldrich extended his hand. Their hands clasped and nothing. He did not pull back in fear or pain. His face was one of polite interest. Aza had grown used to Lorn's recoiling, but Lord Aldrich did nothing of the sort. *Curious, more mysteries indeed* she thought.

"When Lilit and Gravers explained your situation, imagine my surprise in seeing you here in the flesh." He shook his head, disbelief on his face. He turned to Lorn, openly assessing him. "And you, my hunter!" He clapped his hands together, a smile breaking out on his face. "You are alive and well! I know we have much to discuss. I would offer more proper rooms, but I was unsure of how you both would feel about your notoriety."

Lorn faced Aza, leaving the answer up to her. "I wouldn't mind being around your castle, but I would ask that we have privacy and could be left without people gawking at us throughout the day," Aza responded. She flexed and unflexed her fingers, unknown tension building within.

"Very well, how about I set up rooms for both of you. You can rest today and tonight we can have dinner and go over everything from your adventure?" Lord Aldrich's eyes gleamed, a brief glint of green flashed over his dark brown eyes.

"Yes, that would be wonderful. Thank you." Aza knew he was hiding something, something she couldn't discern.

Lord Aldrich led them out of the dingy room and back through all the staircases they had traversed. They walked through the main halls of the castle, and a few castle workers caught glimpses of both Aza and Lord Aldrich. They stared briefly and then averted their eyes. Lorn kept a hand loosely on Aza's shoulder. It was reassuring to feel his presence and he was probably worried about her reaction to Lord Aldrich. What was that? She would mull it over later when they had privacy and time to talk about everything together. Lord Aldrich stopped outside of an elaborate wood door. Carvings of vicious waves adorned its surface. "This is your room Aza." He moved away to lead Lorn to his room next.

"Wait!" Aza blurted out. They both turned to look at her. "I would like a room with a connecting door to Lorn's room."

Lord Aldrich took a step back, "Ahh, if you would like a shared room, you only need to say. There doesn't need to be any secrecy if you are both lovers."

Aza coughed a dry laugh and shot a look at Lorn. He was highly uncomfortable, avoiding her eyes and his cheeks were stained with light pink. "No," she sputtered, "we have been traveling together for so long, it would be strange to be separated in a foreign castle."

Aza caught Lorn mumbling a few words to himself. She heard "Never, Lakesh, my friend." Irritated at Lord Aldrich's assumption she let the chaos take over in her silver eyes. She loosened the leash a small amount to let Lord Aldrich feel it wash over him. Quicker than a breath, she saw Lord Aldrich flash a smirk at her then cover it up with mock sympathy.

"I apologize for the assumption. I can lead you to other rooms more suitable for your needs." Lord Aldrich led them further down the hall to another room. The doors appeared closer together. He opened it, leading her in. The room was extravagant. The bed was giant and inviting, plush blankets and linens draped over it. A door on the left connected to Lorn's equally elaborate rooms. Lord Aldrich left them to spend the day recovering and said he would send someone to escort them to dinner. As he was leaving, Aza felt it again. A stab of familiarity, yet one she couldn't place. It was like Lord Aldrich left a trail of smoke whenever he left the room.

"Lorn, I hope it was alright. I asked for joined rooms. I didn't mean to make you uncomfortable."

Lorn looked at her plainly. "No, I agree with you. It would have felt strange if we were removed from one another." Lorn looked down, staring at his hands like they held the answers for him. "You know a little of my wife, Lakesh. She is...was my everything. There will be no other for me."

Aza wished to touch and reassure her friend, but she sensed he needed to get through what he was saying without interference.

"After she died, I was hollow. I killed creatures to just feel something and every night I dreamed of her. But since that day in the Well, I have something to live for now. A goal I can work towards instead of this never-ending death. You are my friend, and it feels like we have this bond. It is undeniable, and there it is. I feel like we were meant to find each other, and we are not meant to part ways just yet. But you are my friend, and I don't want you to be embarrassed about people assuming we are together."

Aza did not look away. She absorbed the intensity of his look, answering with a soft smile. "I feel the same Lorn. You are the truest friend I could have ever hoped to find." Aza blinked quickly, realization crashing over her. "Lorn! I have so much to tell you." Despite their presumed privacy, Aza glanced over her shoulders to double-check they were alone. "Come here," she beckoned him to a small dining table in her room. Aza went into great detail over the night they traveled and the two women she encountered. She shared with him all the thoughts bubbling through her head, ready to spill out. Lorn listened patiently, not interrupting but intently nodding his head along to the conversation. Aza discussed her thoughts and theories. Lorn sat, absorbing it all.

After she finished, Lorn said the words she never imagined him uttering, "I have met those two women before." Speechless, Aza sat there waiting for Lorn to divulge more. Now they switched, Lorn explaining the group he ran into at the inn before he entered the

Hinterlands. Their brief interaction had lingered with him, despite nothing significant happening. Lorn ended it all with the same question echoing within Aza's head. "What does it all mean?"

Lorn looked just as puzzled as Aza felt. "Do you trust anyone?" Aza asked.

"No." Lorn's voice was chilling. She could sense the detached bloodlust Lorn would subject himself to when killing beasts. This was foreign to her, usually he was the voice of reason, the calm one. Lorn continued, his voice level, "I felt something...off like everyone is hiding information. I never questioned it before, but with you here involved, I'm starting to." Lorn rose out of his chair, a deep-seated sigh easing out of his lungs. Aza watched him walk over to her window and looked out to the ocean below. He ran a hand through his wild black hair and turned to her. "For now, let's try and get answers from Lord Aldrich. We play the gracious guests, trusting no one but each other. Gather information and we'll talk each night." He briskly strode to her and leaned in close. "Trust no one but each other." He straightened up and resumed speaking normally. "Let us clean up and rest, then we can talk a bit before we head to dinner." He waited for Aza to assent, then walked to his room, opening their adjoining door.

While closing his door, Aza caught a glimpse of worry creasing Lorn's brow. She didn't want to cause him worry. She could take care of both of them. Her magic could protect them. This information was more frustrating than scary. The gaps in her memory left her mind in tangles, and her lack of knowledge left her bereft. She had a deep need to figure out the answers swirling just out of reach. For now, she could at least scrub herself clean.

She retreated to the bathroom. It was as breathtaking as the rest of the castle. Colorful tiles in various shades of blue mimicked the ocean and sky outside. The crest of Iyera, waves with a sun, was stamped along the walls.

Aza drew a bath, grateful for the plumbing system the castle had. Hot water poured from the pipe and filled the luxurious marble tub. Aza raided the cabinets pouring in different concoctions of liquids. Scents of lavender, rosemary, and jasmine floated through the air. Aza chuckled to herself seeing the water overflow with bubbles, the rich earthy scents hanging in the air.

She stripped off her dirty clothes and folded them on a small stool in the corner. Although they were dirty, they were precious, from a generous woman in a moment of brief compassion. The clothes Melina had gifted her. She stepped one foot over the lip of the tub with the other following. The hot water was bliss, welcoming her tired and strained body. She lowered herself in, the water lapping over the swells of her body. She attempted to drown out the loudness of her thoughts. They wouldn't let her rest.

Burrowing deeper into her mind, they took a hold, wrenching her serenity away. Frustrated, she submerged deeper into the bath, the water covering her head only leaving her eyes, nose, and mouth visible. She closed her eyes, the water quieting any extraneous noise. She focused on her breath in and out. Counting for each breath. Three seconds in. Three seconds out. Now five. Five seconds in and five seconds out.

Aza stayed submerged, the quiet water atmosphere stilling her racing mind, her breath steadying her. Her body was a buoy raising and lowering with each breath. She succumbed to the flowing movements of the water. It rocked her, comforted her.

She was transported.

Instead of the blue tiles placed around the bathroom, she was staring at the ceiling of some sort of rocky cave. Hot water enveloped her body and the earth above cradled her. She felt safe and protected here. Splashing sounded next to her, she lifted her head to catch a glimpse of who it was, but the darkness of the cave shrouded them.

"My shadows," the husky voice murmured. Their hands played along the edges of her body skimming all her sensitive parts. She was alight. Their mouths met in a soft caress, their naked bodies melding together in the hot spring. The man broke off his kiss to trail more down her neck. She exposed it to him hungry for more. "My shadows," he whispered again, a prayer said in benediction to her and her alone.

Aza opened her eyes. The earthy rock formation was no longer above her, instead she was greeted with the familiar tile of her bathroom. Flustered, Aza pushed herself upright, her head swiveling back and forth. She was still panting, her body aching with need from her dream. What kind of dream was that? A hand fluttered to her forehead preparing for the pounding in her skull. She focused on her breathing to still the cadence of her pounding headache.

She collapsed in the water and rested her head back on the edge of the tub. She closed her eyes again, imagining the rock ceiling and the feel of this lover's hands on her body. Her hand flitted down to toy with her nipple, the dusky tip hardening. Her hand drifted further down to the apex of her curls. She curiously put one finger down on her swollen flesh and gasped. Was it a dream? Her body's reaction betrayed her. She moved her finger in a lazy circle, her hips arching up into the movement. She kept going, a tentative exploration of her own body, her mind confused over what was real or fictional anymore.

Suddenly her mind sparked awake, what was real or not real? Was she really touching herself to an illusion she had just experienced? Momentarily disgusted, she stopped her movements, her passion sputtering out. Hastily she stood and clambered out of the tub, toweling herself off, ignoring the growing need inside of her. Confused and hurt she went to go find some clothes. Aza only had one set of clothes, and the special outfit Melina had gifted her. It lay hidden wrapped in soft linen fabric.

She found a plush robe in one of the drawers and pulled it on. When her aching body rubbed against the fabric in the most delicious way, she hated herself even more. She rapped her knuckles on Lorn's door. A moment passed before the door creaked ajar, his eyes blearily opened. Do you mind sending out clothes to Lord Aldrich for them to be washed by tonight? Otherwise, I have nothing to wear besides my travel stained clothes."

Lorn sleepily nodded his agreement and Aza gathered her clothes to give to him. He paused in his delirious state to look at her, "Would you like to join me in my room and talk?" He must have seen something in her eyes, a frantic desperation to not be left alone right now, but Aza was grateful. She accepted and stepped into his room. He motioned for her to sit at the end of the bed. Their rooms were nearly identical, elaborately furnished and richly decorated. Lorn grabbed a seat at the small breakfast nook and waited for Aza to speak.

Unsure of what to say, she looked around his room. It was the middle of the day but his room was bathed in darkness. He had drawn the heavy curtains closed over his window, hoping to get some rest. He caught her looking at the drapes. "Would you like them open?"

"No...I just don't know where to start." She fiddled with her hands trying to piece her words together. "My mind is frustrating," Aza started, the words coming out one by one as if paving a path in front of her. "I have briefly explained it before, but lately it has gotten worse. I'm often left confused and unsure of myself. I have been seeing images and having strange dreams. At least they feel like dreams." She added, "Being in this place and having all of the extra questions circulating seems to have bogged down my mind and adds to the frustration." Aza's shoulders tensed, rising towards her ears. She mindfully lowered them, stretching them back. "I want answers," Aza finished quietly.

The sleepiness gone from his eyes Lorn studied her thoughtfully. "What things have you seen?"

"When I killed those people in the inn, instead of their bodies, I saw dead soldiers laying on a forest floor." Aza looked into her lap, heat rising into her face. "Right now, I experienced an underground cave...with a lover." She hurried to speak the next part, "I never saw anything, the face was obscured in darkness."

"I see." Lorn's hazel eyes scanned her face. "I wish I had answers right now." He leaned back in his chair, his head hung back taking in the ceiling of the room. "I think we will be here awhile, in El'en. We can search the library for answers, see if we can gain access to any other areas." Lorn straightened in his chair, bringing his forearms to his thighs. "I'm sorry Aza."

Perplexed, she asked, "For what?"

"I was raised in the countryside. I'm glad of the scant education I received, but it was simple. I'm not versed in high lore or ancient texts. I wish I knew more to help you." His eyes brightened. "But we can try to figure it out together. You will not be left alone to shoulder this burden."

Aza gave a grim smile to Lorn. He would shoulder her burden, when he already had so many of his own. She was thankful for this friend in her life. Aza rose and her feet padded across the floor to her door. "Thank you Lorn." He responded with a slim smile, his eyes crinkling at the edges. She closed the door behind her and went to her own bed to finally get some rest.

19

"Gleaned from ancient texts, the five provinces have not always been. If I can understand it correctly, the borders have been altered, many fighting wars over what piece of land they sought to claim. It is muddled at best to try and understand the scarce texts we have preserved from over a millennium ago."
How the land of Ithilia came to be by Ursu of Kreeha

A knock on her door startled Aza awake. She rolled out of bed, pulling her robe tight around herself. Cracking the door open, she peered out. A young man stood outside, outfitted in the crest of Iyera. "Miss, here are your clothes freshly washed as requested." He handed her the bundle of clothes. "Is there anything else I can do for you? Would you like a lady's maid to help you dress or get ready for this evening?"

Aza cleared her throat to speak. "No thank you, this will be fine." The servant began to walk away when Aza interjected, "Wait!"

He turned, waiting patiently for her to continue.

"How soon until dinner?"

"You have precisely thirty minutes until I come to escort you and Lorn to dinner with Lord Aldrich." He turned on his heel and walked off down the empty hallway. Aza closed the door and rubbed the sleep from her eyes.

The heavy curtains blocked the bright coastal sun from filling the room. To help banish any residual sleepiness she yanked them open basking in the warmth. She stretched and put on her freshly washed clothes. They fit her perfectly. Her hands reverently flowed along the fabric. Melina was truly gifted.

Aza headed into the bathroom next, catching her appearance in a small ornate mirror, the edges framed in gold and shaped like the rising tide. Running her fingers through her hair, Aza haphazardly brushed stray coils into place. She had never seen her appearance so clearly before, only catching brief glimpses in rippling streams or stagnant water.

Her breath caught in her chest. She stilled. She had grown accustomed to seeing the other MagicBlessed. They all contained a small spark, an essence she attributed to their magic, but in this mirror she could see why people shied away from her. There was an indefinable glow and attractiveness about her being. She was composed of unique facets when pieced together formed an aura of singularity that caused people to be dumbstruck in her presence.

A soft smile came to her as she thought of Lorn. She commended him. He treated her normally every day they traveled, unlike all of the other people they had come across so far.

Her body was broad, curvy and supple. Her hands ran over her hips, pride flaring over her strong body. It had carried her so far already. She tilted her head sideways examining all the minute details of her face. The smattering of silver freckles and the matching silver of her eyes. The color swirled and shifted like the fog that rolled in on the banks of the ocean.

A knock at the door adjoining her room to Lorn's broke her from her spell. She shook her head, dispelling the focus on herself and went over to open it. Lorn was dressed in the same clothes they traveled in, his also freshly washed. His smooth black hair dripped small droplets of water on his forehead. The stubborn hair fell into his face as he ran an errant hand through it, pushing it back into formation. He raised his eyebrows at her, a question etched between them.

"Ready?"

Aza nodded and with serendipitous timing, the servant knocked on their door again ready to escort them to dinner.

They wound through the empty hallways, the servant confidently leading the way. Aza wondered if Lord Aldrich's castle was always empty or was he purposely guiding them through vacant areas? They did ask for privacy—maybe it was a small request granted.

The servant stopped in front of a large oak door and opened it. A large, private dining room greeted them. The room was cozy with a fireplace at the end of the room, a quaint fire burning within. A table able to seat twelve people lay lengthwise with finely carved wooden chairs situated around it. The servant bowed his head. "My lord, your guests." Lord Aldrich thanked the young man and sent him out.

Lord Aldrich was not the only person at the table— they were joined by Lilit, Gravers, and an old man with shocking white hair.

Lord Aldrich invited them to sit. Aza and Lorn chose two seats opposite the trio of people with Lord Aldrich sitting at the head of the table. Servants entered the room carrying trays of food. They were each placed down on the table and the servants filed out of the room.

Aza dug into her food, her stomach grumbling. Idle chatter filled the room as Lord Aldrich inquired about their trip back. Aza mumbled small responses here and there trying to gauge what kind of person Lord Aldrich truly was. He played the caring, benevolent leader, but she was convinced he had his own hidden agenda. They all did. Why else would he enlist Lorn to enter the dangerous Hinterlands to retrieve a magic item?

"So, Lorn, we need to discuss your compensation for the journey, and I expect your travel plans are to return to your home in Verta?" Lord Aldrich asked.

Aza's fingers tightened on the fork in her hand, and fear spiked through her. Lorn couldn't leave—he was her constant, her lodestone throughout this chaotic time. Lorn placed a reassuring hand on her leg with a gentle pressure, a reminder to keep her emotions masked. Lorn leisurely finished his bite of food, and addressed Lord Aldrich, "Actually I would like to stay on. If that is alright with you Lord Aldrich." His head inclined towards him in a slight bow. "Aza has personally asked me to be her adviser and mentor." Lorn's lie was believable and Aza latched onto it.

Lord Aldrich looked to her for confirmation, "Is that so?"

Aza steadied her voice, a mask of indifference. "Yes of course. He has been my biggest source of help and knowledge."

"Hmm, interesting. Well in that case, Lorn, we are glad to have you here." A tight smile formed on his face.

"What was your hope Lord Aldrich?" Aza's question hung in the air between them.

Confusion riddled his face, his brows furrowing to consider the question. "My hope?"

"Yes. You sent Lorn into the Hinterlands to retrieve a magic item. What did you hope to do with it?" She stared at him, watching for tells, signs of deception or lies.

He placed his fork and knife down beside his plate with a soft touch and considered Aza. Lord Aldrich held her stare, the hint of a smile playing about his lips. "I have studied countless scrolls, tomes, and journals discussing the prophecy of a magic item appearing from the Well. I had no idea what the item could do, only that I needed to obtain it. As Lorn can attest, other provinces would kill for the information. Despite our mutual peace between the provinces, I'm sure other Lords and Ladies wouldn't mind gaining such a powerful item. I don't have a straightforward answer, only that I wished to usher in a new era of peace." Lord Aldrich blinked slowly. "But your immense magical powers are even better."

"And how do you even know of my magical powers? Just how vast and potent are they? Maybe I am powerless," she volleyed back. Aza felt her mask slipping, her voice harsh and biting like a brutal wind in a winter storm picking him apart. She would unearth who he truly was.

"Oh, don't play coy now. Lilit and Gravers already debriefed me on the extent of your power."

Aza cursed herself for displaying her powers so easily. "Fine, I do have power. An overwhelming amount of it." She raised her hand and a flame burst from the end of it. The flame licked around the edges of her hand. She melded and twisted it into different shapes and allowed the size to increase.

She couldn't deny the hunger in his eyes buried beneath his sovereign facade. A glint of green crossed his dark brown eyes. Aza faltered, the flames sputtering out.

"What do you want me to do with it? What is your goal?"

Lord Aldrich opened his hands gesturing to the space out in front of him. " To remake the world."

Aza's magic pulsed in shock and Lorn's hand tightened on her thigh.

"Come now, don't look too shocked. I want to remake it for the better. Everything is orderly, nothing amiss. To rid those who crave violence, those who hurt others, misuse their magic. Is that not an honorable goal?"

Aza's voice was cold and stilted as she replied, "It depends on who you are asking."

"You are not on my side?" Lord Aldrich asked. "Even after I kept your secret of what happened at that inn?"

Aza and Lorn gasped. She was not ashamed of her actions but having Lord Aldrich throw that in her face, she felt heat creep over her.

"How do you know about that?" Lorn's voice was ragged.

Lord Aldrich dismissed the question with a wave of his hand. "I have eyes everywhere, but a group of people disappearing with nothing said. Everything pointed to them not leaving the inn. It doesn't take a master scholar to deduce what had happened. But that's beside the point." He leaned forward, latched onto Aza staring at her, unwilling to let her gaze leave him. "Was that not the same thing? You were ridding the world of them due to their lack of lawful obedience. They touched you and tried to sell you. Would you have granted them mercy?" His fingers came up to stroke his chin mockingly. "Oh wait, you did not. Is my goal not the same thing as yours?"

Aza clenched her teeth. He was right. Was she not the same as him with his re-imagined, remade world?

Lorn whipped his head to Aza and back to Lord Aldrich. "It is not the same thing. Aza did what she did out of defense of my life. They attempted to kill me, and they wanted to sell her. Those are vastly different from you wanting to use and abuse a power you are incapable of wielding. Not to mention the moral implications of your 'good' intentions." Aza's heart lifted at the defense Lorn presented for her. "Do not try to shame her for protecting those she cares for."

Aza felt tears shimmering in her eyes but blinked them back. She needed to be indifferent, uncaring in front of these people. She scanned the table taking in their table audience. Lilit, Gravers, and the man she learned to be Oron, were all taking in the scene.

Lord Aldrich backtracked and spewed mock sympathy. "Now I meant no offense, I wanted you to understand my thoughts for remaking the world. There are many areas of Ithilia that need to be addressed. Areas we could help and improve with your vast magical power." He picked up his fork to resume eating. "Nothing has to be decided right now, Aza. I would love for you and Lorn to come and learn about how I reign within my castle. Feel free to explore and openly talk with me when I'm available." He speared a vegetable and began to chew.

Yes, she and Lorn would explore the castle, and hopefully find the answers she needed. Without giving a proper response, dinner continued awkwardly, small talk filling in the silences of the scraping of dinner plates. Lord Aldrich and his advisers excused themselves, reminding Aza and Lorn to alert them should they require something. They walked back to their rooms in silence. Their pace hurried. They waited for privacy to talk about what happened. When they finally found their room, they looked at each other in disbelief.

"What do you think?" Aza asked Lorn.

"I say we stick to our original plan, trusting no one. We can scout out as much information as possible in the meantime."

After agreeing with one another Lorn departed to the privacy of his own room. The things Lord Aldrich laid out at dinner rattled in her head. Aza was filled with restless energy, pacing back and forth. Realization struck her. She wasn't locked in her room. She was free to explore the castle. Lord Aldrich encouraged them multiple times. They could walk around, and she could defend herself if anyone tried to bother her.

Without a second thought, Aza left her room and wandered the immense hallways. The castle was beautiful. Each slab of marble was neatly stacked, the furnishings and decorations were picked by a loving eye. Maybe Lord Aldrich had good intentions, if not overzealous. His workers seemed content, no simmering hate brewed beneath any of their eyes. He wanted to rid the world of evil. Was that so bad?

Caught in her aimless musings, she found herself in front of a balcony. Glass doors shielded her from the night sky, and she realized she yearned to feel the crisp night air on her skin. She had been too confined. She was born under an open sky—anything else seemed too stifling.

Aza opened the glass doors; a rush of cool night air greeted her. Releasing a sigh, she leaned forward, resting her forearms on the balcony. The stars sparkled overhead. The moon was not visible in the sky. She thought back to when she laid underneath the night sky with Lorn and he taught her some of the constellations. She scanned the sky searching for the hunter and his compass. Spotting them, her hands reached forward to idly trace the outline of each.

"Stargazing?" The voice startled her, and ice sprang from her fingertips, coating the balcony in a thin frosty layer. "Sorry, I didn't mean to startle you."

Aza fixed him with an equally ice stare and turned back to the sky. Having just achieved a sense of tranquility, her peace vanished.

Lord Aldrich joined her at the balcony leaning against the railing, mimicking her posture. It caused his almond-brown hair to brush his shoulders, the soft waves framing his strong jaw. "I am sorry Aza." She ignored him instead focusing on the distant sky, where her consciousness was everywhere and nowhere at the same time. "I am sorry Aza," he repeated. "I have been looking forward to this moment for a long time and I completely blundered it." Aza spared a glance in his direction. He was staring at the night sky like she was, a look of hunger to join the stars above. "Your magic is a gift, and I would like to bring justice to this world. I never meant to spring it all upon you at once, nor bring up the incident at the inn. I understand what you did, and I never meant to use it as a threat. I apologize."

His sincerity rang through her like a clear note, pure and true. Putting her trust in him was foolish, but she could at least be civil. Without turning to face him Aza said, "I accept your apology, but I don't trust you one bit."

Lord Aldrich barked a laugh, the sound resounding into the courtyard below. Aza couldn't help but smirk. It was a truce struck between the two of them. "Very well Aza. Very well." His voice turned silky and sensuous weaving itself around Aza's being. "I will need to change your mind then."

Heat flared in her body, but she tamped it down. He didn't deserve any ounce of desire coursing through her.

"What constellation are you looking at?" he inquired.

"Lorn taught me only two for now. The hunter and the compass." His grip on the railing tightened imperceptibly. There was a tension throughout his body like his magic was singing, thrumming within his body threatening to escape.

"And what did he teach you of these constellations?"

"Very little, but he did mention how the constellations were possibly inspired by the goddesses and gods of long ago." She sidled closer to him, sharing his point of view, and pointed to the sky. "The hunter is named Cruvo, and the compass is named Issi. Once upon a time, they walked this world." A smile filled with awe and wonder plastered her face. "It is very fascinating." Aza knew a silly expression was stuck on her face, but she couldn't help it. The whole universe was infinite, overwhelming, and magical. She moved her head a fraction and saw Lord Aldrich's face staring at her own.

"What?"

Lord Aldrich shook his head from side to side. "You were formed from the night sky, and are a being of supreme magic who cannot recall their own memories, yet you are impressed by constellations of the gods and goddesses of ancient lore?"

Aza shrugged her shoulders, her eyes looking deep into the night sky. It called to her — she looked past the constellations and saw the figures behind it. "It calls to me," she confessed. Maybe it was not wise to be vulnerable, but whatever the repercussions Aza could handle it.

His voice quieted. "Would you like for me to tell you about the others?" He raised a hand fanning it out to the multitude of stars above them.

Aza tried to fight the pleased smile that came unbidden to her face. "Yes, I would like that very much."

Lord Aldrich spent the rest of the night explaining the constellations overhead and the deities attached to them. They talked long into the night, Lord Aldrich even fetched a blanket for them to lay down and gaze up at the stars. As Aza went back to her room, her mind was filled with the stars she yearned to reach and the gods and goddesses that made them real.

20

"Lord Aldrich has often been active in the city of El'en, seen helping his citizens, providing sanctuary for others, and trying to improve the already impressive province of Iyera. However, over the last few years, he has been more secluded and secretive, not venturing out to the city as frequently."
Journal entry from the scholar Trewart of Verta

The following morning Aza and Lorn dressed and ate breakfast in a hurry, eager to explore the castle and find any relevant information. They found a bored looking guard to escort them to the library. It was the perfect day for them to spend an inordinate amount of time searching for information, Lord Aldrich and his advisers were busy with their lordly duties pertaining to the province and the governing of El'en.

While the guard escorted them to the library, Aza asked, "Do you enjoy being a soldier for Lord Aldrich?" The man was middle-aged, slight wrinkles beginning to set in his skin. He risked a quick look at Aza, his eyes widening at the magic pulsing underneath her skin and reverted to looking back down the hallway.

"Yes Miss. I have held this position for ten years. My family has been provided for and he is a just ruler." Winding through halls and past a courtyard, he stopped outside a building and informed them this is the library. Without a dismissal, he scurried from their presence like a mouse under the scrutiny of a hawk.

The massive building swamped Aza's vision. It was separate from the castle, steps leading up to the entrance and framed by prominent marble pillars on either side. Flowers dotted the entrance, and they were greeted by the fresh smell of jasmine as they opened the heavy oak doors. The inside was equally as immaculate as the outside. Wide windows filtered in the light from the three-story building. Bookshelves upon bookshelves encompassed the room, their polished wood shelves gleaming in the sunlight. Their footsteps echoed as they entered, the library swallowing them both up. A few others occupied the library, either reading at desks or searching the columns of books. Aza didn't know where to start. She turned to Lorn, and as if reading her mind, he shrugged. Aza spotted a head of shocking, white hair and drifted towards it. They weren't researching anything that wasn't common knowledge, so she saw no harm in asking him for guidance.

His back was to her. "Excuse me, Oron." He faced them and lit up with pure joy. "Yes Aza. What can I help you with?"

"My memory and my thoughts are often jumbled. I would love your help regarding books about the five provinces of Ithilia. I feel like it would help me sort everything out." Her voice held a note of desperation and earnestness.

Oron nodded sympathetically. "Of course! I actually oversee the library and can provide you with lessons if you are interested."

Looking for confirmation, Aza glanced sideways at Lorn and saw a firm nod of agreement. They needed more information about the land they lived in, it couldn't hurt to study more. Aza agreed and Oron enthusiastically set off to grab books. Despite his curved back and old age, he moved with surprising spryness. He sat them both at a desk instructing them not to move. While they waited he piled book after book into a stack. Lorn chuckled to himself, shaking his head.

Aza whispered out of the corner of her mouth to Lorn, "What's so funny?"

"How many books do you see stacked here? How will we ever get through these?"

"I see your point. He is a bit enthusiastic."

"A bit?"

Lorn and Aza suppressed their laughter in the cavernous library as Oron made his way back with yet another book. Like school children, they forced themselves to stop giggling and keep a straight face. Oron faltered in his steps. "Is everything alright?"

They both fought the laughter bubbling up inside of them,

clenching their teeth. They stiffly nodded. "I think this covers everything nicely for now."

Aza's smile fought to show itself, but she attempted to school her features.

Oron asked in an afterthought to himself, "Was I too excessive?"

The laughter could no longer be contained as it burst out of them. It echoed off the great library filling the vast space. The few people occupying the library sent them swift reprimanding looks, appalled at their behavior. Their condescension caused Aza and Lorn to laugh even harder, her deep belly laughter cutting the knots of anxiety that wrapped through her body. Tears crested her eyes as she took in Oron's perplexed face. His confusion added to the laughter. Her soul felt lighter than it had in many days. Slowly the laughter faded from Aza and Lorn and they spent the next few minutes apologizing profusely to Oron.

Once settled, Oron began teaching the history of the five provinces. Hours had passed but Aza only realized it due to the grumbling of her stomach. Oron finally stopped for the day. Aza was disappointed; she had soaked all of the information like a starving person consumed food. It helped her piece together the vague information and memories she had in her mind.

While Oron packed up, Aza asked, "Can we continue this every day at the same time?"

Oron's craggy face brightened. "Of course, Aza. I would be delighted." He persuaded her to take some books back to her room to study at night if she wished. Both Aza and Lorn thanked him and headed off in search of the kitchen for lunch. Wandering around, Aza noted all of the workers and various nobles. None of them seemed unhappy at being here—they all were pleased, content to be at the Jewel of El'en. Maybe those two women's warnings were false, something to lead her astray.

After asking directions from a few guards and workers Aza and Lorn stumbled upon the kitchen. It was frantic. Fires blazing, smells wafting in the air, people rushing to chop things, everyone was active. Lorn got caught up with the head chef. Aza overheard his conversation.

"Thank you, it was one of the best meals I have ever had."

Aza smiled to herself. The chef, grateful for the praise, pushed more food into their hands, plates overflowing, guiding them on which food to eat first. Aza and Lorn thanked him and proceeded to find a quiet place to eat. The season of summer was fading, and they wanted to enjoy every remaining bit they could outside. Finding one of the many courtyards, with countless flowers and fountains they balanced their overstuffed plates on their laps and dug in, satisfied noises filling the empty courtyard. Aza hadn't realized how hungry she had become during their many hours spent studying.

After moments of contentedly eating, Lorn proposed an idea. "I think I should train you in the afternoons."

"Train? What do you mean? I already know how to wield my magic."

"Physically. Hand to hand combat, swords, weapons, that kind of thing."

Aza mulled it over while chewing her food. "I'm sorry Lorn, I don't really see the point. My magic will always be superior. Why wouldn't I use that instead?"

"Think about it, the more skills you have and use, it will sharpen your reactions, including the precision of your magic. Also, it would give you the added benefit of focusing your thoughts on training, instead of everything else that bogs you down."

Aza considered it, taking another bite of her food. "So, train our minds in the morning, and train our bodies in the afternoon?"

Lorn nodded his agreement. "Plus, you always want to be prepared. What if you were without your magic? What if you ever reached burnout like we do? How you wield your powers is completely opposite to how we do. You use your magic first, relying on its strength. We do the opposite. We will do anything else besides use our magic, because it depletes quickly."

"Okay I see your point, when would you like to start?" Aza conceded.

"Let's ask Lord Aldrich for some clothes, weapons, and an area to train privately and we can start tomorrow."

They finished their meal enjoying the beautiful weather and serenity of the flower filled courtyard. Aza hesitated to share with Lorn that Lord Aldrich met up with her last night. She didn't want to hold secrets from him, especially when their trust was essential to them operating well together.

She turned to him, the words brewing beneath and just spilled it out. "Lord Aldrich met up with me last night on the balcony." She rushed the words out, avoiding the heat which crept into her neck and cheeks, "Nothing happened, we only talked."

"Aza I'm not going to reprimand you. You are an adult and your own person. You make your own decisions." His hair fell back into his eyes, and he pushed it back roughly, an irritated sigh slipping between his lips. "Thank you for trusting me, but I don't trust them. Or any of this. It just doesn't sit right." He shifted to face her, his hazel eyes searching hers. "I only want you to keep your guard up."

Aza tried to fight the defensive attitude rising in her tone. " I know what they are, I know something isn't right. I don't need to be reminded to look after myself."

Lorn nodded curtly. "Very well then."

Shame crept over Aza. Lorn was only trying to protect her and she stomped all over his friendship. He didn't shame her for talking to Lord Aldrich, yet she acted rudely.

Her chest tightened and her jaw clenched. She couldn't hold back the words jumping to be said. "Lorn, I'm sorry. That was ill said of me. I know you are looking out for me, but it can be frustrating when I can protect myself. I am much stronger than you and have held my own so far. It feels belittling when you constantly want me to watch out for myself. I am! I am always on guard." The thoughts spilled out of her and after each word, Lorn shrank down his shoulders curving in on himself like the words were physically battering him.

His voice was barely heard, a soft whisper, "I have lost someone I loved more than the whole of Ithilia itself. I could not bear to lose you as well." He turned his head to look at her, but his eyes moved past her, staring at some unseen person. His eyes crested with silver, a single tear fell down his face. She watched the wet trail on his face. "I am sorry Aza; I don't mean to be overbearing." Another sigh blew past his lips. "You are right. You are ridiculously strong and can take care of yourself. I say these things only out of worry and precaution, never as a sign that you are weak or foolhardy."

Aza clasped his hand, his body gently spasmed as he adjusted to her power. Instead of her raging depths of power, she pictured a calming current of water flowing around him, allowing him to rest among the safety of her waters. She pushed her magic towards him, all the feelings of love, protection and safety, to ease away and diminish his thoughts of worry. It was like he was transparent. Laid bare. The barbed hooks of his fears latched on to him like some sort of sickly disease.

She saw it. Everything that assaulted him. The depression which filled him was a black pool of sludge filling his endless chasms, weighing him down. She surged her magic clearing it out, freeing him from the pains of his own mind. With her eyes closed she focused, pushing her magic, filling in the gaps. A sharp gasp escaped his mouth.

After a time, her eyes flared open. She centered herself in her surroundings, the calm still air of the day, the flowers blooming next to her. While healing him, it was like she was within it. Experiencing his pain, experiencing his sorrow.

"Thank you, Aza," Lorn said quietly, almost too quiet for her to hear. A deep breath expanded his chest as he loosened a sigh and straightened up. "It looks like there is more you can do with your magic." Lorn leaned his head back basking in the sun, his eyes closed in reverence.

Aza watched him as he stood there, steadily breathing with his eyes closed. He was communing with someone or something else. Eventually he opened his eyes, tears shining and a shaky smile on his face. The look he shared with Aza was one of gratitude and happiness. Lorn tipped his head towards her in thanks and walked off leaving her to her own thoughts.

Sitting alone on the stone bench, Aza thought, *Maybe I do have more to learn.* It was time to get to work and hone her skills.

Aza left Lorn to his thoughts and explored the rest of the castle. Whenever she passed by other people, whether it be nobles, guards, workers, or citizens of El'en she was often gawked at. People elbowed those next to them and pointed at her. She tried not to let it bother her, so she continued walking with her head high and shoulders back, but it did irk her, despite her carefully placed exterior. She was not some commodity for them to partake of.

Aza flagged down a server and requested to dine privately in her chambers. Retiring to her room, she ate a solitary meal and flopped onto her bed. After staring mindlessly at the ceiling, she hefted herself up and went to knock on Lorn's door. She wanted to allow him privacy, but she was worried after their afternoon together and she had questions that needed answering. Lorn answered the door, his face lighter and younger than it had been since meeting him. "Can we talk?"

"Yes of course, please come in."

Aza walked in and sat at his small dining table. His meal was already picked apart and eaten, a mirror image to hers back in her room. "I already secured clothes, weapons, and a private room for us to practice tomorrow."

"Oh, thank you for handling that." Aza picked absentmindedly at her fingernails and finally asked, "Are you well?"

Lorn froze. "What do you mean?"

Aza fiddled with her shirt fabric, unsure and awkward about bringing up earlier. "I didn't mean to do anything without your consent or make you feel uncomfortable." Aza stammered, blurting out the rest of her sentence, "Honestly, I wasn't even sure what I was doing."

An incredulous look came over Lorn's face as he rushed over to Aza. He knelt in front of her. He gently took both of her hands, slightly cringing from her power, but forced himself to meet her gaze. A shocked smile appeared on his face as he struggled to find the words. "Aza, please look at me. You have nothing to apologize for. I appreciate you respecting my boundaries, but what you did for me today was something I didn't even know I needed. Your magic, and how you used it today was a gift. I didn't even know something so dark was plaguing my spirit." His hazel eyes pleaded with her, urging her to understand. "I have always been and will always be at a loss over Lakesh, but this darkness that clouded me and held me down has dissipated. I'm no fool to think it is gone forever, but you have provided me a light to follow and a brief respite from the onslaught of negativity."

Chagrined, a joyful smile filled Aza's face. "Good, because I think we should practice. I want to learn how to manipulate my magic in new ways. Train in all facets. With knowledge, physically and mentally."

Aza retreated to her room, her mind filled with anticipation of the busy days ahead. Finally, she felt like she was doing something productive and getting more answers.

Aza luxuriated in the bath again. She was not going to let the novelty of enjoying her bath go to waste, especially since traveling in the woods with little to no bathing. Afterwards her mind was still abuzz, excitement and anticipation trilled within her.

Departing her room, she took up her prior path from the night before and followed her footsteps to the same balcony. The night sky was not as clear as the night prior, puffy clouds covered the stars their brilliance dimmed. Aza didn't mind; she still imagined the constellations and where they would be placed beneath. Her fingers traced the vague shapes, her mind filling in the gaps obscured by the clouds, reviewing the new constellations Lord Aldrich had taught her. Peace and calm enveloped her amongst the dark embrace of the night. She recited them, her mind wandering across the sky. Lost in thought, the balcony glass door creaked open causing her to jump slightly. Aza resisted a smile as Lord Aldrich came to stand beside her.

"Back again?" His voice hid his own smile.

"Mmhmm." Aza's focus remained on the sky even though Lord Aldrich loomed closer.

"Oron told me of your studies, and Lorn approached me about your training."

Aza spared a glance over her shoulder. Lord Aldrich wore a loose white tunic and black pants. The sleeves were rolled up to his elbow and the collar swept into a small vee, revealing a patch of smooth, light brown skin. Aza flicked her gaze back up his fathomless dark brown eyes and he smirked. She rolled her eyes and turned her attention back to the sky. "Thank you for the use of your library. It is beautiful. I'm excited to learn about everything."

"Is there anything in particular you are studying or training for?" Lord Aldrich questioned.

"Everything and nothing," Aza replied.

Lord Aldrich arched an eyebrow at her answer.

"It is difficult to explain my memory and thoughts."

"I see. Well, if there is anything I can assist with, please let me know."

Two things came to the forefront of Aza's mind. "Yes actually, I have a request, and then a question." Lord Aldrich inclined his head to indicate he was listening and for her to proceed.

"I would like to accompany you one of these days during your lordly duties. I want to see what you do and how you operate. If you would like to use my magic, I want to see who you truly are."

"Done. Name the day and you are welcome to join."

Aza's lips quirked. She fought the smile pressing her lips together.

"Now what is your question?" Lord Aldrich's eyes lit up, intrigued by what she was going to ask.

"Why aren't you affected by me?"

"What do you mean?" He leaned closer, like he was testing the limits of her power, further proving her point.

"My power is overwhelming for all MagicBlessed. Whenever anyone contacts my skin, my power causes them to recoil or cringe. Yet when you touched my hands, you betrayed nothing." Aza examined her hands and Lord Aldrich neatly folded his over one another.

"Would you like to try again?" Lord Aldrich offered his hand to Aza. Her eyes flickered between his hand and his expectant face. Facing the challenge, she reached out her hand to clasp his. His rough hand formed around hers and she fought the chill that rose up her spine.

They held each other's hand, each not daring to break the bond or look away. She could feel the magic roiling through his body. He was strong and whatever was beneath lay hidden below the surface. Her magic rose up in response exploring his own. Her eyes narrowed, he was holding back something. His power was immense. He saw her look of skepticism and smirked. Aza kept her tone even, feigning boredom. "Nothing?"

Lord Aldrich yanked his arm forward, causing her to lose her footing and pulling her into his body. He clutched her, his face a mere breadth away. "If you are asking if I feel the need to cringe from you, I would say no. I think it is quite the opposite."

Aza cleared her head and pushed him away, indignation fueling her anger. He chuckled while she stumbled back.

"Tricks don't suit you," Aza huffed and leaned on the balcony, pointedly ignoring him.

"Oh I think they do." His voice slithered around her body, coiling tight. She tried to shake it off, but it gripped her tighter, flaring heat throughout her. He chuckled again and joined her at the balcony. Aza groaned in irritation, refusing to give in.

A few moments passed in silence, when he sighed. "Can we try again?" Lord Aldrich inquired, his voice sincere.

Aza looked at him and cocked her head. "No tricks this time?"

"No tricks, I promise." He held his hand out to her, a truce wavering between them. She gripped it, searching his face for any type of reaction.

"Anything?"

Lord Aldrich closed his eyes, searching for the words to explain. "I feel your power, your magic, it is there, but it doesn't overwhelm me like it does to others."

Intrigued, Aza asked him another question, "Do you mind if I try something?"

"Of course not, please feel free."

Aza closed her eyes, concentrating on her reserves of magic. She sent it over to Lord Aldrich's form, the magic coating him like a layer of pure sunlight. Her eyes remaining closed, his magic rose up to greet hers. It brightened and expanded under her touch. Despite her eyes being closed, she saw the shining outline of his body. His magic melding to hers, embracing it. His magic was a tightened musical string and if her magic touched it, the note rang out pure and melodic throughout her body. She pushed her magic farther, feeling his power, feeling everything.

"Aza," Lord Aldrich's voice was ragged and raw. Her eyes snapped open.

Clarity struck her like lightning from the sky. "You have as much power as me," she whispered. "Why don't you use it? Why do you need *me* to remake the world?"

Lord Aldrich stumbled over his words, choosing them carefully, "It is...tricky. I don't have access to it." Skeptical, Aza kept pushing. "I know what I felt and saw. Your magic is powerful, possibly even more than mine! You are hiding something."

"I cannot tell you, at least not yet."

Furious at the deception Aza turned to storm off. Lord Aldrich reached out, grabbed her wrist, and pinned her in place.

Aza sent a wisp of flame to sear his fingertips. He released his grip cursing to himself. "I apologize for grabbing you, but will you please let me explain?"

Aza didn't want to waste her breath on him. There was something bigger he was hiding. Why send Lorn to retrieve her from the Well if Lord Aldrich had equally strong magic? It didn't make sense. As her footsteps pounded away as she spoke, her back to him, "I knew not to trust anyone, and you proved me right."

Aza didn't even realize she made it back to her room until she stopped in front of the door. She yanked it open and slammed it, leaning her back against the door for support.

Her magic writhed throughout her body, ready to do damage.

Trust no one. Trust no one, she repeated.

She knew this, but she was still surprised at his deception. She walked over to her fireplace, casting her magic to light a fire. She sat down in front of it, watching the flames flicker back and forth. She focused on her breath as the flames hypnotized her. With the flames calling to her, she succumbed, manipulating the flames to create various forms, shapes and animals. The creation of fire helped to bank the power itching to flow out of her. Forms in the flames rose and she molded then crushed them playing with them like dough. Sometimes sparks would fly from the fire, her temper aiding the flame, her magic a bit too much to keep contained.

Good. She could not, would not be contained.

She let herself become lost to the ritual, siphoning her magic off, feeling a small release bit by bit, her mind calming. Finally, her chest had relaxed, the tightness within had made it difficult to breathe or to think. She loosened a breath. If they were to spend a lot of time here to find more answers, she needed to ignore all other feelings. Focus on the task at hand.

They all couldn't be trusted.

After some time, she abandoned the fire and wrestled beneath the covers of her bed. Tossing and turning she eventually stilled her body long enough to drift into a sleep or as close to sleep as she would get.

21

"The mind is extraordinary. Who knows what depth of magic dwells deep within?"

Excerpt from *The Secrets of our Magic* by Yorune of Gara

Aza hiked through the woods. She shielded a hand over her eyes, scanning her surroundings.

Where was she?

A forest greeted her. Not one of darkness and decay like the Hinterlands, but one that teemed with life, vibrant in each hidden corner and uncovered rock.

The light filtered through the leaves as Aza took small tentative steps. A deer pranced between the trees in front of her and darted off. Instinct took over and she decided to chase after it. The deer led her through the woods, running and veering through the trees delicately skipping over the exposed limbs of the tree roots.

Aza followed, her footsteps light and breathing unlabored. The deer halted in its tracks and stared back at her. It was delicate and strong, the fur a light brown with cream-colored streaks running through it like someone mistakenly poured milk on it.

Each step she took carefully, mindful of the branches and twigs snapping underfoot. The deer's soft brown eyes held Aza's own as she crept toward it. Closer and closer, her arm reached out and she almost touched its soft face. The deer waited for her, assessing her.

A distinct sound cut through the forest. A tight string being drawn back. Aza's eyes widened as she processed what the sound was. To her right an arrow pierced the air. Horror filled Aza's face as she realized what was about to happen. She threw a wall of wind to block the arrow and divert its course. The deer, now startled, departed, elegantly prancing through the dense forest. Aza had lost her chance, unsure exactly what would have happened if she touched the deer.

Anger fueled her as she turned on her heels, abruptly scanning the tree line for the person who loosened the arrow. Twigs snapped and crunched as the person revealed themselves and walked over, outfitted in hunting clothes, a bow in hand. It was a man.

He was stunning.

Aza clenched her teeth, willing herself to forget this detail. He had tried to attack a deer that she had a connection with. The man had brown skin, the deep color of chestnuts harvested in fall, and straight, rich brown hair, the same color as his skin, fell to his shoulders. His face was enticing. It drew her in and the air around him seemed to shimmer from his magic. His moss green eyes lit up at the sight of her.

Aza would not be cowed by his good looks. She released her righteous anger and spewed at him, "What in the Darkness below do you think you are doing?"

Taken aback, he retreated a step, his hands up in supplication. "I am a hunter." His voice was like melted honey, smoothing over her, covering her. He repeated slowly as if she didn't understand, "I am a hunter...I was hunting the deer." He gestured to the woods behind her.

Her fury rose. "I understand what a hunter is." Her voice ground out each word. Now it was her turn to act like he was slow in the head. "Why did you shoot your arrow, when I was clearly next to it."

He repeated, a small glint in his eye, "I am a hunter. I hunt things."

This conversation was going nowhere, and he was clearly teasing her. Her magic crackled at the end of her knuckles, begging her to use it. The hunter sensing her magic, tilted his head in assessment, and his own magic swelled in response. She felt the ground shift beneath her feet, the layers of earth waiting for his command to move.

Seething she glared at him. "I'm leaving," she announced. Keeping her anger as a shield she stormed away, her footsteps loud and heavy on the forest floor. The illusion shattered. It was not the peaceful fleeting moment she had shared with the deer. Now she felt like an interloper, like she did not belong here in this sacred space.

"Wait."

She ignored the hunter and trudged on. His silken voice followed her wrapping itself around her. "Why was the deer important?"

Why was the deer so important to her? She didn't know, but it still tugged deep within her, akin to how the night sky beckoned to her. Like she belonged to those faraway stars up above. She whirled around, finding him mere feet away. His beauty was even more stunning up close.

"It doesn't matter why the deer was important, it matters that it *was* important." She flicked her eyes to the surrounding trees and back to his ethereal eyes. They pinned her in place. "You saw me reach out to the deer, saw me..." Aza failed to finish her sentence. Unclear how to exactly explain what occurred. "Yet you released your arrow anyway." Her magic writhed around her arm, and began thrumming within her like the pounding of a war drum, the closer she stepped towards him. She was captivated, but the anger at what he had done was a barrier.

"I am sorry, but I am a hunter. It's in my nature." He stood there unmoving, the bow slung across his back.

She waved her hand in the air dismissively. "Apology accepted. Now I need to leave." She marched away, unsure of the direction she needed to head, but she wanted to gain distance between her and this strange man.

The sun shone directly overhead. The forest trees were a soft white embedded with streaks of brown. The leaves looked like the sheerest paper dappled in oranges, yellows and light greens. A breeze blew through the trees, causing a slight applause from the leaves. This was a beautiful place; it would be a shame to leave so soon.

"Are you lost?" The man followed her, his question slowing her retreat.

"I'm...not quite sure." Abashed at being vulnerable to a stranger, she turned away from him again, taking in the beautiful forest around them. Why was she here? Where was she supposed to be?

"Would you like help?" He appeared beside her, his eyebrow raised waiting for a response. Despite their initial meeting, maybe he could help her return to where she belonged.

Tentatively, she met his eyes and nodded. They hiked through the forest in silence, following winding dirt trails, the trees a captive audience to the two lone beings trekking through its domain.

"What is your name?" Aza's question disrupted the stillness and echoed around them.

"I am called many things but let us avoid those for now."

"Why, what am I supposed to call you?"

"I do not want to call attention to myself, for there are those who seek me." He stated it matter-of-factly, like it wasn't a mysterious and vague answer riddled to confuse her.

Aza rolled her eyes and looked around at the quiet forest. "People will seek you in here?" Her arms stretched to the air around them. He didn't answer the question, only walked beside her, the silence lengthening between them.

He whispered, "I never said it was people."

Aza couldn't fight the shudder that rose up her spine. She sighed, paused her walking and put her hands on her hips, fed up with the mysteries that swirled around her. "Where are we?"

He stopped in his tracks and held her stare, a small smile crept along his face. "Don't you know? This is your mind."

Aza backtracked, her steps faltering as her foot snapped a twig the sound like a bone snapping. Her hand floated up to feel her head, the phantom pain pulsing beneath her palm.

"What?" The question was not for him, but a question for herself, to try and gain some level of composure. Her voice drifted and wove through the tree trunks circling around her. "Why are you here then?"

He took a definite step forward crossing the invisible threshold toward her. "You called me here."

The ground beneath her wobbled, but she forced herself to stand tall, staring at the stranger with his luminescent, green eyes. "No, I didn't, I would remember it. I don't even know who you are!

Aza firmed her legs and squared her shoulders back. She would not lose her footing or her mind. Her magic crackled along the edges of her fingertips urging her to release her power. But if this was her mind, couldn't she just wake up instead?

The man leaned forward, his lips nearing the edge of her ear. She froze. If he touched her, she would incinerate him. His silken voice dropped to a whisper like one between lovers, "You called me here, my stars. If you are unhappy with it, wake up." He pulled back to take in her frustrated expression.

"Fine," she bit out.

He bowed his head slightly and said, "Until we meet again."

Aza couldn't stand his brashness and swaggering stance. She sent a quick blast of magic to knock him off his feet. He flew backward to the forest floor. He rolled, sat up, his mouth agape. She winked at him, shock evident on his face. She swore she imagined before she opened her eyes, a mischievous grin spread across the man's face.

"Wake up," she commanded herself. Bolting up in bed, her head swiveled quickly scanning the room she was in. The same marble castle. The same decadent room in Lord Aldrich's castle.

What had just happened?

The next morning Aza debated telling Lorn about her dream. She mulled over it again and again, deciding whether she was being dishonest if she withheld it from him. Was she losing her mind? All these illusions and dreams bombarded her thoughts every day. She didn't know what to give credence to.

~

Over breakfast, she disclosed Lord Aldrich's hidden depth of power. Lorn had no conclusions why he would have such hidden power and why he never demonstrated it in front of people.

"More pieces of the puzzle," he murmured to himself, running a hand through his hair.

Aza failed to mention her strange dream last night.

Crossing the castle grounds, a thick fog enveloped the entire castle, misting them as they hurried to the library.

Upon entering, Oron already had a table and chairs ready for them. Books lay open on the table with various sheets of parchment and quills. His frail body turned, and his steps quickened in excitement. Aza tried to clear her mind of the prior night, as they sat through another lesson.

Oron taught them about the history of the five provinces. A weathered map lay in front of them. The curling edges were held in place by thick heavy tomes. Oron spoke, his voice even tempered and experienced. He clearly loved teaching and sharing information with others. The five provinces were comprised of: Gara, Iyera, Verta, Kreeha, and Neria. Each province had distinct climates. Iyera was a coastal and temperate climate, Kreeha was hot and arid, Verta was rich in farmland, occasional woods dotting the land, and Gara was a consistently rainy province, their pine trees growing to impressive heights.

Even though the information wasn't too exciting, Aza listened trying to remember every detail mentioned. Oron had failed to teach on one of the provinces. "What about Neria?"

Oron paused and gathered his thoughts. When he spoke, his voice was grave, "There isn't much. They are a remote mountain province. They rarely deign to travel down and interact with the rest of the MagicBlessed. They are ruthless killers and few who travel into Neria come back out." Aza listened to every word Oron said, her gaze unwavering. Oron prattled on about how the five provinces, excluding Neria, traded freely with one another, providing each other with resources including food, minerals, and materials.

If Neria wanted to trade, they would send an envoy down. The envoys would rarely speak, their faces impassive. Oron mentioned it was rare to see a Nerian, but it had not always been the case. Long ago, the people of Neria would travel carefree throughout the other provinces. Only since the creation of the Hinterlands had Neria cut themselves off from the rest of the provinces, resorting to their own resources to survive.

"Why do people not travel to Neria?" Aza asked.

"The mountains are nearly impassable. Only with a guide, someone from Neria, would you be able to traverse it." His wrinkled finger pointed to the map outlining the border of Neria, "See here. All of the mountain passes surrounding the province provide a natural barrier, safety for them."

Aza pointed to the other edge of Neria, the one bordered by the ocean on the western side. "What about access from the ocean?"

Oron shook his head. "The cliff faces are steep. Their ocean does not resemble ours here in El'en. It isn't sandy shores." He shrugged his shoulders. "There just isn't any way to safely enter."

Aza let the conversation steer away from her sudden Neria obsession. She didn't know what overcame her, but it irked her. It was a needle poking at her unexpectedly, and perhaps she should listen to it. Maybe she would receive answers in Neria, the province shrouded in as much mystery as herself. Aza caught Lorn giving her a concerned look. She discreetly shook her head. She would share her concerns with him later after her thoughts had settled.

Oron dismissed them for lunch and Aza and Lorn pushed open the library doors. The fog had lingered obscuring the Wyra Ocean. They steered towards the kitchens greeting the chefs and workers. A few tentative smiles shot their way. Aza smiled to herself. The people were adjusting to her presence here.

After scarfing down their lunch, they went back to change in their rooms. Lord Aldrich had delivered their new clothes to each of them the prior day. Aza folded Melina's clothes with care and tucked them away. She donned the new clothing. It contoured to her body's shape, hugging in all the places it should. It wasn't Melina's craftsmanship, but it would do for now. Lorn was adorned in a similar outfit to hers and they fell in step together toward their private training room. The training room had bright windows filling the far wall, reflecting the white fog outside, the light almost blinding. The wood floors were bare with a weapons-rack and cushions pushed to the corner of the room. Lorn assessed the weapons rack and shook his head.

"Now, I'm not a warrior, but I can teach you a thing or two about fighting and hunting. I don't typically fight people, but I can teach you basics of footwork, hand to hand combat, and some weapons once we get to that." He faced Aza, his hazel eyes locking onto hers.

"Ready?"

~

Aza was exhausted. Her body ached, sweat dripped from her brow. She used her shirt to wipe up anymore that still dripped from her. She lay sprawled on the floor of the training room, the light outside dimming as the evening began. She focused on her breathing, in and out. Lorn did know what he was doing. He ran her through different footwork and punches, what to do if an attacker was in front of her, behind her, to the side. For her first day it was a lot. He was an equal size to her, but his muscles had pummeled her, even though he held back his power and strength.

"You are a bastard," Aza muttered from the floor. Each word was a strain to get out. She wasn't uncoordinated, merely lacked conditioning—unused to the various stances, moves, angles, agility and balance required for real combat. There were so many possible scenarios, it was a challenge to memorize them all.

Lorn barely had a thin sheen of swear after their hours of practice. He chuckled softly. "I used to say the same things when I trained."

Gingerly Aza pushed herself up to a seated position so her upper body leaned back, her palms and arms extended behind her. "Who did you train with?"

"My mom and dad." Lorn walked over, handed her a glass of water, and sat down next to her, his feet planted on the ground, arms resting casually on his knees. "My mom trained me more with hand-to-hand combat and my dad honed my hunting skills." Aza must have looked shocked because Lorn added, "They both trained me, but that was what they focused on." The training room filled with a restless quiet.

Aza dreaded asking the next question. "Lorn, where are your parents?" In the weeks of traveling together, he mentioned his childhood, but she never directly asked that question.

He shifted slightly, the movement small and unsure. "My mom died from an illness that overtook her body." Lorn hastily added, "Our magic doesn't have a cure for all illnesses."

Reluctant to ask, Aza forced herself to do it. "And your dad?"

"He went hunting in the woods and something must have attacked him. I found him with gashes and wounds laced over his body. He was too far gone for me to do any healing." Lorn heaved a sigh.

Horrified Aza thought of her powers. She was sure she could easily have healed both of his parents. If only she was around then. Aza reached out and clasped a hand to Lorn's thigh.

He looked down at her hand, noting the small reassurance she offered. "It was a while ago now. It still stings, but I have dealt with it."

The following question came out of her mouth without thinking. "Was this before or after Lakesh?"

Lorn stilled, his body tense underneath her hand. She let the question linger, not brushing it off or bombarding him with more. Eventually Lorn whispered, "After."

Even though Aza knew it would hurt him, she wanted to pose the question for Lorn to consider. "Will you tell me about her?"

The room was still and darkened slightly as the sun set below the horizon. She waited patiently, not pushing him, but allowing him to come to terms with the idea.

Years of stories poured forth. The love was evident as Lorn told her the story of how he had met his wife and how they had come to live in their small cottage on the edges of Verta. Lorn talked and talked into the night, the two of them resting in the training room as the night sky shone through the glass windows.

Aza absorbed everything, listening to this man share the greatest treasure of his life. His passionate voice wove together the stories they shared. He explained how they met at a market and Lakesh had immediately ensnared him. They bartered over wares, and he was entranced with her sly tongue and cunning mind.

Every month when the market was set up, he would seek her out and their relationship bloomed. Attraction and sharp wit turned into love, and they eventually married. Lakesh lived with him in his small cottage. His parents had both died a little while after Lakesh had met them. The couple had met when Lorn was twenty-one and they were married at twenty-three. They were married for seven years before Lakesh was brutally and abruptly killed by a Howler. Although Aza never asked Lorn's age, she calculated him to be around thirty two. So young for such trauma—still considerably young for the MagicBlessed people who can live up to two hundred years. So much trauma and sorrow for one so young.

As Lorn finished telling his stories, he looked around and realized how late it was. They rushed to the kitchens, begging for a small snack from the cooks and walked back to their rooms. Aza was happy she had asked about Lakesh. There was a lightness to Lorn's features. The shadows that darkened him daily were lightening, if only for a moment. She reflected on what that would feel like. To meet one's soul in the body of another, to have it ripped away from you. For a brief moment, Aza felt like she had experienced that before.

They bid each other good night and departed, ready to bathe in hot water after today's training. She let the hot water soak her aching muscles. The day was long, successful but long, and Aza needed sleep. She climbed out of the tub and groaned. Her muscles would be fatigued and sore tomorrow, Darkness below, even her mind was fatigued. She collapsed into bed, her body limp, ready for sleep to take her.

22

"One must hone their body, their mind, but especially their spirit. Without their spirit, one cannot wield their magic properly. It can be dangerous—an untrained spirit."
Common teachings on magic from Neria

Flowers bloomed around her. Pretty ones in hues of pinks, purples, and whites filled the ground creeping along her ankles. It was a nice cool day, the sun high in the sky with random clouds punctuated throughout. It was beautiful.

Aza released a sigh and glanced around. At the edge of the flower field was the deer. She locked eyes with it and strode purposely towards it. She didn't want to spook it again. This time she would be able to touch it. Her footsteps were muted, the flowers bowing beneath her weight. She neared the deer; its soft brown eyes were as enchanted with her as she was with it like it revered her presence, denizens bowing before their ruler. The breeze shifted and the deer glanced over Aza's shoulder. It turned and bounded off, leaving Aza bereft. She knew who it would be. Clenching her hands she pivoted to glare at the man, the hunter, behind her. He stood still, cocking his head at her with a faint smile on his face. An irritated sound erupted out of Aza as she stalked away from him. "Why are you here?"

He trailed behind her, his voice smooth despite her punishing pace. "Why are *you* here?" he asked.

"It is my own mind. Leave it," she snapped at him.

He was not cowed by her anger, instead he kept following the path she paved through the flowers. "Why are you upset?"

Aza couldn't specifically articulate what frustrated her about the man's presence. She didn't know why the deer was important to her, but it seemed important to reach and that was enough—like it held her unanswered questions. She wasn't going to explain all of this to a strange man inside her very own mind. Needing an outlet for her frustration, she swirled around and sent a wave of wind towards him, to knock him off balance like their last encounter.

The man had learned. He coiled his own magic around him, pulling the earth around his feet to hold him in place. His luminescent moss green eyes sparkled, excited at Aza's challenge. "Would you like to spar?" His voice slid around her, enticing her.

She had enough of him, and she wanted to blow off some steam, both mentally and magically. Her body nearly hopped with the anticipation of the challenge.

Turning to face him, Aza brushed a coil of hair behind her ear, her feet planted. She closed her eyes, the breeze wove around her, coursed through her hair and the back of her neck. She relaxed her body, her mind stilling. She felt the pulse of the life forces around her, the subtle movements of the man across from her. Her eyes flashed open, and she knew the silver roiled within. The chaos she kept reigned within her, she could now release, even if it was only in her mind. The man responded with a feral grin of his own and like a bell being struck they began.

Her magic tingled at his nearness. Aza ignored the sensation, instead she viewed the soft malleable ground around him and crumbled it, the pit a waiting beast ready to swallow him whole. He was fast and easily dodged her attack. She ignored the gaping hole in the ground and redirected her magic. The ground cracked where he stood, the earth splitting in two. He harnessed his own magic and battled hers, stitching together the jagged land, securing his footing.

The look of boredom on his face enraged her and Aza sent wave after wave of magic at him. She was frustrated by her inability to snare him. Then she attempted to encase him in ice. Water erupted up his torso and she began to freeze him in place. He broke out of it either through fire or his strength—she was unsure. The man kept moving and dodged her random attacks, each one chasing after him like a pack of rabid animals. She swirled the wind around him, twisting and trapping him within a tornado, the wind ripping at his clothes. Without any strain, he broke through it, the wind dying alongside him.

Aza would not let herself show surprise at the ease in which he eluded and escaped the assault of magic she hurled at him. With each dodge, he moved closer, each step encroaching on her space. He was toying with her. She thought back to Lorn's lessons. She *did* need to learn to use her body, instead of relying solely on her magic. He wasn't attacking her, only gaining ground. As he avoided each attack, his smirk grew wider. He was within grabbing distance and reached his arm out to her.

Consumed with thoughts of her friend Lorn, she hastily gathered the light within her and blasted it out. The light blinded him as she pulled a maneuver Lorn had practiced with her today. Before he could regain his vision, she spun behind him and wrapped her forearm around his throat.

"Yield." A quietness rippled throughout the field, everything holding its breath waiting for his response.

"Not quite, my stars." Fire burned her forearm and her grip loosened as he sent a blast of wind between them that left her flying backward. She braced herself, using her own power to break her fall. He stood across from her, unaffected, assessing how she would recover from the blow.

Pulling herself to her feet, she sprinted straight at him. His eye held the challenge, and he stood his ground waiting for her to approach. A veiled power deep within her begged for release—a power hidden within a small nook in the deep recesses of her mind. She coaxed it out, calling to that power, encouraging it to reveal itself. She acknowledged it, granting it to rise. She was so close to him. Continuing to sprint, she allowed the power to rise, and shadows enveloped her. Mid-sprint the shadows transported Aza behind him, and she tackled him to the ground.

She straddled him, her hands around his throat. "Yield." Her magic crackled, thriving from the challenge of fighting someone she considered an equal, someone who did not balk from her, someone who welcomed the power thrumming in her veins. Both of their chests heaved from the exertion of the sparring.

"Yield," she snarled, pressing down on his throat.

His mossy eyes flicked to her, and he faintly nodded. She smirked, satisfaction and victory reigning over her. She lessened the pressure and sat up on his lap. Aza became aware of what she was doing. This beautiful man lay before her, and she was straddled over him. She narrowed her eyes, knowing if she asked who he was it would get her nowhere. But it was the first time in a while she felt relief flow through her. The exhilaration of fighting and using her magic to the fullest extent helped to quiet the turmoil in her mind. The stresses that plagued her mind had receded. For now. These strange dreams of hers brought a weird moment of respite.

"You can leave now."

His eyes softened his voice as quiet as the flowers swaying in the breeze, "Is that what you wish?"

A moment of indecision flashed through her mind. He seized his opportunity, hooking his legs around hers and cradling her head as he reversed their positions. She lay pinned beneath him, his forearms cradled on either side of her head. She had no option but to stare straight back at him.

"If you wish me to leave, I can," he conceded. Aza bristled. "But I think this is the first time you have felt the extent of your magic, and I imagine it felt good." His voice caressed her, like warm honey being poured on her skin. Sticky and sweet, she was unable to rid herself of it. He leaned in close to her ear and whispered, "I will be here for you, my stars." He gracefully rose off her body and walked away the flowers yielding to each of his steps. "Until next time."

Aza opened her eyes. Her room in Lord Aldrich's castle was shrouded in darkness. It was still the middle of the night. Her heart pounded frantically.

~

The following week remained the same. Lorn and Aza followed the routine of visiting the library, studying, then training on her fighting skills, practicing hand to hand combat and swordplay. The nighttime strolls disappeared. She forgot Lord Aldrich and instead focused on the mysterious man who haunted her dreams. Each night she was transported to a unique location and sparred with the strange man using her magic. They often bickered with one another, taunting each other, but it was her guilty pleasure. Aza was honing her magic, something she had never considered and something she could never practice with anyone else. Each time they practiced the deer was absent and eventually, she forgot it. When she woke, she never mentioned her nighttime dreams to Lorn. A small wedge of her own making was now separating them.

During their first week at the castle, Aza rarely saw Lilit, Gravers, or Lord Aldrich. She was consumed with her studies, forgetting about her request to shadow Lord Aldrich until he approached her in the library one day. Oron rose with a small bow of his head. "My lord." With begrudging respect, Lorn and Aza rose, unsure of why he was here.

Lord Aldrich turned to Aza. "Would you still like to shadow me for a day to see how my city operates?" Aza was stunned by Lord Aldrich's professionalism, he didn't even appear fazed by their interaction a week ago when she had burned him. Her eyes flickered down to his hand. He followed her gaze.

"Yes, of course," Aza responded.

"Very well. Will tomorrow work?"

Aza nodded, excited to see how the city operated and what the townsfolk truly thought of Lord Aldrich. When Lorn and Aza headed to their afternoon training session, an unexpected visitor lingered in the room. Aza halted, her eyes tilting down to take in Lilit. She picked her nails with one of her daggers, the edges glinting and sharp. "I heard you were training."

Lorn stiffly nodded. "We are, but it is a closed session."

Lilit flicked the dagger, embedding it into the wall. "I offer my services."

Aza brushed past her. "No thanks."

Lilit planted her feet, not retreating. "I'm sure he is a great teacher," she said her voice laced with sarcasm, "but there is a reason you should train with me."

"Oh, and why is that?" Aza replied haughtily, crossing her arms.

Lilit stormed up to Aza and said, "Block me." The punch came so fast Aza almost couldn't protect herself. She formed a solid wall of wind to block Lilit's punch, but Lilit was already moving on to the next. She danced around Aza landing light blows, her speed astounding, Aza couldn't even keep track as Lilit landed a punch, the force knocking Aza across the room. She glared across the room. She readied another blast of magic to teach Lilit a lesson. Then she faltered; Lilit was patiently waiting while Aza lay on the floor.

"See. You need me." Lilit walked over to Aza and crouched before her extending a hand. "My magic manifests differently than most people. I can use it to accelerate my speed and strength. It is rare, and many of us who have this ability are swept into the courts immediately to protect and train among the soldiers."

Pushing her pride aside, she took Lilit's hand and rose to her feet. Lilit did have a point and Aza would learn many beneficial tactics when sparring with her. "As long as it is alright with Lorn."

Lorn reluctantly agreed and their lessons continued. Lilit was to join them when she was available. She was a tough teacher. She accepted no excuses and expected the best out of her student. At the end of the lesson, while Aza fought to catch her breath, Lilit posed a question. "Have you begun training with magic? Or being attacked with both? It is a completely different method of attack." Aza and Lorn shook their heads.

Lorn added, "I wanted her to learn the basics first, then incorporate those tactics." He turned to Aza, explaining, "Right now we are only focusing on the fighting. But if you were truly fighting another person, you would never know what type of magic they have or what they could surprise you with. You could think you have the fight won, but the other fighter might burn the hilt of the sword you fight with or pull the ground out from under you. It presents many challenges when battling."

"We can add that later, when your skill improves."

Aza paused, considering their words carefully before answering. "Thank you for training with us today." Lilit's body tightened in surprise. Lorn and Aza left the room leaving Lilit still behind. Aza spared a glance over her shoulder. Lilit had grabbed another dagger and threw it at the wall. It embedded itself to the hilt, the wooden wall splintering, its cracked lines mocking Aza as she departed.

~

"Will you ever tell me your name?" The sand covered Aza's toes as she and the strange man sat overlooking the ocean. They recently finished practicing, as they had been for the past couple weeks. After each session she felt a relieved sense of exhaustion. Deep in her bones, her magic was spent, being sharpened every day. The man's hand went up to his face considering her.

"I can't." His mouth thinned, he turned to look back out over the rolling ocean. The water rushed up to meet their toes and retreated.

"Okay, then tell me why you are here?"

He sighed and turned to face her. "As I have told you before, you called me here." His eyes pierced her, and she ignored it. They were unsettling, but in a pleasant way. They reminded her of her own eyes, as if something ancient and unknown swirled beneath.

Aza leaned back on her hands and stared up at the sky. The weather shifted, the wind whipping her silver hair into her face, the temperature dropping. Suddenly the clouds broke open and rain poured down on them. They scrambled to their feet, searching for cover. A small cottage materialized at the edge of the beach. They ran for it, sand kicking up behind them as the rain dripped down their faces. Aza pushed her hair out of her face and pumped her arms back and forth, propelling her to reach the small house. The man raced alongside her.

Reaching the small, wooden door Aza opened it without hesitation. It was her mind after all, everything belonged to her. The small cottage was comfortably furnished. A plush couch and comfortable chairs formed a semi-circle in front of an empty fireplace. Aza and the man shared a brief look, her eyebrows raised, and they stepped inside. She lit a fire and used her magic to perform a cursory heating over her body and clothes to dry them. She walked over to the couch. The man followed her with his eyes. She sat, watching the fire crackling in front of her. The flames swirled and consumed, the embers crackling and sparking. The man sat next to her, the small cushion depressing under the additional weight. "Aza." She turned, startled by the use of her name—he rarely said it. They often sparred savagely and left with few words spoken.

She snapped her focus away from the hypnotic flames and met his unwavering gaze. There was no other way to explain his beauty besides ethereal. She supposed other people viewed her the same way. It drew her in, the deep raw power he possessed.

"Why the rain?"

"What?"

The side of his mouth curved up at her response. "This is your mind, why the sudden rain?"

She thought back to where they were sitting on the shore of the beach overlooking the waves. She went still and mumbled to herself, "I wanted to know your name."

He tilted his head reaching out to tenderly grasp her chin, forcing her to look into his eyes. His voice was soft, inquiring. "Why does it bother you to not know?"

She wrenched away from his grasp and turned to face away from him. "Why wouldn't I want to know? This is my mind, and there are so many mysteries consuming me. And you..." Her voice died out. She knew where the frustration stemmed from. Why she truly wanted to know. Her feelings had grown for him, and every time she awoke, she was left more confused than the day before. Her emotions and thoughts were muddled together. Was this all an illusion? What was real? Why was her existence shrouded in endless mystery?

This beautiful, ethereal man was before her, and she only wanted to enjoy this moment without thinking of all the consequences involved. His muscled arm snaked along the back of the couch, his body leaned closer, his eyes locked with hers. Closer and closer, until they were eye to eye. Her breath hitched at the invasion of her space. This close, she noticed his brown skin had a faint luster of gold woven throughout, like the sand sparkling upon the beach. His hand rested upon her cheek, cradling her head.

He repeated his question, "Why does it bother you?"

Because she was an oddity, because she wanted one normal thing and this person's name was one thing she wanted. She wanted to embrace him, but this too would fade. He wasn't real, he was only in her head. She finally answered his question, "It just does."

They stared at one another, their pairs of silver and green eyes locked together. A question lingered, and Aza nodded her agreement. Keeping his hand resting on her cheek, he leaned in, his lips softly brushing over hers. It was electric. This kiss was not a soft exploration but a wild joining similar to their contests of magic. They melded and moved together, her hands coming up to yank him closer. Their bodies met. She opened her mouth, an invitation for him to go further. His tongue entered slicking against hers. She was breathless.

This was ecstasy.

Aza's hands moved to the back of his head, her fingers flowing through the silky, dark brown strands. They were only kissing, but it felt like a rejoining of two broken pieces of glass. It was natural. Their magic and power washed over one another.

When she finally pulled away, Aza could feel her lips bruising from the kiss. Heat flared through her body. He looked wild, feral, like the kiss had been an undoing. His eyes glowed an even brighter green, the power pulsing around him. They both breathed heavily, taking in the other. A small voice sounded within her, *Aza don't.* It was faint, but she heard it. She needed this, needed him. He was a match and her body understood it. And yet...the voice wriggled its way in, placing a seed of doubt.

"I need to leave," Aza announced out of breath.

He widened his eyes in surprise. He leaned back, allowing her space and quickly masking his surprise with feigned indifference. "As you wish."

Aza cursed herself for leaving. She felt torn, unable to decide, but she had already told him she was going. She might as well follow through.

"Until next time, my stars."

Aza opened her eyes, finding herself in her room, alone.

23

Aza woke sore and tired. She tossed and turned in bed thinking only of the passionate kiss from her dream. Heat spiked throughout her body, pooling low. She begrudgingly rolled out of bed and freshened up in the bathroom. Aza tossed water on her face and checked herself in the mirror. There were no signs of anything marking her skin or her face. Nothing to show her encounter with the strange man. She was fooling herself, after all, no bruises or marks from their spars ever revealed themselves the following morning.

But she knew it was real, that kiss. Her fingers absentmindedly drifted to her lips caressing them, reliving the feel of him against her.

A knock on her door broke her from her spell, and Aza rushed over to open it. A servant bearing the Iyerian crest stood there. "Miss, if you and Lorn are ready I can escort you both to Lord Aldrich."

Aza nodded.

They followed the servant, keeping a swift pace behind him. Aza fought the yawn rising within her, covering it with her hand. Lorn leaned next to her. "Long night?"

Heat rose to her face, but she fought to hide it.

"Yeah, couldn't sleep." Aza didn't want to disclose the reason why and Lorn didn't pry.

The servant led them through hallways until they reached the throne room. Two chairs were pulled aside next to the main seat. Lord Aldrich perched near the edge of his throne and upon seeing them, met them in the middle of the room. Dismissing the servant, he faced them, his regal appearance forcing Aza to arch an eyebrow.

Typically, Lord Aldrich wore more casual clothing, but today he looked every part the ruling lord. The Iyerian crest was stamped along the back of his resplendent robe with shades of blues and whites to depict the Wyra ocean that bordered Iyera. The jacket was outlined in small bits of gold thread. His outfit alone must have cost a small fortune.

A crown forged from silver rested upon his brow. It mimicked the rise and fall of the ocean waves so exactly, Aza expected to see whitecaps piercing the top of each watery peak.

Lord Aldrich took a turn looking at Lorn and then Aza. A glint appeared in his eye and they flicked down to Aza's mouth and back up to her eyes. Aza's mouth thinned and her eyes narrowed at him. What was he playing at?

"Once a month, I hold an open forum for the people of my city to come and make requests, complaints, or any other matter they see fit to bring to my attention. I thought it would be a beneficial time for you to observe me." He gestured to the chairs placed on the edge of the room. "I only ask that you act as true shadows and only observe the proceedings. Do not interrupt or disrupt us." He looked to each of them for confirmation. Aza and Lorn agreed and headed over to their seats.

The throne room was beautiful. Aza had only caught brief glimpses of it in passing since other duties had kept her occupied elsewhere. Enormous glass windows filtered in the radiant light of the morning and highlighted Lord Aldrich's beechwood throne. Each piece hewn and gnarled like the ocean itself spat out the wood.

Guards stood around the room waiting for Lord Aldrich's orders to open the door and escort people in. Lilit and Gravers marched in from an adjacent door and took their place among the guards. Lord Aldrich seated himself on the large beechwood throne and motioned for the guards to open the doors. The outfit blended in perfectly with the throne, like he was the ocean upon which the throne buoyed.

Doors swung open, a cool blast of morning air filled the room. A queue of people lined up outside patiently waiting to see the Lord of Iyera. Aza and Lorn sat through the procession. Many were typical complaints about their houses, their land, their businesses.

Aza noted how Lord Aldrich ran his affairs. He listened to the people trying his best to come up with solutions. He gave the citizens all his attention, never once straying. Aza was surprised how well he kept his attention. It was tedious, and as the day wore on, Aza forced herself not to squirm in her chair.

Everything progressed smoothly, and Lord Aldrich was about to call a close to the forum when two women walked in. They were coated in dust, their clothes slightly tattered and frayed at the edges. They held something in their hands that Aza couldn't see.

Both women inclined their heads towards Lord Aldrich. One had short blonde hair, the sides shaved, her brown eyes sharp and shrewd. "My Lord, my wife and I run the vineyards for most of Iyera." The blonde woman motioned to the short woman beside her, her long brunette hair woven back into multiple braids out of her face, and her curvy figure outfitted in soft linens.

Lord Aldrich nodded, encouraging them to continue, his light brown hair falling along the side of his face.

"We came across something recently. We think you should see." Lord Aldrich rose from his throne and strode over to the two women. In their hands they cradled something precious, their fingers unwilling to open and show what was inside.

Lord Aldrich tried to coax them with a soft smile. "Ladies, I will need to see what you are holding if I am to help you."

The blonde woman audibly gulped and began prattling on, her voice filling the throne room. "We were tending to our grapes, as we usually do, and we thought this was a fluke, but when we came out later, all of our grapes are beginning to look like this." Her fingers unfurled, revealing the precious grapes beneath. The grapes, normally a purple hue, had darkened, to black. Only a few were left on the cluster.

"Where are the rest of the grapes?"

The woman cleared her throat. "That's the thing, my lord. They had turned into ash on the vine. They are gone."

The people in the throne room audibly gasped. Lord Aldrich tried to hide the shock from his face. Aza turned to Lorn, confused at why everyone's skin was paling. Even Lorn looked sickly, his body still. The guards glanced at one another, fear residing in their faces. Aza had no choice but to watch the scene in front of her to try and gain more information.

Lilit and Gravers approached as Lord Aldrich gently took the grapes from the woman's hand. He whispered something to them, and they dispersed. "Please do not panic," he assured the gathered crowd. "We will figure out what is happening to your crops." Lord Aldrich went on expressing his sympathy and ushered everyone out of the throne room. While busy trying to smooth things over, Aza and Lorn slipped out, heading to their rooms.

Lorn nudged her past the door frame and swiftly shut the door behind him. Aza waited for him to explain as he searched the room, closing windows and drapes. Something was wrong. Something was deeply wrong.

"Something is wrong," he announced, his thoughts echoing her own.

She stepped close and mimicked Lorn's hushed tone. "Why? I don't understand."

Lorn only looked at her frantically seeking something. "The Well. It is the reason for our prosperity, why our people, the MagicBlessed, are never left wanting." Nausea built in her stomach. She knew what he was going to say next would change everything. "If something is happening to our crops, it means the magic is failing." Loud buzzing filled her ears. She could barely hear what Lorn said next. "Something is wrong with the Well."

24

"Are not all empires built upon secrets? I think it is a requirement to be considered a leader of a province."
How The Land of Ithilia Came To Be by Ursu of Kreeha

Lorn stayed in Aza's room. They sat on the edge of her bed, stunned. A sharp knock broke them from their stillness, and Lorn went to open the door. Gravers' weathered face peered in, and he gruffly said, "Come with me."

He led them through the twisted hallways, the beauty of the outdoors shining in, a mockery of their own turmoil. Aza's heart pounded with each step. What did it all mean? Why did she feel at her core that she was inexplicably connected to it all? Gravers led them into one of Lord Aldrich's many studies. Lilit, Oron, and Lord Aldrich were already seated in the room, their expressions grim.

Lord Aldrich lifted his head to greet them, the crown slipping down and the silver glint catching upon the marbled room. "Thank you for coming. I felt this information was related to both of you." The withered and twisted grapes lay in the center of the table, an ominous threat to the prosperity of the provinces. Aza and Lorn filed in, found two vacant seats, and sat down. "Something is happening to the Well." Lord Aldrich stared at Aza. She had to fight to keep from flinching under his unrelenting gaze. "We aren't sure what is happening, but we will continue to keep an eye on it. This is the first we have heard of crops failing. If it progresses, the five provinces could descend into chaos." His statement lay thick in the room like a noxious fume.

Lorn interrupted the stillness, "What is the worst that could happen?"

Oron faced Lorn, his bright blue eyes dim and defeated. "If it progresses, we might lose our magic altogether."

"Do you still have your powers?" Lord Aldrich directed the question at Aza.

She bristled. "Yes, of course." She did a cursory scan of her body. Her magic lay there dormant like a sleeping beast waiting for her to awaken it.

"Good, let's take that as a good sign so far." Lord Aldrich looked at each of them in order. "We keep this a secret, and we research why the Well is failing us. We do not want mass panic."

"The gossip will be hard to manage in the city my lord," Gravers asserted. Aza briefly forgot he was Lord Aldrich's private guard.

Lilit nodded her agreement.

Lorn sat still in his chair. Aza could see his mind whirling through everything, filtering through why they were here. Finally, he addressed Lord Aldrich, "Thank you for sharing this, but why did you invite us here?" Lorn challenged Lord Aldrich, seeking truth.

"I did it as a sign of my good faith towards the both of you. I do not seek to use you." Aza schooled her face to remain neutral but internally she scoffed at such a remark. She saw how he viewed her power, like a hungry beast waiting to devour it the moment she let her guard down—the nights on the balcony probably a ploy to gain her trust.

"We are going to research this as much as possible. If it is as I suspect, we may need to hone Aza's magic to defeat it." Lord Aldrich's eyes sharpened on her, as if seeing the raw magic potential underneath her skin. She fought the chill that skittered down her spine.

Lorn leaned forward, placing his forearms on the table. "And what do you think she will be facing?" his voice demanded.

Lord Aldrich stifled a response, "I... cannot say yet. But if it is what I fear, we are all in trouble." A heaviness settled in the room and a pit formed in Aza's stomach.

Oron's craggy voice broke through the stillness, "Keep to your studies, Aza. We will keep an eye on everything and let you know what we discover." Oron nodded his head towards Aza and Lorn.

Lord Aldrich dismissed them and Aza and Lorn walked back to their room in stilted silence. Aza opened her large wooden door, the hinges creaking, grating on her ears.

Once in the safety of his rooms Aza turned to Lorn. "What do you think it is?"

Lorn ran a hand through the hair falling down his forehead. "I have no idea." He paced the room, releasing the frantic energy that built up during their meeting. It was like he needed the physical exertion to work through all the thoughts and ideas in his head. He stopped, searching her for answers. "Like I have told you before, I am not as highly schooled as the people here within this court. I have no idea what could cause the destruction of magic within our land. I didn't even know something like this could happen." He took Aza in, assessing her as if she held all the answers. His voice was soft, probing. "Do you feel different? Or anything amiss?"

Aza gripped her body like it might reveal an answer. "No, nothing has changed." They trudged to the edge of the bed, defeat slumping their shoulders. "I hate admitting Lord Aldrich is right, but let's try not to focus on it and we will learn more within the coming weeks." Hope rose in her voice. "Maybe my training will come in handy."

"Yes, let's stay focused on our training, and let me know if you feel anything change or diminish with your magic." Lorn's eyes creased with determination. "We still have half the day left. Would you like to go now?"

Aza agreed to his offer, the need to focus on her physical body was overwhelming. She wanted out of her mind, the ceaseless thoughts careening around leaving her with little rest. They headed to the training room and spent hours focused on fighting maneuvers and strengthening.

Exhausted and drenched, they trudged back to their rooms. As they turned the corner in sight of their rooms, Aza realized they hadn't eaten yet. She turned to leave, motioning for Lorn to go rest. She didn't mind grabbing food for the both of them. The torchlights in the hallway flickered as she navigated her way towards the kitchens. She could have asked for a servant to grab the food for her, but she preferred to grab it herself and mingle with the kitchen staff, allow them to become acquainted with her and acclimated to her power.

Hushed whispered voices carried to her along the corridor. Aza stilled, silencing her steps.

"You need to hurry this along," a furious voice grated.

"I'm well aware of the timing, Lilit." The voice was quiet but firm.

"Clearly not enough! The grapes are a sign. We need to do this, it will only worsen."

"I cannot move any faster than I am. We need her willing. She is too skittish right now."

The distinct sound of a blade being pulled rang through the hallway.

Lilit's voice rasped, venom coating her every word, "I. Want. Him. Back."

Lord Aldrich's voice rippled throughout the corridor. "Remove the blade from my throat. If you kill me, you kill him."

The snick of the blade sounded as it went back into the sheath. Aza remained quiet. If they found her here, what would happen? Footsteps stomped her way, Aza scrambled to a dark alcove hoping the shadows and the angle of the torchlight kept her in the darkness. Lilit marched past her hiding spot, unshed tears glistened in her eyes. Aza released her magic, coating herself in darkness using the familiar caress of long hidden shadows to shield her silver hair and eyes from being spotted. Lilit paused in the middle of the corridor, turning back and forth as if tracking Aza's footsteps. A muscle ticked in her cheek then Lilit continued on.

When she was gone, Aza loosened a pent-up breath, reeling back her magic, the shadows dimming. She turned from her alcove back into the hallway. Her breath caught in her throat as Lord Aldrich stood across from her. His casual stance belied the fact that his eyes swallowed her whole. He was a hunter, and he had caught his prey.

"Out late to be wandering the castle?"

"Why do I need to explain myself to you? You gave Lorn and I permission to explore." Aza would not let herself submit to him.

"It was only a question."

She approached the situation with a cavalier tone. "I'm grabbing food from the kitchen for Lorn and I."

Lord Aldrich eyed the alcove, his eyebrows raised in a silent question.

"I thought I saw something of interest on the wall and went to check it out." She crossed her arms surveying the marble walls and flickering torchlights. "You know your castle is very impressive, I hate to miss all of the architectural details." She sauntered over to him, keeping her expression cool, her attitude cocky. Maybe her irreverent attitude would conceal the beating of her heart. Of what she had overheard.

A smirk crossed his face as his eyes scanned her.

"Do you mind, *my lord?*" She nodded for him to move aside so she could squeeze past. His eyes stayed locked onto hers. Unmoving. Aza counted her heartbeats. One. Two. Three. Slowly, he stepped to the side allowing her to pass.

"Always a pleasure, Aza."

Aza brushed by him, keeping her steps even despite her desire to run. She would not turn around. Instead, she would show how little concern she had for her back being exposed. Aza left Lord Aldrich in the corridor, the feel of his eyes boring straight into her.

Only when she had made it down to the kitchens, a multitude of corridors between her and Lord Aldrich, did relax. She leaned back against the wall, the cool marble calming her, allowing her to focus on the feel of it beneath her skin. Her eyes shut. She focused on the rhythm of her breath. She needed to rush back to Lorn. She needed to know who Lilit wanted back and why would Lord Aldrich kill him? They wanted to use her for something, and she was determined to find out what it was.

With her breathing under control, she slipped into the kitchen and left carrying platters of food on her arm. She carefully made her way back to her rooms, pausing to listen if other people lingered in the hallways. Once in her room, she pounded her fist on Lorn's door. He opened it, his eyes widening as he took in Aza's panicked expression. He ushered in her, locking the door behind him. Aza laid the food out on his dining table and sat down in a chair. She folded her body, her forearms resting on her thighs, head hung low.

Lorn rushed to her side crouching next to her. "Aza, what is wrong?"

Aza straightened back up and saw the frantic desperation in Lorn's face. She took another steadying breath and said, "We have another problem to deal with."

* * *

~

When Aza finished, Lorn leaned back in his chair across from her. His hair fell again in front of his face, the inky black strands covering his eyes. He hastily pushed it back, the hair forced back into submission. "We need to talk to Lilit, find out what she knows."

"When?"

Lorn considered for a moment. "We typically see her during your training. We have privacy. Let's try to broach it then."

Aza hesitated. Her lips pressed together.

"What are you thinking?"

"Lilit isn't the most forthcoming individual," Aza said diplomatically.

Lorn huffed a laugh, "Yeah, but we will have to risk it."

"What if she tells Lord Aldrich?"

Lorn paused. "I thought about that too, but if she was threatening him in the hallway, maybe she might use some discretion."

"Lilit, Gravers, and Oron are still loyal to him. We can't forget that."

Aza nodded, lost in her thoughts. After bidding Lorn good night, she retreated to her room seeking refuge in sleep. When her head hit the pillow, all thoughts of the court intrigue and Lord Aldrich slipped away.

25

"What is real? I often have dreams that feel as real as the ground beneath my feet. The visions I have compared to the reality I wake up with, compete with one another. I am starting to prefer the fantasy of my dreams compared to the cold, stark reality upon waking."

Unknown philosopher from the province of Gara

Storm clouds gathered on the horizon. The voluminous masses of purple and gray knit together like a blooming bruise, expanding across the sky. Aza peered out through the window, the meadow grasses outside blowing viciously in the impending storm. She spotted wildflowers around the edge of the cottage creeping up into the bottom of the window, their colorful petals brushing against the glass. Aza turned away from the storm, taking in the cozy room she occupied. A small kitchen lined the wall to her left, with a tiny breakfast table seated for two nestled next to it. It was accompanied by a fireplace roaring on the opposite wall with a couch and chairs encircling it. Rough woven blankets lay strewn about the room. Down the hall, a door stood ajar leading into a bedroom.

A loud crack echoed through the tiny house as Aza swiftly turned back to the window. She scanned the incoming clouds, the threat of rain and lightning looming closer and closer. Amongst the loud crack, she heard a soft bleating. She closed her eyes, listening. There, the bleating sounded again. Aza clenched the rough wooden windowsill. Her heart raced beneath her chest, the sound pounding in her ears.

Bleat. Bleat. Bleat.

Another soft bleat sounded, a cry made directly to her. She needed to find the source of it. Racing to the ramshackle wooden door, Aza flung it open. The wind outside gusted in, sending her clothing swirling around her, and nearly pushed her back with its force. Her eyes darted around and spotted a pair of worn leather boots inside the door, she shoved her feet in them and ran into the impending storm.

Beside the small cottage, a meadow lay open with pine trees jaggedly lining the outside of the property. The wind whipped at her hair and silver strands fell into her eyes. She roughly shoved them back, her eyes frantically searching the surroundings. Unsure of the source of her intense desire to find the soft sound, she cast aside any thought and sprinted for the tree line as a loud crack blasted overhead. Instinct caused her arms to cover her head.

Rain poured down in sheets, obscuring her vision. Where was it? The rain slowed her down, the thick heavy droplets weighing down her clothes, her boots becoming heavy. Each step filled her with more desperation. She whipped her head back and forth, searching. She found refuge in the pine trees, their dense needles helping to block most of the rainfall. As the clouds moved overhead, the sky darkened further nearly eliminating the threadbare light. Another loud crack startled her; her bones rattled from it. Then, lightning flashed down, the forest illuminated with twisted shadows. She strained to listen for the soft bleat, for a sign of life.

Please, please, please, she muttered, a repeated prayer. The tortured cry of the injured animal continued, and Aza clutched her head falling to her knees. She cradled herself as the rain poured down, a watery cloak covering her. The soft bleating was relentless. Her head pounded in rhythm with it.

Worthless, worthless, worthless. Can't save it. Need to save it. It needs me. Where are you? Where are you?! The words circled through her head like vultures picking at discarded carrion. Shivering overtook her, and sobs wracked her body. *I need to find it. I need to find it. Where are you? Worthless. Worthless. Worthless.*

Aza didn't use her magic to warm her, didn't use her magic to shield her from the pouring rain. She didn't deserve it. She didn't deserve the power flowing through her veins if she couldn't find the injured animal. It was in distress, it needed her, and she couldn't help it. Lightning struck the ground around her. She didn't move. The smell of burnt earth floated through the air and the feel of ether surrounded her. *I need to find the deer. I need to help. It needs me.*

She wasn't enough to help it.

She wasn't enough.

She couldn't do it.

Suddenly she was lifted.

"Shit, Aza." The strange man cradled her to his chest. He moved easily as if she weighed nothing. "What are you doing?"

She nuzzled closer to his chest, her head resting on part of his deep brown skin. His tunic was soft, the fabric like a blanket against her cheek. Everything was numb, the rain and chills seeping through to her core.

He prattled on, a clear attempt at distracting her. "Were you so scared of sparring with me? I know I have been dominating you lately." His chin dipped down looking at Aza's curled form, his green luminescent eyes faintly glowing, a beacon within the storm. The man's footsteps were hurried but remained light, not jostling her. Approaching the door he shifted her weight, his hand pushing back the door which flapped madly in the tempestuous winds. He crossed the threshold, kicking the door shut behind him.

He laid Aza gently on the couch and crouched in front of her, his brown hair dripping water. "Aza, we need to get your wet clothes off you. You are soaked and clearly don't want to use your magic. May I remove them?"

Aza, numb, nodded. Her eyes stared ahead unseeing. She remained still while he worked. Methodically, he yanked off her boots, the suction between her foot and the shoe causing it to stick. He then moved to her pants carefully guiding out one leg out followed by the other. Her underwear clung to her skin, the rain making the fabric sheer. He averted his eyes and peeled the underwear from her, keeping his gaze at her feet.

She didn't move, didn't assist him. Keeping his gaze locked away from her, he smoothly grabbed a blanket nearby, tucking it around her hips. Now covered, he moved to her shirt. The fabric clung wet and heavy to her. Coaxing her to sit forward, he propped her up with his arms and had her raise her arms.

She was hollow. Something was terribly wrong and being unable to explain her feelings caused her to descend into further madness. The sound of the injured deer, a distressed bleating and her inability to find it haunted her.

With her shirt discarded, he moved on to the band around her chest. He tilted his eyes to hers, keeping his focus on her face never once glancing down to her bare body. The band slipped over her head, and he kept a hold on her back, slowly lowering her back down to the couch. He grabbed another blanket nearby and tucked it over her chest.

Now that Aza was dry, he faced the fire, and added some nearby logs to it. The flame kicked up higher, sparks rising. Aza took in everything he did, unmoving. The chills in her body began receding, the warmth of the nearby fire and blankets warding off the perpetual chill that overtook her. It was like the warmth and heat offered her a ladder to bring her back from this pit of despair her mind had created.

He gave her a quick look and walked to the back room. She heard his wet clothes being removed, and he walked back out in new, dry clothes, a white shirt, and loose, brown pants. His bare feet padded over to her, and he gripped her chin forcing her to meet his gaze. "Aza, you need to tell me what is wrong." His voice commanded her, and she could feel herself submitting to it.

"The deer," she croaked, her voice sore and tired.

His brows knitted together in confusion.

"I needed to find the deer. It was injured and crying."

The man cocked his head at her, considering her words. "Aza, I didn't hear anything."

Anger sharpened her voice. "I know what I heard! It needs me."

The man's eyes softened. "How can I help you, Aza?"

The softness in his tone and his empathy broke her. She felt the tears spill out onto her cheeks as she choked out the words, "I'm worthless, I need to find it. I don't know why I do, but I feel this pull." Her hand lingered on her stomach, her fingers tapping down. "Right here."

The man leaned forward. His lips followed the tears trickling down her cheeks and he kissed each one. He pulled back and whispered, "You are not worthless Aza."

She was shocked by the intimacy of his actions, and the words caught in her throat. "I need to help it. I need to find it."

He kept his eyes locked on hers, never looking away. "Do you hear it now?"

She shifted on the couch. The blanket on her chest slid down, revealing the top of her chest. Readjusting, she clutched the blanket to her, pinning it in place. She strained to listen. "No, I don't hear it anymore."

"Maybe it is gone. Or maybe it is healed."

Aza made a noncommittal noise in her throat. She didn't feel like the deer was healed or gone. She knew deep within it was hurting and it needed her. It wasn't anything she could vocalize or explain.

"You need rest, Aza." The man retreated to an adjacent chair. His legs spread wide, he leaned back, his arms resting on the sides.

Aza propped herself on her elbows glaring at him. "What do you think I'm trying to do right now? When I go to sleep, it isn't exactly restful now, is it?"

He grinned. "Fair point."

Aza grumbled to herself, pushing plastered pieces of hair off her forehead. "The least you can do is tell me your name." She scanned his elegant body, the thick muscles of his thighs still showcased even in his loose trousers. Even his plain shirt showed the fine cut of his muscles hidden underneath. His wet hair was slicked back, the ends brushing the tops of his shoulders.

Aza maneuvered herself into a cross-legged position, the two blankets sliding around as she adjusted them. Brief flashes of her bare skin revealed themselves. Aza caught glimpses of the man's eyes widening, his jaw clenching. His hands firmly gripped the edge of the chair.

The energy between them pulsed and crackled, their magic and power unable to be restrained. Aza hid her smile and readjusted allowing the blanket to slip lower around her shoulders. His grip tightened on the chair, the wood creaking from the force. Aza's eyes flashed to him, pleasure radiating throughout her body. It was fun to torture this man across from her. Aza knew she had been rescued by him. He had revived her from the descent of madness. The search for the hurt deer overrode any other thoughts, but he pulled her back. She needed something else right now. A single answer. A single moment of joy and release.

Aza bit back the growing smile on her face and readjusted again, the blanket slipping. "I have an idea."

His face remained tight as he ground out the words, "Let's hear it."

"I want to know your name."

"You have stated your desire before. Multiple times."

"Oh, I know. But this time I will be successful. Do you know why that is?" She tilted her head at him, inviting him to respond.

"Why?"

"You are attracted to me, and I am attracted to you."

His eyes devoured her as the hint of a smile appeared on his face. "Is that so?"

"Yes, but I won't let you act on it, unless you tell me your name." Aza rubbed the soft fabric of the blanket covering her, peering around it in mock concern. "I don't think I will need these anymore."

His eyes narrowed, the smile disappearing.

"Here's the game. I will remove these blankets and start touching myself." She held up a finger indicating there was more. "However, you must sit there and watch."

The man looked murderous. His stare pierced through her, and heat pooled low within her core. She would not let herself blush; she needed to keep the upper hand.

"But if you choose to tell me your name, you can leave your chair." Aza pursed her lips. "Understand the rules?" Unwilling to wait for a response, she replied, "Good."

Aza needed this right now. She needed a distraction, something to pull her out of the despair she had just flung herself into moments ago. She fought the urge to laugh as she took in his face. His ethereal eyes glowed as he scowled at her.

Her heartbeat began to accelerate. Without giving it much thought, Aza plunged forward. She could take charge. She needed to right now. No more mysteries. She needed an answer, something to make sense for once in her chaotic life.

Boldly, she dropped the blanket covering her shoulders and chest. It pooled around her lap, her breasts exposed. She watched as he scanned her body. His breath stilled. His eyes flashed to her. Hunger showed within.

Aza's hand playfully danced across her collarbone, trailing across her skin. She flicked her eyes down as if enraptured by her own movements. Keeping her head down, her fingers moved across her skin, and she asked, "Ready to give a name?"

Silence.

"Okay let's have more fun." Her fingers drifted up and down her sides, tickling her ribs. One hand moved under the swell of her breast. Touching the delicate skin caused heat to spread throughout her body. The bud of her nipple tightened underneath his gaze. Her hand gripped the swell of her breast, lingering there as her index finger poised. She flicked her eyes back up to him. His grip on the chair had tightened more somehow.

"Would you like to give me a name?" Her voice had become husky, her own ministrations causing her to tremble. Goddess, his eyes — they devoured her. His movements were stiff. His tongue darted out, licked his lips, and he shook his head no.

Aza gave a slight shrug. "So be it."

Her finger brushed against her nipple and she arched her back, releasing a soft moan. She couldn't help it, the touch felt too good even though she needed to remain in control. Her other hand joined as she kneaded and teased her sensitive skin. She could feel her thighs getting slick. Her eyes closed allowing herself to enjoy the pleasure she gave herself, lost to it. She dared a look at the man across from her. He had readjusted in the chair again, his teeth clenched so hard a vein became prominent in his cheek. She noticed a large swell in his pants and almost smirked to herself.

He would fight this. Determined and stubborn, he would try to resist telling her his name. The secrecy of his name meant that much to him. But this wasn't about him. She needed answers and this one thing needed to be discovered.

Aza couldn't deny he was incredibly handsome. His wet hair remained slicked back from the rain and a few loose strands fell around his face, framing his strong jaw. Each muscle in his body was taut, preventing him from leaping across the room to her. Seeing him like this increased her desire, the heat in her body near exploding. She couldn't stop her hips from undulating, and she needed more.

The second blanket remained bunched around her hips. She needed it gone, needed more contact. She barely asked her question, her breath a mere rasp, "Name?"

Without a response, she flung the blanket off her lap, baring herself completely to him. She wanted to draw this out, take it slowly, make him beg, but she couldn't fight her own rising desire. Aza forced herself to pause, her hand trailing down to the soft curls of her sex. They were a brilliant silver just like her eyes and hair. Her fingers teased around the top, catching sight of the man across from her. He was barely restrained, and Aza felt triumphant. She could do this and not give in to the desire crashing through her. She needed a name and an answer, then she could give in. Her fingers waited poised. She quirked an eyebrow at him awaiting an answer. "Would you like to come over here and do it yourself? Or do you prefer to not answer and watch me continue?"

His first words since she had started, struggled to get out, his voice a low menacing threat, "Aza..."

"What? You knew the rules of the game. If you would like to come over here, you must tell me the answer to my question." Her hand descended and her fingers began playing with her sensitive skin. Her breathing hitched. She felt his stare heat over every inch of her. His magic radiated from him. He was at his breaking point. She knew she just needed to go on a bit longer. She released a deep, throaty moan and heat spiked through her. Her breathing was erratic, so she forced herself to slow the pace. She leveled a stare at him as her finger lowered to her core, a momentary pause to see if he would concede. He would not succumb, and her finger plunged into her warm heat and she gasped. She needed to hold off, she could feel the release building up within her. Only a little longer, he was bound to give in.

His name. She only wanted his name. Such a small request.

Suddenly she felt magic build around her body, wind and air pushing and pulling in places. Her nipples were being softly touched as if the air was being manipulated around her body and playing with her. She glared at him. "No cheating, pull back your magic."

His eyes glinted at her. "Do you really want that?"

Another swipe of his magic across her breasts had her moaning. The pumping of her hand into her core, the wetness and slickness coating her. The feel of his magic across her chest had her near her peak. "You make such delicious noises when I do that. Tell me to stop again and I will." His moss green eyes held hers as another swipe of air and wind pressed against her swollen flesh.

She nearly buckled at the sensation, both foreign and fantastic. Aza needed to regain control. She couldn't give in, wouldn't give in. Not yet.

"Tell me, Aza." His low voice wrapped around her seductively. Another swipe of his magic across her had her moaning loudly. She was lost to the sensation, this feeling. It was fantastic, it was ecstasy. Her eyes closed, feeling, and savoring every touch across her body, every caress with his magic, wishing his body was there instead. A name. She needed a name.

"Stop," she barely whimpered. She didn't want the feeling to end.

His magic ceased instantly. She slowly peeled one eye open then the other. He rose out of his chair, regal and elegant, the fire in his eyes growing.

"I win," Aza breathed out. "You aren't supposed to get out of your chair." She was beginning to become disoriented from the senseless heat flowing throughout her body. She needed release and soon. As he stalked towards her, she stopped touching herself. Her eyes widened, not in fear, but anticipation.

"No, my stars, I think I won." He used his magic to pull her arms over her head and he bound them together with a thin band of ice. Her legs were bound in a similar fashion to the couch. She was completely at his mercy, her legs spread wide to him. Aza knew she could escape easily, but she wanted this, wanted him.

He walked in between her legs looking down at her. "You don't play fair." He knelt, his calloused hands gripping her thighs. He looked up at her through his dark brown lashes, the moss green of his eyes standing out even more. She was bewitched and couldn't look away. He held her gaze as he leaned forward and licked her from her core up. It was slow and leisurely, and Aza felt every bit of it. Sounds of pleasure rippled out of her. He took his time savoring each taste, watching her writhe in anticipation. She could barely move. The ice chains kept her shackled and spread for him. The coolness of the ice brought a flood of sensations through her body. The combination of cooling and heat from different points of her body converged, heightening everything. The man knelt before her and worshiped her. He found every spot, every area that elicited sparks from her. He played around, keeping her climax right within reach. Satisfied she had had enough, he sent her over the edge. She tried to writhe and twist with the overwhelming feeling coursing through her. Her eyes closed tightly, she saw starlight sparkle back at her.

Once she had come down from her high, he released the ice bands around her. He gripped her as she lay languidly back on the couch. He kissed a trail up her body allowing her time to recover. When he reached her ear, he bent in, teeth nibbling the outside of it. "My name is Cruvo."

Aza opened her sleepy eyes and cocked her head to look at him. The name sounded familiar, but she couldn't place it. She could sort out his name later. What she wanted right now, was him. She grabbed his shirt and attempted to pull it off over his head, but Cruvo chuckled, lifted her effortlessly off the couch and walked her to the bedroom. He laid her down on the bed and stepped back, removing his shirt and pants. He pinned her in place with his eyes, and Aza stifled her breath. Cruvo was gorgeous, his body lean and sculpted. "Say what you want, Aza."

"I want you. Now."

The command released any reservations he had. Cruvo prowled over to the foot of the bed and peppered her with kisses starting at Aza's feet. He made his way up her body with soft kisses along her thighs, her hips, up the center of her chest and along her neck. Aza let him, each touch grounding her and leaving her wanting more.

Cruvo kissed along her neck, small scrapes of his teeth bringing Aza to the edge again. She was ready for him and wanted to stop this slow, torturous pace. His kisses went all the way up to her ear as his breath softly played around the outside of it,. Chills went down Aza's spine.

"You are fucking exquisite, my stars." He leaned back, his forearms propped alongside her head and stared into her eyes. Cruvo dropped down kissing her hard, leaving her breathless. On their next kiss, he positioned himself at her entrance, the tip of him teasing her. She lifted her hips up to him, eager for him to do it. He chuckled near her lips and pulled away. "So impatient." She scowled at him, and he went in for another kiss. Their tongues slid around each other, exploring, going deeper, and Cruvo did the same. He entered her slowly giving her time to adjust, and Aza wanted more. He had built up the fire inside her once again and she wanted to fan the flames.

She wanted everything here in this moment, every feeling, every desire. She was present and not plagued with the heavy thoughts that followed her in her real life.

Once he was seated to the hilt, Cruvo moved at a languid pace. Aza met each movement, her hips, her mouth meeting Cruvo's own. Their bodies glistened in the fading night, only the candlelight in the room outlining each other. Cruvo's deep brown skin melded with Aza's own black as the night itself. Along with their bodies, their magics blended finding the edge of each other, embracing each other.

When Aza was at her peak again, Cruvo picked up his punishing pace, Aza could feel it everywhere in her body. The heat spread, waiting. Cruvo reached a hand down in between them. His eyes found hers and he kept her gaze as his fingers rubbed her sensitive bundle of nerves. Aza exploded. The stars and nighttime embraced her as her whole body clenched and tightened while Cruvo kept his pace.

Still coming down from her climax, she felt Cruvo go faster and then he joined her over the edge. He leaned over her, head hung down, his brown hair curtaining his face. His hand ran alongside her cheek caressing her. Both of their breaths exhausted, he leaned down kissing her fully. They stayed entwined around each other, until Cruvo removed himself and placed his forehead against hers. This was her equal in so many ways, both could feel it. Their joining felt destined, even in these strange circumstances.

Cruvo gently removed his forehead from hers and rolled beside her. They lay on their sides staring at one another. Aza traced the planes of his face, his brown skin glistening with an underlay of gold. "So, Cruvo huh? That wasn't so hard, was it?"

The side of his mouth titled up slightly. "But wasn't it more fun to wait and see. I think you enjoyed yourself much more this way."

"Maybe."

Cruvo huffed a laugh, "Maybe? Will I need to prove it again?" He leaned in to nuzzle her neck, and heat reformed again. Aza pulled his head up to meet hers and joined their lips together.

Aza wake up.

Aza broke off her kiss with Cruvo sitting up.

Aza you need to wake up. Lorn's voice echoed in her head.

Aza please, I need to see if you are okay.

Cruvo looked at her, resignation in his face. "Go," he said quietly. "I will see you tomorrow night." He broke into a feral grin, his eyes ravenously scanning her body.

Aza pressed one more kiss to him and woke up.

Lorn's familiar face hovered over her bed, his hair falling down in front of his panic widened eyes.

"Thank the Goddesses and Gods. I thought something had happened to you." Before letting her speak, Lorn said, "I received a warning."

26

Lorn knew he was dreaming. He was back in his home in Verta, the woods surrounding him in a comforting embrace. The familiarity of his home life lay around him beckoning him back.

This was a memory. The proof emerged before him as Lorn exited his house, the old wooden door creaking when he closed it as it always did. He grabbed his bow and arrows off the side of the house and went to join Lakesh. The poppies bloomed in wild abandon. Appreciating the small beauty, he smiled and went off to join Lakesh at the haystacks. If they had any leisure time, they would gravitate over to their makeshift shooting range and practice shooting together to keep their skill honed. Oftentimes it turned into a competition, each betting the other to see how far they could get their arrow to fly. Lakesh had a wicked shot and she usually beat him, whereas he would usually come out on top in swordplay.

Ever since meeting Aza, his dreams had merged and become living memories. Cherished memories of his time with Lakesh. Each day he found himself eager for sleep, ready to relive the happiest moments of his life. Instead of gripping him in the past, the memories were a cathartic experience allowing Lorn to slowly move past the numbness which overrode every part of his life. He was facing his grief one step at a time.

But here. Here in these dreams, he came alive.

Lorn raced out to the haystacks surveying Lakesh's work. Their homemade arrows were embedded in the targets. Lorn stood there expectantly waiting for Lakesh to reveal herself. She should have been here already. The edges of his surroundings wavered, like the ripple from a pond, confirming that this was a dream and not reality, and his time would soon be ending.

Typically, he would not be pulled from his dreams so soon. He furrowed his brows, looking past the targets and the cluster of trees. Something wasn't right.

He spun around coming face to face with a gorgeous woman. Her white blonde hair fell unbound down her back, the edges fluttering from a phantom breeze. Her skin was an alabaster white and her eyes a cerulean blue. Everything about her appearance was heightened and extreme. It was almost too much for Lorn to look upon her. She was quite tall, matching Lorn's height, but slimmer, her shoulders narrow. The strange woman wore a simple dress, a deep red which slashed across her shoulders hanging off one side. It fluttered down to the ground. Lorn's eyes trailed down her body. She was unarmed and barefoot. Who was she?

"Lorn, you need to save her. She is being pulled under by him." Her voice filled the field around them, both deep and powerful, while remaining soft and light. Her full lips pushed together in frustration.

Lorn struggled to speak, stunned by her presence. The woman's voice tugged at a memory within, something he couldn't quite place.

"Save who? From him? And who are you?"

"You must save Aza from Cruvo. You might not know me, but I have been with you throughout this journey. I have been protecting you and guiding you." She gestured to herself. "I am the Goddess Issi."

Lorn allowed her words to sink in. His eyes narrowed at her. "Why should I believe you?"

Issi stared at him, her cerulean eyes heightening in their glow. "I don't have much time. Believe me or not, but I have been helping you this entire time." She strode towards Lorn, her eyes level with his. "She is being enchanted by him. He will use her. You must stop it. It might already be too late."

"What do I need to do?"

"Warn her. Get away from the god, Cruvo. He wants her and will do everything to get her." Issi clutched at her sides and doubled over in pain. "His power already is too much for me to be here. If he takes a —" Issi released a scream and disappeared. His head snapped around to take in the field around him. The fields were being swallowed by the ground underneath, everything falling out into the void below.

~

Lorn jumped out of bed, wrenched open the door and ran to Aza's side. Assuming the god, Cruvo, was accessing Aza the way Issi accessed him— through dreams— Lorn needed to wake her up immediately. Aza remained in bed, a slight smile on her face. Maybe Issi was wrong, she didn't seem in distress or any pain. He knelt before her and voiced his concerns, begging her to wake up. She needed to come back, come back to this reality, and come back to him.

Aza's silver eyes flashed open. She wasn't pleased but he needed to be sure she was okay. "I've received a warning." Aza's eyes widened and he beckoned for her to join him.

Lorn lit a few of the torches and candles around the room and waited at Aza's small dining table a perfect replica to the one in his room.

Aza sat across from him expressionless. Lorn plunged ahead explaining his dream and the encounter with the Goddess Issi. Aza's lips parted when he explained who appeared in his dream. "She warned me about you and someone named Cruvo."

The silence lay heavy. Lorn knew to be patient and let Aza process everything he had said. She was keeping something from him, and he wanted to be a source for her to confide in. "Can you tell me what she is talking about? Or if it is even accurate?"

Aza worried her lip and released a pent-up breath. "After our first few days here, I began to dream, and this person would appear in them. He was annoying, but soon I realized I could spar with him." Aza's eyes lit up the silver brightening to a near glow. "Truly spar. Use my magic in a way I could never imagine." She mindlessly rubbed her temple and continued speaking. "I never knew his name. Never questioned anything because it was happening in my head. This last time..." Aza broke off a slow blush crept up her neck and cheeks. Lorn could imagine what happened next, especially if the god Cruvo was as ethereal and beautiful as his companion Issi. "I learned his name and we slept together." Aza held his eyes unashamed. "Afterwards...that is when you called me back." Aza leaned forward placing her forearms on her thighs, head resting in her hands. Her voice came out muffled as she said, "I thought knowing his name would solve something, but it has created more tangled webs for us to unravel."

Aza bolted upright. "Cruvo is a god." She placed her fingers on the bridge of her nose and inhaled a deep breath. "Cruvo is a god, the god of the hunt. How did I not see this? It was clear, everything about him." Lorn didn't want to interrupt her thoughts. He knew she was working through everything that had occurred to her. He sat there as a silent supporter, present if she needed him. Aza shot him a glance, "Wait. I thought Issi and Cruvo were partners? Destined to be with one another. Why would she warn you about him?"

Lorn shrugged his shoulders. "What is true anymore? All these stories and folktales. I dismissed as false, but here we are talking to the gods and goddesses in our dreams." Lorn gestured to Aza. "You appearing from the Well is a myth I would never have believed." He rolled his shoulders back and wove his fingers together in a contemplative manner. "Issi could be lying. Cruvo could be lying. There isn't a lot of information pertaining to the gods anymore. I thought they were only a myth or story told at night by fearful parents." Lorn paused thinking back to his lessons with his parents. "I think the gods and goddesses have been gone for close to one thousand years. The records on them are also sparse." Lorn leaned forward, his hand on the table reaching for Aza. "Issi mentioned Cruvo was using you or deceiving you for your power. What do you think? How do you feel?"

She closed her eyes considering his questions. He pictured her going back through her memories like flipping through a book hoping to snag on anything helpful. Her eyes opened slowly like a gate being raised. "I don't know what to think anymore. The biggest issue is he refused to give me his name until recently. Cruvo said someone or something would find him—was hunting him." Aza shifted in her chair, her arms cradling each other. "It didn't feel like deception. He was straightforward with his answers, didn't seem like he was hiding anything."

Lorn's stomach twisted as he looked at Aza. He hated thinking about someone using her for her power, but he needed to speak his thoughts. "What if Cruvo is that skilled of a liar?" Lorn's voice softened, he could see Aza's face falter as she considered the same thing. "What if it all was a deception to gain your trust?"

Aza's jaw clenched and tears glistened unshed. Her voice was quiet, he could barely hear her at all. "I will think on all of this, but I need some time alone."

Dismissed, Lorn stood up and walked to his adjacent room. Aza sat there still as a statue, the lit candles casting her in shadows. All he saw was her consumed by the dark, the faint traces of her silver hair shining through. He didn't want to leave her alone, not right now. Respecting her wishes, Lorn went back into his room, his mind whirling with everything he couldn't solve.

~

The following morning Aza and Lorn didn't discuss what had transpired the prior night, each partaking in surface-level pleasantries. Lorn could feel the void within Aza, as if each edge of her had hardened. He didn't know how to proceed. Should he give her space or talk about the painful subject with her? They engaged in their morning studies with Oron and trained together in the afternoon. There was no mention of the disease that overcame the crops and Lilit didn't show up to their training either. Breathless at the end of their practice, each of them sat next to each other on the polished, wood training-room floor.

Aza turned to him. "We need to talk to Lilit about her incident in the hallway. Maybe we can get answers from her."

Lorn nodded. He would follow Aza to the end. If she wanted to talk to Lilit and discover what she knew, he would be at her side.

~

The summer heat began to dwindle away, replaced by the cool, brisk fall mornings. The city of El'en was often blanketed in a thick fog obscuring the rolling ocean from their morning walk to the library. Another month had come and gone. Lorn and Aza trained and studied every day. Lilit failed to join them at their training, despite her offering, and Aza was starting to get restless. During her free time, she paced the castle hallways searching for her, but she was nowhere to be seen.

They remained with the same questions they always had, no closer to solutions. The corruption of the crops hadn't been mentioned again. The disease had not gone any further. Aza felt like her and Lorn were frozen in time, doomed to repeat the same actions of each day again and again. She needed something to change, something to shift.

Since learning of Issi's warning, Aza vowed to never see Cruvo again. Yet every night, he plagued her dreams. She tried to banish him at first, but he was persistent even in her anger. He soothed her with words— then actions—as they met in a passionate kiss. His hips ground into her and she remembered their recent coupling. Her body craved him, despite the anger funneling through her veins. Cruvo had pulled away, a glint in his eye, cocky in her body's submission to him. Her anger would rise like a spark catching fire, and she began sparring with him. Her magic chased and consumed him. It wasn't enough. She allowed her magic to drain her anger as she channeled it towards him. He fought her off easily enough letting her release her anger, her frustration. When they were both exhausted from their fights, they joined together in a frenzied kiss. Aza wanted to argue with her body and her mind, but it felt right. They were destined to be together. Their powers melded and molded to fit one another. Maybe Issi was wrong? How could one so wild yet tender be deceitful to her? Aza vowed it would not go too far. She would not allow her heart to be taken with him. Instead, she allowed her body to enjoy this feeling, this ecstasy with him.

Each night was the same. She fell asleep, and in her dream, he would be there waiting for her. Mad at herself for giving in, they would spar and then make love. Aza would wake up flush, her body craving the feel of Cruvo's against hers. Then guilt would slam down upon her. Lorn never asked her if she ended her nightly meetings with Cruvo. He trusted her and her decisions too much to question them.

The guilt tore through her, as they walked together every day, studied together, trained together. She ignored it, placing it into the back of her mind. Aza justified it. It was only her body—she was not giving him her heart, or her magic. She had control of the situation. She wouldn't let it get carried away.

Aza was as restless as Lorn. They could feel something brewing. She waited for a sign, a change, anything.

Finally, something changed.

Aza caught sight of Lilit within the castle. She abandoned her route and stalked Lilit shadowing her footsteps. Her last two months of training enabled Aza to silence her footsteps and move with stealth throughout the castle. Lilit turned the corner and Aza sprinted to catch up. Keeping her footsteps light, her breathing quiet before she peered around the edge. Lilit was steadily making her way down the hall. No servants, no one was walking by. Disregarding the need for caution, Aza decided to act.

She snuck up behind Lilit and pushed her against the wall utilizing her body weight to pin her. Lilit surged Aza backwards, her prowess in fighting outweighing Aza's meager skills she had learned so far. Lilit spun her around, so she was now pinned against the wall. Aza felt the rush of Lilit's magic swell around her. Lilit's hand encircled Aza's wrist and began to squeeze. Her magic manifested as physical strength and her wrist began to protest under the crushing weight.

Lilit sneered, "I see your lessons aren't doing anything for you. I think you deserve to be punished for sneaking up on me. I'm Lord Aldrich's Captain of the Guards." Her grip tightened and Aza fought back a gasp. Her bones were close to being pulverized under Lilit's strength. Despite their disparity in height, Lilit had to pull her head back to stare at Aza, her gaze was no less fierce. Her cold gray eyes hardened waiting for Aza's response. "No answer? Hmm pity."

"Wait!" Aza blurted out. Lilit paused. "Where have you been?"

"I don't answer to you, no matter how much Lord Aldrich likes you." She sighed with annoyance and answered, "I do have various tasks I have to go and check on."

Aza was speechless. Such a simple answer to Lilit's whereabouts. She had thought that her lack of presence at court indicated nefarious intentions. Lilit's grip loosened and she moved away from Aza.

"You need more practice. But it was a good stealth attack." Lilit walked away, a clear dismissal. Aza's pride flared at the small praise from Lilit.

Remembering the conversation between Lord Aldrich and Lilit, Aza blurted out, "Wait! Who do you want released?"

Time slowed as Lilit turned back to her.

"What did you say?" Lilit asked quietly. Her eyes held Aza's waiting for her to respond.

Aza faltered. "A month ago. I overheard you and Lord Aldrich arguing. Lilit, I can help you. If you need assistance, Lorn and I can help." Aza backed up. Something was terribly wrong. Lilit marched up to her cold fury fueling her steps. She pinned Aza to the icy marble wall.

"Never, ever mention that again," she snarled quietly. Her voice came out in a hushed whisper, her head darted back and forth scanning the hallway. "You know nothing. You need to be smart, Aza. This world is not what you think it is. Our history, everything, is warped. Everything is a lie." Lilit's hand gripped Aza's wrist again, her fingers gently rubbing against the tender bones. Her eyes flickered back to Aza hardening once more.

Aza knew she could easily dismantle Lilit with her magic, but something within bade her to stop.

"I am not your friend. You owe me nothing. But just as a reminder Aza, be smarter. Be shrewd. Be cunning. Stop thinking the best of everyone." Aza couldn't rationalize her words. She was threatening her yet trying to help her. Lilit held Aza's eyes as her grip tightened like a vice, snapping Aza's wrist in one squeeze.

Pure, blinding pain lanced through Aza as Lilit pulled away from Aza's body. She slumped to the floor in a heap. She wanted to scream but only a wordless cry came out of her mouth.

"Take this broken wrist as a warning."

Aza choked out her words, "I could destroy you with my magic."

Lilit's eyes filled with a deep unknown sorrow. "I know, but you won't."

She left her on the floor of the deserted hallway. Aza cradled her wrist to her chest and closed her eyes focusing her magic on the bone, knitting it together, fixing the breaks. Even though Aza could heal quickly, didn't mean it wasn't painful. She felt the breaking of her bones, the ease with which Lilit squashed her wrist.

Aza picked herself off the floor and dusted off her clothes. Any runaway tears she wiped off her cheeks. Lilit needed help. Aza wouldn't abandon her, despite all her warnings. Setting off down the hallway, her thoughts were full of questions on how to help the woman who just broke her wrist as easily as swatting a fly.

~

During their afternoon training, Aza explained in hushed whispers to Lorn all about her interaction with Lilit. When Aza finished, Lorn's mouth set in a thin line, his eyebrows furrowed. He reached to examine Aza's wrist, turning it back and forth. "Are you okay? Why didn't you use your magic?"

Aza dismissed him quickly. "I'm fine. I was more shocked than anything." Aza thought back to her interaction with Lilit. Something within told her not to react, not to give in to Lilit's bloodlust. "I didn't need to use my magic. I think she wants me to... wants me to end her."

Lorn had no sympathy in his eyes as he grumbled, "I want you to end her too. What in the Darkness below is her problem?"

"We need to help her."

Lorn loosened a sigh, his expression softening. "Aza, what can we do to help? She warned you to stop trusting people, to stop being so kind to everyone. Yet you want to do this?"

"Yes." Aza knew she only needed to say one word and Lorn would follow her.

"Okay, but she is not our priority. If we can help her, we will try."

Satisfied, Aza grinned.

Lorn rolled his eyes. "You shouldn't be so happy about someone who knowingly and willingly broke your wrist."

27

Journal from a prophet located in the Hall of Prophecies in Kreeha

Weeks passed. Aza and Lorn went about their days consisting of library, training, and sleep. The routine was starting to make Aza's skin itch. Something unknown shifted and was about to begin.

She could feel it. They needed a change. They weren't bound to stay in El'en. Maybe they could travel elsewhere? Receive answers in other provinces. However stifling the castle became, it was still comfortable. The servants treated her with respect, they didn't ogle anymore. She felt less and less like an oddity walking around. But something called to her. She needed to follow it.

Aza only saw Oron daily while he tutored her and Lorn in the library. Lord Aldrich and his other advisers she saw only in passing. She needed to speak to Lord Aldrich and tell her of her plans to leave. Lorn already agreed with her. There wasn't much they were achieving here and Lorn told her if she felt like she was needed elsewhere, he would follow her. Aza worried her lip, concerned over helping Lilit. She had scarcely seen her around and she hadn't figured out how to properly assist her. If an opportunity presented itself, she would do it.

Tonight. She would find him tonight and tell him.

After dinner, Aza strolled around the castle. She walked out on the same balcony where she met Lord Aldrich at the beginning of her stay. Opening the glass balcony doors, she walked to the railing, gripping it tightly. She was nervous to tell him about her plans of departure, but it was necessary. The warm summer nights had faded away, replaced by the brisk cooling nights of autumn. The Wyra ocean provided a thick chill in the air. The wind casually whipped around Aza's clothes, the coldness causing her skin to pebble. She rubbed her hands together, cursing herself for forgetting a jacket. She released a fraction of her magic to warm her body. The coldness dissipated and was replaced by a warmth that radiated throughout her.

Aza tilted her head back taking in the expansive sky overhead. A pity. The voluminous clouds blocked many of the stars and constellations she loved learning about. Ever since Oron's tutelage her breadth of knowledge had increased. She loved it all, taking in every detail, every piece of information.

Lord Aldrich leaned his body next to her on the railing. "I have not seen you for some time," he said.

"I could say the same to you." Aza kept her face to the sky.

"I have been busy."

Aza gave a noncommittal noise in her throat. She decided to be blunt and tell him of her intentions. "I'm leaving. I am going to travel to other provinces."

"Is my castle and city unsatisfactory?" They remained staring up into the sky.

"No, you and your people have been fantastic..." Aza hedged unsure if and how she wanted to explain, "...but I have a feeling I need to follow."

"Will you promise me to stay a little longer? I'm hosting a meeting with all the delegates from the five provinces. At the end of the week, it will end in a ball." His voice grew soft, a question posed on the air. "Will you stay until then?"

Her relationship with Lord Aldrich was tricky. He was charming and magnanimous, his every move focused on political gain. She couldn't forget his initial declaration that he wanted to remake the world, or of his private conversation with Lilit, or his omission about his immense magical power. Despite all of these reasons Aza couldn't help but feel like she owed him an explanation.

Aza forced herself to remember all of these things, and not forget in a moment of weakness, however she could see no harm in waiting a little longer. It was even more convenient for her to do so. She could meet these new delegates and potentially travel with them. She mused over this new information. The silence stretched between them. Aza finally agreed and made ready to leave. Lord Aldrich reached for her fingers. He took her hand and bowed his head to kiss the top of her hand. She froze, startled by the sudden intimacy.

Lord Aldrich pulled his head back to look into her eyes. "You will be missed here in El'en." Aza met his dark brown eyes, completely jarring compared to the rest of his face. They were unsettling like something else was hidden underneath. A flash of green replaced the brown and Aza took a hesitant step back.

"Is something wrong?"

"No, it's nothing. Probably my head. Good night." Aza left, speeding down the hallways back to her room. Her head pounded. She forced herself to take slow breaths. The consistent pounding subsided with each exhalation. She could last a few more weeks. After the meeting with the five provinces, she would leave El'en and find answers elsewhere.

~

As if on cue, the next day the castle was bustling with servants bearing decorations and crates of food to be prepared. Aza usually only passed a handful of people in her daily routine, but now the hallways were packed with people, seeming to appear out of the air itself, to accomplish their tasks around the castle. Many of the servants talked in hushed whispers about the other delegates from the other four provinces showing up. Most of the residents of El'en have only seen Lord Aldrich and no other ruler.

The anticipation built within Aza. Each day she saw the castle being prepared and each day she grew more and more excited to see the delegates from other provinces and to leave this castle, to find the answers she sought.

At the very least the gathering would break up the mundane routine she had built for herself and would be a proper send-off while she left and traveled the rest of Ithilia.

Aza and Lorn continued about their routine, talking discreetly about their upcoming departure. Lorn admitted to her, he had never witnessed a lord or lady from another province. He mainly traveled throughout the rural areas to dispatch unwanted creatures and was nervous about the upcoming dignitaries. Aza was surprised when he shared that information—not about meeting important officials—but about his nervousness. Lorn always portrayed a calmness and levelheadedness in challenging situations, which she envied. His face never betrayed his nerves. Upon Aza's explanation, Lorn released a quick breath, his face relaxing upon learning how she perceived him.

"Good, I feel out of my element every time I am in a court." An easy smile softened Lorn's face. "You know my upbringing. It is nice to know I don't stick out so easily among all these people."

"Is there any information you can tell me about the leaders of the other provinces?" Aza entreated him to share.

He shook his head sadly. "You know as much as I do. Everything Oron taught us is all I know as well." In their morning lessons with Oron, and in preparation of the upcoming visit, he had taken care to teach them about the dignitaries from each province. Crestfallen Aza nodded her head in understanding.

~

Any lingering traces of summer were banished over the following weeks. Autumn had fully taken over, the morning air crisp and biting, and the nights a chilling cold. The fireplaces within the castle were kept stoked with a burning fire, providing a brilliant warmth throughout the marbled sanctuary.

Lord Aldrich had supplied additional clothes for Aza and Lorn, their summer attire no longer suitable for the decreasing temperatures. They were given long sleeve tunics, pants, coats, and cloaks made of warmer materials so they wouldn't freeze in the cold hallways. Aza pulled her thick coat tighter around her body, warding off the incoming chill that seemed to stay with her.

She paused in the hallway and peered through the window next to her. Nearly every morning the castle grounds were blanketed in a thick layer of fog, obscuring any vision to the crashing ocean waves below. Yet today the fog had cleared early allowing Aza an unobstructed view of the Wyra ocean below. The clouds were painted thick, their forms providing a backdrop for the morning light to puncture through. Glory rays outlined each cloud, their shapes merging and colliding over each other. Aza stilled herself, her eyes shuttered closed, locking away the beauty she witnessed. She seared the image to her soul, tethering it there. The following morning would bring about a whole new slew of problems and situations to maneuver.

When Aza finally deigned to open her eyes, the Wyra ocean was gone, replaced by towering pine trees, her legs dangling over a ledge on the precipice of a mountain. The clouds and sky mimicked the viewpoint of the ocean she had back in the castle of El'en. The same rays of sun pierced through the vibrant sky in front of her. Her fingers tightened around the rough rock below her, and she looked down in surprise. The slab of rock jutted out into the open air, the surface scraping into her legs and palms. She didn't mind the sensation. It brought her back to this moment, breathing in the quiet morning air around her. Aza had the feeling her chest had been wound tightly for a long time, and only now had it slightly unspooled, each string loosening turn by turn.

She could breathe freely.

Footsteps shuffled behind her as a man sat to join her on the edge of this rock. If she pushed herself forward, it would be a freefall into the blue-green pine trees below. Their impressive heights jutted up into the air but could still not reach the great mountain they sat upon. The wind whipped through Aza's hair, clearing her mind and her eyesight to appreciate the view before her. She leaned forward, uncaring about the vast height as she sat above these trees. She yearned and envied the trees, to be so rooted in ground below them, yet to feel so inspired to grow and tower up to the skies above.

"It is beautiful," the man uttered. Aza was unsure of whether this statement was said for Aza's benefit or simply a slip of the tongue because he was equally overwhelmed with the vastness before them.

Aza strained to turn and look at the man beside her. Curious as to where she was, and who she was with, she wished to see him. Yet she couldn't. Whatever vision she was in, it prevented her from looking at the person sitting beside her. Her only view was the trees before her, and his thick legs swinging in tandem with hers over the precipice of the cliff.

A deep sadness bloomed in Aza. She wanted to see this man next to her. No. Needed to see him. Why couldn't she turn to look? Only one more glance. She should have just one more look. The mountains and trees before her wavered like smoke before her eyes. She scrunched her eyes, clearing away the remainder of what lay before her.

Aza was back in the castle in El'en. The overlaid image of the mountains seared into her mind. She stared blankly at the Wyra ocean before her. The window constricted her line of sight as she followed the ocean waves rolling back and forth. The man's voice in the vision was familiar and Aza searched her mind, the undulating waves a mocking reminder of everything she knew being washed away and replaced. Aza closed her eyes, shutting out everything around her and replayed the man's sentence. Over and over.

"It is beautiful." The voice echoed within the deepest chambers of her mind as she thought.

Aza's eyes flashed open. She did not know of the man who spoke, but she had heard his voice before. It had whispered to her on her first night here while she was in the bath. A vision of a cave and water and a man whispering, "My shadows."

Aza had been overwhelmed with past illusions before, but never had one felt completely real. She had lost herself within it. Her daily life had become a mishmash of figuring out illusion compared to reality. Images from a time before constantly overlaid the images from now.

Aza paced through the hallway, the corridors blurring past her as her mind focused on the two scenes which replayed through her head. The cave and the cliff. The man was the same in each vision, and each time she never saw him clearly. Only his voice wove through her, her body tightening with need and longing, and a deep chasm of sorrow she was too scared to pierce the surface of. Besides their first night in El'en together, Aza never disclosed her visions to Lorn and now was the time.

As night descended, Aza found Lorn lounging in his room. Aza explained the constant dreams and hazy images which overtook her. Lorn sat up with a thoughtful look on his face as he listened to the new information.

When she finished, Lorn leaned forward, his eyes focused on the ground, a hand placed underneath his chin. Aza let the quiet permeate around them, patient to hear Lorn's thoughts. Even though Lorn dismissed his own intelligence, Aza knew this man was observant of his surroundings and able to piece together obscure bits of information. She respected his mind and how it worked vastly different from her own. Even though he discredited himself, his rural upbringing did not hinder her appraisal of him.

After another beat of silence, Lorn eye's cut up to meet Aza's own. "What if these visions or dreams are not either of those things?" His voice softened as he reached out to clasp Aza's hands within his own. He flinched discreetly over the overwhelming power of her but held her gaze. "Aza what if these are memories?" The question floated through the space in front of her. "You have briefly explained your memory to me in the past. What if these are a part of that?"

Aza turned her head to the side, unable to look anymore into the sincerity of Lorn's eyes. He wanted her to have answers. She worried her lip between her teeth and hissed an exhalation. "It's possible..." Aza trailed off. "But I don't know how to explain it properly. It doesn't feel like me. I can't even see myself or what I look like." Aza shook her head dismissing her line of thinking.

Lorn released her hands and sat up straight. "We are so close to leaving Aza. We have little time remaining. With the incoming delegation, hopefully we can get new answers and have a more pointed search of where to go next. But we remain in this together." Lorn paused and placed one hand atop hers. "I can't imagine how frustrating everything is for you. I want to find answers too. We need a bit more time. We can do this."

Aza nodded, doubt creeping into her veins like a vine grabbing and rooting her down. She was thankful for Lorn's optimistic outlook. He would be by her side supporting her despite the outcome. He had nothing left in his life; they could at least have the friendship of each other.

Soon.

The delegation would come soon and with it, Aza was determined to find her answers.

28

"Getting prepared for an event is similar to donning armor for a battle. Instead of preparing for swords and arrows, one must be prepared for the salaciousness of gossip, rumors, and slander against oneself."

Excerpt from *The Battles of Court Intrigue* by Yasmine of Kreeha

Electric energy coursed through the entire castle. It was the day of the delegation's arrival. In anticipation, Lord Aldrich had sent Lorn and Aza to his seamstress to have clothing readied for them.

The morning of the event, Aza laid out the clothes in front of her deciding upon which she should wear during the formal announcement of each province. The clothes provided for them would never be called shabby, however the clothes before her now were more delicate and beautiful. Aza ran her fingers over each article of clothing, the fabric smooth between the pads of her fingertips. Her typical daily outfits were built for practicality, for her to be able to train in, and to sit for hours in the library studying. Aza decided to wear a tunic and pants. There would be time later in the week to wear more formal dresses. She wanted to appear serious, but not overly so. She would need to be able to discuss leaving El'en with these leaders.

Lord Aldrich's seamstress had wanted to embed the royal insignia on the clothing, but Aza had refused, not wanting to appear like she belonged to him or his court. It was bad enough she was here at his court. Besides, other leaders might not take too kindly over the affiliation.

She slipped on the clothes. They melded to her body like a second skin. Both the tunic and pants were black, because she didn't wish to stand out any more than she had already. Although the fabric was understated, there was elaborate detail along the pant legs. The artistry of the seamstress was unmatched—except for Melina. Aza glanced at the wrapped package Melina had gifted her. She had peeked at the precious clothing within. Aza wanted to wait for the right moment to don the dress.

Along the black tunic, Aza noticed faint weaving of silver thread throughout. The effect was a slight glimmer when she walked. Aza went to the mirror, checking the outfit and herself reflected on its surface. The seamstress was indeed skilled. The outfit by itself was not distracting, but with Aza modeling it, the colors matched her perfectly. The faint silver shimmering throughout mimicked the silver of her hair, eyes, and freckles. Her breath caught at her reflection. She was every bit the ethereal, mysterious figure people believed her to be.

A knock at her door brought Aza out of the bathroom. Lorn stood on the other, side resplendent in his outfit. He wore black pants like hers, with a dark green tunic that highlighted the golden hues of his skin. Gold thread embroidery was decorated throughout his shirt. The sword he carried with him and trained with daily was attached to a scabbard on his hip.

Her eyes drifted to the ornate scabbard. It was encrusted with small jewels and the hilt of his sword was framed with a decorative gold piece. Aza raised her eyebrows at him and looked him up and down.

He followed her line of sight and grinned while rolling his eyes. "I know, it was at Lord Aldrich's insistence. I am to look the part of a well-cared for guest. An *honored* guest." Lorn paused, taking in Aza's outfit. He stood unmoving, stunned. He reached out a hand, palm up waiting patiently for Aza to reciprocate. She placed her hand in his as he bowed and gently kissed the top of her hand. "You are stunning today," he whispered to Aza.

A smile filled her face as she quipped back, "Only today?"

He returned her smile, "Everyday, but today you look especially *subtle*." He looked her up and down.

Aza playfully hit his arm and let out a laugh. "Yes, subtle is exactly what I would call it."

Lorn led her back into his room and motioned for her to sit. Aza waited patiently while Lorn rummaged around in his room. He bent down under the bed and pulled out a long, rectangular black box along with a smaller box resting on top. Both boxes were wrapped together with a red bow.

"You have been training so well the past few months, I hope you like it." He placed it tentatively on the table beside her and waited for her to reach for it.

Aza grabbed the satin box and pulled an end loosening the knot. The ribbon fell away, and she gingerly clutched the top box. She removed the lid. Inside was the most beautiful dagger she had ever seen. Aza gasped, lifting it into her hands. It was forged of iron and silver, both metals twisted and twined around one another, their metals marbled. The dagger was light and delicate in her hand, the blade was sharp and glinted back at her. Gemstones were inlaid within the grip, each gem placed by an expert hand. Aza didn't know the name of the gems, but they were absolutely beautiful. They had a smooth surface with the color swirling, each gem glowing from within. It was a prism of warm light which shifted from gold to silver and back, like the essence within the gem could not be contained, but rather burst forth to be free and display its qualities.

Before she asked, Lorn answered her question. "The gemstones are called stardust gems. They are incredibly rare and gathered from the mines deep underground in the province of Gara." Aza nodded, recalling her geography lessons with Oron. The province to the north, Gara was renowned for its robust mining operations and was a prosperous province due to their rare minerals. "It is called the stardust gem because of its light. It will slightly glow from within and change colors. It will typically range between shades of gold and silver, but some claim it can embody any color. They grow deep underground where not even the light of day reaches. The miners claim the stardust gem creates its own light to remind itself of where it came from." Lorn cast his eyes upward, a brief smile on his face as his eyes drifted back to Aza's face. "They reminded me of you and our first meeting."

Aza's heart burst with joy, as she reached forward and clasped her friend in a giant hug. "Thank you, Lorn. Truly this is beautiful."

"Open the next one."

Aza released Lorn and opened the next present. Inside was a replica of the dagger in the form of a longsword. Aza removed the sword from the confines of the package and laid it across her lap, admiring the beautiful work and craftsmanship. A thought pierced through as she nearly shouted, "Lorn how did you pay for all of this?" He chuckled and Aza lowered her voice reminding herself not to accost him. "If these gems are rare and this sword and dagger so well made, how did you pay for it? And why? You don't need to waste excessive money on me!"

Lorn held up a hand, motioning for her to relax. "My agreement with Lord Aldrich stipulated that, upon retrieving you from the Hinterlands, I was to be paid handsomely. It is my money to do as I see fit."

Aza clumsily pushed the weapons back towards him. "I can't accept this. They are lovely, but Lorn, I can't have you spend that sort of coin on me."

Lorn looked thoughtfully at Aza and reached to one of the packages. Hidden inside was a leg tie for her dagger. He grabbed it and knelt before Aza. He reached for her leg, pulled up her pant leg so her calf was exposed, and took the sheath along with the leg ties and fastened it around. Without speaking, he reached for the handle of the dagger and reverently sheathed it. The blade slid smoothly and soundlessly into the sheath. Aza sat, stunned, watching him equip her with her gifted blades. He reached up again, and his fingers curled around the handle of her sword. His hand opened expectantly for her, waiting for her hand to mirror his. She brought her hand forward and he placed the sword hilt in her palms. Still kneeling before her, he stared into her eyes. There was no room for questioning, no room for doubt. He had commissioned these items to be crafted for her. He guided her fingers to curl around the grip of the sword, his eyes locked with hers. Lorn's voice was soft, yet a command lingered underneath. "It is a gift. Keep it."

Aza nodded, tears threatening to spill down her face. Her friend, who knelt before her, who looked past her magic and power, he never balked, never doubted, and always supported her. He showed his support now and throughout her journey, never mocking her, and always displayed patience. There was something tethering them together, and Aza hoped that bond would never break.

Wordlessly, Lorn rose from his position and offered her his arm. She placed the sword within its sheath and attached it to her hip. Ready to depart, she wrapped her arm within his. They walked together, down the castle halls to meet their future below.

29

"The five provinces and their respective leaders rarely gather. First, it is a security nightmare to have to try and protect all our great leaders gathered together. Secondly, the operation of a kingdom is a full-time job. They rarely have any time to escape."

How The Land Of Ithilia Came To Be by Ursu of Kreeha

Every corner of the castle was cleaned and decorated. Servants and workers passed by each more finely dressed than the last. Aza and Lorn gave polite nods as they walked by, quietly acknowledging their efforts in the castle's finished look. Aza knew everyone would be on edge this week with the visiting dignitaries, everyone poised to be on their best behavior. Hosting the leaders was not the only reason for their rare gathering. This included discussions, but also a measure of boasting and showcasing their respective provinces. Excitement fluttered within Aza with each step. She gripped Lorn's arm tighter. He returned a reassuring squeeze.

They walked into the throne room and Aza stifled a gasp. It was beautiful. The throne room was covered in brilliant colors representing the autumnal countryside of Iyera. Rich blends of reds, oranges, and yellows covered the ceiling, and Aza could barely see any white marbled castle beneath. Aza craned her neck back to admire the handiwork of whatever artist Lord Aldrich had employed to carry out this impossible task. Trying to discern what was on the ceiling, she realized the flowers merged and crested, the colors jostling one another and forming a picture. She blinked, her eyes adjusting to the vibrancy overhead. It was Iyera's crest of the riotous waves. The lighter yellow, near-white flowers were placed strategically to create the depth of color to each wave. Despite autumnal flowers being used for the display of the ocean, it was clear what it was depicting.

Aza turned to look at Lorn. His face mirrored hers, a look of awe plastered on his face. He felt her looking at him and returned her gaze. They both smiled, a smile of shared amazement, and wonder.

Aza straightened herself and turned to take in the rest of the room. Beautiful and intricate sculptures were placed throughout, each depicting a different scene. Aza reminded herself to check each one later after the guests had entered. She noticed a few curious glances cast towards her. She was an oddity among them. She could feel their eyes upon her.

The throne room was filled with people. Everyone stood shoulder to shoulder eagerly awaiting the incoming dignitaries. Guards were on alert. They formed a line, parting each side of the throne room, keeping the townsfolk separate from those incoming.

Aza spotted Lilit standing at the entrance, fully outfitted in her captain's garb. Various filigrees and adornments were displayed proudly on her jacket indicating her military prowess. Even though her jacket was filled with a plethora of awards, Lilit was not overwhelmed by it. She filled and embodied it despite her smaller stature, the very picture of Iyera's Captain. Her face belied nothing, stoic and still. Her feet planted, awaiting what came next.

Gravers found them entering the throne room and placed them near the dais, directly adjacent to Lord Aldrich's gnarled, beechwood throne. Close in proximity, but not close enough to overshadow his presence. Aza thought he kept her power close to prove to the other provinces what he had acquired and used it to boast to the rival leaders.

There was an electric buzz in the room as if everyone and their magic were collectively waiting. Aza could feel the pull within her own well of magic, the overwhelming desire for hers to combine and grow with all these other people around her. They were a blend of people, their magic reaching the edges of others, pushing, pulling, enticing one another—a mirror image to the ocean outside.

A silence settled over the room as a door to the side of the throne room swung open and Lord Aldrich walked out, two guards accompanied him on either side. Collectively the citizens of Iyera hushed as they took in their grand leader. He strode towards the dais and throne, his regal smile reeling the townsfolk in. The silver crown rested upon his brow, the metal shaped and warped mimicking the waves of the Wyra Ocean. It rested delicately against his light brown hair, the hair loose falling in soft waves to his shoulders. He wore a long sleeve tunic, white trimmed in gold, the material sparkling and shining off the marbled castle walls. Lord Aldrich's pants were tailored to fit his body exactly, the blue so dark it almost resembled black. His sword was attached to his hip, the pommel and guard equally as grand as his outfit. The gold of the sword gleamed as he walked forward.

His steps to the dais were slow and measured. Lord Aldrich surveyed the crowd, acknowledging them with gracious nods. If Lord Aldrich was dressed to such lengths, Aza failed to imagine what the rest of the incoming leaders would look like.

Lord Aldrich ascended to his throne. Before sitting, he announced, his voice smooth and unwavering, "Thank you all for attending and greeting our favored guests from our neighboring provinces. Your presence is a display of the strength and solidarity of Iyera." A deafening cheer filled the throne room, the sound echoing off the walls.

The crowd fed from his outstretched hand like a starving dog. The borderline worship this man endured was disgusting. Aza's face easily showed her inner thoughts and she fought to maintain some composure.

Lord Aldrich lowered himself into his throne, his hands glided over the beechwood throne, and motioned for the guards to open the doors. Aza assumed the invited parties were waiting outside, ready to be ushered forward.

A collective hush filled the room, everyone holding their breath in anticipation of the incoming envoys from the other four provinces. A herald dressed in the finery befitting Iyera announced the first contingent entering the throne room. "I present Lord Ravinder and Lady Sarava of Verta."

The presenting couple wore complementary mixture of greens, yellows, and browns like the earth itself draped them in life-given color. The couple displayed a jolly exterior. Lord Ravinder met the gaze of each citizen and flashed them a pleasant smile. His ruddy complexion reddened with each indulgent grin at the crowd. Paired with his rust-colored hair and a trimmed beard to match, he had the appearance of a portrait whose artist splashed too much paint on a canvas. Whoever their tailor is had picked their colors well; the green and browns toned down his natural redness. Walking in stride with him was his wife, Lady Sarava. She displayed a gracious demeanor, yet Aza spotted her eyes, which held a shrewdness hidden within. Difficult to discern age in the MagicBlessed, Aza guessed they were years older than Lord Aldrich, possibly around sixty. Yet, with the long life given to MagicBlessed, they appeared youthful with very few lines marking their face. The crowd devoured the couple's positive energy, their cheers and praises rebounding throughout the room.

When they reached the end, each gave a nod of respect to Lord Aldrich who responded in turn. Lord Ravinder and Lady Sarava both cast curious glances at Aza. Even though they tried to hide their curiosity, she caught the surreptitious looks passed between them. Aza fought to keep her face neutral, but an instinctual anger flared at their scrutiny. She needed to thicken her skin, people would always gawk at her.

Behind the Lord and Lady of Verta, their contingent and guards followed. Aza spotted Verta's crest on one of their guards—a trio of wheat stalks with an accompanying scythe. The sharpened scythe loomed over the wheat like an imposing threat. Lord Aldrich's guards ushered the Verta group off to the side where a collection of chairs and tables were prepared for them.

Once seated, the herald moved on to the next group, his voice reverberating through the room, "I present Lord Sune of Kreeha." A broad-shouldered man strutted through the room, his head held high as he casually scanned the people gathered. He differed from the Lord and Lady of Verta, uninterested in earning the praise of the people, yet simply accepting it as his right. His skin was a rich brown, with long braids draped down his back each decorated with crafted pieces of gold and jewelry. With each step, he created a soft, musical jingle. He commanded the presence of the room as people looked on in awe. His contingent of guards and nobility stationed behind him, granting him the courtesy of basking alone in the spotlight.

Aza noted how he furtively peeked at the man to his left. She recalled Oron's teachings of the five provinces and how Lord Sune, while not married, maintained a relationship with his male consort, Ryu. Aza was surprised at the stifling difference between the two. If Lord Sune was the embodiment of Kreeha—desert, strong, powerful, unflinching—Ryu was the opposite. The Lord of Kreeha's consort was rail-thin, his body lacking any muscular definition. His ink black hair was styled and pulled back into a bun. Thin-framed glasses rested upon his straight nose. Aza marveled at why the two of them were together, yet when Lord Sune looked back at Ryu, she saw a warm smile light up Ryu's face. Aza's questions vanished. They clearly held a great affinity for one another, despite their appearances. As Lord Sune surveyed the crowd, his eyes traveled over to Aza. He paused, his footsteps faltering only slightly, then progressed forward faster. Lord Sune stopped in front of Aza, his feet planted, shoulders rolled back his self-assured stance revealing his cockiness.

She eyed his extravagant wardrobe, his body cloaked in gold and silver. The fabric expertly draped him covering his arms, the billowing fabric loosely draped around his arms and chest highlighting a body hardened for fighting.

Lord Sune's voice was lowered so only Aza, Lorn and Lord Aldrich could hear his statement. His voice rolled out smooth and rich as he said, "I see Lord Aldrich caught the true prize." Out of the corner of her eye she saw Lorn bristle at his statement. Aza loosened the restraint on the roiling wildness within her. She sent a tendril of magic to enfold Lord Sune's body. It crept like a vine, rooting and taking hold then prodded at him.

Aza kept her voice low and even, her eyes not straying from Lord Sune, "I would be careful how you address those infinitely more powerful than you." Her magic flickered around him. She knew he could feel the intrusion of her magic threatening to swallow him, engulf him.

Lord Sune's rich brown eyes flashed in alarm, the only part of him reacting to Aza's stealthy attack. He bowed his head slightly, a mischievous grin flitting across his face. "I see you are a worthy match indeed." He moved over to Lord Aldrich giving him another slight bow of the head. "It will be an interesting time together, Lord Aldrich."

Lord Aldrich appeared bored, disinterested in Lord Sune's

interaction with Aza. He returned Lord Sune's bow of the head, and their contingent was ushered to an adjacent table. The back of their guards' uniform was embroidered with a blazing sun, the crest of Kreeha.

The crowd's cheers died down as the Kreehan contingent sat at their table. All heads turned towards the open door, awaiting the herald's next announcement. He cleared his throat which was heard throughout the weighty silence. "I present Lady Rasmina of Gara." A striking woman entered the room, her unblemished, porcelain skin shone like a freshly polished gem. Her straight raven black hair framed her heart-shaped face and flowed down her back unbound. Lady Rasmina's heels clicked across the marble floor. A blood-red dress dragged upon the floor, the train taking up space behind her. The lace sleeves covered her arms, and the dress hugged her body and flared out at the hips, the copious amounts of tulle and fabric creating a barrier between her and the people around her. The dress was cut up to her throat and the lace trailed down leaving her with expertly exposed pieces of skin.

Upon announcement of her name the crowd had cheered, but as she walked further into the room, the cheers died down, her severe countenance quieting the room. Unbothered, she was flanked by her guard, their faces as hard and unflinching as their revered leader. Aza spotted three women trailing her, presumably her daughters. They each were a copy of their mother, their postures and faces unyielding. Two of them appeared identical to their mom, their skin and hair the same color. Only their eyes were different colors, both having varied shades of brown.

Lady Rasmina's eyes raked over Aza. She suppressed the urge to shudder. Her eyes were like vapor, the lightest shade of blue she had ever seen. It gave her the quality of a phantom given form. As she approached, she noticed her third daughter, the one with differing looks. Her hair was equally black yet held a thick curl to it. Her skin was a shade darker than her sisters' and mother's, a skin tone that would darken instead of burn if exposed to the sun. Aza noticed her because despite her opposing appearances, her demeanor was vastly different. She openly smiled to the crowd around her, shooting small waves to those she gazed at. Aza was startled to find she had inherited her mother's shocking light blue eyes.

Before Aza even realized it, Lady Rasmina halted in front of her. Standing so close to each other, Aza was able to discern fine lines around her eyes and mouth like small cracks in a fragile tea set. They each assessed the other. Lady Rasmina maintained her indifferent facade. Her lips matched her dress, almost eerily so. Aza couldn't help the morbid image of Lady Rasmina recently feasting on a corpse before attending the event. She waited expectantly for any words to come out of this terrifying woman.

Without anything being said, Lady Rasmina turned, dismissed Aza and addressed Lord Aldrich. She did not bow or incline her head in respect. Her light blue eyes unwavering, she appraised the man who sat in front of her. "I see you are getting older."

Lorn Aldrich shifted forward in his seat. "I could say the same of you, Lady Rasmina."

Her guards behind her, bearing the crest of a tree with its roots splayed and spread into the ground below, tightened their grip on their swords. A disquiet and hush filled the room, people bobbing their heads to peek over their companions, eager to see the leaders exchange harsh words. Their gossip would fuel the chatter on the streets for weeks. Lady Rasmina peered over her shoulder, a subtle nod to her guards to stand down. "Funny, how one's looks can hide who one really is." Surprise sparked through Aza at hearing Lady Rasmina's voice. It was soft and light, a stark contrast to her demeanor. "A pleasure as always, Lord Aldrich."

Lord Aldrich imperceptibly tightened his grip on the throne, but he leaned forward and inclined his head towards her, keeping up with courtly pretenses. With that, she left to seat herself and her daughters at Gara's designated table. The crowd murmured unsure how to interpret the comments made between the two leaders. Aza mulled it over herself. Her comment seemed to be veiled in hidden meaning only Lord Aldrich could understand. What else was Lord Aldrich hiding and how was Lady Rasmina involved?

The crowd rustled and moved, everyone awaiting the fabled Nerian's entrance. Aza recalled her lessons with Oron. The Nerians rarely interacted with those outside of their own province and didn't travel far outside of their own borders. The herald prepared himself for his final announcement, the crowd eager to see a true Nerian within their court.

"I present the emissaries Xira and Anwin of Neria."

Aza gasped. Lorn stiffened beside her. Their faces never faded from her memories. She knew the two women who walked through the archway. They were the ones who met her in the dead of night, in an orchard grove warning her away from El'en, away from Lord Aldrich.

30

"Never cross a Nerian. It will be the last thing you do."
Common saying around the five provinces

Xira and Anwin were not affected by the fashion of the courts and held no pomp over this event. They were dressed in worn leather and outfitted with a baldric of knives along their chest and back. Many oddities singled them out, such as where they hailed from, how they were dressed for battle, the myths of their existence, but also the fact that they were alone. All the other envoys were packed with nobles and servants clamoring to be a part of the gathering. It was a grand and highly sought-after affair. Thus, everyone traveled heavily packed in regard to their travel companions and outfits.

Yet the two women casually strode into the room, their expressions stoic. They embodied every bit the harsh Nerians they were expected to be. Aza schooled her features. She saw Lilit cast a sharp look in their direction and swiftly turn back to monitor the room. Aza fought the urge to stare at Lorn, remembering he too had met them before.

The two women made their way to the throne, their faces as sharp and unyielding as the mountains guarding Neria. Their hair was pulled back into intricate braids both tiny and large twisting around the crown of their head. They needed no elegant jewelry to exaggerate their self-importance. They exuded pure power. These were not the same women she met with in the orchard, open and unguarded. These were Nerian warriors, the message they sent to the surrounding crowd was clear.

As the women stalked forward Aza turned to see Lord Aldrich's reaction. Being placed at the base of the dais, Aza was able to make out the fine details of Lord Aldrich's face; his jaw was clenched tightly, a small vein protruded from his forehead. A depth of darkness flashed within his eyes and Aza startled. One foot lost its balance and awkwardly scraped the floor. Lord Aldrich noticed the disturbance and the angered visage disappeared. She cursed under her breath for drawing attention to herself. She wanted to see Lord Aldrich's true intentions that brewed beneath the surface. Aza was expecting Xira and Anwin to stop and say a few words, but they brushed right past her, not even acknowledging her presence.

They halted in front of Lord Aldrich's dais, their heads held high, expressions unfaltering. They were not a people to bow before anyone. Before they could speak Lord Aldrich interrupted with a question, "Where is he?"

"Busy with Nerian matters," Xira replied.

"Consider yourself lucky that the two of us attended, " Anwin spat at him. The knives and daggers covering them were not only for looks. She believed the two women could wield each one of them with impressive skill.

Xira and Anwin saw themselves to their own Nerian table. Comparing their size of contingent with the other provinces would have been comical, if not for their deadly expressions. They sat, assessing the other groups, their expressions aware, calculating and weighing everyone.

They still did not look towards Aza or express any interest in her. Maybe what they offered that night in the orchard was no longer. Their offer retracted and rescinded. Or she was not as important as she thought herself to be. Whatever the reason, Aza squared her shoulders, ignored their lack of interest, and looked out over each contingent. The welcoming faces of the Verta province, the arrogance of the Kreeha province, the austere Gara province, and lastly, the cold and cutting Neria province, all converged here in the province of Iyera at the shining jewel city of El'en. This would indeed be an interesting gathering. Which province held answers for her? An uneasiness flared through her body tinged with a touch of excitement. This would not be a simple or even enjoyable task, but her future called her to move past this city and into another.

Lord Aldrich rose from his throne. The crowd quieted, ready to soak in his every word and spread it throughout the city. Aza understood the crowd's reverence. His image and words boasted that of a generous, wealthy leader—something they one day could aspire to be. He addressed the crowd first. "Thank you for being here to welcome our neighboring provinces. We are all part of Ithilia, and we need to remain united." He turned, his gaze taking in his fellow leaders. "We will have much to discuss over the coming week. I thank you for taking the time to join us." Lingering on the Nerian table, he blinked and shifted back to the crowd. "You are all dismissed."

The hushed silence broke like glass shattering on the ground as the crowd of voices rose, each talking over one another. The Iyerian guards led the citizens out and servants scattered to show leaders of each province to their rooms. Aza remained near the dais waiting for each group to disperse. This would indeed be an interesting time together. She could see friction, furtive looks, and angry glares between the provinces. Once the last of the groups filed out of the throne room, Aza said, "I hope you put each group far away from each other in the castle." Lorn chuckled beside her.

Lord Aldrich descended and stood next to her, his shoulder right next to hers. "Don't worry, nothing like a little political intrigue to stir everybody up."

Lilit stormed up to Lord Aldrich. "We need to talk." She gave Aza a dismissing look and Aza took the hint. Without rising to the bait, she led Lorn away back up to their rooms. There was much to discuss.

~

Within the safety of their rooms, afraid of the increased occupancy in the castle, Aza whispered to Lorn, "Explain everything that happened when you met Xira and Anwin."

Lorn stuttered, caught off guard. "How do you know Xira and Anwin?" he countered.

Aza's eyes widened in alarm, worried he forgot she had already met them too. "They were the women in the orchard! Remember? The ones who warned me about coming here." Understanding crossed Lorn's face. He nodded slowly, trying to piece all of the information together. Aza lightly shoved him, breaking him out of his reverie. "Now explain to me again how you met them." Aza reminded herself to keep her voice down. She had no idea who could be listening to them.

Lorn took a steadying breath. "Before I entered the Hinterlands, I stopped at the ShadowAcre Inn. The one we stayed at before we left the town." Aza nodded, the inn faintly weaving itself through her memory. "The night before I entered the Hinterlands, they entered the same inn." Aza listened patiently as the story played out in front of her. "There were four of them. I was dining alone when they entered the room. I always thought it was curious that they took an interest in me. Maybe they knew where I was going and what I was going to do." Lorn paused, reflecting on that night.

While he paused, Aza jumped in with a question, "Wait, there were four of them?"

"Yes, two men and the two women— Xira and Anwin."

"Who were the men?"

"I only caught one of their names, Reed." Lorn shook his head, chuckling to himself.

Aza couldn't believe Lorn was laughing at a time like this, when so much seemed warped around her, and she was left not knowing which way was up or down. "What's so funny?"

"I still can't believe I interacted with a group of Nerians."

"What do you mean?"

"Aza, they are ruthless. Known for their brutality and strength." He gestured to Aza, exasperation laced through his words. "You remember Oron's lessons. They do not mingle, and they keep to themselves high up in the Nerian mountains."

"Yeah, I see what you mean…The night in the orchard, Xira and Anwin, they were more…" Aza searched for the word to match their actions. "Open. Vulnerable."

"I understand completely. When they entered the inn, they were charismatic, fun." Lorn ran a hand down his face groaning. "They were probably playing me, and I fell for it. They asked me pointed questions, tried to get information from me. I divulged a bit but not enough." A panicked look took over Lorn's face as he gripped Aza's shoulders, his fingers digging into the back of her arms. "We need to get you away! They want you for their own power and purpose. Why else would they persuade you to not come to El'en?"

Aza mulled over everything Lorn said. It made sense logically. But there was something unknown, something hidden that she couldn't quite place that made her question whether the Nerians were as bad as they were being portrayed. A small doubt wriggled itself within her, the roots spread and took hold. Right now, she needed to reassure Lorn as the worry was controlling him. She knew it was from a place of concern—a deep, dark place within him where he lost the love of his life in front of his eyes. She gently removed his hands from her shoulders and held them within her own. She contained her magic, needing this physical connection with him. He needed something solid and present to keep his fear at bay. Aza peered into his hazel eyes. "Remember, I can fend for myself. You have trained me with blades, and I have been practicing my own magic. Magic which can rival and top anyone else's abilities." She squeezed his hands, pushing any and all reassurance she could through to him. "We will stay here. I will not run and cower from the potential enemies surrounding us."

Lorn blew out a breath and released his hands from her grip. "You are right. I'm overreacting." He ran a hand through his hair pushing the loose strands out of his eyes. "I know you can handle yourself. As I have told you before, I'm worried about people using you for your power. I really thought seeing the leaders of these different provinces would provide answers. Yet they are all MagicBlessed people with a position of power. They all have their flaws and motives. We need to be on our guard."

"We will be. We can handle ourselves. Remember there will be a welcoming ball held tonight. Our goal is to get to know each of them." Lorn nodded his agreement. "Let's go walk around and see if we can catch anyone wandering the castle." They left the sanctuary of their room, Aza propelled by a new mission to find the answers she so desperately sought, by questioning their new guests.

31

They descended through the castle hoping to bump into one of the leaders. Many were sequestered in their rooms, taking the time to relax and prepare for the night's festivities. Disappointment tinged Aza's steps as they found the castle relatively empty, except for some hurried servants running to and fro.

Lorn noticed her sour mood and playfully bumped his shoulder into hers. He kept his voice down as he spoke, "Chin up. We have plenty of time to talk to them. Plus with each of their *winning* personalities, maybe they are doing us a favor by not meeting us yet."

Aza cracked a smile and nodded. He was right, there was plenty of time to have a moment together with these leaders. Impatience flared through her and she attempted to tamp down the flames that licked at her. Ever since the five provinces gathered, an internal clock began ticking within her. A countdown of sorts, one she wanted to dismiss, yet couldn't cast aside.

"I saw each of them look at you Aza. They will be the ones to come to you." Aza followed Lorn as he led her to the gardens. A few people milled around taking in the beauty of the gardens, but all the leaders were absent. A marbled bench, the legs chiseled with the waves of the ocean, lay vacant. Aza and Lorn sat, a small moment of respite after the hurried day. Despite the bright clarity of the sun, the air held a distinct chill of autumn.

Shifting in her seat, she asked Lorn, "What do you think of each of the leaders?"

He pressed his thin lips together, the motion causing them to almost disappear. " I honestly don't know. I am not cut out for politics. All of the double meanings and backstabbing..." He trailed off, his gaze locked on the vibrant sky above them.

Her hand clasped his shoulder in a supportive manner. "You do not have to follow me if you do not wish it." A lump formed in Aza's throat. Even as she said the words, she didn't wish for Lorn to take her up on the offer. She would miss him dearly. "If you wish to return to your life prior to hunting, I will understand."

A small, dry laugh escaped from Lorn. "I cannot return to my life prior. There is no life prior. We are tethered together, Aza. For good or for bad." He turned to look at her, mirth dancing in his eyes. "I can put up with the different courts. Hopefully it will not be forever."

Aza relaxed. She did not want Lorn to leave her side. He was her rock, unmovable and unyielding. She needed him.

A dark shadow descended over them. Alarmed, Aza looked up at what was blocking the sun. Lord Sune towered over them, a smug look plastered on his face. "I apologize for interrupting such a tender moment between the two of you."

Lorn stood abruptly and inclined his head in a bow. "Lord Sune." Aza refused to rise to this man's bait. Aza remained, lounging on the bench. She lazily met Lord Sune's gaze. He raised an eyebrow at her lack of respect and turned to face Lorn. "Lorn of Verta, I have heard great tales of your hunting." Lord Sune extended an arm towards Lorn. Lorn's eyes widened in shock as he lifted his arm to clasp Lord Sune's, their hands gripping around the other's, their forearms parallel to each other. Behind Lorn, Lord Sune and two of his guards were stationed a fair distance beyond him. Their armor was vastly different from the armor worn by the Iyerian guards. Instead of heavy metal covering their body, they seemed to be draped in a thin, white-gold material. It extended down to their wrists, the material thin and wispy like spider webs. Attached to their waist were curved swords. Their golden hue caught the rays of suns and winked towards Aza. She faintly heard the conversation between Lorn and Lord Sune in the background and brought herself back to their conversation.

"I see you admiring my guard's armor."

Aza relinquished her cavalier exterior and responded, "Yes, I haven't seen anything like it." Lord Sune ushered one of his guards forward. Aza rose from the bench to catch a closer look at the unfamiliar material.

Not wanting to be too forward she asked the guard for permission to touch the material. Giving his consent, her hand brushed the armor examining the delicate yet strong feel of it. It glistened as she ran a finger down it. Lorn's head was right next to her, intently examining the armor. "I have heard rumors of this, but have never seen it in person," Lorn whispered.

"What is it?" Aza asked, her curiosity getting the better of her.

Lord Sune's voice cut through the quiet garden, enveloping it in his deep voice. "It is extremely rare, called Goldenring. Only a select few of my personal guards wear it. It is a rare material harvested from deep within Kreeha and only around the Midsummer Festival. We don't truly know why or how it happens, but our scholars believe the strength of the sun and the power of the Well combine to help make the material."

"How is it harvested?" Lorn asked, his hand running along the material again. Aza did the same. It felt light and heavy. Soft yet hard. The material itself seemed to be a paradox.

Lord Sune grinned. "I can't be sharing all of our secrets, but it is very time consuming."

The guard wearing the armor shook slightly, and a light sheen of sweat dotted his forehead. Aza pulled back her hand inspecting the material. "I'm sorry, I didn't mean to cause you any discomfort." The effect was immediate as she pulled her hand away. The guard relaxed and let out a soft exhale.

"Nonsense." Lord Sune laughed and clapped his guard on the back causing his shoulder to buckle under the weight of his hand. "Hanu, I'm sure you can handle her touch." The guard stiffened, caught in a precarious position not wanting to disagree with his lord and not wanting to offend Aza.

Aza stepped in to prevent the guard from making that tough choice. "Many are overwhelmed by my touch. My magic tends to consume those around me." She met Hanu's eyes and gave a small nod. "I apologize, I tend to forget my own power." The guard nodded back and looked desperate to join his companion some distance away from Aza. Lord Sune dismissed him and sent a curious look at Aza.

"Will you both accompany me for a walk in this garden?" Aza hesitated. This was what she wanted. She needed to meet and talk with each of these leaders, but his cockiness upon their first meeting rang through her mind. He viewed her as a prize, nothing more.

"Why would you value time with someone you view only as a prize?" Aza's tone was sharp, reprimanding. Despite needing Lord Sune's time, she couldn't betray her pride.

Lord Sune's cocky demeanor faltered. "I misspoke when I saw you this morning. It was callous and unwarranted. I apologize." His silver tongue twisted, his words adapting to his new obstacle.

Aza marked how easily this man swayed, his personality effortlessly shifting like the sand traps hidden around Kreeha. This was the start of the game. Aza needed to be on guard and find the answers she sought. "Apology accepted." Aza and Lorn led the way with Lord Sune falling in step beside them. People passed by the outskirts of the garden, nosy eyes and ears eager to pry on their conversation. Aza already garnered too much unwanted attention. Her striking features and commanding presence caused people to stop dead in their tracks. The three of them strolling in a garden—the famed Lorn of Verta, Hunter of the Hinterlands, Lord Sune of Kreeha, and Aza, gossip was bound to spread.

Aza hoped upon meeting the lords and ladies of each province, it might trigger one of her memories. Maybe a flyaway comment could ignite a feeling or something buried deep within. There were a multitude of unanswered questions, and she hoped the secret to unlocking the knowledge lay within the other provinces.

"You are quite a mystery, Aza." Lord Sune conceded. "Do you mind sharing your story with me?"

"There isn't too much to tell. I was formed from the Well, and Lorn found me there." Aza knew she would receive questions about her origins and kept it purposefully vague.

"Ahh yes, the famed Lorn of Verta." Lord Sune clapped Lorn on the back, "You must regale me with tales of the Hinterlands. You are the only one who has entered and emerged sane and without injury. What was it like?"

Lorn had shared small stories of the Hinterlands with her, but most of it was still a mystery to her. Lorn's face shuttered. "The tales of the Hinterlands are too dark for the likes of this lovely day. Maybe another time, when recounting the horrors within will feel more bearable." His eyes lost the light within, his essence slowly leaching away from him.

Lord Sune cleared his throat, catching the cold look in Lorn's eyes. "Yes, maybe some other time."

"The Hinterlands itself was suffocating. The forest was not healthy. The wood twisted, decayed, rotten. Right now, you can feel the flare of your magic within your body like the beat of your heart. Within the Hinterlands, it was withered, smothered. It is a feeling I never wish to experience again."

Usually adorned with his arrogant demeanor, Lord Sune was suddenly uncomfortable with Lorn's frank assessment of the Hinterlands. He averted his eyes staring out over the Wyra ocean, "I see what you mean Lorn. Thank you for sharing." Immediately, he regained his composure and changed the subject. "I hear you are a formidable fighter! I would love to see you against my own guards." He turned to Aza. "And your magic prowess I've heard compares to no one else. Would you mind doing a demonstration?" Aza considered him, his handsome muscular physique, the gold links wrapped in his braids glinting in the sun. She would concede, if only to play the political game and gain advantage.

They both agreed to demonstrate their skills the following morning. Lord Sune's eagerness was noticeable. After the brief mention of the Hinterlands Lord Sune navigated the conversation to banal, common subjects, never straying into anything remotely exciting. There were no memory triggers, nothing revealed. Aza tried not to let the minor defeat weigh her down. It was only just the beginning.

As the afternoon wore on, they departed to ready themselves for the giant feast planned for the evening. Aza knew it would be a lot of the same. Many would comment on her extravagant power or want to see a demonstration. She wanted to get to know these people, but she only had a week's time. She would make do with what she had so far. *The feast tonight will be interesting,* she thought.

Aza decided to change her outfit, instead donning a dress in a similar shade to her tunic and pants—the same black material with hints of silver winking through. It suited her and there would be plenty of other times she would have to dress up and parade around like a colorful bird in front of the other guests. As she walked, she felt the press of the hidden dagger under her dress, the cold metal flush against her skin. With the pretense of civility among guests, weapons needed to be discreet. Her regretful thoughts traveled back to the beautiful longsword left in her room. *Plus,* Aza thought ruefully, *she didn't need one if there was trouble.* Lorn had also left his sword on the table, but he had secretly equipped daggers as well. He reassured her that most of the people would have hidden weapons. Except for the guards, everyone else would be weaponless as a sign of good faith.

Aza and Lorn awaited in their rooms until a knock at the door ushered them back to the throne room. The servant who escorted them was nervous, her eyes darting between Aza and Lorn unsure of who to look at. Aza hoped the other lords and ladies were treating the staff well. If not, she may have to go have a personal word with them.

With the crowd of Iyerian citizens gone, the throne room was replaced with a massive table spanning the length of the room. It was covered with plates of food. It was a demonstration of Iyera's strength and prosperity. Aza was surprised the wood table didn't buckle under the weight of all the food gathered on top of it. Platters of roasted meats encrusted with herbs, vegetables heaped with mounds of golden-yellow butter, bowls of nuts, and fresh fish caught from the Wyra ocean laid on the table. Aza spotted more and more food, her mouthwatering. One of the perks of eating in the castle was receiving the best food throughout all of Ithilia. After traveling on the road, she had grown accustomed to travel rations and meager portions that they had hunted near each town. Aza would never take this delicious food for granted.

The servant brought them over to their designated table seated as guests of honor next to Lord Aldrich. Oron, Gravers and Lilit were already seated at the table. Both Gravers and Lilit were dressed in their uniform. Lilit held all the regalia of the Captain of the Guard, her uniform bedecked in medals. Aza faltered, a sadness swelling up within her. She had not figured out how to help Lilit yet, despite her vehement warnings not to.

Oron smiled widely as they both sat down. Gravers gave a faint nod in their direction and Lilit barely deigned to give them a glance. Lord Aldrich still wore his elaborate garb from the morning and turned to greet them. Aza knew everything about his performance was perfectly crafted from his smile to including them in the conversation. He was putting on an act for the other provinces, letting them see how kind and benevolent he was to his honored guests. Aza played along. Biting back a frustrated sigh, she forced her gaze over the guests. Unwilling to entertain the duality of Lord Aldrich's personality was at once charming and maddening—with a conniving calculation he bounced between them effortlessly.

The other guests filtered in, finding their seats amongst the tables labeled for each of their respective provinces. Everyone wore the same outfits as before, only having used the brief interlude to freshen up in between. Lord Aldrich stayed in animated conversation with Aza and Lorn, his questions and statements hiding their banality. Lorn politely followed along, and Aza made vague distant replies to the conversation, her vision following those who entered the room. She caught sight of Xira and Anwin making their way to their over-sized table. She willed their eyes to meet hers, but they never strayed over to Lord Aldrich's table.

Once all the tables and provinces had filed in, Lord Aldrich pushed himself up from his chair, the bottom legs scraping the floor. The room quieted as people began to nudge each other and point in his direction. With the room silent, Lord Aldrich's voice boomed, "Welcome." The sentiment rang out. "Welcome my friends from afar. All of you have traveled a great distance to be here, and it is noted and appreciated." His head swiveled slowly, a sincere glance toward each province's table. "We will begin our feast shortly, but first I have two very important introductions."

A ripple of conversation poured out among the tables. Lord Aldrich cleared his throat and Aza clutched Lorn's leg under the table with a tight squeeze. She wasn't expecting a formal introduction in front of the whole audience. "During the summer I tracked down the famed Hunter of Beasts. Lorn of Verta." Lord Aldrich motioned for Lorn to rise. Lorn shakily stood, his eyes glancing around unsure of what was expected of him. Aza could feel the hesitation rippling off him.

"He emerged victorious from a task no other could complete, no other would even dare to even try." Lord Aldrich's voice rose, deepening and booming throughout the throne room, enticing those around him. "He who was brave, and steady of heart and mind was able to enter and escape the Hinterlands!"

A collective gasp rippled throughout the throne room. Everyone cheered. The applause was deafening. Aza noted the faces that beheld fake countenances, those who were obligated to clap, but held back their bitterness. Lorn was uncomfortable with the praise but held his shoulders back and feet planted on the ground. He was not one to call attention to himself. Aza knew Lord Aldrich was making him uncomfortable. "I sent Lorn of Verta to travel deep within the Hinterlands in hopes of bringing back an item of magic. Instead of finding an item of magic, Lorn brought back Aza of the Well."

The applause faltered, the crowd uncertain how to react. Lorn was famed and revered. Many dreamed, fantasizing of being hero. One able to enter the Hinterlands and return unscathed. However, to praise Aza, an unknown entity who appeared from the Well, that was a dangerous affair. Flickers of fear, suspicion, and awe flashed across the guests' faces. Some that knew who she was were not surprised, like Lord Sune. But for the rest, a deep-seeded paranoia deepened in the room.

Their collective stares and judgments held her frozen in place. Lord Aldrich pulled her from her chair, her daze interrupted. Aza stood tall, her eyes sweeping the room and meeting every wary look with one of coolness. The curious looks from earlier had turned on her. She knew this would happen eventually. She wanted to ignore it. Ignore this.

Lorn was right, the people would view her with suspicion. Aza had grown comfortable within the safe confines of Lord Aldrich's castle and the real world outside of this sanctuary would prove difficult. The judgment and envy from the crowd was a noxious fume leaking towards her. Blinded by her innocence and companionship with Lorn, she forgot the utterly cutthroat nature of the people around her. Unless people had the power for themselves, they would always be fearful of it. And she was the very definition of power.

Lord Aldrich continued speaking, but she didn't hear the words. Instead, she caught the looks between people. Aza debated releasing her power, letting the crowd have a feel of what her magic could do, but that would not be how she wanted to be remembered—someone who inspired fear and lorded their power over others. Instead, she plastered a vacant smile on her face and reigned her magic in, pulling it in tightly so that none could escape.

Disappointment flashed across Lord Aldrich's face. Aza thought she had imagined it, because she immediately saw him don his lordly mask and forcefully clap for her. The room was stunned into near silence. Only pockets of whispers remained.

It was more and more tempting to stay within the comfortability of El'en's castle. To be looked upon as different and separate from those around her was uncomfortable. As Aza searched the crowd she saw two faces stand out. Xira and Anwin. Their faces were contorted into a look of disgust. Aza wanted to bow her head in shame.

Lord Aldrich bade everyone sit and begin eating. Servants rushed to grab trays of food for their respective tables and food was laid in piles upon plates. Everything appeared delicious. Lord Aldrich's cooks had outdone themselves, but Aza could not eat, knowing it would taste like ash, the nausea and unease slithering throughout her body. She would never be accepted by the MagicBlessed, and it was something she didn't want to dwell on. Yet the proof lay in front of her. All of the tables looked at her with outright suspicion.

Lorn shifted in his seat and his hazel eyes found hers. His voice was soft, barely a whisper yet Aza heard it clearly. "Are you well?"

Mad at succumbing to her emotion, tears of frustration swelled beneath the surface. "No, I am not." Her voice wavered as she fought down her rising emotions. Lorn gritted his teeth, his eyes holding Aza's own. He did not look away, trying to silently support her while the bevy of onlookers gawked and judged.

Aza was forcibly twisted the other way and was suddenly facing Lord Aldrich. He leaned in close, his face right next to her ear. The heat and power he exuded trailed along the side of her face. "Fuck them all. Do not reign in your power. It is their choice to be scared, not your duty to appease them. You are fucking exquisite. Do not dampen your power. Be who you are, Aza."

He pulled away and Aza was bereft. Her tangled feelings for Lord Aldrich confused her. One moment he was threatening Lilit, and the next, he was empowering her and uplifting her. Something was so familiar, she couldn't place it. But he was sincere. A stab of heat flashed through her. She couldn't respond so she nodded her head.

Lord Aldrich pulled away from her and resumed his conversation with Gravers. Before Aza began to eat, she couldn't help but notice

Lilit. A look of pain and anger twisted her features, then disappeared. The clatter of silverware echoed within the room, along with the chatter of gossip among the provinces. Aza could not shake the look of pain on Lilit's face. She wanted to leave this mundane dinner and find safety within the sanctuary of her room. Aza forced herself to stay at the table, nibbling bites of food which slid down her dry throat.

Musicians began setting up in the corner, a combination of string instruments and a female singer. Her golden curled hair was swept up with a beautiful ruby-inlaid comb. The singer's body was draped in a deep-green dress which hugged her sumptuous curves. The full-figured singer stepped forward; the tables hushed in anticipation.

Lorn leaned next to her. "I hear she is the best singer in all of Iyera." Aza was ready for a distraction. She only wanted to be another MagicBlessed citizen enjoying the beautiful singer in front of her. With the throne room silent, the musicians began.

A slow, mournful song played, the notes eerily resonating within Aza's soul. She closed her eyes, allowing the music to wash over her. It called to the magic held deep within her, tugging it forward. She acknowledged it. The notes rose and fell. Her magic, her very being was lost in it. Once the singer added her voice to the music, Aza's eyes flashed open. Her haunting soprano voice paired beautifully with the string instruments. Aza thought of the Wyra ocean, how the waves crested and fell, the song unfolding in front of them echoed that feeling. Aza's eyes drifted closed again, allowing herself to become one with the sounds.

The story depicted the people's obsession with the moon and how their obsession turned deadly. The moon in its grace and glory bore the obsession until the townspeople turned deadly. The moon instead focused her love on the stars, her twinkling companions. With greed in their heart the townspeople ripped the stars from the moon's embrace, seeking her glory only for themselves. With this final betrayal the moon turned her full fury upon those who sought her, wreaking destruction and chaos. Left with only herself, the moon mourned the loss of her friends and cursed those that pursued her.

Aza lost herself to the song. Her magic swelled and dipped with the lyrics. The sound swept through her. Her magic felt lightweight, effortless, and it wanted to join along in this song of mourning and triumph. She released the tight hold on it, and it unspooled in front of her.

Whispers spread, the song interrupted by hurried chatter. The singer's last note was drawn out as the instruments mimicked her voice. Deprived of the beautiful music, Aza's eyes finally opened. She was glowing. Floating orbs of light drifted throughout the entire throne room, casting a romantic hue on everything. The whispers were not filled with hate and suspicion, but with beauty and awe. People pointed at the floating lights, their faces filled with wonder. The music had pulled out this beauty in her magic, like a gem being uncovered from the rock surrounding it. It was fragile and beautiful. Aza relaxed, a rare, genuine smile filling her face as she beheld the beauty of her magic. The moment was suspended in time. Aza indulged a moment longer. The lights floated gracefully overhead filling the dark cavernous areas of the throne room. With a snap of her fingers, the orbs exploded. Soft trickles of radiance fell like a waterfall from each explosion, like a flurry of fireflies had occupied the room. The lights sparkled and twinkled. Aza caught a brief, self-satisfied smile on Lord Aldrich's face before she turned to the crowd before her.

A soft applause filled the room, everyone heavily blinked as if recovering from a daze. The singer nodded in Aza's direction and another song began playing. This was more upbeat and encouraged dancing. Servers expertly removed plates and tables out of the way so guests could dance.

"I have never done that with my magic of light." Lorn's face beamed with pride. "Would you like to dance?" His hand reached out expectantly.

She was taken aback; for some reason, she never expected Lorn to know how to dance.

Reading her mind he responded, "I know how to dance, and I must admit I am rather skilled."

Aza clasped her hands in the familiarity of his and joined him on the dance floor. Spurred by their confidence, other couples joined. Lorn placed one hand on her waist and the other delicately held hers. The music lifted and they took off. Lorn guided her, his feet swift and agile as they twirled. He swirled and dipped her with the music, their bodies moving quickly and nimbly across the floor. Aza didn't care about the other couples around her; she savored this precious moment with her friend. Lorn wasn't lying about his dancing skills. Aza let herself go, with only Lorn and the music to guide her, she felt secure. The music picked up speed, and they flew across the floor. She was breathless. Her laughter rang out, unencumbered by the weight of her problems and the weight of her fears. It was laughter of triumph and friendship. It was laughter reminiscent of their escape from the Hinterlands, one of complete abandon. Lorn smiled in response, his own face mirroring her joy. Too soon the song came to an end. Aza froze, her chest heaving from exertion, a silly smile stuck on her face.

Lorn escorted her off the dance floor. Aza caught Lord Sune with his consort Ryu heading up to dance. He discreetly sent her a wink as they passed. Refreshments lay on the other end of the throne room and with her arm wrapped around Lorn's, they made their way to get a drink.

Aza sagged against the wall, her shirt sticking to her with perspiration. Lorn returned to her side, two glasses of sparkling liquid in his hands. "This is a famed drink of Ithilia, typically partaken at special events. It is called Starwine, because the type of grapes used to brew this are only harvested on very specific days of the moon's rising. I hear it can be extremely tricky to harvest. This particular bottle is from Lord Aldrich's personal vault."

Thirsty, Aza reached for the glass, the liquid almost clear with a faint silver glow to it. She took a sip. The Starwine was light and crisp, and absolutely delicious. Aza tilted her head back, consuming the whole glass.

Lorn chuckled. "You should slow down, Starwine is very strong and can have adverse effects."

Aza disagreed. She felt wonderful. It filled every part of her body. She was light and buoyant. She left Lorn to grab more Starwine from a server. Upon her absence people surrounded him instantly. She must have been keeping his admirers at bay, the people too frightened of her to approach the famed Lorn of Verta. He shot her a dismayed look as she returned one of mock sympathy. Aza flagged down a server and they brought her another glass. She decided to take her time, slowly savoring each sip. She tucked herself into a corner, wanting to detract attention from herself and scan the room. The musicians played on, the throne room filled with their jubilant sound, the singer weaving her voice throughout each of the songs.

A light, breathy voice caught her off guard. "Your magic is

impressive."

32

"Luckily, we do not have to deal with many magic-related incidents. With the diminished power of the MagicBlessed over time, their magic had reached a point of not being able to do any impacting damage."

Guard entry from the garrison on the border of El'en

Aza whipped around. Lady Rasmina of Gara stood next to her. Standing so close gave Aza a better view. Her porcelain skin was flawless and her features even more beautiful up close. Despite the compliment, Aza sensed the Lady was scrutinizing her as one would an enemy on the battlefield.

Aza gave a curt reply, "Thank you."

Lady Rasmina didn't even acknowledge the response. Her eerie blue eyes scanned Aza from head to toe. Aza bristled at the inspection. "It is a shame."

"What is?"

"That you are his pet. Something to be *kept*."

Aza's magic reared at the insult, and she tamped it down. It wouldn't do well to harm a leader of another province during a time of peace. She could only grunt out a word through her clenched teeth, "Whose pet?"

Lady Rasmina's voice remained light, unaffected by Aza's demeanor. "Why *his* of course." She inclined her head toward Lord Aldrich. "There are rumors and whispers. With as much power as you have—why are you here?" Aza tightened her hands, the nails embedding into her skin. She focused on her breathing. This woman was trying to rile her, trying to get her to respond in front of a crowd of people. Lady Rasmina carried on. "Of course, there are other reasons you might stay. Rumors abound, even in the other provinces." Aza furrowed her brows in confusion. Who she was had become widespread knowledge? "Oh yes, all of the provinces and their courts know of you, have waited to meet you." Lady Rasmina leaned in conspiratorially. "Are the whispers true?" Lady Rasmina's eyebrows slightly lifted awaiting Aza's response. Her red lips curved like a predator realizing it had cornered its prey. Try as she might, Aza couldn't walk away. She had been lured by Lady Rasmina's venom. "Many say you are his whore." Aza's magic flared, but if Lady Rasmina felt it, she indicated nothing. "I had my spies receive word of many interesting things. Maybe you are not only his whore, but also Lorn's?"

Unable to control it, Aza's magic exploded. She could tolerate the slander of her own character, but not of her friend Lorn. She knew what he had gone through, his terrible life experiences. She would not have Lady Rasmina insult him too.

A blast of wind erupted from Aza. Lady Rasmina slammed backwards into the wall and crumpled to the floor, her tiny porcelain figure looking broken. The people surrounding them clattered to the floor, scrambling on their hands and knees. People screamed and the music abruptly halted. The room filled with stillness, then people rushed into motion. Lady Rasmina's guards encircled Aza, swords held to her throat. One of the guards shouted, "Check on Lady Rasmina." A guard knelt beside her feeling for a pulse. Lady Rasmina's eyes flickered open, her hand reaching up to the back of her head. She pulled away, blood coating the white fingers. Her face showed nothing, no shock, no pain. She only held Aza's eye's in a silent challenge.

Aza held her hands up in supplication, letting them know the conflict had ended. Lorn pushed people aside, racing to get to her. Her eyes caught Lady Rasmina's three daughters. The older two held looks of disgust, while the youngest only looked impossibly sad.

"What happened?" Lord Aldrich's voice parted the crowd.

Wanting to speak before others skewed the story, Aza answered. "I lost control of my magic," Aza muttered, heat creeping up her face.

The guard helped Lady Rasmina to her feet. "I'm sure it was an accident. Everyone can put their swords down. Come help me to my rooms." Her innocent voice and tone attempted to endear those around her to rally to her side. Lady Rasmina's daughters assisted her out of the room, the guards trailing in their wake. The nobility of Gara followed her out in a show of solidarity, revulsion on their faces.

With the Gara contingent out of the throne room, gossip and muttering spread. Aza couldn't look anyone in the eye. Shame crept through her. Aza cursed herself. Lady Rasmina wanted to appear innocent, and she wanted Aza to appear unhinged and incapable of handling herself. She wanted people to view Aza as a threat. Having accomplished her goal, Aza wanted to scream at being played so easily.

Whispers bounced around the room.

"If she can't control herself, she's a danger to everyone around?"

"What if she attacks us without being provoked?"

"This is not safe, I'm leaving."

"You should have a leash on that pet, Lord Aldrich."

Lord Ravinder of Verta marched up to Lord Aldrich. His typically jovial demeanor was replaced with blatant fear. "Lord Aldrich, how can we all be here in good faith when we have a person with unchecked magic able to fell any one of us? This is hardly sensible for us to stay here when our safety is our biggest concern."

Lady Sarava joined her husband, linking her arm with his. "I agree with my husband. The safety of our people is our highest priority."

Lord Aldrich nodded, listening to their concerns. "Aza has occupied this castle for the last two months. She has never exhibited any behavior like this before." He scanned the crowd making eye contact with every person gathered. "I trust her to not lose control again."

His declaration barely appeased the crowd, who looked ready to throw her in the dungeon. No longer wanting to stay at the party, people dispersed back to their rooms. Looks of suspicion and loathing were abundant. Aza didn't have the heart to look into their eyes as they left. She heard the whispers. The thin veil of illusion was pulled from her eyes; she could see how the people truly viewed her. Something to be feared. Something to be kept. Something to be used.

Before she knew it Lorn's arm was around her shoulder guiding her back to her room. She didn't have the energy to keep her magic contained and despite the pain Lorn must have been experiencing from touching her, he did not falter. No words were spoken. Overwhelming frustration filled her. She knew better than to rise to the easily laid bait of some political opponent. And yet, she had fallen for it.

Unwilling to talk, Lorn left her. The hesitancy of his steps indicated his silent opposition. Once in the privacy of her room, Aza stripped off her beautiful clothes and climbed into bed. The coldness of the autumn air crept into the room. She allowed it to, numbing her to the feeling of her inadequacies.

~

Aza stood in the center of a wheat field, the stalks swaying in the soft afternoon breeze. She tilted her head up to the sun above, letting the heat wash over her skin. Any moment he would be here. The crunch of wheat stalks underfoot sounded behind her. She didn't even greet him.

Instead, she turned and freed her magic. The anger. The hatred. Every emotion intrinsically tied to herself and her magic she let go with wild abandon and released it at Cruvo. The smile Aza didn't even care to see, vanished. The entire wheat field caught on fire from her magic. Cruvo responded. His own water doused the wheat. Aza crumbled the ground beneath him. Cruvo jumped aside and formed a ledge out of the dirt. Frustrated, Aza sprinted at him, her magic forming sharpened icicles ready to skewer him. He easily melted them and dodged the attack. Cruvo only stayed on the defensive, letting Aza release all her anger and frustration. They darted around one another. One attacking and one defending. Her reserve of energy was not draining. If anything, her anger was growing.

"Aza!" Cruvo shouted. "Talk to me. What happened?" He tried to restrain her body, trapping her in ice, but she easily broke free and went to attack him again. He was the only one who didn't view her as a monster. *That's not true,* a voice whispered to her. She was a monster, look at her. She was fighting a god and he was her match. Even *he* was tiring under her relentless onslaught. She kept attacking him, and he diffused them. Maneuvering to gain ground and finding an opening, he sprinted towards her. Aza's magic grew frenzied, shooting out wildly around her. Cruvo clasped her wrists, his hair whipping around in the wild torrent of air that Aza cast around.

"Aza!" His piercing green eyes searched hers trying to find something to hold on to. His magic pushed against hers, enveloping it and warping it. He was trying to calm her enraged spirit by blending it with his own. "Aza," he breathed out her name and the wild wind around them calmed. Cruvo's strong hand cradled the curve of her face, his eyes beseeching Aza to listen to him.

Her voice felt detached as she whispered, "They only see me as a monster."

"You are anything but that," he countered.

"They will never see anything else," she muttered. Tears threatened to spill out.

Cruvo gripped her chin, forcing her eyes to meet his. "You have power, Aza. Everyone will always fear it. It is something you must embrace." A tear dripped down her face and he traced the wet trail of it with his finger, clearing it away. "You are able to battle a god, and honestly you wear me down. I do not know what you are, my stars. But I never want you to be ashamed of your powers. Never of that."

"They all cower before me. I can't bear it. There is genuine fear in their eyes."

"It is not up to you to manage their fear. They look upon you and see power they will never have. That is not something to be afraid of."

"I hurt someone today. They used their words against me, and I lashed out in anger. I didn't control myself. They orchestrated it perfectly and made me appear like a dangerous monster."

"Then next time, beat them at their own game. Outmaneuver them, out manipulate them. You can do it. You just need practice."

He kissed her gently, his lips caressing hers. Her mouth opened in invitation, and he explored further. She relaxed, allowing him to guide the pace. The frenetic energy channeled from anger to something else. Needing a release, she let him continue. His hands moved to the rest of her body, igniting her. Aza's body arched into his hands. His fingers deftly moved over her breasts teasing her nipples. Ripping the shirt off over Aza's head, he moved lower, his mouth hovering over her nipple. His tongue swirled around the tip, eliciting a deep moan from Aza. He supported her body as she relaxed into his grip. She loved watching him as he worshipped her body. Cruvo broke contact and looked back into her eyes. "As I have said before, you are fucking exquisite, my stars."

Aza froze, her body instantly still. "What did you say?" she whispered more to herself than to him. Aza pushed him away. She grabbed the discarded shirt off the ground and covered herself.

Cruvo remained where he was, confusion warring over his features.

"What did you say?" Aza repeated louder. His green eyes followed her. Aza clutched the shirt to her chest as a useless shield of protection from the god across from her. "No, no, no, no... Wake up!" she yelled.

Aza sat up in her bed, the coldness of the room seeping into her soul. She grabbed the pillow from underneath her head and screamed into it, her rage and betrayal resonating within her enclosed chamber.

33

*"In this time of great peace amongst the MagicBlessed, spies
are considered a rarity. Who would need to resort to such a
thing in a time of prosperity?"*

Ripped out entry from a scholar's notebook.

Lorn didn't know how to comfort Aza. Last night did not go well.
Lady Rasmina was clearly pulling some political schemes to portray
Aza in a negative light. Anyone with half a mind could see that,
however Lorn feared how successful it was. Aza had taken it
personally, not responding to his knock on her door.

It was difficult for him to organize all the different thoughts and
feelings that filtered through him. He did not view Aza as this
untouchable entity—over time she had become his closest friend. Her
powers, her abilities, those were a part of who she was, but she was
changing. Shifting. Altering into who she truly is. Lorn struggled to
remember the first time he met her appearing from the Well, her
demeanor and understanding of the world limited, her spirit still
caught in an in-between state, like she was still lost among the stars.
Being here and training in El'en, Aza had found part of herself—who
she truly was. Lorn saw the glimmering facets of her personality
shine through, the trust she had in others, her drive, her
overwhelming sense of feeling towards others. It was a stark contrast
to her brutal nature that night in the inn. She had lost her ability to
act first, instead of becoming thoughtful and more calculated, instead
of demonstrating pure strength. Lorn worried it would be her
downfall. As her grit and toughness eroded like the stone below this

castle, it left her vulnerable. *That* Lorn couldn't abide. When her trust shined through, it was so radiant the sun balked from its brightness.

Trying not to be hurt by the snub, he left to find breakfast for himself. On his way down to the dining hall, Lord Sune intercepted him. "Lorn of Verta, how Fate keeps placing the two of us together." Lorn fought the urge to roll his eyes. "Are you up to a demonstration this morning?" Confusion must have lingered on his face because Lord Sune elaborated, "Yesterday morning we discussed a sparring demonstration, one to show off your skills." Lorn had completely forgotten about the demonstration, his mind wrapped up in the previous night's drama. He absentmindedly nodded his agreement and Lord Sune clapped him on the back. "Good man. I hope to see some of the skills you are rumored to possess."

Hopefully the sparring would clear his mind. Too much, everything was beginning to be too much. Aza's face flashed in his mind, her joy while they danced. He believed it was the unrestrained joy and freedom that made her shine. Usually she always held back, something deep within, something she was probably unaware of—held her back, weighed her down. Weighed down her soul. Maybe it was her power, but it could have been something else, something she needed to discover.

All of the leaders' ambitions and schemes left Lorn with a tension that nearly overwhelmed him. Lorn needed to figure out where Aza's answers could be located. He found a secluded area of the dining room to eat quietly, to allow his thoughts to settle. His peace was shattered quickly as nobles approached. They all were polite and greeted him cordially. Many wanted to shake his hand and hear a small story from the famed Hunter of the Hinterlands. He was humbled by the attention, but he couldn't ignore the fact that many of these smiling faces were the same that viewed Aza with such suspicion last night.

After appeasing the groups of admirers, Lorn excused himself and escaped to his room. After readying himself for his sparring battle, he listened at the door connecting his room with Aza's. Lorn heard nothing and decided to leave her alone for a little more time. It was a dangerous time for Aza to exhibit a blatant display of her magic. Yet, frustration warred within. She should have the freedom to decide.

He strapped his sword to his belt and grabbed his bow. This was where he excelled. This was what brought him comfort. This is what allowed him to escape the political intrigue and hostile whispers that permeated the castle. Racing downstairs, he was ready for the exhilaration and focus that came with training. He wanted to focus on a single target, a single opponent, and to show them his skill, earned from his years of dedication and practice. This political scheming frustrated him to no end, yet he had vowed to stick with Aza. There was nothing else for him.

Lorn made his way to the training ring, located near the stables around the back of the castle. He was thankful for the inconspicuous location—he didn't need flocks of admirers coming to watch him practice. Fame was something he would never adjust to. He thought back to his dreams of becoming a hero as a child. How silly. The reality was tiring. Most of the people meant well, but it was perpetually tiring, having to appease these people who thought they knew the depths of your character. They would approach him with exaggerated stories of his achievements. Only he knew the truth of his experiences. People boasted of his encounters with excitement, while only he knew the rage and hollowness that consumed him on those journeys. Everyone was curious about the Hinterlands too, but the memories of what he experienced were still raw. It was tricky to give details without exposing too much of what he went through in those dark and twisted woods. When he spoke of the Hinterlands, an imaginary diseased hand crawled along his arm, sinking its rotting nails into his flesh. No, he did not wish to return to that poisonous land in thought or in person.

Lorn rounded a corner coming upon the immaculate stables that started his journey. The familiar huffing of horses caused him to take a detour through the stables. When the castle life became too unbearable and he needed a return to his home and farm life in Verta, he would visit them. Their movements and smells transported him to his quaint life from before.

Animals, he understood their motives, their behaviors. He did not have to explain himself or put on a show for them. Instead, he could share their steadfast companionship without repercussion. The horses eagerly rushed to the front of their stalls, familiar with Lorn after the months of his presence at the castle. He rifled through a burlap bag of food, fished out some carrots and apples, greeted each horse with a pat on the head, and offered them a treat. The horse master would disapprove of early morning treats for his horses, but Lorn couldn't summon the energy to care. They calmed him, and he wanted to reward them for such friendship.

Bidding the horses goodbye he left the earthy smell of their stables and walked in the brisk autumn air. The Wyra ocean coated the castle in a seaside chill. Lorn picked up his pace in an attempt to warm his body, before entering the training ring. He turned the corner and halted to a stop. A giant crowd was encircled around the training ring despite the small size. The guard barracks were located on the outskirts of the city, so the practice grounds here were offered as a small reprieve for the guards stationed here, and any rogue citizen who would want to practice in their free time. The training grounds was dwarfed by the sizable crowd. Lord Sune broke free of the crowd, his braids pulled back from his face with a leather wrap. He changed his attire from the previous day. Lorn noted he was dressed equally as lavish, but his clothes were more suited for training. Lord Sune wore a simple shirt, and tight-fitted pants, in the Iyerian fashion unlike the loose, billowing fabrics and style of Kreeha. He wore similar boots to Lorn, the toe scuffing the dirt of the training ring. Despite Lord Sune's dressed down appearance, he was still as regal as the prior night with people fawning over him. He had an indefinable quality about him. One couldn't help but stare, and Lord Sune used it to his advantage.

"I apologize for the large crowd." He waved his arms theatrically at the throng.

Knowing his words to be false, his face reminded Lorn of a child who had taken too many sweets. Word had gotten out about the demonstration and Lord Sune had fanned the flames.

Lord Sune was a difficult man to assess. He was the epitome of a political leader, his words and actions in constant opposition to one another. "I cannot help that word had spread of the famed Lorn of Verta doing a demonstration." Lord Sune peered around Lorn. "Is Aza not joining us this morning?" Lorn shook his head saying nothing further. He would not give this man more fodder to spread among the people, the insidious gossip spreading like wildfire. "Ah, a shame! Seeing her magic last night left me wanting more. Maybe another time."

Whispers spread as Lorn stepped through the crowd. At the far end of the training ring, he spotted a set of targets and several of Lord

Sune's personal bodyguards waiting. "Would you rather start with bow and arrow or swords?" Lord Sune asked. The crowd awaited Lorn's response.

"I'm sure your guards will be able to out-shoot me. I'm no expert in archery. Let's start there." He walked over to the marks on the ground, aware of all the eyes following him. Even when he helped rid villages of the wandering beasts from the Hinterlands, he had never had an audience. It caused his neck to itch in irritation, as if the eyes burrowed deep underneath his skin. Lord Sune's guards stood beside him, eager to have their chance to rival the famed hunter. A slew of guards bearing the crests from the other provinces joined, wishing to be included in the competition. The Iyerian garrison supplied all the soldiers with bows and arrows. Lorn noticed a few guards had their own bows, their hands gripping the well-worn wood—the intricate woodwork apparent and cherished.

A mark was made on the ground from where they had to shoot from. Lorn detached himself from the noise and commotion. He thought back to his mornings when he and Lakesh were able to practice and hone their skills. A friendly competition, where Lakesh typically dominated in archery and Lorn would win in hand-to-hand combat. The background melted away as he gripped the bow in his hand, his eyes focusing on the target and nothing else. He nocked an arrow and let it fly. It hit the target dead center. He moved to the next, and the next, and the next.

He returned his awareness to his surroundings and smiled humbly. All three of his arrows were embedded dead center in the targets. Over the last few months, Lorn had made it a habit to include archery in his training. He didn't want to lose the skill he had acquired over so long a time. His mind trailed back to when he last used it, when he fought the twisted bear in the Hinterlands. His skill had saved his life.

Lorn stepped aside for the others to participate. They all clamored forward, impatient to take on Lorn of Verta. Most were skilled archers. Their place within each of their respective province's guard was well deserved. Many were close to Lorn's skill, but no one hit all three targets with the precision he had. Unsatisfied, many called for the targets to be moved back farther. Lorn hit each with equal accuracy. Wanting to escalate the challenge, the guards and crowd argued for introducing moving targets.

Still, Lorn was successful.

After a multitude of failed attempts to match Lorn's skill, Lord Sune interrupted, his strong hand clapping Lorn on the shoulder. "It is like you have had multiple lifetimes to hone your skills." Lorn had never considered his skill in combat to be anything extraordinary. His parents had trained him from a young age, but now he was unsure. Before he could dwell further on the comment, Lord Sune announced, "The day is carrying on, let us move on to swordplay." The crowd cheered their agreement. Lord Sune turned to the eager crowd. "I will pick my best swordsman, and he will face off against Lorn of Verta. The rules are first to yield, draw blood, or step foot out of the ring. No magic allowed. Understood?" He raised his eyebrows at Lorn, awaiting his agreement. Lorn nodded. He couldn't fight his rising excitement. He prided himself on being a skilled swordsman, but he had never fought soldiers from Kreeha, their weapon of choice a scimitar. Maneuvering around and defending against a scimitar would be different from a traditional longsword.

Lord Sune strode among the line of his guards. Each of their faces were stoic, battle-trained, but an eagerness to prove themselves glinted in their eyes. They each wanted to be chosen for the demonstration. Lord Sune paused and pointed at one of the guards. Lorn was shocked to find it was the guard from yesterday — Hanu, the one Lord Sune pulled forward for them to inspect his Goldenring armor. Hanu was outfitted in the same Goldenring armor. His wheat-colored hair was pulled back from his face in a low ponytail. Hanu met Lorn with a cool gaze and pulled out his golden scimitar from its sheath. The scimitar appeared to be made from the same material as his armor. *Kreeha must be gilded in gold for everything to be gold-touched,* Lorn thought. The growing crowd rushed to the edges of the training ring. Following tradition, Hanu and Lorn walked to the center of the ring and bowed to each other. The crowd silenced, straining to watch. They straightened, Hanu's grip familiar around the hilt of his scimitar as was Lorn's around his own sword. A sharp whistle from Lord Sune pierced the silence and the fight began.

Lorn assumed Hanu had more experience battling against a longsword compared to Lorn battling against a scimitar. His goal was to draw Hanu in, watch how he attacked, and observe how he favored the weapon. It was clear why Hanu was picked by Lord Sune. He moved fluidly like the flow of water over stones, both light, graceful, but hidden, untapped strength behind his attacks. He was able to move the scimitar quickly compared to Lorn's movements with the longsword. Keeping a slow retreat, Lorn blocked Hanu's attempts while trying to anticipate what his next move would be. Lorn's balanced feet trailed in a circle, dragging Hanu after him. Confident with being able to read Hanu's moves, he feinted right, lured Hanu in, and attacked his exposed shoulder. Hanu was caught off guard, but quickly reestablished his footing. They continued, swiping and striking, countering with blocks and feints.

Hanu gained ground on Lorn, pushing him back up against the edge of the circle. Lorn could only defend himself, the scimitar moving too quickly for Lorn to take the offensive. His sword was heavy in his arms, his labored breathing slowing him down. Hanu slashed again. Lorn barely recovered and brought up his sword in time to block. His eyes darted to the edge of the training ring. Hanu was battering him back. Neither would yield or draw blood. The only option was forcing him out of the ring. Hanu let a rare, triumphant smile cross his face. He used his body weight and slashed one more time to push Lorn out of the ring.

He saw Hanu shift his weight and knew what was coming next. Lorn needed precise timing for this to work.

Hanu pressed his elbow against his side and lowered his shoulder to knock Lorn out of the ring. He bulled forward.

With grace and quickness that made their previous night of ballroom dancing look clumsy and slow, Lorn side-stepped, spun, and with a step so fast no eyes could follow, he moved behind Hanu, their positions now reversed. Hanu balanced precariously at the edge of the ring, a look of shock on his face. Lorn took advantage of the moment and used his sword to clip the leg that held most of his weight. Hanu sprawled awkwardly to the ground and out of the ring.

"Match," Lord Sune shouted. The crowd erupted and cheered.

Lorn let a small smile crack and reached for Hanu's hand. He pulled Hanu forward, raising his hand in the air with Lorn. The crowd's roar grew, their cheers encircling them. His body ached from the exertion of the fight, but he wouldn't let a soldier's wounded pride fester. He leaned closer to Hanu, some of his hair escaping into his eyes. "You will have to teach me how to use a scimitar."

Hanu's eyes widened. "If I teach you how to use a scimitar, you will be unbeatable. I need to retain a shred of pride so we can one day battle scimitar to scimitar. Hopefully then I can beat you." Lorn let out a good-natured laugh and Hanu followed suit.

Scanning the crowd, Lorn was surprised to see crests from each province represented among the people. Lord Ravinder of Verta beckoned Lorn over and pulled him aside from the roaring crowd. People reached out, wanting to touch him. Lord Ravinder's ruddy face loomed near Lorn like a friend conspiratorially sharing secrets. "Great performance, Lorn! Great performance! You make Verta proud by your display. I would love to share a meal with you, and I want to invite you to dine privately with Lady Sarava and myself." Lorn absentmindedly nodded, his attention distracted by distant movement by the stables. With all the commotion by the training ring, what would someone be doing by the stables? The figure seemed familiar, and he couldn't help but follow them. He thanked Lord Ravinder, agreeing to the meal, and rushed away. The crowd slowed him down as everyone congratulated him and wanted to speak to him.

He gently parted the crowd, not wanting to lose sight of the mysterious person. Their vague outline slinking around bothered Lorn like a thorn caught in his leg. Catching up to the edge of the stables, the roar of the crowd quieted down as he turned the shaded corner. Lorn paused, listening to his instincts. He wanted to ignore the warnings to stay still and instead race ahead, yet years of tracking animals forced him to remain still. He crouched down, the worn gravel path shifting under foot. He lifted his feet and brought them down silently, edging slowly into the stables. The familiar warmth of it hit him as he crept. The horses brayed their dismay. He was glad he had listened to his instincts. The stranger was here somewhere. The faded light filtered through the windows, his vision dim and hazy.

Lorn took a calming breath, drowning out the distracting afternoon he had and focused solely on the stables. The horses' hooves pawed at the ground, nervously shifting from leg to leg. He silenced his breathing and listened intently.

A quiet shuffle sounded next to him, and everything happened at once. The figure emerged from their hiding place aware of Lorn's scrutiny. They knocked Lorn off balance. He faltered, throwing out a hand out to catch himself. The strength behind the push was vaguely familiar. Lorn swore and hauled himself back to his feet. The figure sprinted away, cloak billowing behind them. He pulled the dagger strapped to his leg, whispered a quick prayer and whipped it at the person's retreating back. Before the stranger could turn the corner and disappear beyond the castle grounds a soft *umph* sounded. The blade had met its mark. Lorn sprinted, searched for the person and found them lying face down on their obscured face. Grunts of pain came from them. Lorn kneeled beside them and flipped them over, unconcerned with the dagger's handle sticking out of the person's back.

"You!"

His anger stoked into a fire, building, cresting into a rising inferno. There before him was the man who had sneaked into his room in the middle of the night. The man who had assaulted him and ran away through his open window, scurrying away like a rat in the night, the spy who wanted information on the Hinterlands. Lorn remembered how he escaped, the man's magic manifested as strength and speed. He grabbed a second dagger from his leg sheath and jammed it into the man's shoulder, targeting the same spot Lorn had hit while at the inn. If this man was too injured to summon his magic, he couldn't escape again.

This was the same man, his pale skin, brown hair, and forgettable brown eyes. His face was neither memorable nor notable, one that can easily blend into a crowd. Lorn would not let him escape this time. Blood leaked from the shoulder wound and puddled behind his back. The stables were only a few steps away, and Lorn didn't want anyone to discover him hovering over an injured man. Straining from the effort, he pulled the man into the dark safety of the stables, away from prying eyes. The man tried to maintain composure, but his wounds caused groans of pain. Lorn dumped the man against the floor and pushed his body weight against him, pinning him to the floor with no way for him to escape. The horses stirred, unsteady and unsure from the metallic scent of blood filling the air. Lorn didn't have much time before this man bled out. He needed answers before the man died, an outcome Lorn wanted to avoid at all costs.

"Who are you?" Lorn's voice remained calm and steady. He did not have to resort to weak words of anger, when the threat of death lingered over this man's head.

The man's voice gurgled, blood leaking from his mouth.

"The faster you talk, the faster I can heal you."

The man's voice was rough, Lorn hated admitting it, but he relished the pain the man was suffering. Spying on him and attacking him in the night left Lorn feeling no pity for this man. But he needed answers, and the man had no right to die. Not yet.

"I will die anyway," the man groaned.

"I swear upon my life I will heal you and not kill you afterwards."

"It's not you I'm worried about," he gurgled blood pooling out of his mouth. His eyes softened as if resigned to his fate.

Lorn's mind raced through this man's potential list of employers. "Who?"

His voice strained as the wounds bled on to the hay-covered floor. "You would never believe me, and I would never tell you." The man's eyes closed. Lorn cursed, he would not let this man die when he needed answers.

Lorn accessed the familiar feel of his magic and summoned it forth. He quickly assessed the man's injuries and concluded; the man's knife wound in his back was causing the most damage. From Lorn's small medical knowledge, he knew removing a blade from the body was usually frowned upon. The item typically kept the blood within the body, but once it was removed the blood would flow freely and the person would hemorrhage. He would have to be quick, and not make any mistakes.

Lorn's magic flared, as if sensing the urgency. He placed his hand around the wound on the man's back and whispered a quick prayer to the goddesses and gods. Simultaneously, he yanked out the knife and flashed his magic, willing the remaining magic to staunch the wound and begin to knit the flesh back together. Sweat beaded on his brow and dripped into his eyes. Still, he pushed his magic towards this man, imagining and willing the wound to heal.

The mind is a powerful ally when it is used in magic. He thought back to his days of magic training, his mother guiding him. *For the magic to be successful, you need to imagine it. If you imagine it, you bring it into being and thus it is true.*

Lorn pictured the body healing, the blood slowing, the skin, muscles, and sinew slowly melding back together how it should be. His head pounded with effort. Lorn wished for Aza's abundant magic, her well of power never-ending. Yet the typical MagicBlessed held only a kernel of her raw power. If pushed too far, it could result in unconsciousness, headaches, nosebleeds, and loss of bodily functions.

His head pounded, but Lorn held firmly onto the man, to prevent him from harming his open wound. The bleeding from his back had ceased, and Lorn lowered him to the ground. He fumbled for his neck checking the man's pulse. It was present and steadily growing. A sigh of relief loosened from his mouth as he eyed the dagger sticking out the man's shoulder. He would have to leave it for now. The injury was not ideal, but also not life threatening. White spots danced in the corner of Lorn's eyes as his vision blurred, his magic consumed. He needed someone he could trust. He needed Aza and now.

Lorn shakily stood and looked around the stables. He hadn't paid any attention to the horses, who were now panicking, neighing their displeasure at the blood and intruders within their sanctuary. Streaks of blood coated his pants and hands. If anyone saw him, they would instantly become alert and suspicious. Lorn yanked the man into an empty stall and tried to place hay about his body to hide him from view. Lorn staggered, forcing himself not to lose consciousness. He slammed the stall door and peeked out from the stables. Most of the people were still at the training grounds occupied by their nobles.

With no one in sight he ran. He hoped no one was looking out of windows, wondering what the *famed* Lorn of Verta was doing running around the castle of El'en. Through sheer luck no one was in sight as Lorn sprinted through the exterior of the castle heading towards a more private entrance. He aimed for one where the corridors were less conspicuous, the visiting dignitaries were unlikely to use such a secluded walkway. Spotting a handful of people on the edges of the courtyard walking in groups, he slowed his steps to a more leisurely pace, hiding his bloodstained hands from view. The small, unassuming wooden door was within sight. He yanked it open and when the door clicked shut behind him, he set off on a sprint. His head pounded with each footstep as he propelled himself forward. The only people who used this passageway were the servants, and they were all overwhelmed with taking care of the other needs in the castle.

He was almost at Aza's door, his breathing rough and erratic. It was draining to lift his feet and if he slowed down he feared he would collapse on the floor. Lorn's fist pounded on the door. No sound, nothing stirred inside. "Aza, are you in there?

He pounded on the door again, hoping Aza would come quickly. He assumed she was still in her room. Panic flared through him, what if she wasn't even in her room? His head beat in time with his fist on her door. He could feel himself losing consciousness, his body heavy and his awareness diminishing. He needed to fight the urge to pass out. The use of his magic had drained him, paired with the adrenaline of racing here to find Aza. He was at his limit. A flash of silver caught his eye as he slumped against Aza's door, hoping the strong door would support his weight

"Lorn, what in the Darkness below is happening?" A grip firm on his elbow lifted him and the pounding in his head began to subside. Aza was healing him and feeding her magic to own. She easily pulled him up and helped support him. Losing his balance, Lorn reminded himself of why he was here at Aza's room. Aza was always beautiful, but around her eyes he noticed the lines and the angry firm set of her lips. Something was troubling her, but first he needed to tell her about the intruder downstairs.

"I need you to come with me. It's urgent." Aza asked no further questions and only sent out a warm embrace of magic. It helped to quell the rising tide of unconsciousness that had threatened to consume Lorn.

She motioned for Lorn to wait and disappeared into her room. She came out with two cloaks clutched in her hands. "I figured we would need to be discreet." Thankful for her quick thinking, he threw the cloak over himself. With Aza by his side Lorn's strength slowly returned. Although she had healed his injuries, he still needed rest. She helped support some of his body weight while they hurried down the corridors. If anyone saw them, it would be comical. They were caught between a run and a walk, afraid to be conspicuous yet not wanting Lorn to lose consciousness.

Under his breath he uttered, "To the stables." Aza nodded, and half dragged him to it. While her magic helped to bolster his energy, he needed to sleep and recover. Lorn had depleted his energy by sparring with Hanu, then using his magic to heal the man in the stables.

Like a blanket being tossed over him Lorn felt Aza's shadow-magic shield him from the light, the shadows entwining with them, coating them like delicate hands. With barely any time to register his shock, he couldn't focus on this new information. Shadow magic was rare for the MagicBlessed, like his light magic. However helpful, her darkness and shadows could only block so much during broad daylight and wouldn't be able to hide them completely in the open hallways they traversed, but it would be enough to discourage people from seeing them or quickly trick an overcurious eye.

They burst into the courtyard, their breathing heavy. People milled around, finished with the distraction of the training ring. Lorn heard Aza swear under her breath and they halted. Immediately, Aza straightened her posture, forcing Lorn to rise. Her arm which supported him quickly moved to wrap her arm within his, a picture of two people enjoying the lovely gardens. Luckily, the weather had turned, the clouds darkening the sky above and the wind whipped around them. It wouldn't appear odd if they both donned their cloaks while on a walk. He hoped to keep a distance between himself and any other people strolling the gardens. Blood was still smeared across his hands and pants, but Aza used her cloak to cover his exposed hand.

The stables were within sight. Impatient, Lorn willed themselves to go faster, but they needed to be discreet. Aza pulled him forward. They entered the calm warmth of the stables, the horses greeting their entry. They were the only people in here. Aza kept her voice low. "Okay. What is it?"

Lorn disentangled himself and stumbled to find his footing. Reaching for the stable door he wrenched it open. Lorn could feel Aza loom over his shoulder peering into the stall with him. Shock coursed through him. He couldn't move, could barely breathe.

The man was gone.

34

"The MagicBlessed's gift of healing cannot fix everything. It can stanch bleeding, help fight infection. But to bring someone back from the brink of death—one should call upon the gods or goddesses from myth."

Excerpt from *The Secrets Of Our Magic* by Yorune of Gara

Lorn muffled a curse as he covered his mouth. He was so close to receiving answers, yet the man had slipped away. He bent down, haphazardly chucking hay pieces aside, searching for a trail, a hint of blood, anything to indicate where the man had gone. Nothing seemed disturbed besides the faint impression of the man's body on the scattered hay. All the bloodied hay disappeared as if it hadn't existed in the first place.

"Lorn..." Aza's concerned voice cut through to him. He couldn't handle the pity and confusion that laced through her voice. "Lorn, if you tell me what's going on, I can try to help." Lorn stood abruptly, almost bumping into Aza, not realizing how close she was to him.

"He was here. We were about to have answers!" Lorn wanted her to realize how important this was. Ever since accepting the quest to enter the Hinterlands, a woven tale of mysteries and questions had plagued them both. Finally, he had seen an exposed thread and if he pulled, he could unravel it all and find the answers they both sought. He was frustrated, but even more so for Aza. He saw how she shouldered the daily burden of mysteries and unanswered questions. If he could only solve this one, it might create a ripple effect on others.

He paused and took in the concern etched upon Aza's face. Forcing himself to take a breath, soothing the erratic pace of his heart, he opened his mouth to explain what happened, when they both heard voices right outside the stables. Lorn pulled Aza out of the stall and they scrambled over to the nearest horse, feigning inspection.

"Let's see these fine horses you brag about so much, Lord Aldrich." Lady Sarava of Verta's voice carried into the stables.

"We might have to see about acquiring some of your fabled horses," Lord Ravinder's booming voice joined in.

"I'm sure it is something we can discuss later."

Lorn kept his focus on the horse in front of him. He didn't want to imagine the rumors that would circulate if he was caught with blood coating his hands and clothing.

"Oh, I see we are not the only ones who wish to see the beauty of these horses," Lord Ravinder commented, their footsteps coming to a scattered stop.

Lorn glanced at Aza and realized their cloaks were still concealing their features. He pulled the hood off and turned to face the Lord and Lady of Verta. His fingers fidgeted unease coursing through his body. Lorn bowed his head towards the Lord and Lady of Verta, sure to keep his bloodstained clothes and hands out of view.

"My Lord and Lady, what a surprise seeing you here," Lorn kept his voice smooth and even, forcing his face to betray nothing.

"Ah! Here's where our famed Hunter of the Hinterlands ran off to," Lord Ravinder chuckled. "It was quite a display of skill out in the training grounds. I'm proud that a man of Verta stepped up to the challenge." He nudged Lord Aldrich. "Although we all get along, it is nice to boast in front of the other provinces."

Lord Aldrich clenched his jaw and a tight smile forced itself on his face. "Indeed."

Stepping forward, Lady Sarava softly placed her hand upon her husband's shoulder, her shrewd eyes looking past Lorn. "Who is your companion?"

The air around Lorn thickened and tingled with the familiar feel of magic being loosened. Aza stiffened beside him and pivoted slowly, removing the cloak from upon her striking silver hair.

Lady Sarava released a soft, "Oh," while her husband took an unsteady step back. Clearly the lack of control from last night was not forgotten. The two were uncomfortable in Aza's presence.

Lord Aldrich looked between the two of them, curiosity evident on his face. His eyes flashed between Lorn and Aza. No one spoke, and Lorn heard the faint cracking of knuckles. He risked an innocent glance towards Aza. Her whole body was taut. Lorn felt the embrace of magic around him like a fog drifting in from the Wyra Ocean. Why was Aza allowing her magic to come undone? What game was she playing at?

The magic drifted over him and coursed towards the three nobles, like the crackling of ether, the warning lick of an errant flame, the fear of an unsteady step near a cliff. Panic seized Lorn. He couldn't have Aza lose control. Not again. If she attacked another Lord or Lady she would be an outcast. No one would trust her. Lorn jokingly placed his arm around Aza's shoulder. "We were only admiring the fine horses here. It is nice to have a sanctuary amongst such fine animals."

Lorn had to stop himself from crying out in pain at her touch. Her magic was torturing him, as if his skin was being burned and boiled from the heat generated. Fighting the urge to cower in fear, her eyes were the brightest silver he had ever witnessed verging on becoming white. Pure disdain and anger radiated from her, and her magic mimicked it. Aza's eyes were locked on Lord Aldrich's. Lorn needed to diffuse the situation before anything irreversible happened.

"Aza, let's leave them to inspect the horses." Lady Sarava's eyes flicked between the two of them, noticing the underlying dissent—her lack of control betrayed her. She narrowed her eyes at the two of them, her mouth about to open and say something ill-advised, when Lorn interrupted her, "Let's head back, Aza. We can scour the kitchens for some much needed food." He steered Aza out of the room, her body unwilling to move and cooperate. After some subtle nudging, verging on a shove, Lorn was able to coax her out of the room. Snatches of small conversation started up as soon as they left.

The weather had shifted fully, transitioning into a brutal autumn storm. The wind tore at their cloaks, and the courtyards were empty. No one wanted to be caught in a downpour. Lorn yanked his arm from around her shoulder. The heat and power of her magic left a line of raw, red skin and blisters, even through the thick sleeve of his clothes. Wanting to avoid a scene to any prying, unseen eyes, Lorn cursed under his breath and stepped in front of Aza.

"What was that?" he seethed. Lorn loved Aza as his closest friend and companion, but he couldn't condone the amount of magic and power she was about to recklessly release upon Lord Aldrich and the Lady and Lord of Verta. Aza's face was contorted into one of rage, and Lorn hadn't the faintest idea of how to help or what was going on.

A loud boom sounded overhead. It was the call to the skies above. A sheet of rain slammed down on them both, drenching them instantly. The rain seemed to shock Aza out of her intense focus, and he could feel the tendrils of her magic reign back in, like a lover being coaxed back to bed. She blinked a few times and turned to him. "Lorn?" Instead of the anger he expected, she was tired and resigned.

"Aza, what's going on?" He peeled back his layer of clothes and shoved his arm in her face. He repeated himself, throwing the proof that her magic inflicted pain on him. "What is going on?"

Her eyes widened and she reached for his forearm, delicately touching and inspecting it. "I did this?" He nodded his head, keeping silent. He wasn't going to punish her, he knew she would punish herself. A gentle flare of magic pulsed along his arm and the raw skin and burn marks vanished. It was such a difference between the malevolent magic that pulsed, ready to destroy.

The rain coursed down his face and the wind coupled together to form a chilling storm. He didn't care. He would stand here and figure out how to help Aza and figure out what happened to her.

"I can't talk about it right now." Aza's voice was firm and steady.

"But–"

Aza held up a hand to indicate she wasn't finished. "I promise, I will tell you about it soon."

Lorn clenched his teeth, choking on the words he wanted to say to her.

"Will you go train with me right now? Her eyes dimmed the internal fire quieting for now. "I need to move and fight and get *this* out of me now." The desperation in her voice lanced through him, and he could only stiffly nod his head in agreement.

They headed to the indoor training room, the one they had practiced in for months. They didn't bother to change out of their wet clothes, but discarded their cloaks, a wet plop sounding on the floor. Lorn retreated to a corner, his only role as support for her. Aza grabbed a sword and began going through her training motions. She sliced, stabbed, and maneuvered around the room while Lorn watched. When she was ready, Lorn joined her. They stood across from one another, their blades drawn and in their opening position. The spell was broken, and Aza rushed forward, slashing and swiping at him. Lorn took the brunt of the attack, knowing she needed this release. She needed something to funnel her anger and pent-up energy into, he was it. He defended her excessive onslaught, blocking her blows and occasionally parrying. Aza easily dismissed his attacks. Although he was worried, pride also swelled through him. She had learned so much in so little time. She wielded the sword like she had been doing this her whole life.

Fatigue was wearing Lorn down, but he kept up the pretense of battling her. He was exhausted and needed rest, but Aza needed this. He went for a move he knew could disarm her. Aza left one of her sides exposed and Lorn always admonished her for it. He attacked, knowing she was faking the vulnerability — she left it exposed to draw him in. At the last moment he feinted and spun around going for the other side in hopes of it being unguarded. As he brought the sword in closer to her vulnerable side, she threw up a shield of ice. His sword clanged off it and Aza spun around, pulling her sword up to his throat. He couldn't help as his mouth stood open. She had been practicing and he had underestimated the skill and damage she could unleash.

"Yield." Aza held the blade to his throat. He could feel the slight nick in his skin as blood trickled down his neck. It wasn't only anger in her eyes, he thought he imagined the faint glimmer of wetness.

"Impressive." Aza lowered her sword and they both turned to see who stood within their training room. Xira stood in the doorway still in her leathers with an array of knives tucked into her baldric. Her jet black hair was plaited down her back. Though she was significantly shorter than both Lorn and Aza, she had a fearsome presence. She commanded the room as she walked into it, sizing Aza up and asked, "Want a real fight?" Aza said nothing as she held Xira's stare. The challenge hung between them.

Lorn took his cue to back away. Aza was more than capable of handling herself. Finding a corner of the room to sit in, he leaned against the wall and watched the duel unfold. Aza and Xira faced each other, taking their places.

From a sheath Lorn never noticed until now, Xira pulled out her sword. It was beautiful and slim with a delicate handle. White gemstones were inlaid only on a small part of the hilt but everything else was kept plain. The metal was a darker color than Lorn had ever seen for a sword. Unable to discern what metal it was, he presumed something mined from the mountains surrounding Neria.

Aza charged Xira. Lorn believed he was an exceptional sword fighter, but nothing prepared him for the beauty of the Nerian swordplay. She was beyond skilled. Effortlessly parrying, blocking, attacking. She disarmed Aza, her blade held to Aza's throat. Aza's sword clattered to the ground.

"Yield." Her command was quiet.

"No. Again."

Xira considered her request and backed away from Aza lowering her sword. Aza reached down to grab hers and they squared off again. They rushed and attacked, sword clanging against sword. Aza moved faster than he had ever seen her—whatever was brewing inside was about to erupt.

Lord held his breath while he watched, willing Aza to gain the upper hand. But anyone could see Xira was highly skilled. She would never be beaten. Aza only had three months of training. Despite how far she had come, she just wasn't skilled enough to take out a born and bred Nerian warrior. Xira was about to pin Aza in place, her sword cutting through to find her mark. Before the sword made it to Aza's throat, a blast of wind threw the swing off course. Xira didn't even bother looking surprised, effortlessly flowing into her next move. Xira simply continued as if the burst of air had never appeared. She fought against it, swerved around, and aimed for another vulnerable spot. She swiped down and Aza fumbled, again relying on her magic. She seared the hilt of Xira's sword, causing the warrior to curse and drop it. In one smooth motion Xira rolled and pulled a dagger from her boot. Aza had the stronger weapon and farther reach. Seeing an advantage, she moved to Xira, hoping to get an edge on the hardened warrior. Lorn saw Aza regain her confidence, her strikes and blocks surer and stronger.

If Xira were not a fighter, Lorn thought she would have been a graceful dancer. She blended and moved effortlessly, anticipating Aza's moves as if Aza was loudly declaring each one. Lorn witnessed an opening for Aza to strike. Xira ducked and Aza swung down to knock the Nerian unconscious, but something odd happened. Aza faltered like her body weight was pulled forward. Xira's small dagger was held against Aza's throat.

"Yield, my lady." Xira's voice was calm, waiting for Aza to concede.

Upon the utterance of Aza's title of respect, she blinked her eyes refocusing on where she was. "Yield," she whispered. Xira lowered her dagger, sheathing it.

"What was that?"

Xira stared at Aza for a length of time and finally said, "You used your magic in a last-ditch attempt to recover. I used my magic in a strategic maneuver to win against an opponent." Aza bristled at the criticism, but Xira continued, "I can manipulate earth and the materials that come from it. I was able to control the metal in your sword and throw you off balance. How long have you been training?"

"For about two to three months."

Xira nodded her head like a general assessing a promising recruit. "Do you feel like you made the right choice?"

Lorn didn't know where the conversation was turning to, but it wasn't about the training anymore. He curiously watched Aza awaiting her response.

Aza paused, brushing aside an errant silver coil of hair, reflecting on the question. "It was neither right nor wrong. It simply was. Your cryptic message in the orchard did not help me to decide. How am I supposed to make a choice with only a thinly veiled warning?" Aza's eyes flashed in a quick anger. Lorn agreed with her. How was she supposed to make an informed decision based on half-truths and conjecture?

Lorn had to commend Xira. She was not cowed by Aza's spurt of anger and held her ground, looking thoroughly unimpressed. "With everything you know *now*, everything you *think* you know about *him*. Would you come here?"

A deep and wounded pain bloomed slowly over Aza's face. Xira had hit her mark. Aza didn't respond, the weight shifted under her legs as if the ground beneath her gave way.

"He has his claws so deep within you, and you don't even know it," Xira hissed at Aza and turned away, shaking her head in disappointment. "My offer still stands, despite how this has turned out." The Nerian warrior left the room, leaving Lorn and Aza in silence.

302

35

"There are those Fated to be together. It can be joyous or disastrous."

Excerpt from *The Secrets Of Our Magic* by Yorune of Gara

Aza left Lorn, excusing herself by feigning tiredness. She saw the tightness around Lorn's eyes at the deception, but without a word, he let her go, sensing her need to be alone. She needed to find Lord Aldrich. She couldn't stand it anymore and she needed to confront him. Aza had never set out to find his personal chambers, but she knew where they were located after living in the castle for over three months. Through necessity she didn't want any nosy nobles to overhear their conversation, so she sought out the privacy of his personal room. The servants and guards, knowing who she was, let her pass. Awaiting Lord Aldrich, she sent a messenger to find him as soon as possible and to have him meet her here.

Aza blushed while waiting, thinking about what Lady Rasmina had told her the other night. People assumed she was physically involved with Lord Aldrich and with Lorn. Now she was standing here in Lord Aldrich's bedchamber. Her unbridled anger pushed away those shy thoughts. Let them think what they want. Anger had propelled her here. Taking deep, measured, breaths she waited for him to enter, but the curiosity of his room had her inspecting it. It was surprisingly sparse. Little items of sentimentality around the room compared to the grandness of the castle.

A massive bed lay in the middle of the room draped with a gauzy canopy. Strange. Aza stepped forward to inspect the bed. Leaning over, she found above his bed along the ceiling an intricate star-map, a realistic, detailed painting of the night sky. She spotted all the constellations she had learned, except one near the edge the paint luminescent, near glowing. Unwilling to lay in his bed Aza craned her neck to see the constellation, set apart from the others.

A sound startled her, and she turned around. A plain wooden cabinet lay adjacent to the bathroom, with the door popped open. She crept closer, checking over her shoulder in case anyone was coming. She heard no footsteps and darted for the cabinet. Her hand enclosed upon the iron knob, and she tentatively opened the door. It was stacked with scrolls upon scrolls. The pages were more delicate than she could ever imagine, their edges curled and frayed. She searched for the source of the sound but found nothing. She assumed it was the door cracking open. The top scroll lay unfurled. Tempted, she grabbed it, interested to see the contents of what Lord Aldrich had kept hidden.

It was a prophecy, written by the prophet Ulmina of Iyera.

Aza scanned the prophetic poem and noted the ink written hastily in the margins. *Who could this refer to? When will this happen? Is this the time? Who can break it?*

"Lord Aldrich, Aza is waiting inside your chambers."

Aza heard the conversation right outside the door. She hastily shoved the scroll back into the cabinet and yanked it closed.

"Thank you. You are both dismissed for now and please ensure no one disturbs us."

Aza stepped quickly away from the cabinet and faced the door.

Lord Aldrich entered, his eyes traveling over to Aza and the interior of his room.

"If you wanted to see the inside of my bedchamber you could have asked a while ago."

The fury that brought her to this room resurfaced. "How dare you!"

He raised an eyebrow at her waiting for her to continue.

Aza fumbled with her words, her fury overriding what she needed to say. *You are fucking exquisite, my stars.* It repeated. Again and again. She couldn't stop it.

The silence stretched between the two of them as she finally spoke her words carefully, and slowly. "Who are you?"

Lord Aldrich tilted his head. "What do you mean?"

She stalked up to him, putting her face right next to his and repeated herself, "Who. Are. You?"

His fathomless, brown eyes held hers, unmoving. A flash of green appeared and went away. Aza did not imagine it. It was there. She had seen it. It wasn't her imagination or a figment of some long-forgotten memory. "No, you cannot be." She shakily backed away, as she sought to find level ground, her legs wobbling beneath her. "It is not possible." Aza shook her head, denying the truth that lay in front of her.

"Just answer it. You know who I am." Lord Aldrich stalked towards her, and she retreated until he trapped her against the wall.

"It can't be. How is this even possible?"

Lord Aldrich reached for her hand and Aza's magic unraveled.

Pure energy exploded from her and sent him against the far end of the room. He hit the opposite wall and crumpled to the ground. Her breath quickened as panic began to descend. How could this be him? Lord Aldrich rose to his knees. His arm reached out to her as a last vain attempt to persuade her. Blood streaked down his face. "Come now, my stars. You know I love our foreplay before we get to the main event, but voice what you already know." When Aza stayed silent, Lord Aldrich beckoned her forward, "Say what you have always known but choose to ignore."

Aza encased his body in ice. "No, you cannot be...how is it even possible?"

Lord Aldrich immediately burned through the ice and the gash on his forehead healed. He rose to his feet. "You never liked it when I begged. I won't start now. If you give me your hand, we can stop this charade. I can show you it is me."

The lies, the deceit, everything in her life since coming from the Well was muddled. The rage at being deceived overwhelmed her. She sent a burst of fire spreading around him. He immediately quelled it with a match of his own power, his air taking the oxygen from her ring of fire.

"Aza, enough! Give me your hand." His hand reached forward as a peace offering. Aza considered it, staring at his hand, willing it to give her the answers.

Frustrated, Aza stomped forward and touched his hand, the light brown skin disconcerting when she was used to a darker skin color in its place. She bit her lip to prevent herself from speaking further. He wanted her to touch his hand. Fine, she could do that.

"Please, close your eyes. I need you to channel your magic to me. Act as a conduit."

She glared at him. "How do I know this isn't another trick?" His hand came up to cradle her cheek, his eyes softening, albeit a different color than what she was used to. "You will have to trust me, my stars."

The affectionate name caused her grind her teeth, but she would submit. She wanted to see what would happen and get the answers she so desired. With one hand interlaced with hers and the other cradling her cheek, Aza closed her eyes. Her magic rose to the forefront, and she guided it towards him, allowing him to tap into her deep power.

A soft whisper nudged her. "Aza, open your eyes."

There before her stood Cruvo. His luminescent green eyes stared back at her, his deep brown skin faintly glowing in the light of his room. One hand drifted up to his face, running fingers through his loose wild hair, following it down to the tops of his shoulders. Immediately, she crouched down and knelt in front of him.

Cruvo chuckled. "Come now, you don't need to bow before me. You have never done it before."

In one fluid motion, like Lorn had taught her, she unsheathed the dagger attached to her thigh and aimed upwards, the point held against Cruvo's throat. Aza could barely acknowledge the satisfaction she gleaned from seeing the shock on his face. She pushed her weight against him, pinning him against the wall. The end of the blade glistened as it pointed at the front of his throat.

"Tell me why I shouldn't do it?" Aza pushed the blade into the skin, nicking it. A trickle of blood drifted down his throat and Aza trailed it with her eyes.

"You would not kill me, merely the host I am inhabiting."

The image of Cruvo faded in and out of view like the sun being shielded by the clouds. She could faintly see him and knew he was behind the veneer of Lord Aldrich but hidden beneath the depths. Aza faltered, the vigor behind her threat losing its weight. "What do you mean host?"

Cruvo's visage reappeared. "Merely that. Lord Aldrich is my host."

"So you took him against his will?" Aza pushed the knife back up against his throat, torn between slitting his throat and blasting him with her power.

"Just so you know, Lord Aldrich was willing. He invited me into his body. I cannot do so without a proper invitation after all."

"Explain," Aza hissed between her teeth.

Cruvo glanced down at the blade lingering just before his throat. "Do you mind removing the blade?"

She smiled sweetly at him. "I'd rather not."

"Looks like your training with Lorn has come far." He cocked his head in annoyance. "You already know I am a god–"

Aza cut him off, "Yes I know that, but there are so many other questions. Why are there no gods and goddesses around now? Why don't you have your own body? Why are you inhabiting Lord Aldrich's?" Aza rattled off the list of questions finally ready to receive some answers.

"All of these questions would take a long time to answer fully, but I can give you a brief summary. All of us, my fellow gods and goddesses, cannot take physical bodies anymore. Even this," he gestured to his body below, "is quite difficult and takes a lot of power to do. The host must be willing. To reiterate, Lord Aldrich invited me to take over his body."

"Is he still alive?" Her voice was soft as she asked the question. She did not think she could be with a god who so carelessly killed and disposed of someone.

Cruvo rolled his eyes. "Yes, the mortal is still here. He lies dormant. I can sense him, and he can sense me, but I am the one in charge. I unfortunately have to don his appearance, because I cannot fight the power holding us back."

What Cruvo explained made sense with everything she had witnessed so far. The way his green eyes would flash in place across Lord Aldrich's brown. How her magic and her touch had no effect on him and didn't overwhelm him. How sometimes she was left confused over her feelings for him. He was simply Cruvo in disguise.

"Why can't you take a physical body? It was rumored the gods and goddesses used to walk among us and be a part of our society. What happened?"

Anger rippled over Cruvo's face, and he snarled, "The Hinterlands."

Her dagger faltered slipping from his throat, as she processed the information, not expecting the haunted woods to be the source of so many problems.

Cruvo saw the shock on her face and explained, "Ever since the Hinterlands appeared, the gods and goddesses were banished from their physical bodies. Many do not seem to mind drifting in a non-physical form around the land. I do not prefer it."

"Is that what all this is for? Recruiting Lorn, finding me, duping me into helping you and seducing me?" Aza's voice cracked at the end of the sentence. She refused to allow her emotions to rise and overwhelm her. She briefly forgot about the dagger held carelessly in her hand. Her grip had softened during his explanation. The answers to many of the questions she had prevented her from proving her threats. She tightened her grip, her anger at being used like a pawn in his game. *Did he even care about her? Or was she simply a means to an end?*

Cruvo's eyes narrowed in anger. "Yes, you are part of the equation, but never think for a second that I do not actually care for you. Like I have said so many times—you are fucking exquisite, my stars. You are the answer to everything. I have been searching for you and attempting to figure out the vague riddle of the prophets."

"Why not tell me? Why keep me in the dark?" Aza tried to ignore the hurt that bloomed inside her chest, its vines coursing through her and curling tightly around her heart.

"Don't you think I wanted to tell you!" At his sudden burst of emotion the image of Cruvo faltered, replaced with Lord Aldrich. He took a breath and Aza forced another push of magic towards him. The guise of Cruvo returned. "Every day I wanted to tell you, I waited and wondered what would happen if I did. Aza, if I told you everything right when you showed up, you would have left with Lorn and never returned. You could decimate my entire court and I would barely be able to stop it in this form. My power is greatly reduced. But with your close proximity, I'm able to enter your dreams and we can be as we truly are."

His intertwined hand gripped tighter, like he was afraid she was a phantom who could vanish into the night. "Aza we are true equals. I was lucky we could connect in your dreams, and you have clearly seen how compatible we are." He smirked at her and scanned her body slowly. Aza fought the urge to punch him in the face. She was torn. So much information to absorb and she didn't know whether this was Fated, or some grand manipulation orchestrated by Cruvo since the dawn of the Hinterlands.

A single thought struck her, and she voiced it immediately, "How do you return to your body?"

Cruvo paused, taking a breath and when he looked back at her, his shoulders sagged in resignation. "You need to banish the Hinterlands."

The statement hung between them. Her magic seemed unbeatable and all-powerful to her, but she could not fathom it taking apart something so utterly destructive and invasive as the Hinterlands.

Aza finally relaxed the dagger away from Cruvo's throat. No more could be expected of her. How could she possibly do such a thing? Get rid of the Hinterlands? She shakily stepped back, giving herself distance from this god who had orchestrated so much of her life without her consent. She shook her head in disbelief, unable to face this anymore, unable to look at him. She turned around and aimlessly paced away, fighting the urge to hide her face with hands.

"How?" It was a plea, not even meant for Cruvo. Only a simple plea uttered to the universe to see if an answer would appear.

Footsteps sounded behind her and she didn't bother to turn. "You don't even know the extent of your power, what you are capable of. If anyone can do it, it would be you."

"And then what happens?" Aza questioned. She turned to face him, her anger rising again. "What happens if I *can* banish the Hinterlands? All the gods and goddesses return and what happens to the MagicBlessed? I'm to believe all of the gods and goddesses of before were kind-hearted souls who took care of their people? Or would they use their immense power to wreak havoc over Ithilia?"

"Aza, we can talk hypothetical situations all day, but you know the Hinterlands. Lorn barely speaks of the Hinterlands—that's how terrible is. It is a blight on this world. Don't you think if you could take it away, you should try?"

Aza considered that it could help people, and if she could remove the reason why Lorn lost his wife so others wouldn't go through a similar fate, then why not?

She took a stabilizing breath and clutched a hand to her forehead.

"It is a lot to take in right now. But I will think about it."

Cruvo nodded and brought his hand up to her shoulder. They stood eye to eye looking at one another. It was jarring to see him here and not in her dreams. She had grown accustomed to only seeing him there, and she was having a hard time deciphering what was real or not anymore. Her memories had always blurred reality for her. But his touch right now was real and solid, something she needed and craved. His fingers stroked her arm down to the dagger in her hand. He softly gripped her wrist, his eyes flicked to hers. "Are you still wanting to slit my throat?"

She curved her lips. "Still debating it."

"Mm, well I will have to change that opinion." He brought the hand that held the dagger up to his lips and gently kissed up her arm. This was the one thing that centered her, the melding of their bodies and magic. It felt like a meeting of two equals as he put it, their magics bowing in unison to each other. Cruvo's lips reached her neck, his kisses slow and leisurely, taking the time to properly savor the moment.

She closed her eyes allowing his ministrations to make up for all of the deceit and the betrayal, for all the secrets. Her dagger clattered to the floor as Cruvo guided her shirt off her body.

"Do I need to prove my devotion further?"

Aza said nothing, her mind warring with her body, but Fate above, she did not want this crushing sense of responsibility. Instead, she deserved to revel in a moment with someone who was her equal. She didn't answer and Cruvo added, "I guess I will need to prove it further."

His fingers pulled down the leather around her chest, exposing her breasts. "Much better." Cruvo lazily descended his kisses trailing down her body while his hand came up to cup the underside of one breast. His fingers teased around the center causing her to ache, the fire pooling low in her belly. She moaned low and deep, the need growing inside her. He leaned down and took the darkened bud into his mouth, flicking his tongue over the tip. Aza's head lolled back, allowing him to support her body as she relaxed into his grip.

In her dreams it had always felt real, but here and now it *was* real. Cruvo made his way over to the other side. "So responsive," he murmured against her skin. "Do you remember the first night we lay together? You forced my name from me and made me watch while you pleasured yourself? I have always thought about paying you back in kind. I dreamed about it, having you here in my arms forcing you to wait, overwhelmed with the pleasure I give you." His fingers teased her while he spoke. Aza couldn't stand it. It was torture to have him here in person, yet he kept playing like a predator that had finally captured its prey. "Do you know I had to stay away from you? I couldn't bear to see you wandering the castle. You were so close to me, yet I was patient. I waited until night came for us to reunite within your dreams." Cruvo faced her, his lips drawing in towards her ear. As he whispered, one hand drifted lower. He found the waistband of her pants. His hand crept towards her core, and he cupped her gently, his fingers unmoving.

Aza panted, urging him to move, to do anything except keep still. His breath caressed her ear as he whispered soft as a lover, "Did you dream about me during the day? Were you as wet and eager for the nights as I was?" Aza tried to push her hips into the hand cupping her, wishing for some friction. "Tsk, tsk, I need you to answer out loud. Did you crave this as I did?" He moved one finger up her slit, causing her to buck against his hand. "You can have more when you answer the question, Aza. Were your thoughts consumed with me? With how our magics intertwined together, how our magics are made for each other?" Aza failed to respond, needing more of his touch. Her body was on fire, unfulfilled, and she needed more. Cruvo released her hand from her core, the warmth dissipating.

"Wait," Aza breathed.

Cruvo pulled his face away from hers and watched, his luminescent green eyes holding her own. "Yes?" Cruvo asked innocently, while his fingertips danced lightly over her skin causing her to tremble. "You need to play the game to get the reward, my stars."

Aza could barely think straight as desire spiked out of control in her body.

Cruvo smirked like he knew her thoughts and repeated his question, "Were your thoughts consumed with me during the day? Were you begging for the night to descend and your dreams to release you?"

"Yes," Aza sighed.

Cruvo stepped closer, his hand teasing down to her core again. "Yes what?" His hand cupped her again awaiting her response.

Deep within her, Aza hated admitting such a weakness. Falling asleep and into her dreams with him was the highlight of her day. Ignoring her traitorous body, Aza went throughout her day trying to rid herself the thoughts of him, but she was lying to herself if she didn't accept that Cruvo was what she wanted. He was addictive, like their powers were an intoxicating blend of heady wine. She caved and admitted her weakness towards him, the thoughts that consumed her daily were of him. "Yes, I thought only of you," Aza confessed.

Cruvo gave Aza a quick, feral smile. "Good girl." Without a warning, his finger plunged within her, and his mouth descended upon hers. His tongue and finger followed the same rhythm one above and one below. Aza was lost to the sensation, her moans incoherent, her eyes closed, enjoying the pleasure he gave her. Her back hit against the wall, adding additional support and adding another level of pressure for her to push against. Cruvo pulled his finger out and brought to the front, circling her sensitive bundle of nerves. He kept up the slow pace, building up the heat within her. Without warning, Aza fell over the edge. Her body tightened as Cruvo kept up his punishingly slow pace.

Cruvo stripped her pants off and hastily pulled off his restrictive clothing. Both bare to each other, he lifted her by the hips, and she entwined her legs around him. In one thrust he embedded himself to the hilt. Both of their gasps filled the quiet room. Cruvo used the wall to help support Aza's body as he slowly thrust into her, filling her up. He kept up his deliciously slow pace, helping to rebuild the heat within her. Their mouths met in a ravenous and sloppy kiss, teeth hitting as their tongues intertwined around each other's.

Between their shared breaths Cruvo said, "This is why we are meant to be together, my stars. Look how well you take me. Look how well we fit together." He thrust again causing Aza's head to rock back, her eyes closed in pleasure. "We are made for one another."

Aza had reached her peak again, and Cruvo followed her. They both tightened, holding on to each other as they came together. Aza and Cruvo's magic blended, expelling outwards into the room. A blast of wind knocked all his belongings off their shelves. The cabinet of scrolls rocked against the wall, the paper contents crinkling inside. Their foreheads rested against one another. They slowed down their breathing. Cruvo pulled his forehead away from hers and regarded Aza, his soft, hypnotizing voice wrapping itself around her heart. "We were made for each other, my stars."

36

And so she found herself alone at sea
With nothing to cling to
Resigned to her fate
She floated
When her body no longer fought
The ocean claimed its prize.
Excerpt from the poet Harmina of Gara

Aza found herself sequestered in a secluded corner outside the castle on a damp patch of grass, the chill seeping into her. She welcomed and craved the cold, dousing her alert. It enabled her to sift through her thoughts. Her back rested against the hard marble exterior of the castle.

The night sky tonight was rare.

The autumn season brought forth a brutal coldness to the air and with it perpetual clouds blocking the sky.

Except tonight.

Tonight, the heavens burst forth as if weary from being shrouded in the dreary bleakness of the gray clouds. Aza wondered if the sky above knew of her inner turmoil and provided her with this small shred of beauty to still her racing thoughts.

Cruvo was here. Cruvo wasn't only inhabiting her thoughts and dreams but had a physical form. Well, not entirely. She tried to wrap her mind around the concept of banishing the Hinterlands. Even the mere thought of the twisted woods caused her magic to cringe and retreat. She sighed, a drawn-out long-winded breath, in a weak attempt to dispel everything weighing her down. Aza couldn't help but think back to her afternoon with Cruvo. It was difficult to argue with his logic. She couldn't deny the feeling of their synchronicity. Every time they came together, it was a force beyond anything Aza could imagine. The power, the magic, the perfect blending of them together both physically and magically. Even now, her eyes betrayed her as she closed her eyes and replayed their afternoon together, the mingle of their bodies, the feel of him within her, the heat spiking through her body. No, she couldn't deny what they had together.

However, there was more hidden beneath the surface. Cruvo is a god who has existed since the dawn of time, with a hidden trove of secrets he hadn't divulged. A deep tug within Aza's stomach confirmed the truth about his deceptions. Even in her dreams, he refused to tell her his name. She had to force it out of him after countless interactions. Yet, the feral look as he gazed upon her, the strength of his magic, and the wildness of his spirit, Aza yearned for — it was simply a mirror of herself.

If she banished the Hinterlands, then the gods and goddesses would be able to take physical forms. It wasn't only Cruvo she was bringing back, but all of them. What sort of consequences would result?

Frustrated, she ran her hands through her hair, releasing the tension on her scalp. In all of her lessons with Oron, he never showed any literature about the divine forces from long ago. Many were rumored to be just that, a rumor or a story told among the MagicBlessed. Maybe she would be able to extract information from the other provinces? They were all gathered here. They might have more information than the libraries of Iyera.

The stars were luminous overhead. Were the divine among the stars? Or were they vaporous beings drifting among the MagicBlessed, lacking corporeal forms. Aza hugged her knees into her chest, the constriction bringing comfort to her scattered thoughts. She was exhausted. The last few months had drained her. She closed her eyes again, seeking a much-needed reprieve.

Aza's mind latched onto a singular sound—the thrashing ocean waves below. Back and forth they recklessly crashed against the rocks supporting the castle, their water retreating and returning, locked in the endless cycle.

"The one who has been crafted from starlight." An ancient and powerful voice wrapped itself around her mind. Aza's eyes remained closed, the voice at once alluring and devastating. "Let me look upon you woman of starlight and the night sky."

Like a mouse in front of a snake, Aza couldn't help but obey, a deeper pull on her limbs causing her to release her knees from her chest and rise to her feet.

"What power in one so confined." The hypnotic voice caressed her cheek placing a finger under her chin, leading her on. Aza glowed with pride. In this moment, she felt like a speck in front of this ancient voice that beckoned her forward. She could do nothing else but follow. She was spurred on by the need to obey with an undercurrent of implied punishment if she did not.

"Child of magic, child of our creation, what a worthy prize you are!" Aza beamed, her footsteps blindly following the voice leading her. Her eyes squeezed shut, afraid to open them and lose the voice that called to her. Deep in her mind, Aza knew she was standing on a patch of grass near the edge of the cliff. It would take only a step or two and she would fall.

Her instincts rang out in fear, but the voice soothed and calmed her. She stepped forward with her eyes tightly shut. Her heel was supported on the ground, but the toes hung off the edge of the cliff.

"Woman of starlight, are you ready to meet me?" Aza readied herself to dive into the ocean below. Aza could hear the distant crashing waves, the jagged rocks awaiting her arrival. She needed to get down there. It would be thrilling, the weightlessness as she dove through the air. A small smile crested on her face. She would meet the ancient being soon enough. One little leap and it would be exquisite.

"My lady!" Aza fell through the air and was tackled onto the cold grass below. The foreign presence of the ancient voice disappeared like a snake gone back into its hole.

Aza opened her eyes.

Bereft, Aza's hands roamed her body, clutching at it. Her body wasn't ready to be tackled and it took a painful moment for Aza to regain her bearings and suck in a deep breath. Aza groaned and rolled onto her back once again admiring the night sky above her. She sucked in another breath the dampness of the grass seeping into her top.

What had come over her? She shuddered from the thought of swan-diving off the cliff into the Wyra ocean. Powerful or not, she would have been dashed against the jagged rock face below. Her head lolled to the side, curious to see who rescued her from her nighttime possession. "Thanks."

Loose red hair fanned around her head like a halo, her breathing erratic. Anwin gave a faint smile, her breathing leveling out as she muttered, "Whatever you were doing, please don't do it again." Anwin readjusted herself coming up onto her elbows. "Touching you when your magic is out of control is quite painful."

"My magic was out of control?"

"Yeah, it was like..." Anwin paused her head dipped back to look at the night sky above to clear her head, "an ember."

Aza raised an eyebrow at her, waiting for Anwin to explain further.

"An ember that caught out of control and began blazing brighter and brighter. When I pulled you back, your magic felt like a raging inferno." "

Aza propped herself up onto her hands, cursing the pain blossoming in her ribs. "I didn't hurt anyone did I?"

Anwin chuckled lightly to herself, "No, my lady You didn't. Your magic never manifested as anything real, it was more of the feeling. Like your magic was leaking out to your surroundings, ready to consume and devour anything within its radius." Anwin shifted and winced slightly.

Aza raised a skeptical eyebrow at Anwin's pain. "So, I didn't hurt anyone?"

"I figured you meant anyone else. But yes, like I said, touching you with your powers unleashed hurts something fierce."

"Well at least let me heal you." Aza held both her hands out expectantly waiting for Anwin. A look of doubt crossed her face and whatever internal battle she was waging, Anwin conceded and placed her arm within Aza's hand. Aza closed her eyes, this time directing her magic towards someone who needed her. There were small scratches and bruises around Anwin's body particularly where she took the fall, but Aza sensed something deeper, almost like an internal burn. Her magic spread over it like a healing salve to soothe the pulsing heat within Anwin.

Anwin gasped, causing Aza to open her eyes to look upon her patient. "Thank you," she whispered in awe. "I have never come across magic so powerful. It is indeed a blessing."

Aza gave a noncommittal response, the last few days proving otherwise. She would not want to go without her magic, but she also didn't want to go around accidentally hurting people.

"Would you like to talk about it?"

Aza put up a guard, schooling her features. "What are you talking about?"

Anwin shrugged, a very casual expression for someone who most MagicBlessed feared. "Whatever is eating you up inside. I can see it within you, my lady."

Aza gave no further information, allowing the silence of the autumn night to fill the void between them. Without any further explanation, Anwin bounced to her feet, shaking off the tension and soreness. "Xira's offer still stands," Anwin announced, and she disappeared into the night, rounding a corner of the castle.

Aza let her arms give out, her back thumping against the hard ground. She wanted to linger only a few moments longer, the constancy of the earth below her, grounding her in the moment. How she must look right now, laying down upon the hard ground like a star fallen from the night sky above. As Aza lay there letting the cold brisk winds turn bitter and fierce with the turning of the night, she realized she never questioned one thing—why and how was Anwin out here to save her?

37

"We often place nobility above us — thinking they are above petty squabbles. The truth is always a shocking reveal."
Excerpt from *The Battles of Court Intrigue* by Yasmine of Kreeha

The visiting dignitaries were not only here for parties and festivals. Oron explained before they came to visit how the week would transpire. Most of it was for the benefit of the lords and ladies to snoop on one another, boast about their superior provinces, and check if anything was amiss in their neighboring provinces.

Among the many dinners, there were serious discussions which took place. Aza accompanied Lorn to one of their first meetings, in which Lord Aldrich insisted they both be there, even though Lorn asserted they had no say in the makings of the provinces and rules or regulations. However, Lord Aldrich insisted and here they both were marching towards the giant conference room, large enough to hold all of the lords, ladies, and their selective guests.

They followed the low chattering until they came upon a rounded room. All of the other leaders were seated waiting for Lord Aldrich. Aza was overwhelmed by the people present but not wanting to cower before them she stood up straighter forcing her eyes to meet everyone who stared her down. Many averted their gazes, not wanting to be caught in the eyes of the mysterious woman who appeared from the Well.

Aza could barely look Lord Aldrich in the eye now that his guise had returned. Although she knew Cruvo was hidden inside, it was disorienting to face someone else knowing they were trapped within their own body. Aza chewed on the inside of her cheek worried over not disclosing the revelatory information with Lorn. He deserved to know, but with the last few days and everything going on, it hadn't felt like the right time. She wasn't sure how he would react upon finding out he had been duped by a god this entire time. A specific god he had been warned to stay away from by the goddess Issi. Aza wondered why the goddess hadn't made another appearance, if Cruvo was here, where was she?

The bumbling Lord of Verta flushed as she met his gaze, his ruddy cheeks becoming even more pronounced. Lady Sarava's eyes flickered away pretending she wasn't caught sizing up such an unknown variable.

Lorn disclosed what transpired earlier. While she sat questioning her and Cruvo's relationship, Lorn had privately dined with the Lord and Lady of Verta. He recalled nothing of importance happened, yet everything felt strange. "Off," he explained earlier. "Many times, the conversation circled around back to you, and who you were or what you could do. I had the feeling they were trying to be friendly but had an underlying purpose to their questioning."

Aza didn't know what to expect from the Lord and Lady of Verta. They seemed friendly enough, cordial, but they looked upon Aza with open suspicion since the night she accidentally hurt Lady Rasmina of Gara. She wondered if Lorn wasn't simply being overprotective of her. She didn't sense any malicious intent, only those trying to protect their own from an unknown entity.

But she wouldn't back down either as she entered the room. While she hated people fearing her, she would not conform to their standards. She double-checked her magic, making sure she had control over it. With coincidental timing, her eyes locked onto Lady Rasmina. They both knew what had transpired was a ruse. Aza fought to control her emotions, not allowing the hurt to spear across and tell everyone how she truly felt. They did not deserve to know her inner workings and what haunted her.

Lord Sune sat leisurely sprawled out on one side of the table. He grinned mischievously at her and sent her a wink as she entered the room. Xira and Anwin sat adjacent to Lord Sune and his advisers—stoic and ever watching. They didn't even bother giving Aza a glance as she walked by. The women she interacted with in private were so vastly different from the ones who were around these groups of people, Aza could only wonder which Xira and Anwin were the facade?

Aza and Lorn found their place around the front of the round table closest to the door. It was the only spot vacant, and Oron already occupied one of the chairs. Oron's eyes light up as Aza bent down next to him and asked, "May I sit here?" He clapped his hands together excitely and gestured for Lorn and Aza to sit. Oron was oblivious to the strange stares and whispers that preceded them. He might be only concerned with the information he gleans from scrolls and ancient texts instead of idle gossip.

Forcing her stiff shoulders to relax, Aza reclined into the velvet lined chairs. Oron chatted about pleasantries, since Aza and Lorn had scarcely seen him over the past week. They used to visit him every day for his lectures in the library but since the arrival of the other four provinces their tutoring had gone away.

While Oron talked on, Aza noticed a large map of Ithilia unfurled in the middle of the circular table. It was expansive, giving details of each province, locations, streams, mountains. The map was painted in beautiful shades, highlighting the distinctly unique beauty held within each of the respective provinces. Aza couldn't tear her eyes away from it. She scoured it without appearing too absentminded towards Oron's conversation. If the map edges gave any indication it was quite old, the edges tattered and fraying, a dark russet brown creeping along the edges and vined towards the center. But the colors of the map drew her in. Brilliant watercolors were brushed across the paper with an expert hand. It highlighted every positive quality of each province and many, if not all the cities around Ithilia, were included in it.

Framing the edge of the map were the crests of each province in a repeating pattern— the sun and crashing waves of Iyera, the three wheat stalks and scythe of Verta, the deep-rooted tree of Gara, the radiant sun of Kreeha, and the mysterious mountains of Neria. The craftsmanship was beautiful, and Aza wanted the rest of the room to leave her in peace so she could spend the rest of the day admiring such work. It allowed her to feel like she was traveling to each province and enjoying their distinctive perspectives on life.

The room silenced jarring Aza out of her musings. Lord Aldrich entered the room and took a seat beside Oron. Lilit and Gravers accompanied him, flanking him on either side. From Aza's lessons, there wasn't one province in more power than the others, they were all viewed as equal, yet Aza got the impression that Lord Aldrich had called them all here and was the one leading. Without any precedence, they plunged ahead and began discussing trading and the distribution of magic, how their peoples were sustaining and what was going successfully in each province. Remaining as a spectator, it was interesting to see how the leaders interacted with one another.

Aza wasn't surprised Lady Rasmina was particularly tight-lipped, her porcelain features displaying nothing of the inner thoughts brewing inside. She often donned a bored expression, but Aza caught how her eyes flicked between different people talking; she was soaking in every bit of information to make a calculated move later.

Lord Sune was often as loud and boisterous as his personality. Aza gleaned the provinces of Kreeha and Gara made the most money. They cultivated precious gems, minerals, and supplies that were traded to the other provinces. Verta and Iyera were mainly reliant on trading their food sources, since their land was richer for growing the wheat, fruit, and vegetables provided for the rest of the five provinces. Lord Sune and Lord Aldrich put forth the most vigorous arguments, one wanting more and the other not conceding. The Lord and Lady of Verta volleyed a few thoughts backing Lord Aldrich since they were on the same side, supplying food for the rest of the provinces gathered. Curiously, the Nerians stayed silent, never trading or offering to with any of the other provinces. Lady Rasmina kept her thoughts silent, only observing. After many lengthy discussions Lord Aldrich dismissed everyone for a quick break with the cooks and servants bringing trays of pastries and sandwiches from the kitchen.

Aza made idle conversation with Oron and Lorn and ignored talking with Lord Aldrich. She was filled with uncertainty, unsure of how to proceed with him in public. No one knew he was the god Cruvo. Her strategy was to dismiss the pointedly growing heat pooling within her body at the mere thought of him and turn her attention to Lorn.

Once their hunger was satiated and people took the necessary breaks, Lord Aldrich began with his next line of questioning.

"Has anyone noticed anything odd within their province?" The meeting room silenced as if a death was announced. People awkwardly shifted in their seats and stole furtive glances at one another. Bartering and trading with each other was common practice, but admitting a weakness within one's province, that is a line many of them wouldn't cross. Lord Aldrich waited for a beat and then spoke breaking the silence. "Our grapes have been corrupted and withered from the inside out." His voice was low, and it carried throughout the whole room. Everyone sat still their movement ceased when Lord Aldrich shared the burden of Iyera.

"What do you think it means?" A young man standing behind the Lord and Lady of Verta spoke up. He appeared to be in the in-between stages of transitioning from a teenage boy into a man, his sandy blond hair pulled back in a short ponytail away from his face. Despite his young age, there was an intelligent set to his eyes and his face as he questioned Lord Aldrich.

Lord Aldrich hesitated and said, "We haven't come to any conclusions yet."

Ryu, Lord Sune's consort, interjected, "When did it happen?"

"Roughly a month ago," Oron answered.

Everyone grew quiet as they connected the dots of Aza's timeline. She knew it looked suspicious. Upon her arrival from the Well magic was being altered and corrupted.

Lady Sarava brushed a hand along a runaway strand of hair and admitted, "We have had reports of wheat being ruined."

Lord Sune added in, his head nodding methodically, "Us as well. Some of our precious fruit trees are dying, a similar effect to what you described." His head inclined towards Lord Aldrich.

"This is all very convenient." Lady Rasmina had finally opened her mouth and it was only to damn Aza further. Aza's gut soured as Lady Rasmina spoke further. "You are all thinking about the timing of such a thing. Why now? We have the answer." She gestured to Aza. All eyes snapped to her. Aza hoped her face portrayed boredom, she did not need these to give these nobles an additional thing to gossip about over their breakfasts.

"What are you saying Lady Rasmina?" Lord Sune turned, his braids clinking slightly as the gold jewelry knocked against one another.

"I am saying, *Lord Sune*, that since her appearance from the Well, corruption is now taking place in our land." Her posture altered as she leaned forward, pulling everyone into her trance. Her sweet voice was misleading, it was the overly honeyed taste of something poisoned. "The magic that supplies our food and keeps our lands prosperous is starting to fail. What else could I be insinuating?" Her icy blue eyes met Lord Sune's as they stared at one another.

Lord Ravinder interjected before Lord Sune could reply, "Surely you are not suggesting the Well is failing? How could it be? We are still doing fantastic. Only a meager handful of crops are perishing. Something that is unfortunate but not indicating the end of our magic."

He chuckled and the weak laughter died off as no one joined. Lady Sarava's hair was swept up in an elegant bun, her warm brown hair pulled back from her simple beauty. She cut in, her fingers squeezing against her husband's arm, " I know many of us are wary of Aza's powers, but surely she cannot be the cause of such disruption."

The table quieted and Lady Rasmina responded immediately, "How can you argue she isn't the cause? You all have seen the extent of her power. Power, that is frankly unheard of in any MagicBlessed." Lady Rasmina's icy gaze scanned the entire room savoring the suspense of everyone hanging on to her every word. "How can we trust something so unknown?"

Everyone considered the statement and Lord Aldrich interrupted, "Why don't we let her speak for herself."

Expectant eyes landed on her. Aza refrained from shifting in her seat, uncomfortable with the weight of everyone looking at her. "There is no reason why I believe I am behind this. At least, not intentionally." She forced herself to meet everyone's face, delving to find the pride and confidence in herself to radiate out. "I am like you. I do not know exactly what power lies beneath my veins, but I don't use it willingly and without consequence. I have few memories, but I am not some evil force at work if that is what you are insinuating." Aza fought to keep her voice level, stooping neither to anger nor sarcasm. She needed them all to see her true self and how she viewed the situation. Some of the people were mollified by her explanation and others remained suspicious. She would not be able to win everyone over to her side, but this was a start.

Lady Rasmina barely acknowledged Aza's heartfelt sentiment and plunged ahead. "How can we even be safe around her unchecked power?" Her delicate hand pointed towards Aza accusing her.

Aza's magic rose in indignation. This woman dare accuse her and create this fear mongering among these other people of power. How dare she? Before Aza could spiral into a descent of rage, Oron interrupted, "Were not the gods and goddesses from before, present with indescribable and unimaginable powers?"

Lord Sune scoffed. "Surely you do not put any weight behind those folktales? Those are bedtime stories we tell our children at night. There is no merit behind them." Lord Sune leaned forward checking each person's expression around the table, crossing his arms. "However, I don't agree with Lady Rasmina's argument. I do believe Aza can be trusted; she has not proved otherwise."

Lord Sune's praise was comforting, but Aza couldn't deny the cold fury that sparked within her. For this conversation to even exist in her presence was unthinkable. How dare they question her sanity like she was some rabid animal to discuss the possibility of being put down. Xira and Anwin sat next to Lord Sune, detached from the conversation their faces impassive. How Aza yearned to know what was going on inside their minds.

Lord Aldrich glared at Lord Sune, his deep brown fathomless eyes flashing green for a brief second. " You would do kindly Lord Sune to not discredit one of my highest acclaimed scholars in all of Iyera."

Unphased by the danger lying in front of him, Lord Sune leaned back in his chair holding up his hands in mock supplication. "I mean no offense Oron of Iyera." He arrogantly looked at his peers and pressed on. "But are we all here speculating the truth behind whether the gods and goddesses of long ago are actually real? We have better things to waste our time here today than some made up stories of long ago."

Lady Sarava interjected, "He's right, whether you agree with his sentiments or not, the true discussion is of Lady Rasmina's claims towards Aza." She paused, assessing each person in the room. "Do we trust her? And do we trust her to not use her magic against us?"

Lord Aldrich cleared his throat bringing the attention back to him. "We will cast a vote. If we all are in favor of Aza remaining unrestrained, free to go about without fear of her power or if we will place restrictions upon her and a guard or some form of watch if the vote goes the other way." A unison of head nods agreed with Lord Aldrich's diplomatic approach.

Quiet throughout the whole meeting except now Lorn jolted forward. "Please Lord Aldrich, surely this is unnecessary." His face was pinched with contained fury. "You should all be ashamed. Judging and trying to restrain someone who you are afraid of simply because she is different. Simply because she holds more power than all of you combined."

Lady Rasmina's eyes narrowed and addressed Lord Aldrich. "Why don't you contain your glorified farmer. Surely he is reaching beyond his means."

The Lord and Lady of Verta wheeled on Lady Rasmina, the well-aimed dig at Lorn's upbringing hitting its mark. "Lady Rasmina, apologize at once!" Lord Ravinder demanded. "I must have misunderstood the jab you made towards Verta, especially since we just agreed to provide Gara with the food needed to continue supporting your province."

Lady Rasmina waved a dismissive hand towards the both of them. "I apologize toward the slight on Verta. This doesn't negate the question of can we trust a man who has spent all of this time with this woman? She could have him in her thrall. We all know his heartbreaking story. She could have manipulated him to meet her own needs. After all," she eyed Lorn up and down, "I don't blame her. I would love to have him as my whore too."

Aza's magic flared in rage, her hands fisted at her side. Trembling. She was trembling.

Lady Rasmina shot a look towards Aza, and she forced herself to back down. This is what Lady Rasmina wanted. She wanted Aza to lose control and unleash her magic upon a room full of leaders. She wanted a deep-seeded suspicion sprouting in the hearts of them and rooting into their minds. Aza could not play into her hand, despite how crass she was acting. Her anger only grew as she saw Lorn blush and sputter over his words, unsure of how to address such a statement.

Voices whispered to each other, the nobles enjoying every bit of drama unfolding in front of them.

A strong voice cut through the noise silencing everyone. "Lady Rasmina, I do not trust you need a tongue to go on living. I will free you from it. If you wish." Chaos filled the room with Xira's threat.

Lady Rasmina's daughters gathered around her, their magic crackling, like ether gathering in the room. Xira was unbothered as she pulled out one of her wicked sharp daggers always adorned on her body and began cleaning her nails with it. The daughters blocked Lady Rasmina pointing fingers and shouting for blood. Xira's honey brown eyes flashed up to the group throwing curses and insults at her. Lord Sune saw the bloodthirsty glint in Xira's eyes and inched away from her. Quick as lightning Xira threw the dagger right in front of Lady Rasmina's seat, embedding the tip of the dagger deep within the round wooden table.

Magic erupted.

The daughters released their magic in retaliation towards Xira . Ether crackled in the room and all the other leaders and guests ducked for cover. Anwin threw up a shield of wind blocking Xira from any attacks the daughters tried their way. Through the chaos, Aza noticed the two daughters who looked most like their mom, Sapphire and Ruby, threw what little magic they had at the Nerians. The youngest daughter, Pearl, her curly hair pulled back, knelt beside her mom, offering comfort. She appeared upset about the situation but wasn't doing anything malicious towards Xira and Anwin.   Once the daughters' limited magic was depleted, Anwin released her shield of wind wrapped around herself and Xira.

"Lord Aldrich and everyone gathered here today, isn't this proof of how ridiculous their argument is? They complain about Aza's unpredictability of magic, yet they release an attack on us." Anwin's clear voice rang throughout the throne room.

"Well, you did threaten their mother," Lord Aldrich replied drily.

"And does Lady Rasmina not answer for the venom she spews at others? The implication of Lorn of Verta and Aza together is uncalled for, and everyone here knows the baseless claims she lays for you all to step in and submit to."

"Like we would ever trust a Nerian, "Lord Ravinder whispered to Lady Sarava.

Too late. Xira and Anwin both heard it, their bodies stiff and turned to face the offender.

"What did you say?"

The room quieted, the tension thick as Xira stood up and stalked over to Lord Ravinder, genuine fear shone in his eyes. Aza was disgusted by his actions, such bold words to only cower before someone you spoke ill of.

Xira and Anwin were both terrifying, decked out in their leathers, dressed ready for battle, swords attached to their hip and an array of daggers decorated across their chest. Xira was a foot away from Lord Ravinder, her back bent over to look him straight in the eye, leaning on the table in front of him. "You know nothing of which you speak, I would hold your tongue as well, unless you wish to be free of it too."

Aza fought the chill that raced down her back. Oron's teachings on Nerians had been correct—they were terrifying. Luckily Aza had seen them in a different aspect and was able to reconcile the two differences between them.

"I thought so." Xira walked away from Lord Ravinder, her back exposed to him. A subtle mockery at him. She didn't even consider him enough of a threat to keep facing him.

Lord Ravinder didn't say anything, fear swallowing up his words. The only sound was Lady Rasmina's daughters bickering over the injustice Xira and Anwin had done to them. Lord Aldrich released a long-suffering sigh, weary of the petty squabbles before him. "Enough. There will be no demands for justice, no blood on anyone's hands. Everyone is at fault here and we will let it lie." Xira leveled a bored look at him and turned to give a slight nod to Anwin.

"No matter the argument, we need to cast a vote."

Aza couldn't help but feel hurt as he said those words. Cruvo was the one in charge, why couldn't he defend her and tell them all to not worry about it? She knew he needed to maintain his facade, but to do it this much? Each group grumbled and returned to their seats. A servant walked around handing out papers to each leader and they cast the vote amongst their own people of their province. Aza sat in disbelief as the fate of her freedom and life hung in the balance of some puffed up political leaders. She took a tortuously slow breath to ease the magic roiling in her veins. It begged her for release, to be able to do something and put something into action.

Lord Aldrich gathered the paper after the leaders furiously whispered their answers and scribbled it onto paper. Five simple slips of paper would decide her fate and how the people viewed her.

Lorn leaned over in his chair and whispered next to her, "I am with you, no matter what. Always." Aza fought the smile that came unbidden to her face. She didn't want to be playing into the hands of what the nobles thought of her.

Lord Aldrich examined the papers and announced, "In a three to two vote, Aza will remain unburdened and free to do as she likes." Aza was relieved but not at the ratio. She imagined at least Lady Rasmina would vote against her, but there was someone else at the table who did. She tried not to dwell on the thought of someone else out for their own ends. Who was she fooling? Everyone was out for their own agenda.

"How about—"

A guard of Lord Aldrich bearing the Iyerian crest on his right arm barged into the room, "Lord Aldrich!"

Startled, he turned to address the guard. "What is it?"

His eyes were wide with shock, his face becoming paler as the guard searched for the words. "The Hinterlands, it is out of control! It is rumored to be morphing and engulfing neighboring towns and areas."

38

"Our current MagicBlessed have only a minuscule amount of power compared to those who came before. We do not even know the depths of which our magic can reach. Who knows what we could be capable of?"

Excerpt from *The Secrets Of Our Magic* by Yorune of Gara

"You need to try."

"I don't know if I can."

"At least attempt to banish it."

Lord Aldrich had quickly dismissed everyone, their faces leeched of color and worried. Malcontent and grumbling followed, agreed, they would return later that evening to discuss it further once they found out more information. Everyone filed out of the room, casting paranoid glances at Aza. The credibility she had just built for herself crumbled like a patch of loose sand. Once everyone except Lord Aldrich's inner council was gone, Lord Aldrich immediately turned to Aza, pleading for her to try and banish the Hinterlands.

Lorn interrupted, walking and standing next to Aza supportively, his presence a steadying energy Aza needed right now, "What are you talking about?"

Aza faced him, her lips set in a thin line. "He wants me to banish the Hinterlands."

His eyebrows furrowed in confusion. "What do you mean?"

Lord Aldrich answered, "Exactly that. She has the power to get rid of the Hinterlands entirely."

Lorn's eyes glistened, his voice quiet almost too low to hear. "So, all the threats would be gone? All the people, families, animals....no one would be in danger anymore?"

There was so much hope in his voice, Aza couldn't bear to tell him the other consequences. How could she crush what little hope he had of letting other people live out their dreams of being with their spouses and loved ones? The not-so minor detail of freeing the gods and goddesses into the world ran through her mind.

Lilit broke the silence. "You need to do it, Aza. What is the point of even having you here if you can't do something with your power?"

Lord Aldrich scowled, but Lorn's icy glare drew her focus. "Aza is not some tool to use for her power!"

Lilit scoffed and strutted up to Lorn, her eyes flicking between Aza and him. "Then why is she here? What is all this for? Don't you want her to destroy the beast that killed your wife, the thing that ruined your life?" Her voice was quiet, but her words hit their mark. Aza knew he would want to get rid of the Hinterlands. He would never ask it of her, but the longing was there. She saw the frantic desperation in his eyes, the hope to rid the world of something so monstrous.

Indecision warred over his face. He didn't want to admit Lilit's cruel, calculated assessment was correct, but the craving to have the Hinterlands banished surpassed it. "Could you do it?"

Lorn's voice nearly shattered her — the soft plea from her friend. Frustrated, Aza pulled away from the group, her hands flaring out at her sides, "I don't even know if I can do it!"

"But you could try?"

Aza tried to drown out the potential consequences. She didn't know if she could betray his trust by telling him Cruvo existed within the body of Lord Aldrich.

Hating the feeling of indecision, she decided it was time for her to act. Worst case, she wouldn't succeed, but if she did, she would have to hope the resurrection of the gods and goddesses was less devastating than the Hinterlands.

Damn all the options—the Hinterlands was spiraling out of control. Lord Aldrich disclosed to them the reports from soldiers among Iyera. Most people were evacuated, but the Hinterlands had morphed and changed, as if the very wall of forest had chosen to expand. Darkness was creeping over the lands, engulfing the surrounding territory and land.

Her thoughts wandered to the people she saw throughout her travels. Although not all of them were pleasant, they were still people. People who loved, fought, played, lazed about, and cherished one another. They were people to protect because of who they were and their right to exist. Yes, she could try and defeat the Hinterlands so that those people could live without fear of the Hinterlands swallowing them whole.

Aza clenched her eyes, her whole body tightened as she heard herself whisper, "I will try."

Aza heard nothing further as the roaring in her ears drowned out everything else. She was so rarely affected by anything, but her body had already rejected her decision. A cold sweat began to bead on her skin, Aza ignored her body's reaction and turned to face her spectators. "What do I need to do?"

Lord Aldrich clapped his hands together and led them deep within the castle. They took mysterious turns and back ways that even Aza hadn't even explored in her months of being here. The ways were darkened with only the faint glow of torchlights to guide them into the descent of the castle.

They all walked in silence, Aza's thoughts consumed with the impending task. Lorn's apprehension and worry radiated off him, despite his overwhelming desire for her to banish the cause of all his pain. She was grateful for his concern and that he valued her well-being above the threat of the Hinterlands. With each step, her worry grew. Sweat formed on her skin like a shroud.

She had never feared death up until this point, but now she was beginning to question it. If she failed, would she die? Would the weight and darkness and despair of the Hinterlands consume her soul? Would she return to the Meadow of the Undying, or would she return off into some unknown existence before she had materialized from the Well? She couldn't let the existential dread flood her. Using her breath to steady herself and provide a buoy for her to rely on, she pulled herself out of the impending doubt. They turned together onto another narrow staircase, and it spiraled even further into the darkness.

Loosening her magic to guide them, she illuminated the dim staircase. Lorn breathed his thanks as he casually slipped on a loose stone. Aza gave a shaky smile in return. His face grew concerned and he walked closer to her. Lord Aldrich loomed in front of them with Lilit, Gravers and Oron bringing up the rear.

"Hey, you don't need to do this."

The narrow staircase allowed no room to fully turn and face him, so she casually whispered back over her shoulder, "I've got this."

"Aza, I know we rely on your powers a lot, but don't think for one second I would risk you over everything else."

"How can you say that Lorn? Why is my life worth more than all the others that the Hinterlands consumes? If I have a chance for people to keep people alive. I will do it."

"You are not responsible for their fate," he hissed back.

The response hit a part of her heart hidden from view, a part she didn't even fully understand. She *was* responsible for their fate. If she could prevent this terror from happening, she would. "I have the power to do it, then I shall try." Aza's voice was a command and Lorn obeyed. He dropped the subject, their footsteps becoming a drumbeat to her death march.

The staircase widened at the bottom into a great void. Lord Aldrich grabbed the nearby torch and held it in front to provide light. He turned to face them, his face full of grim excitement. "Is everyone ready?" There were no responses, a word of dissent did not echo.

Single file they entered the room and a great cavernous opening expanded out in front of them. Lord Aldrich skillfully navigated the room, lighting various torches until the room was lit with a harsh glow. The flames flickered with an absent wind. The deep cavern below the castle did not match the opulence Aza was accustomed to. It was drab, with a thick moisture in the air. The walls were a smooth black, almost obsidian, like all the light had been sucked out. If Aza strained, she could hear the faint crashing of waves against the walls. With how far they had descended, she assumed they were below sea level.

She thought of the other night and the trance she suffered, from the voice beckoning her downward. She had told no one of it—had completely forgotten about it. Only Anwin knew. With the flurry of activity, and the tumultuous meeting, she hadn't spared it a second thought with all that was happening with the Hinterlands. It was another strange occurrence in a long list of things. Who would even be able to solve the problems that plagued her when only *she* had the power to abolish them?

She pushed the memory from her mind and stepped forth into the cavern. Once her eyes adjusted to the dimness and faint flickering of the flames, an imposing slab of rock stood in the center of the room. Lord Aldrich circled it and stood waiting for the rest of them to approach. Aza hesitated, her steps unsteady. She had to banish the Hinterlands here?

Lorn echoed her thoughts. "What is this place?"

Oron spoke, his old voice carrying throughout the cavern, "It is an ancient place. One of power. Power long before the MagicBlessed existed. We think this is where Aza can finally banish the Hinterlands."

"On some rock?" Lorn questioned. He neared the slick, black stone and ran a finger down the length of it. It looked to be hewn from the earth itself, coming up in a smooth rectangle, perfectly centered within the obsidian room. Aza caught flickers of sparkles and swirls glittering back at her. They were faint in the light, but it gave her hope. Hope that it wasn't an empty black abyss meant to swallow her up, but that beauty remained and fought for survival.

She could return from this.

Lord Aldrich spoke, causing Aza to jump. She had been in such deep concentration on the stone table. "This is a special type of obsidian formed deep. Within the earth. Within the ocean itself. Oron is correct, it holds special properties that no one in this room knows about, even me." Aza took note of the additional statement as reassurance. Despite how long-lived Cruvo is, he still doesn't know all the answers.

"We don't have time for this, Lord Aldrich. The Hinterlands needs to be dealt with now." Lilit hissed at him. "Enough with the history lesson. Get her on the table."

Lorn stalked up to her, his expression eerily calm. "She doesn't have to do anything you ask. If she wants to say no and leave, she will."

Lilit's gray eyes hardened and didn't hesitate as she said, "Then many families and people will die. Do you want that to happen again? Do you want their blood on both of your hands?"

"You will not shove your misplaced guilt onto us." Lorn's stance was firm, his feet planted, with his hand dancing around the outside of his sword hilt. A calm boundary set.

Lilit's smile was as sharp as her sword. "You want to go, ohh *famed* Hunter?"

"Enough." Aza marched between Lorn and Lilit. She kept her back on Lilit—she could deal with her easily. Her eyes held Lorn's own. "Leave it."

His jaw unclenched and Aza led him away from Lilit and towards the table. With her back to Lilit, Aza claimed, "If you want to fight Lilit, I don't mind stepping up." Aza sent a flame to encircle Lilit, trapping her within the heat. A muttered curse echoed in the chamber. Only after Aza reached the obsidian table did the flames recede.

Lord Aldrich sounded bored as he ordered, "Lilit, Gravers, please keep guard. Oron, come to me and help Aza get situated."

At his command everyone moved. "Aza you will need to lay down on the table."

Aza approached the obsidian table, the deep power within rippling off in waves. Lord Aldrich leaned next to her whispering, so only she could hear, "We believe this will amplify your powers and extend your reach." Aza brushed a finger against the surface of the table. Immediately, her magic reflected back to her. She felt strength, power, and something else hidden within. It came at her in waves. She quickly pulled back her hand from the table, her eyes locking with Lord Aldrich's.

"Yes, he confirmed. "I feel it too."

Resolutely, Aza squared her shoulders. She would not let any weakness show. She needed to do this. To rid the Hinterlands from all of Ithilia. She hoisted herself up onto the table, the impact causing her to recoil the echo of her own magic. She braced herself as she lay on the cold, smooth stone. It was rough and firm against her back, offering little support. Nothing lay in her vision except for the yawning chasm of darkness above her with brief glimpses of Lord Aldrich and Lorn within her periphery.

"What do I do?"

Oron said from a distance, "You must focus your thoughts on the Hinterlands, and use your magic to vanquish it. Imagine it as something that needs to be cured. Like an infected wound, surround it with your magic and heal it."

Aza tried to keep the puzzlement from her face as she thought through how she would accomplish the task Oron had just described.

Her magic often took the form of elements and while she had physically healed Lorn, she had never attempted something like this before. She didn't even know if it would work. The chill and wrongness of the Hinterlands seeped through her — she didn't want to succumb to such darkness. Firm with resolve, she breathed out, and nodded.

Lorn moved closer and peered anxiously over her, "You can back out at any time Aza. Please know that."

"I know, but I must try."

Aza forced herself to close her eyes.

~

When she reopened them, she was standing in a dream-like reality. Wisps of fragmented smoke lay in front of her. She tentatively reached out a hand and intertwined her fingers with the smoke, the haze of it drifting in and out of focus. It wasn't smoke. No, it was darkness weeping out of the air in front of her. She felt sorry for it, like it needed a reprieve from the despair it had been subjected to. Aza wanted to comfort it and protect it. She urged her fingertips forward just a bit more—only enough to touch the darkness and prove that she too, was one with the dark. Upon impact, she released a feral scream.

A roaring filled her ears and drowned out all other sounds. She faintly heard Lord Aldrich from eons away shout, "Now, my stars!"

Lorn screamed, "Aza, stop this!"

But they were a distance—a lifetime away from her, and she was here in this unrelenting torture. The darkness writhed within her, coursing through her veins, filling her magic, her power, with fire. It was agony. She felt like she was being boiled alive. The darkness wrapped around her, filling her.

She cried out in pain. Cried out for someone to come save her and stop this agony. It was endless. The darkness found her heart, it wrapped itself around it, like a snake coiling around its prey. It squeezed tightly and with each squeeze, Aza found herself unable to breathe. Images of despair flashed through her mind. Sorrow was her only companion. This was unbearable, this overwhelming sadness and anguish. It was pure mental and physical pain.

Why was she here? What was she meant to do? In the recesses of her mind, she remembered she had a purpose here. She wasn't meant to be here, but she was. She searched and searched, the pain a reminder and a motivation to keep going. She had a purpose to be here. She would find it.

A flash of clarity broke through the torrent of pain. This festering darkness was the Hinterlands, and she needed to banish it. Heal it. The place was in pain, the same pain it was causing her right now. Aza forced herself to view the pain through a separate lens, a detached perspective. She needed all of her focus, all of her energy spent on using her vast magic to heal this monstrosity.

Her magic swelled and the darkness receded from her. She felt stronger. The darkness was kept at bay. She tried again. Her magic pushed harder, like venom being sucked out from her body, the darkness departed. It drifted aimlessly in front of her, and she looked on dispassionately. Her magic expanded, encapsulating the darkness around her. But it was never-ending. She strained against the edges of it, trying to coax and maneuver it. Sweat gathered across her brow and dripped down into her eyes. Her fingers were stiff kept in their perpetual state of clenching, her jaw locked.

Aza screamed.

It was a scream of rebellion, of love, and of light. A battle-cry for courage to kill the darkness infecting their lands, a scream to keep the citizens safe. It was a scream of anger at not being able to protect Lakesh from dying at the hands of a Howler. It was a scream of primal rage, and strength, and love.

Her magic encapsulated the shimmering darkness in front of her. She had it in her thrall and she could squash it now. One more press of her magic and it would be obliterated. So close. It was right there.

Out of the shimmering darkness, a figure emerged. It approached her with a steady slowness. The pace was excruciating as Aza kept the darkness at bay, yet she held it and watched as the figure solidified in her sight.

Aza nearly lost the grip she had on the darkness. It was the woman from the Hinterlands. Her onyx black hair was braided and coiled around the top of her head, framing her angular face. She still had the same sallow brown skin as before, the Hinterlands sapping her of any warmth. Her hood was down, revealing the thin, geometric tattoos on her cheeks.

Aza weighed her options, unsure of this person's intent, but the woman strode forward unencumbered by the darkness surrounding her. She paused on the threshold of light and darkness, her eyes searching Aza's.

They stood, each staring at the other, unmoving and unspeaking. Aza didn't know what to do, her magic straining to withhold the darkness. Was this woman the cause of it all?

"Free me." The woman's voice was both young and old. She did not plead to Aza. It was a simple command. She stayed on her side of the darkness, not yet encroaching into the light.

"Get out of the darkness! Come to me and I can help you," Aza begged the woman.

The woman shook her head sadly. "You are not ready yet," she simply stated.

"Come with me." Aza reached forward trying to pull the woman to her. Damn her stubbornness. She would save her no matter what.

As if a torch was blown out, the woman's features changed from resignation to pure fury. Her head cocked to the left, a predator assessing her prey

"Get out of here now!" the woman screamed.

The darkness broke through Aza's magic and swallowed her whole. She could barely stifle a scream as pain, sorrow, and anger filled her.

39

And so, I watched as she was torn away from me
Horrified I could not look away
Nor could I take her pain away
I was stuck
In between
Forever in between
Author unknown, scroll covered with burn marks

Lorn couldn't stand it. Her scream rang in his ears. It was a nightmare. He squashed down the haunting memory of Lakesh being slashed by the Howler, but Aza's piercing scream brought it to the forefront. They needed to stop this. Why wasn't anyone doing anything?

Lorn didn't miss the quick sentiment between Aza and Lord Aldrich. Something was deeply amiss, and he didn't need her to pay the price with her death. Fuck sacrificing herself for Ithilia. She didn't need to be some fabled hero. She needed to stay alive.

"I'm taking her out of here, now!" Lorn reached for Aza despite the swells of magic pulsing off her in waves. His head pounded with the force of her magic, but he needed to pull her out of this.

As he reached for Aza, Lord Aldrich's voice cut through her screaming, "You will do no such thing." He didn't even need to raise his voice to be heard over her screams of pain.

"The Darkness below, I won't!" Lorn paid no heed and reached for Aza. Before he knew it, his arm was wrenched behind his back, his wrist bent in pain. A hand grabbed his hair and pulled him away from Aza. He was dragged back, away from her, when she needed him most. "Stop it! She's in pain." He tried to wrench free, but Lilit and Gravers had restrained him and held him easily at bay. They kicked his struggling legs out from under him. He slammed down onto his knees, Lilit's arm wrapped around his throat.

"She will be fine, Lorn. Trust in her abilities. She is combating the Hinterlands as we speak," Lord Aldrich reassured him. He appeared completely unruffled, watching Aza scream and her back arch from the pain inflicted on her.

"How do you know?" Lorn struggled to speak, Lilit's arm had reconfigured to be around his neck, cutting off his air. "How are you so sure?" He strained against Lilit and Gravers, his voice hoarse.

"She is more powerful than you can imagine." Lord Aldrich walked so he loomed over Aza's head, his hands reverently placed on either side. But Lorn noticed how Lord Aldrich flinched ever so slightly, and his posture lost its confident pose.

"If she is so powerful, then why isn't she out yet? Why is she still screaming?" Lilit's grip tightened around his throat and his vision began to blur, the edges darkening. "I can see the doubt in your face, Lord Aldrich." Lilit's forearm clamped against his windpipe cutting off any further speech. Lorn had reached his limit, if he died here defending Aza, so be it. Any strength he had left he put forth into his magic his light blinding Lilit. Lilit stumbled releasing the hold on his windpipe and he forced her hands away from him. He scrambled to his feet, legs aching as he raced towards Aza. She lay there screaming on the obsidian table, the black stone swallowing her, and he couldn't stand it any longer. He sprinted, faltering slightly as jagged fragments of air raced back into his lungs. He gasped, plunging forward determined to break whatever trance she was in. Only a little closer.

Oron stood on the edge, uncertain and unmoving, a grim expression on his face. Lord Aldrich just watched Lorn advance, unconcerned. Lorn was consumed with a singular thought, helping Aza off this table. She didn't deserve this torture.

His hands firmly clasped her arm as her body writhed. "Aza, listen to me! You need to come back!" One final scream ripped through the cavern. It was a scream of death. He froze, his voice small as he called her name into the giant, undersea cavern, "Aza?"

Silver eyes flashed open. Before he could breathe a sigh of relief, a giant blast of wind crashed into him, sending him flying into the wall. As he tumbled through the air, he caught glimpses of the others being tossed like leaves in a gust of wind. Aza rose from the obsidian table, her magic rippling off her in powerful waves, pushing them all. Her silver eyes were filled with untempered anger and a deep unmitigated sorrow.

She was lost to them.

Something had happened.

This was not Aza.

Lorn could not comprehend what was happening. The blast might have broken some of his ribs, and his breathing was still ragged from Lilit trying to crush his windpipe. He winced, clutching his sides, blood trickled down his temple, the wetness seeping into his eyes. The back of his head smarted, but he needed to reach her. Aza sent another pulse of magic out, but this time Lord Aldrich responded, redirecting the magic to an empty spot in the cavern. A resounding boom shook the cavern, and Lorn fell to his knees as he attempted to clamber to his feet. Their magic was too strong. His head throbbed, the room going in and out of focus. Lorn forced himself to his feet and spotted Lilit and Gravers doing the same thing in a far corner of the room. Oron lay unconscious in a separate corner of the room. Aza and Lord Aldrich faced off against each other. Their magic volleyed back and forth.

Aza was possessed, unseeing and unfeeling to what she was doing. Lorn had never seen anyone combat with magic the way Aza and Lord Aldrich were doing now. It was like the fabled battles of MagicBlessed heroes from long ago, able to freely use it without fear of a burnout. He couldn't help but stare as their magic blasted across the room. Aza sent a blast of fire to scorch Lord Aldrich, and he quelled it with a douse of water and wind at the same time scattering the ashes of her power.

"My stars, stop!" Lord Aldrich barely shouted the words as another onslaught of attacks happened.

Aza did not hear him or chose not to. Lorn couldn't decipher which it was. She sprinted at him, raining down shards of ice and torrential blasts of wind, sending the razor-sharp icicles straight towards Lord Aldrich's chest. He burned them away with a blast of his own fire. Lord Aldrich only defended, never attacking Aza.

Lilit and Gravers stood on the edge, equally slack-jawed at their confrontation. Lorn didn't know what to do. Was he supposed to join Aza in her attack or bring her back from the brink of whatever precipice she stood over? Lorn had always acted as her guide helping her to use restraint. Yet with his wounds, Lorn struggled to keep standing. His misplaced ribs poked as he fought for breath.

He took in the vast cavern. It wouldn't withstand much more. The walls were groaning with the strain of withholding the immense ocean beyond its barrier.

Aza's sprint brought her near Lord Aldrich. She feinted in one direction and rolled to the other, skillfully drawing her dagger. She thrusted it at him, swiping viciously, each slash a near hit. Lord Aldrich backpedaled, traversing the whole cavern, giving himself space to avoid Aza's attack. She held no mercy in her strikes, her newly acquired skill of using her magic and dagger, a deadly combination. Aza struck, advanced, her magic reigning down different torments. The ground twisted below Lord Aldrich's feet, wind and solid air struck him, water attempted to flood his throat, fire burned his body, and light blinded him. Yet still he held his ground, defending and blocking her attacks. She was relentless.

Darkness swirled around her and enveloped her. She appeared behind Lord Aldrich, her dagger swiping at his calf. She finally struck true, Lord Aldrich faltering to one knee. He blocked her next attack and healed himself instantly.

Lorn dragged himself over to their fight, his breathing labored. He couldn't even register shock at her shadow magic disappearance. Only once had he witnessed use of shadow magic in such a particular way. Every step was painful it felt like an arrow in his side, but he needed to reach her. He needed to stop the madness that consumed her.

"Aza." His voice strained and was barely above a whisper. They didn't stop and twirled about the room, locked in their deadly dance.

"Aza, stop. Why are you doing this?" His words tried to whittle away at her possession. She flinched, her silver eyes losing the fiery focus they had a minute ago. It didn't last long before she lashed out again at Lord Aldrich. "Aza, please! Come back to yourself. Let go of whatever this is!" Lorn shouted as much as he could, his voice giving out.

Aza froze mid-strike and turned to face Lorn. She crumbled in on herself. Her hands clutched her silver hair, gripping the coils as if she was grounding herself in this reality. Through clenched teeth she moaned, pain laced throughout each word, "It hurts, Lorn. I need to get revenge. The darkness needs an outlet. It needs him." Aza pointed a shaky hand at Lord Aldrich.

"You can fight it Aza! You are stronger than this pain!"

Aza eye's shuttered closed, the edges creased in pain.

"Keep going Aza. Push it away. You are stronger than you know. Focus on my voice, forget everything else." Lorn nudged himself forward, the black spots in his vision threatening to take him down. "I know what it means to want to destroy, but you need to stop. You need to fight it." He was thankful the others didn't interfere. They were silent, staring in anticipation. He was an arm's length away, the ground beneath his feet threatening to tilt and upend him. Lorn could do this. He could reach her. Aza floated towards him like a lost soul looking to cling to the nearest life form. "Aza, no more," Lorn reasoned. His hand reached towards her, providing her sanctuary and relief from the tide of emotions swallowing her. She copied him, her hand reaching to close the gap. Their hands clasped. Lorn was overcome with relief. He fought to keep their hands together, he would provide her with the support she needed. He couldn't fail her now. Her demeanor shifted, like a heavy weight being removed. A sigh of relief broke free. Lorn gave a feeble smile. "Better—" Before he could finish his sentence the cavern released an earth-shattering crack.

The ocean battered in, sweeping Lorn off his feet. His head cracked against the obsidian table and darkness claimed him.

~

Freed from the chains of her pain, Aza blinked in astonishment at Lorn, their hands clasped together. Her friend attempted to smile, his face concealing his pain. Before she could respond the walls broke, bringing in watery chaos. Lorn was ripped from her grasp by the rush of water. She heard faint screams and cries from the others. She needed to contain this. Otherwise, the whole cavern would collapse, and they would drown. She was so weary. Aza wanted to lay down and rest, her magic nearly spent. Whatever happened while she was in her trance, it had nearly drained her vast reservoir of magic. Aza scrambled and splashed for a better position in the room and pulled up any last dredges of magic she had. The water was strong, pulling, demanding.

She would not yield to it.

Her magic gripped the water, attempting to form it to her will. It fought her, wanting to fill in the vast cavern, claiming them all as its victims. The salty brine filled her nose, the cresting waves crashed against her legs, pulling her deeper.

A familiar voice entered her head. "Daughter of starlight, why have you evaded me?"

Aza tried to ignore it, but the voice pushed deeper, like a current pulling her into the sea. The voice was only in her head. It did not reverberate throughout the room. The briny voice beckoned to her and her alone. She gritted her teeth, still focused on containing the water in the room, the crack in the cavern widening from the pressure of the ocean. "I am not evading you," she said through clenched teeth.

"They will all die here. They are worthy sacrifices." The voice slithered over her like hidden sea snakes that cower in their coves.

"They are not yours to take!" Aza shouted to the ocean surrounding her.

"If I cannot have you, I must have someone else." The voice paused in consideration and the waves crashed harder in outrage. "I should kill you all now!"

"Why?" Aza gritted her teeth, pain threatening to sweep in and claim her. Exhaustion weighed her down. She was so tired. But not yet. Lorn needed her.

"How dare you offer yourself to Cruvo, and not me?"

Enraged that this entity would dare try to own her, Aza had to bite her tongue and calm herself down. She didn't want to make their situation worse.

"Pull back your water."

"Why would I do such a thing, woman of the night sky?"

She kept trying to manipulate the water, frantically searching for Lorn. She couldn't see much; the torch lights faded out one by one with the thick moisture in the air.

Aza thought quickly and replied, "I can offer you a deal."

Lord Aldrich waded his way to her, carving his path in the water with his magic, pulling the waves apart, separating them. "Aza, who are you talking to?" She caught a glimpse of his luminescent green eyes and reminded herself that Cruvo stood beside her right now. He could help. It wasn't Lord Aldrich with his limited capabilities, but Cruvo, a god of near unlimited power.

Without warning, she clasped his hand, allowing their powers to meld. She was overwhelmed with the wild, raw power and used it to manipulate the water away from her companions.

"I am not patient, daughter of the night. What is your deal?" The water was relentless. They would not be able to hold out much longer. Another murky ocean wave crashed into the cavern. Aza redirected it with Cruvo's help.

When the ocean let up, Aza hurriedly explained to Cruvo, "I don't know, it is a voice inside my head. I hear it when I'm near the ocean. They want to make a deal otherwise it will kill everyone in this room."

Cruvo released a long-suffering sigh and shouted to the crashing ocean waves, "Go back to your tempestuous sea, Eonas. You will not make a deal with Aza today!"

The voice residing in Aza's head filled the entire room. "You do not give me orders, Cruvo, God of the Hunt. If there is no deal, sacrifices will be made."

The water kept spilling into the room. There was little time left. Lorn and Oron were missing, possibly dying, Lilit and Gravers were not much better.

Cruvo leaned close to Aza whispering, "I will distract them. Use our combined power to push the water out and seal the crack."

Aza gritted her teeth. She was near exhaustion, her magic and body drained. She needed this one last push, for Lorn and Oron floating unconscious in this whirling pool of water and ocean debris.

"Eonas, are you jealous? I didn't know you were one to care for such things, things of the flesh." Cruvo glanced at her, leering. "Well, I do understand your infatuation. She is the embodiment of the night sky," he prattled on. "Do you feel it? The undeniable pull towards her." Cruvo ran the back of his hand down the side of Aza's face.

Ignoring the intensity of Cruvo's gaze, Aza focused. Now was the time for Aza to draw from any reserves of her magic and force this entity out of the depths of the castle of El'en. Her hand clasped tight within Cruvo's. She was renewed with a refreshing amount of magic and her weariness ebbed. She could force it into a deep corner of her mind, for her to face later.

"Did you know, Eonas, that I have tasted her? Do you yearn for the same thing? It's a shame you don't have a physical body to inhabit, no one wants your briny ocean particles to take over their body."

Eonas was furious as the water gushed in with even more force. It wrapped itself around Aza and Cruvo, winding its way up to their faces to drown them in the very substance he mocked. Cruvo used this moment to distract Eonas. All his focus would be on getting retribution, so Aza closed her eyes. Her power pulsed around her, a bright full moon in a dark endless night. She held on to it. With all her strength and all of her practice, she forced the water to make an unnatural retreat through the crack in the cavern. An invisible wall led it away, pulling it away from them. The water fought, crashing at different points along her shield, but her shield did not relent. The ocean was forced back through the crack and with a finishing touch Aza dredged up any remaining energy to seal it. She manipulated the cavern walls together, like a hastily stitched wound. With the tattered remains of her energy, she forced the water out and the wall closed, with the ocean violently thrashing on the other side.

A resurgence of energy rebounded around the room extinguishing any remaining torchlights. Pitched into complete darkness, Aza collapsed to her knees.

Cruvo's heavy breathing filled the eerily silent cavern. She had grown used to the slushing of water and cresting of waves. The silence seemed like death settling over them. A faint glow emitted from Cruvo as he crouched beside her, worry creasing his brow. He still had the appearance of Lord Aldrich, but how he had spoken to Eonas made Aza call him Cruvo.

"Lorn." Aza's voice was strained, memories battered at the back of her mind. This seemed too familiar, the pain jolted through her.

"Lorn," she pleaded again to the empty room. Footsteps scuffed the ground behind her. Cruvo looked up, giving orders to Lilit and Gravers. "Find Lorn and Oron. Check their injuries and bring them back upstairs."

Aza couldn't fathom how they would ascend the spiral staircase with both Lorn and Oron's bodies. "Lorn." Her wild eyes searched the yawning chaos of darkness, searching for her friend. He couldn't be dead. He wasn't. She would not allow herself to think that way.

Aza dragged herself past Cruvo, desperately searching the emptiness for Lorn. Everything ached. It was too much. Trying to destroy the Hinterlands was folly. It had nearly destroyed her in the process. She dragged herself forward once more, her legs scraping against the hard-formed ground. She struggled to say anything. Her throat was dry, her body ached, her head throbbed.

Darkness was not only looking back at her, it became her as she succumbed to unconsciousness.

40

"Memories can be the greatest gift, or the greatest burden."
Journal entry from the astronomer Lilia of Gara

Clashes of swords. The whoosh of magic passing through. A forest consumed in flames, the mix of oranges and yellows dancing in front of her. Bodies littered the ground. The weeping blood a fertilizer for the pine-ridden forest floor. Screams, endless screams from people. No, not from other people. From her. It ripped from her soul. It was too much. Everything was too much. Why? So much death. Too much death. Too much power, she had too much power. It was all wrong. Everything was wrong. Everyone would pay. Never again. This could never happen again.

Deep ragged breaths were forced from her chest as powerful magic splintered through her, breaking her into jagged pieces. Pieces that would never be reconfigured again. They were lost, shattered, missing — just like her.

~

Aza gripped the silken sheets below her, jolting upright. The blaring, clear white room shined back at her causing her to shield her eyes. Her chest heaved from the terror plaguing her dreams. Aza forced herself to breathe a steadying breath. She closed her eyes to clear, to recenter herself. She reopened them and took in the room around her. Everything was in shades of white. The gauzy curtains filtered the early morning light through the clear glass windows. The floors and the walls were marbled white that echoed the rest of the castle.

Last she remembered, she was in the bleak darkness of the undersea cavern. Where was everyone?

Lorn.

Her throat dry from disuse croaked as she attempted to shout his name, "Lorn!" She swung her legs to the side of the bed, surprised at their nimble movements. The pain inflicted on her body and her mind was only a memory now. She was fully recovered. Unaware of how much time had passed, she planted her feet on the ground, steadying herself before taking off. "Lorn!" She scanned the room for a glass of water to relieve her parched throat.

"Aza."

Her back was to the doorway, and she slowly turned. It wasn't who she wanted to see right now. Lord Aldrich filled the door frame, still donning his opulent clothes and appearing every part of the dutiful lord.

"Where's Lorn?"

Lord Aldrich's lips thinned into a small line, his fathomless brown eyes searching hers, searching for the words to say before finally speaking. "He is fine. He is eating breakfast."

"Let me see him." Aza marched right up to him, looking to move past him.

"Aza, please sit first."

Anger and worry had fueled her, but she paused, taking in Lord Aldrich's appearance. He was haggard, equally worried—she saw it in the fine lines around his face and the shadows under his eyes. She forced herself to consider his plea and retreated to the side of the bed.

Lord Aldrich joined her, his shoulder brushing against her own. He turned slightly toward her, taking in her appearance. "How do you feel?"

Frustrated with the question, Aza swiped her hand in front of her dismissing the question. "I'm fine. You know I am."

He pushed further. "Are you sure?"

"Yes! I'm fine, I only needed to rest. Why?" Aza made to stand up and leave Lord Aldrich behind, but his hand shot out to stop her, clamping down on her thigh.

With his physical connection to her, Lord Aldrich's visage disappeared and Cruvo replaced it. Aza started. She sometimes forgot, the god she had grown to care for was buried deep within this lord's appearance. His wild, ethereal eyes stared at her before continuing, "Aza you have been asleep for three days."

Whatever was poised on her tongue dissolved with his statement. Three days. She, who was rarely affected by anything, was forced to recover for three days.

Cruvo watched the realization settle in. "So, you see why I am concerned."

"Lorn?" Aza could only whisper her question. If she was out for three days, how was he?

Cruvo shook his head. "Like I said, he is completely fine and healed. I healed him myself. His injuries were physical. Easy to manage. Yours..." He didn't finish his thoughts.

Aza knew. She understood the depth of damage inflicted upon her, the mental and emotional onslaught from the woman of the Hinterlands and the God of the Ocean. Both of those attacks together had been a deadly combination. She had reached her bottom, used up the last dredges of magic to stop the ocean from consuming them all and to force herself out of the trance inflicted upon her.

"What happened?" Cruvo asked. His hand tightened upon her thigh, as if checking she was still there and wouldn't disappear under his fingers.

It was Aza's turn to shake her head, a myriad of confusing images and memories conflicting with one another. "I won't be able to stop the Hinterlands."

Cruvo released a disappointed breath through his nose. "We will figure it out. How long has Eonas been in contact with you?"

Aza recalled the slippery ancient voice calling to her, wanting her. Everything seemed to want her—she was growing tired of it. "Not very long."

Cruvo pursed his lips and warned her, "Careful of that one. They tend to get what they want. Be wary of the ocean, that is their home." An uneasy silence descended upon them before Cruvo asked, "Is there anything important that happened when you were on the obsidian table?"

How to answer that question? Everything had happened when she attempted to face the Hinterlands. "I'm not sure I can talk about it right now. There was too much. It was like time was suspended." Aza needed time to gather her thoughts and figure out their next course of action. What would happen if she couldn't banish the Hinterlands? "I will share more with you when I have had some time to sort through it all."

Cruvo nodded and ran a hand through his hair. "You are right of course, my stars. I will give you time to recover." He leaned forward and gave her a tender kiss on her temple. She wanted to weep from the softness. Cruvo was a jewel with his many faceted sides; she didn't know which one she would get in each moment. Below in the cavern, he was resolute, focused on his goal of banishing the Hinterlands. Now, he was tender and sweet-hearted. In her dreams, he was feral and wild with his power and his love.

Even after three days of rest she cursed her body's reaction to him. Heat spiked through her at his proximity, at the tenderness with which he kissed her. She decided to return his chaste kiss with one of her own, her lips meeting his. It was not filled with the passion often riddling her dreams, but one of caring and companionship. It was slow and steady, after the chaos of their prior days together. After some time, Aza broke apart from him and without a word, only a flush in her cheeks, she departed from the room and set off in search of Lorn. She spared a brief glance back at Cruvo, his lips curved up in a slight smile. At their broken contact, his image faded like wisps of smoke disappearing from a blown out candle and was replaced with Lord Aldrich.

~

True to Cruvo's word, Aza found Lorn uninjured and looking especially healthy. She came upon him dining alone in his room, munching on a piece of toast. Mid-bite he scrambled to his feet and embraced Aza in a tight hug. Lorn debriefed her on what had happened, most of it from Lord Aldrich's point of view. All three of them—Aza, Lorn, and Oron were carried back up the countless stairs by other guards, and Lord Aldrich personally healed Lorn and Oron. Lorn hesitated when touching the topic of the old, withered man. Aza bade him to continue, and he shifted in his seat, uncomfortable with what he was about to disclose. "Oron was hurt badly. I think Lord Aldrich rescued him from the brink. It was your blast Aza…when you were not yourself."

Guilt gnawed at her. She thought of the kind, old mentor, his wrinkles carved with the passage of time. At least he had survived thanks to Lord Aldrich's fast thinking. "How bad?" Aza muttered, uncertain if she wanted to hear his answer.

"He is still bed-ridden."

Frustrated at how everything had happened, Aza clenched and unclenched her fist. "This wasn't what was supposed to happen."

"I know, Aza. You tried and when you are more prepared you can try again." He ran a hand through his disheveled hair, sweeping the straight black hair back. "Or you can say screw it and someone else can try to deal with the Hinterlands."

"But—"

Lorn leaned closer, his hazel eyes holding her own. "Aza, you have done enough." His tone brooked no argument. "Plus, from all of the reports Lord Aldrich has gathered so far, the Hinterlands seems to have been contained for now."

"Contained?"

"It hasn't expanded again, and that is promising."

"But Lorn, what if it does change?"

"I know, Aza, I do. But we cannot stretch you too thin, even if you want to attempt it again. You were bed-ridden for three days!" Lorn shifted uncomfortably in his seat, breaking his eye contact with her.

"What?" Aza questioned. She had known Lorn long enough to guess he was hiding something.

He didn't answer the question, instead directing his attention to the decorations in the room. He scanned the interior while Aza waited patiently. She knew if she interrupted he would never share his thoughts. "Aza, when you were on that table…it was excruciating."

"I know—"

"No, you don't."

Aza sent him a withering look and Lorn immediately backpedaled, "I'm sure you do, you experienced it. But Aza, watching what you experienced and the trance you were in when you came out. It was terrifying." His hand rubbed his arm like a random chill had entered the room and settled over him. "And…"

She waited for him to find the words, but when he wasn't answering she pressed further. "And, what Lorn?"

"They wouldn't let me try to save you. I begged them, Aza. Begged them to pull you out. They didn't care, didn't listen. Lilit and Gravers nearly caused me to black out at the beginning. I had to listen to you screaming and writhing on the table. I fought Lilit and Gravers, and once I was at the table, Lord Aldrich and even Oron just stood by, uncaring. I pleaded with you to return, to stop this madness." Lorn's voice shook, he paused to take a steadying breath. "Then your eyes flashed open, and you were lost. Goddess above, Aza. You fought Lord Aldrich to the death. I have never seen anything like it." Lorn reached forward and gripped her hands within both of his, his eyes silently beseeching her to listen. "You can make your own choices. You know I will follow you until the end. But to do something so heedless again is madness. You might die, or you might kill everyone around you."

Aza took in everything he said, each word like a solid stone being tied down in her stomach. Everything he said rang with truth and she could not ignore such sound advice.

Lorn released the grip on her hands, the emotional moment broken as he leaned back, assessing critically her. "Now, there is something you aren't telling me, *my stars*."

Her stomach tightened. She knew this moment would come. Lorn discerned too much. Cruvo was too careless in the cavern and their battle together was no ordinary fight. She wouldn't lie to him any further. She searched the ceiling above for any answers before she began her explanation.

Aza was impressed. Lorn sat through all the details, everything she had learned about Lord Aldrich and Cruvo's cohabitation, with a rigid calm. At some points his eyes would widen in alarm, but overall, he maintained his cool composure.

"Well, I already found out earlier this month the gods and goddesses are real." His black hair dropped in front of his eyes. He brushed it back quickly with his fingers. "Cruvo inhabiting Lord Aldrich as a vessel doesn't seem too much of a stretch."

"And what about the Hinterlands?"

"What about it?"

Aza worried her lip before speaking. "If I truly were to banish the

Hinterlands the gods and goddesses would return. Is that the wisest decision?"

Lorn leaned back in his chair, crossing his arms across his muscled chest. "I'm sure we could sit here for another millennium discussing what is the wisest course of action. The problem right now is the Hinterlands shifting and moving out of control. I think we need to take care of that first, and if the gods and goddesses cause problems we will deal with that after."

How Lorn phrased everything seemed logical. Aza wished for her mind to not be so overwhelmed with her choices, decisions, and regrets. "Okay, fair enough." Aza made to rise from her seat, but Lorn reached his palm out indicating she should remain seated. Surprised, she thought they were finished with their discussion.

"Aza, I want you to think deeply about what I ask next and if you answer true to your heart, I won't question it again."

She cocked her head at him, her eyebrows drawn together in confusion, but motioned for him to proceed with his question.

"With everything that has happened—Lord Aldrich summoning me, sending me to the Hinterlands, returning with you, Cruvo appearing in your dreams, training you, Issi's warning against him, Cruvo using you to banish the Hinterlands..." Lorn slowly ticked all of the events on his fingers. He looked at Aza in between each. "Do you trust him?"

Ever since their arrival in El'en, Lorn had worried that no one in this court was trustworthy. It was his biggest concern, and one trait in others he valued above all else. Lorn, who often relied on only himself and never anyone else. She wanted to be honest and give him a straightforward response, but she paused not wanting to mislead Lorn.

Cruvo's image flashed through her mind, his piercing green eyes, and cunning smile. The way he had entered her dreams and her life without any warning. His veiled mysteries and questions left unanswered. Their shared passion. Everything filtered through her mind as she weighed her response. Their undeniable bond, their melding of magics. How he saved her in her dreams from crumbling, and in reality from Eonas. Yet...there were more secrets he held.

Lorn patiently waited for Aza's response, watching her mind work. "I do care for him, but no, I do not trust him." The reality of her truth clanged through her like a coin being dropped into a well. The revelation pierced straight down to the bottom.

She lifted her eyes to meet Lorn, a firm smile on his face. "I agree with you, Aza."

The revelation unearthed a deep truth she never wanted to face. She did not fully trust Cruvo. There was too much hidden underneath the surface, too many unanswered questions. She could not deny the feelings she had for him, but she couldn't let that cloud her mind. They needed time, yet time was not available to them.

Too many things needed to be done. Banish the Hinterlands, bring back the gods and goddesses, stop the decay of magic, and find out answers about who she is. The list keeps growing. The only words she could manage. "Now what?"

He ran an appraising eye down her body. "You need to get dressed for tonight. There is a giant masquerade ball, and everyone is expected to attend." Aza groaned, more performing in front of people who assumed the worst of her.

41

"The constellations are in perfect harmony with our world, reflecting our own battles and turmoil. We have only to tilt our heads back to the sky to observe and reflect."

From Oron of Iyera's private journal

Sequestered to her room, a horde of servants prepared Aza for the masquerade ball. Lorn informed her that while she had been recovering over the last few days, the masquerade ball was the final celebration with the visiting dignitaries. After the ball, over the following week, the leaders with their respective attendees would depart back to their own provinces. While she was recovering, Lorn told her of the dissent spreading throughout the other leaders.

"They are all panicking," he explained. "This masquerade is a farce. Everyone will put on a brave face, party and forget their worries, but I think they are conspiring. Keep on your guard." Lorn was able to share this information before Aza was whisked away by harried servants ready to be done with their charges.

Aza preferred getting ready alone. She often didn't spend copious amounts of time on her appearance. She knew what she looked like, and she never wanted to garner any more attention than necessary. Despite her protests, the servants washed her, scrubbed her, and placed makeup on her. She swallowed her cries of outrage after a few minutes, when they repeated the same sentiment of, "Lord Aldrich requested this for tonight." The servants held a beautiful dress in front of Aza expecting her to wear it. This one request she denied, instead veering for the dress Melina made for her. The servants filed out the

"

door with one leaving a black box on a nearby credenza with the instructions for Aza to don it tonight at the ball. With a towel still wrapped around her, she withdrew the delicately wrapped dress.

The pure white linen wrapping slid open with a soft whisper as she reverently unwrapped the treasure within. For some unknown reason, Aza had only briefly peeked upon the dress Melina had gifted her. She knew there would be a moment, an event that called for such a work of art, freely given from the hard work of Melina. Aza held up the dress, stifling a gasp. The dress was liquid silver. Her fingertips ran over the fabric, rubbing the impossibly soft fabric made from the highland sheep of Gara. Melina the seamstress, was indeed gifted.

Aza eagerly shed her towel and pulled the dress on. It curved to her body effortlessly. The fabric smooth and sheer. The material did not weigh her down or limit her movements. The dress was held up by two thin straps the fabric cupped to her body as it showcased all of her luscious curves. It was a simple and elegant cut, the fabric gently pooling around the base of her legs. As she walked a sensuous slit revealed her muscular, toned thigh. Aza readjusted her dagger to the other leg. She raced back to the blue-tiled bathroom and truly looked and appreciated herself in the mirror. The dress had a modest cut in the front, only relying on the suggestive curve of her body to enhance it. When she turned around, the back was cut out revealing midnight skin. As she moved and admired herself, the dress rippled.

She was starlight incarnate.

Aza remembered the black box gifted to her from Lord Aldrich. She brought it back into the sanctuary of the bathroom and lifted the cover. Inside was a jet black mask. It was only a half mask, but the details on it were exquisite. Small black diamonds dotted the border and eye-line of the mask, and a simple silk tie brought it all together. Curious to see how the completed outfit appeared, she tied the mask to her face and checked back at the mirror. The unassuming look of the mask paired perfectly with her dress and her appearance. Aza was already startlingly beautiful. Anything additional would appear over the top and take away from her overall beauty. With only the simple black mask, her eyes, hair and dress popped.

She was radiant.

Although Aza was resistant to the method of being washed and prepared by the workers, she was beyond pleased with the results.

Even the makeup applied by the workers was tastefully done, emphasizing her natural beauty without detracting from her.

A knock at the door startled Aza from her reverie. Her movements were slow and unhurried. With all of the chaos happening, she wanted to enjoy this night, no matter what transpired. Aza pulled open the door, her mouth forming the words ready to greet Lorn. She froze mid-greeting.

Lorn of Verta stood across from her. He did not resemble her friend anymore. Gone was the rough exterior carved from years spent living on the edge of the Hinterlands. Gone was the man who wore grief on his face. Here was the famed Hunter of the Hinterlands. Tapered black pants framed his lean body while a deep rich green coat hid his muscular chest. The coat was inlaid with threads of gold, in different whorls and textures. Underneath it, Lorn had a simple, white-buttoned tunic tucked into his pants. Her eyes trailed up to the mask he donned. The pattern in his coat was gracefully mimicked in his mask. He wore a half-mask similar to hers, with the base color the same deep green and golden whorls as his coat. The gold and green mask brought out the dimension of color within his hazel eyes. The mask fit his angular face perfectly, accentuating all the curves of cuts of him. Even his faint scars seemed to glisten in response to his beauty. Lorn's loose black hair, which always fell into his eyes, was slicked back with some gel. Lord Aldrich had spared no expense. Even Lorn's boots were new, the leather a shiny and untarnished rich black. Spotting Lorn's new boots, Aza remembered to slip on her own flats. Somehow, they blended in with her dress, as if Lord Aldrich had known what Melina's dress looked like.

"Ready?" Lorn raised an eyebrow at Aza.

She glanced about the room, searching to make sure she remembered everything. The sword Lorn had gifted her lay across her bed. She had no way to discreetly wear it with her skintight dress, so she chose to forgo it for this evening. Aza mournfully looked at Lorn's sword hanging gracefully from his waist. She looked down to where her dagger hid next to her thigh, thankful to at least be able to carry that down to the masquerade.

Lorn held his arm out expectantly waiting for her to join. Before Aza entwined her arm with his, she paused gripping his shoulders with her hands. "Thank you for everything Lorn. Lakesh would be proud to see you here now. You look extremely handsome." Aza saw a muscle feather in Lorn's jaw, his eyes piercing into hers, before he bowed his head and took a slow inhalation.

He raised his head back up to look at her and whispered, so quietly Aza barely heard it, "Thank you, Aza."

So Lorn and Aza walked arm in arm down to the masquerade ball, unaware of what Fate had planned.

~

Over the last few months Aza had adjusted to the grandeur of the castle. Extravagance was one of the many things Lord Aldrich partook of. He appreciated the craftsmanship of his citizens deploying a diverse range of their art pieces around the castle. He also boasted the finest food and drink available. Thinking back on the first day of welcoming the leaders, Aza was blown away by the beauty of the throne room. From Oron's teachings and some subtle comments made about each of the leader's egos, Aza knew if they were in charge of hosting a gathering, each respective leader would try to put everyone else to shame.

This masquerade ball was no different. She tried to stifle her gasp as she walked arm in arm with Lorn into the throne room. Instead of a magnificent swell of flowers in the shape of the ocean, she was greeted with a sea of candles. The long thin tapers suspended from the ceiling in varying heights each held precariously by some magnificent engineering and magic. The thousands of candles paired perfectly with the darkened stormy clouds gathering on the Wyra ocean that she saw outside the large glass windows.

Her face betrayed the simple joy children experience daily—one of awe and wonder, at the beauty of life. A dazed smile was stuck to her face as she scanned the ceiling, taking in the beauty of the romantic lighting set out over the decadent floor, casting everything in a joyful glow. Aza was enamored. She looked to her partner to share in the wonder and found his face mimicked hers. They each quietly led the other through the constantly revolving door of people. It was like time had slowed, and Aza was able to ignore the feeling of being ostracized and appreciate the moment for what it was—pure beauty. They both found their table without a word, not needing the encumbering display of words to weigh down their experience.

Most people avoided her. The stigma surrounding her involvement with the Hinterlands and her overall mystery had people questioning their proximity to her. She didn't mind. Not tonight. The guarded looks and hushed whispers rolled off her back like droplets of water.

A band assembled near the throne dais and the piercing sound of a violin chord cut through the chatter in the room. A beautiful, slow tune began, and people began coupling off and dancing in the center. Before Lorn could offer his hand, Lord Aldrich scooped Aza up, twirling her out of her chair. He effortlessly swept her over to the dance floor, one hand protectively draped around her revealing, low-cut dress, the other clutched in her hand guiding her through the steps. Although Aza favored Cruvo, she could not deny Lord Aldrich's visage was attractive. His light brown skin glowed in the overhead candlelight, drawing attention to his mask. Aza was taken aback. She had expected him to be in something resembling the ocean, yet he wore a full mask resembling that of a stag. The mask was beautifully crafted, golden horns protruded from the top in a natural formation. The rest of his tunic was a mixture of earth tones. The results were startling, forcing Aza to focus on the golden stag mask.

Aza tried to give an easy smile. Her time with Cruvo was complicated. Only this morning, she was entwined with him, leisurely kissing him and enjoying the taste of him. After her talk with Lorn, her experience had soured, like the feel of too much wine sitting in her stomach. She did care for him, yet she didn't trust him. It was difficult for her to resolve the two glaring truths.

Lord Aldrich twirled her effortlessly as he leaned in and breathed out, "You are exquisite, my stars." While she was cautious with his flattery, it still was lovely to hear and caused her belly to stir in response. She responded with a genuine smile. Words would only be a waste. They twirled and floated on the dance floor and Aza allowed herself to enjoy this moment with him. Even though it was Lord Aldrich's appearance, Aza pictured Cruvo instead. His wild, feral eyes raking over her, devouring her. "It is a shame..." he murmured.

Unable to ignore his unfinished sentences Aza asked, "What is?"

Pulling her close for another spin he whispered in her ear conspiratorially, "That the throne room is full of people."

"Why?"

The music reached a crescendo causing Lord Aldrich to dip Aza. His hand supported her back, as his eyes roved over her body. He finished by locking eyes with her. "So I can properly undress you right here and make you moan my name." A flash of green crossed his irises as Aza tried to hide the heat flaring throughout her body. Like he could sense her arousal, Lord Aldrich's eyes strayed to her breasts hovering below his face and he smirked. He smoothly lifted her out of the dip, the music coming to a halt. Aza fidgeted with her hands, unsure of where to place them. Lord Aldrich leaned in one last time and placed a chaste kiss along her cheek. "I will have to wait until tonight and taste you later." Aza bit her lip. Her pull towards Cruvo was too much. It was undeniable and Aza hated herself for it.

The room was filled with the shuffling of feet and people excusing themselves from the dance floor as the band prepared the next song. Lord Aldrich left Aza, heading to mingle with the other political figures. It wouldn't do well for him to be seen around her constantly. Vicious gossip would spread. Her stomach twisted with hunger pains. The day had been hectic, with her waking up from her injuries and fatigue only this morning. She never truly replenished all her spent energy. On the edges of the throne room, there was a large wooden table covered with food. Her mouth watered simply looking at the extravagant buffet. She made her way over to it, ignoring the judgmental stares from the other visiting nobles. The food smelled Goddess-blessed, and Aza immediately grabbed a plate and piled it full of food. Two figures swooped down on either side of her, their clear porcelain skin and black hair were clear indicators of who stood beside her—Lady Rasmina's two elder daughters. Ruby and Sapphire were dressed in their respective colors, their dresses and masks both elaborate and stunning. They inherited their mother's gorgeous looks and deadly personality. They put on the farce of grabbing food on their plates all the while whispering their venomous words to Aza.

"What you did to our mother is inexcusable."

"You should watch your back, lest you find a dagger in it."

"Without your power you are nothing."

"There will come a day when we repay what you did."

"Watch your lover-boy hunter, he might find himself on the end of a blade."

They took turns, alternating their threats and hate. Aza sighed and stepped back from the table so she could clearly see them. They were indeed great beauties, both in their early twenties. It was difficult to discern age in the MagicBlessed, but Aza would not tolerate such slander. They quieted when Aza stepped back. She calmly turned her head from side to side. "I do not lie back and take idle threats against myself or my friends. If you are so brave to threaten me, would you like to see the consequences?"

Aza needed to maintain control of her powers. It couldn't appear like she was hurting these women. They only needed a small reminder to not tangle with forces stronger than the both of them. She relaxed the tight leash, allowing her power to pool around her being. It leaked towards them, poking and testing the exterior of each woman. She was impressed. Each of them held their ground, only allowing a small glimpse of fear to twinkle in their eyes. Aza's magic crept over them. In one fell swoop she yanked the air from their lungs. They both clutched their throats, their eyes widening in fear before Aza returned their ability to breathe. Red blotches of anger dotted their faces.

Aza stepped forward to retrieve her plate of food on the table. She looked at them as if they were of no importance, like mere bugs on the ground she needed to squash. Echoing Xira's sentiments, Aza said, "If you cannot control your tongue, then I will do it for you." As Aza turned and left to find solitude back at her designated table, she heard the tell-tale sound of the women squabbling. A small victory. Aza was able to punish them without anyone in the room being aware of her involvement. She strode through the throne room and found her seat, but Lorn was not there.

~

Lorn watched Aza dancing with Lord Aldrich. He let out a long-held breath. He did not doubt Aza's ability to handle Lord Aldrich. However, the god that inhabited him—Cruvo, she cared for him and that would be tricky to navigate. Lorn forced himself to look away from their skilled dancing. He refused to be her minder and lead to any festering resentment.

Instead, Lorn took in beauty of their final gathering. The throne room was awe-inspiring. Living his quaint life on his farm in Verta, he had never imagined that he would ever experience such a lavish night.

To be among these lords, ladies and nobles, and to be considered an equal. He silently wished for Lakesh to be here. She would have held a secretive smile at Lorn's elegant outfit, his hair freshly slicked back, her arm squeezing his for support. As the transcendent music played, he began to daydream, picturing Lakesh in a full gown the color of liquid gold. It would pair well with her golden brown skin, playing off her rich skin tones. Her mask would be a reflection of her dress. They would dance throughout the whole night, her rich hearty laughter filling the chasm of his heart and the surrounding space. Lorn's fingers would dance over her farm-honed body, the two of them filling the dance floor.

Growing up in the rural outskirts of Verta, Lorn and Lakesh loved to attend their giant dances. Often held in the ramshackle barns of the host, they would gather their paltry few instruments, but the joyous beat of music would reverberate off the wooden walls. In the warm months, their gatherings would take place outside, the families and children dancing amongst the long wild grasses neighboring their farms. Lorn much preferred the contentment of their simple dances, and their ragtag group of musicians. However, for one night he would have cherished seeing Lakesh and he dressed up for a fancy lord's masquerade ball.

He scanned the dance floor, appreciating the beauty of all the couples. He spotted Lord Sune dancing gracefully with his consort, Ryu. Lord Ravinder clumsily stepped onto Lady Sarava's feet. Although he didn't agree with the politics and heated debates of the politicians, he still enjoyed the unique MagicBlessed moment happening around him. He wanted all the people of Ithilia to enjoy themselves and be who they were without the fear of monsters or other people endangering them.

Near the back of the room, something familiar caught his eye. The man had a full mask obscuring his features, but his body, his gait, how he held himself triggered an alarm within Lorn. He had relied on his instincts to guide him for years and now wasn't any exception. He rose steadily from his chair, keeping an even pace, feigned curiosity as he circled the room. The strange man was doing something similar, his focus on the people gathered.

Lorn stood an arm-length away from the man, and with a feigned familiarity he flung his arm around the man, faking a laugh and leading him away from the throne room. The man stiffened under his touch. Lorn leaned in like he was telling a secret or a joke. "If you struggle and make a scene I will kill you here and now." Lorn had stealthily slid his dagger into his hand, and it was pointed firmly into the man's back, right over his kidneys. Lorn remembered how the man's magic had manifested as strength. He recalled how the man had miraculously healed from two stab wounds and escaped from the stables. He would receive answers and he would not let this slippery man get away again.

The man's eyes flickered, taking in their surroundings as Lorn led him down a secluded hallway. The sound of music faded away with each step. He had the appearance of a caged rabbit and Lorn knew in a panic rabbits could accidentally kill themselves trying to escape.

Lorn found an empty room and led the man in there. It appeared to be a spare dining nook, possibly for visitors or for workers. He pushed the man into one of the wooden chairs and cast about the room for something to tie him with. Luckily, a faded and stained tablecloth was hastily discarded on the floor. Lorn grabbed it and tied the man around the chest to the chair. It wasn't perfect, but it would have to do for now. Lorn flipped another chair around and sat on it facing the man. He didn't know what he was doing. He had never interrogated a person before, but right now the idea dangled in front of him, a tempting thought he might have to consider. Although Lorn would never intentionally kill someone, this man didn't know that. Lorn wanted to use it to his advantage. "I won't hesitate to stab you in the shoulder wound in the same spot as before. I will impale you with it and continue my questioning without healing you. I'll make sure it's not fatal, just painful. Keep your magic restrained and I won't have to resort to that." Lorn yanked off the ridiculous mask obscuring the man's face. "Let's start with a name."

The man heaved a breath and hung his head down, defeated. He sighed, "Brafter, my name is Brafter."

The name wasn't familiar to Lorn, but he wasn't surprised by that. He rarely knew the people who operated within the confines of each province. "What province do you work for?"

This was the question Lorn wanted to know. He had a deep suspicion that Brafter worked for the Gara province. Lady Rasmina did nothing to hide her disdain. He only needed confirmation from the spy.

Brafter held his silence. Lorn sighed, and repeated his question, "What province do you work for?"

"I told you, I am not afraid of you. There are worse things out there that will harm me."

Brafter held no suspicion in his face, no forced calculations. He spoke frankly with Lorn. It was time for a change of tactics. "What could be worse than your imminent death right now?"

Brafter's eyes bulged with a surge of fear. "Kill me now and be done with it. I will not share any other information other than my name."

Lorn did not want to torture the information out of him, but he needed the answers. His bravado was swept away in one quick exhalation. Lorn was no torturer, but he could play the part. Considering his options, Lorn stared at the dagger in his hand and raised it up, ready to stab the man in his prior injury.

While Lorn fought his conflicting feelings, Brafter burst from his chair. He grappled with Lorn. His dagger clattered to the ground. Brafter had his magic of strength. Lorn was forced back against the wall, his breath knocked out of him. Lorn struggled for air as Brafter wound up and punched him in the jaw. His head snapped to the side. Lorn's vision blurred. He became disoriented. Brafter forced his forearm against Lorn's throat, cutting off his limited air supply.

His plain features lit up in enjoyment. "What would happen if I killed the famed Hunter of the Hinterlands?" he mused. "I don't know if they even need you. I could kill you and beg for forgiveness later." Brafter's eyes were wild, lost to the madness of bloodlust and victory. His forearm began to push harder against Lorn's throat.. Brafter's strength was too much for Lorn to combat, so he summoned his remaining magic to create a bright, piercing light. Brafter faltered briefly enough for Lorn to regain his balance and leverage. He wouldn't let it go to waste.

The door crashed open. The familiar clanging of metal sang through the air as a sword came down upon Brafter, cutting him to the floor. Blood pooled under his body as Brafter's eyes fluttered closed. He was finally dead.

He lost the precious opportunity to question Brafter, but he couldn't complain that this intruder had saved his life. Lorn swore under his breath and looked up to meet his savior.

"We need to leave," a voice demanded.

42

"Patience is paramount when hunting." Cruvo's private journals

Aza watched as another dance unfolded in front of her. She patiently waited for Lorn, scanning the room but unable to find him. She assumed he would return. He was probably swarmed with admirers and people inquiring about his experience in the Hinterlands. A brush of air blew along her back caused her to look over her shoulder at the disturbance. Aza spotted Anwin's familiar red hair done up in elaborate braids, her mask and sleek dress the deepest black of night. Her dress was cut in a flattering shape, embracing Anwin's statuesque height and warrior-honed body. Aza noted Anwin still had a number of daggers and swords attached at different points around her body.

Anwin approached her and leaned down. "My lady, I'm sorry to interrupt you, but there is something you need to see."

Curious about what Anwin was so desperate to show her, she rose from her chair, joining Anwin's brisk pace across the perimeter of the throne room. She disappeared down an adjacent, abandoned hallway. Aza followed, watching the ease of Anwin's movement in her dress. They were the only ones who occupied the hallway, not even accompanied by the stray patter of workers' feet on the marble floor. Anwin navigated the large castle with ease, leading Aza down halls. She paused considering her actions, Lilit had warned her not to be naive and trust everyone. She was blindly following a Nerian down a deserted hallway. Aza froze, and voiced her doubt, "What do you need to show me Anwin?"

Anwin had gained distance down the hallway, but at Aza's hesitation she backtracked. "My lady," her soft green eyes appraised Aza, considering before she answered, "it will be the answer to all of your questions."

Frustrated at receiving a vague response instead of an answer, Aza pulled back and stood firm, her feet rooted to the floor. "I need a proper answer, Anwin. I can't go with you any further until I know."

Her eyes flickered with impatience, checking over Aza's shoulder for intruders. She released a sigh and began to persuade her, "Aza, we know of what plagues you. The constant questions. Questions about your origins, questions about memories that haunt you, questions about who you are and the source of your power. I cannot properly explain where I am taking you, but it will answer everything." She quickly whispered these words, hurrying through the explanation. "I do not have much time, and people cannot catch us here right now. Your missing presence will be noted. Are you joining me or not?" Anwin extended her hand, awaiting Aza's decision.

Aza did not want to be the gullible child following someone blindly into a deserted corridor because they asked. However, Anwin's sincere explanation piqued her interest. How long has she waited to learn of these answers? How long has she desired to know more about herself? Aza could defend herself no matter the situation. She placed her hand within Anwin's, letting the tall red-head lead the way to all the answers to her questions.

Anwin barely cringed against the onslaught of Aza's magic, but Aza felt a sharp prick against her hand and released her grip. She inspected her hand briefly, confused over what had poked her. There wasn't a break in her skin.

"Everything okay?"

Aza nodded absentmindedly, pushing the irritation from her mind. Anwin stopped in front of an unassuming door. She opened it, ushering Aza into the barely lit room. A window faced the Wyra ocean and Aza could lightly discern the white tipped waves in the distance. Another person occupied the room.

Xira stepped forward, dressed in the exact same attire as Anwin—both of them adorned in the deepest black of night. "Aza, thank you for coming. We have wanted to talk to you privately for some time."

The door shut behind Aza and the room was swarmed with

darkness. Uneasiness crept throughout her body. "What is so important, you must tell me with such secrecy?" Aza demanded in a quiet tone. They might still have some information to offer her, and she didn't want to risk being overheard by some stray party guest. The eerie darkness of the discarded room bothered her, and she sought to conjure a flame to the empty torch.

Her magic was sluggish, reluctant to come when she called. She had never struggled with it before, and the feeling was as unfamiliar as being able to stop her beating heart. It was her lifeblood. Her magic never failed.

Except now.

Something was terribly wrong.

Before Aza could question what was wrong, Xira moved quickly. Too quickly. She grappled Aza to the floor, her limbs were contorted and she cried out in pain at the assault. Xira held her there in an expert grip. Aza called to her magic again and again, but it was smothered. Dampened. She could not feel its constant presence around her, comforting her, strengthening her. Instead, there was only emptiness. A hollow void in her soul. She fought back frustrated tears at her lack of magic and the pain that lanced through her body.

"I'm sorry, my lady, but time is running out," Xira said, a sincere sorrow lacing her words. It did nothing to quell Aza's fury. She did not need pity from someone who operated in half-truths and deceptions. Inwardly Aza cursed herself for her stupidity. Lilit was right, she did believe the best in people.

The rattling of a doorknob brought Xira and Anwin to attention. Their heads snapped towards the sound and Anwin positioned herself ready for attack while Xira tightened her grip on Aza. She attempted to fight Xira's grip, but it held too firm. She was a seasoned warrior, and Aza had only begun training a few months ago. Despite her exceptional progress, it was not enough.

She opened her mouth ready to scream when the door swung open without a sound. The scream died in her throat as she saw through the faint gleam of the window, who was illuminated in the faint glow.

Lilit's small, lithe body appeared in the doorway, her sword unsheathed and ready to attack. Anwin stood ready to attack a sword drawn. Her imposing figure towered over Lilit and Aza fought to see her. She was her only salvation against whatever plot was unfolding.

Anwin growled out, "Lilit of Iyera."

Aza struggled against Xira's grip, but trying to escape using the maneuvers Lorn had taught her was fruitless. She could only plead, "Lilit, help, please."

Still Lilit made no move to attack. Aza understood the Nerian warriors were impressive, but so was Lilit's skill. She couldn't understand why Lilit did nothing. Her cold gray eyes flickered between Anwin and Aza. "I warned you Aza. I warned you. Did you listen to me?" Hoping for mercy, Aza only received disgust. "I have no desire to save *you*." Her voice wobbled at the end.

Aza's vision clouded, all resistance released from her muscles. Even though they had a strained relationship, she never thought the captain of the guard could be so cold. Lilit was Lord Aldrich's Captain of the Guard. She had the responsibility to oversee everything in Lord Aldrich's province, including Aza's safety. He wouldn't tolerate the treatment and whatever potential damage these Nerians wanted to do to her. All she could ask was "Why?"

She sneered at Aza, turning her sadness into fuel for her anger. "You can barely see past your own nose." Lilit sheathed her sword, her head jerking towards Anwin addressing her, "I will not fight you" Anwin kept her sword raised in front, not daring to risk whatever plan they had concocted.

Lilit clenched her jaw and refocused on Aza. "Have you been with him?"

"Been with who?"

Lilit nearly lost it at Aza's question, her rage palpable. "Do not be so thick Aza. You are smarter than this." Aza's mind raced at what she was saying, too many things were happening at once. Redrawing her focus, Lilit snapped her fingers impatiently. "I saw you two together. I see how he looks at you."

While Xira pinned her to the floor she struggled to make eye contact with Lilit, but Aza lifted her head determined to fix whatever disparity was going on. Aza couldn't fathom who Lilit was talking about and only repeated her question, "Who?"

"Lord Aldrich!" Lilit hissed, fighting the urge to redraw her sword, her fingers curling around an invisible hilt. "You do not listen. I tried. Tried to warn you. You crossed a line, Aza. It was never supposed to go this far. But I can see the guilt in your face. You have been with him."

All the pieces began to click into place. Lilit was in love with Lord Aldrich. And perhaps Lord Aldrich was in love with her too—not Cruvo—but the mortal hidden within.

"Lilit, no it isn't like that—" Aza begged her to understand.

Lilit's grip tightened on her hilt while she interrupted her, "I know what he is!" she shouted. Her anger reverberated in the room, hollowing Aza. It was all so confusing. Yes she had slept with Lord Aldrich, but he was actually Cruvo. Clearly that didn't matter to Lilit. "Do you know what it's like?" Lilit whispered. "How maddening it is to watch his fascination with you. To watch him toy with you. And just like he planned, you fall for it." Lilit's hand clutched her own hair the strands choked between her fingers.

"You were supposed to be fucking smart Aza."

Aza couldn't respond. She didn't know what would console Lilit and what might cause her even more anger. She could only shake her head.

"We were together, you know, before Cruvo took over his body. I didn't ask for this. Lord Aldrich…he thought it would better Iyera. He had a plan. But Cruvo seduced you and you fell for it? How can that help the province? How will that bring about change?" Lilit shook her head in disbelief. "So no, Aza, I will not help you. I hope whatever these Nerians do to you will be comparable to my pain." Lilit lowered her hand and walked out the door, leaving Aza to the mercy of Xira and Anwin. With one final glance over her shoulder Lilit shook her head and whispered, "I tried to warn you."

In her compromised position Aza fought to shout, "Lilit! Stop!"

The door slammed shut. Her opportunity for rescue simply walked away.

Frustrated at Lilit's refusal to help, Aza dismissed her words as a love-blinded woman. Aza and Cruvo's relationship went much deeper than the superficial eye that Lilit saw it through.

Racing back to Xira's side, Anwin kept her sword at the ready. "We don't have much time," Anwin muttered.

Xira shifted her weight on Aza's back. "He will be here soon. Have faith."

Within a few minutes two pairs of feet were running down the hall.

They both charged in their breathing heavy. Aza's eyes widened as two people entered the room.

Lorn stood next to a man with brown skin and locs hanging down his back. Aza's eyes widened in recognition as she shouted, "Lorn!"

Lorn's breathing was ragged, but he attempted to spin bringing forth his sword, but before he could react, the man beside him knocked him out with the butt of his sword. Lorn's body slumped to the ground beside Aza.

A guttural scream erupted from Aza. She fought Xira's hold with every ounce of strength she possessed. She called upon the nonexistent magic around her, but nothing responded. She was completely weak. There was nothing she could do to save her friend.

"Time to go," Xira said.

A darkness swirled around her, caressing her body with loving care and in a snap of space and time she was no longer in the small storage room with Xira pinned on top of her. Her face smacked onto a shoddy, wooden floor. She was unsteady. Was she dreaming? No, she was unsteady because she was on the ocean.

Aza had been transported to a boat.

Here she was no longer constrained by Xira's bodyweight on her back. She scrambled to her feet looking around for an escape route. They were in a small smuggler's boat in a cavern, in what appeared to be beneath the castle of El'en.

"I do apologize, but I can't have you leaving." A deep male voice filled the cavern and before she could see the face it belonged to. She was slammed to the floor of the boat; unconsciousness took her.

~

Aza's head pounded as her body lifted and fell with the swells of the ocean. Her awareness trickled back in. She fought the urge to groan and clutch her head. She felt for the magic always present at the edge of her being and found it absent. She nearly cried from the emptiness of it. Her magic was a part of who she was and to find it completely gone was devastating.

Xira and Anwin had betrayed her. They kidnapped her. Where were they taking her and what was their overall plan? She feigned unconsciousness in hopes of catching a glimpse of their conversation. She only heard the waves slapping against the edge of the boat before Xira's smooth voice said, "He will come for her."

"We have enough of a head start to cause confusion," a voice she was unfamiliar with replied.

"We need to return home. She has much to learn," Anwin's lilting voice added.

Aza tried to maintain the steady rise and fall of her chest, yet Xira must have caught some shift in her body. "We should hold our tongues for now. She is stirring."

Since they already knew of her wakefulness, Aza's eyes flashed open to take in the three people on the boat. Light lavenders, and oranges swept along the horizon, with the weak light of the morning sun. The third person standing next to Xira and Anwin was the same man who knocked Lorn unconscious. Lorn.

"Where is Lorn?" Aza croaked, her throat dry and parched.

"He is fine. A bit sore, but fine," the man answered.

"Show me!"

The man gestured behind her his locs swaying with the motion. "I cannot. He is not here."

Foolishly Aza rolled to search for Lorn resting beside her. There was nothing. Aza fought the tears that crept in place.

In an attempt to forgo her vulnerability, her anger rose up like a viper instead. "Where are you taking me?"

No one spoke, their eyes flickered behind Aza as a man appeared coming into her vision. She felt the power radiate from him, his magic overwhelming. It made her miss her own. She should have it now and be able to combat these people. In their grips so was no greater than a child, helpless to their whim.

The man held a distinct air about him, utter confidence in his abilities and strength. He looked to be about her height, his dark brown skin outlined in a light glow from the unobstructed early morning sun. His hair was shorn close to his head with intricate designs shaved into the sides. Beneath the typical black attire of his fellow Nerians was a muscular body hinted at in the cut of his clothes. His eyes scanned her, the deep rich brown searching her before speaking. "I am sorry about the head wound, Aza, and your lack of magic."

He crouched before her, and Aza could not deny the man's pure beauty and strength that emanated from him— except he was the enemy. These people had taken her against her will. They took away her choices no matter how polite they pretended to be. They took away her magic. No, she would not be submissive to them. Cold anger burned through her as she put her icy fury into the gaze of her captor.

"I am Rune of Neria." His warm brown eyes held Aza's own, and suddenly a flash of gold dashed across his eyes. Aza gasped. No, she couldn't be held within the thrall of another god or goddess.

He smiled sadly back at Aza, confirming what she knew was correct. "But you can call me Nivet." He stood back up, his head swiveling, searching the distant horizon. "To answer your question, we are going home."

Home. To the harsh lands of Neria with these gruesome battle-hardened warriors. She was trapped with another god inhabiting a MagicBlessed body.

No one spoke. Aza let her body and mind be quieted by the soothing ocean waves.

She would find a way to escape.

She would get away from these Nerians and this other god.

With or without her magic, she would find a way back.

Acknowledgements

This story was a shot in the dark. It was an act of me keeping my cards close to my chest afraid of failure. I want to gratefully acknowledge everyone I have shared this story with. It is always difficult revealing a vulnerable part of yourself and being open to criticism. This story means so much to me and I could not have gotten here without the help of my husband. You have always pushed me and encouraged me, no matter how frustrated I became. I also want to thank my daughter, who hopefully won't read this story for a very long time. Your child-like optimism and perspective on the world always encourages me to keep trying, and to remain humble. A huge shout-out to my family. When you learned of my completed book, you jumped in with editing expertise, and storyline feedback. Lastly, thank you to anyone who has completed the book (whether you liked it or disliked it). I appreciate any amount of time spent on something written from my heart.

About the Author

Author portrait by cloudycitrus
@cloudy.citrus

A.N. Fox is a schoolteacher who writes fantasy in her spare time. She lives in California with her husband, daughter, dog, and her three cats. For fun you can find her playing board games, reading fantasy novels, or binge-watching anime. Incarnate is her debut novel.